The Nyctalope
and The Master of Life

IN THE SAME SERIES

Jean de LA HIRE

The Nyctalope
and The Master of Life

translated by
Michael Shreve

BLACK COAT PRESS

ISBN 978-1-64932-116-9. First printing: March 2021. Published by Black Coat Press, an imprint of Hollywood Comics.com, LLC, P.O. Box 17270, Encino, CA 91416.

TABLE OF CONTENTS

Jean de La Hire

Introduction

Le Maître de la Vie (translated here by Michael Shreve as *The Nyctalope and The Master of Life*) was first serialized in the daily newspaper *Le Matin* from 11 September 1938 to 17 January 1939. It was never reissued in book form by any publisher until this translated edition.

For those who have just joined us, Leo Saint-Clair a.k.a. the Nyctalope was a relatively minor French pulp hero who did not gain the recognition of, nor survive the test of time as well as, Arsène Lupin, Rouletabille and Fantômas—at least, not until the undersigned dragged him out of literary limbo to appear in our yearly series of anthologies devoted to French pulp heroes, *Tales of the Shadowmen*.

Jean de La Hire, the creator of the Nyctalope, was born in Banyuls on January 28, 1878, into a relatively obscure, aristocratic family which had long been impoverished by various social upheavals. His birth name was Adolphe-Ferdinand Célestin d'Espie de La Hire. His family claimed descent from one of the knights who fought with Jeanne d'Arc, although its most famous member was the mathematician and astronomer Philippe de La Hire (1640-1718), who has a theorem and a lunar mountain named after him.

La Hire began his literary career with high ambitions, selling his early work to Fernand Xau, the editor of *Le Journal*, and to the humorous periodical, *Gil Blas*. He worked for a while as secretary to Colette's husband, "Willy," and wrote a brief memoir of that time.

Vernian fiction had become popular enough to warrant the founding of specialized magazines, such as the *Journal des Voyages*, and although it moved steadily downmarket, it did benefit to an extent from the importation into France of the enlivening influence of H. G. Wells. By 1907, Wells himself had given up scientific romance, and the entire genre was in steep decline in England, but its less pretentious equivalent was still healthy in France.

La Hire's first serial for *Le Matin* was *La Roue Fulgurante* [*The Fiery Wheel*] (1907)[1], the extravagant account of an alien abduction by a spacecraft which appears to anticipate the notion of "flying saucers." *La Roue Fulgurante*, however, must have been judged a little too extravagant for *Le Matin*'s readers, because La Hire soon reverted to more Earthbound adventure fiction.

His most enduring creation was the Nyctalope, one of the first modern superheroes in the history of popular literature. Leo Saint-Clair is a crime-fighter who can see in the dark and, as it was later revealed, also sports an artificial

---

[1] Available in a Black Coat Press edition, ISBN 978-1-61227-217-7.

heart. To modern comic book readers and filmgoers, the Nyctalope is bound to seem rather feeble as a proto-superhero. His only superpower seems trivial by comparison to the abilities possessed by the likes of Superman and Spider-Man. Even in the context of an ensemble, like the Avengers, he would today have difficulty qualifying even for a minor role. The Nyctalope does illustrate the primitive nature of La Hire's understanding of the logic of superheroes, but his power is ultimately less important than his symbolic status as a paragon of moral and scientific enlightenment.

La Hire's first venture into the proto-techno thriller genre was *L'Homme qui peut vivre dans l'eau* [*The Man Who Could Live Underwater*], serialized *in Le Matin* in 1909. The water-breathing "Icthaner" is not the hero of the novel, but merely the subject of a biotechnological experiment carried out by the villains. The hero is an engineer named Severac, the inventor of a new kind of submarine. One of the minor characters who assists Severac is, however, a man named Jean de Sainte-Claire.

When the arch-villain of *L'Homme qui peut vivre dans l'eau* joined forces with a whole company of evil masterminds for a more ambitious Martian adventure in *Le Mystère des XV* [*The Mystery of the XV*], serialized in *Le Matin* in 1911 (translated as *The Nyctalope on Mars*),[2] he was again opposed by a Sainte-Claire, this time Leo, Jean's son, a fearless explorer whom we are told is known as the Nyctalope because of his ability to see in total darkness.

La Hire reverted to more orthodox Vernian fiction in the *Le Corsaire sous-marin* [*The Submarine Pirate*] (1912-13), which features one of many clones of Verne's Captain Nemo, but soon thereafter, *feuilleton* fiction suffered one of its frequent *bouleversements*, its consumption and development inhibited by the Great War of 1914-18. La Hire was not reduced to inactivity in those years, however; *Le Matin* continued to appear and he continued to supply it with serial fiction, including the long futuristic fantasy *Au-delà des ténèbres* [*Beyond Darkness*] (1915-16), whose protagonists employ suspended animation to escape the woes of the 20th century, awakening in the 30th.

After the Great War, La Hire continued his science fictional experiments with a explicitly Wellsian novel, *Joe Rollon, l'autre homme invisible* [*Joe Rollon, the Other Invisible Man*] (1919)—one of several works he issued under the pseudonym Edmond Cazal—and it was at this point that he apparently became convinced of the viability of superheroism as a device of literary crime-fighting.

In 1921, the Nyctalope returned with a vengeance in *Lucifer* (translated as *The Nyctalope vs. Lucifer*).[3] There, the hero fights the megalomaniacal Baron Glo von Warteck, who tries to enslave humanity with his devilish teledyname.

---

[2] Black Coat Press, ISBN 978-1-934543-46-7.
[3] Black Coat Press, ISBN 978-1-932983-98-2.

Other novels in the same vein soon followed: In *L'Amazone du Mont Everest* [*The Amazon of Mount Everest*] (1925), the Nyctalope discovers a hidden Tibetan civilization of Amazons. In *L'Antéchrist* [*The Antichrist*] (1927), he faces Leonid Zattan, evil incarnate. In *Titania* (1929), he is opposed by Zattan's ally, the Red Princess, Diana Ivanovna Krasnoview, Queen of the Hashishins. In *Belzébuth* (1930), Leo fights Diana's son, Hughes Mezarek. And in *Gorillard* (1932), he battles a villain who is an arch-enemy of his family.

L'Assassinat du Nyctalope [*The Assassination of the Nyctalope*] (1933) (translated as *Enter the Nyctalope*)[4] is a retroactive origin of the Nyctalope, in which we learn of an early assassination attempt that endowed Leo with his powers and an artificial heart.

In *Les Mystères de Lyon* [*The Mysteries of Lyons*] (1933), the Nyctalope fights Alouh T'Ho, a Chinese Empress who steals people's lifeforce. In *Le Roi de la Nuit* [*The King of the Night*] (1943) (translated and included in *Return of the Nyctalope*),[5] Leo travels to Rhea, a wandering planetoid, and settles a war between its day-siders and night-siders.

One of the last Nyctalope stories was the novella *Rien qu'une Nuit* [*Only One Night*] (1941) (translated as *Night of the Nyctalope*),[6] in which Leo appears to have succumbed to the charms of collaboration with the Nazis, retroactively making him the first superhero to have actually gone bad in his old age!

The Nyctalope, even more than Rocambole, Lupin or Fantômas, was the first, full-fledged superhero in the history of French pulp literature. What made him so were not just his superpowers, secret origins, and devoted band of fearless assistants, but also a colorful rogues' gallery that even Doc Savage or The Shadow would envy.

After World War II, La Hire was arrested in May 1945 for having collaborated with the Vichy régime and was tried in December; the judgment confirmed his permanent exclusion from the world of French publishing. He escaped from custody in February 1946 while being transferred to a hospital, but was condemned *in absentia* in 1948 to ten years' imprisonment and the loss of his citizenship rights. He never returned to serve his sentence, and was still in disgrace when he died on September 6, 1956.

La Hire was, however, survived by his great hero, the Nyctalope, the penning of whose adventures was taken over by his son-in-law, according to a pattern that has since become more or less normal in popular culture. A 22-volume reprint series of his works was published from 1952 to 1955 with covers by renowned science fiction illustrator René Brantonne.

Then, it and its creator fell into literary oblivion, until, after an absence of fifty years, the character returned in *Tales of the Shadowmen*, where it proved

---

[4] Black Coat Press, ISBN 978-1-934543-99-3.
[5] Black Coat Press, ISBN 978-1-61227-211-5.
[6] Black Coat Press, ISBN 978-1-61227-102-6.

immediately popular. Several translations of the original works have since followed, and today, the Nyctalope has reclaimed its title as one of the pioneers of superhero fiction.

New readers may be surprised by some Harlequin-like aspects of the story. One should remember that, in the United States and England, pulp magazines at the time were bought mostly by men. However, in France, a daily newspaper like *Le Matin* had a sizeable female readership, often comprised of secretaries, salesgirls, etc. Therefore, it was important for any author of *feuilleton* fiction to incorporate both adventure and romance in their serialized novels.

Now, read on!

Jean-Marc & Randy Lofficier

Updated Bibliography
(only first serialization and first book publication are listed.)

I. Main Series

I. Le Mystère des XV
1. 23 April-17 July 1911. *Le Matin* (serial).
2. *Le Mystère des XV + Le Triomphe de l'amour*. Ferenczi, 1922.
Note: *The Nyctalope on Mars* (translated by Brian Stableford, Black Coat Press, 2008).

II. Lucifer
1. 25 November 1921-30 March 22. *Le Matin* (serial).
2. *Lucifer + Nyctalope contre Lucifer*. Ferenczi, 1922.
Note: *The Nyctalope vs. Lucifer* (translated by Brian Stableford, Black Coat Press, 2007).

III. L'Amazone du Mont Everest
1. *L'Amazone du Mont Everest*. Ferenczi, 1925.

IV. L'Antéchrist (a.k.a. La Captive du Démon)
1. 28 January-21 April 1927. *Le Matin* (serial).
2. *La Captive du Démon + La Princesse Rouge*. Fayard, 1931.

V. Titania
1. 20 April-23 July 1928. *Le Matin* (serial).
2. *Titania + Écrase la vipère !* Tallandier, 1929.

VI. Belzébuth
1. 12 February-9 May 1930. *Le Matin* (serial).
2. *Belzébuth + L'Île d'Épouvante*. Fayard, 1930.

VII. Gorillard
1. 2 October 1921-9 January 1932. *Le Matin* (serial).
2. *Gorillard + Le Mystère Jaune*. Tallandier, 1931.

VIII. Les Mystères de Lyon
1. 22 January-30 April 1933. *Le Matin* (serial).
2. *Les Mystères de Lyon + Les Adorateurs du Sang*. Tallandier, 1933.

IX. L'Assassinat du Nyctalope
1. *L'Assassinat du Nyctalope.* La Renaissance du livre, 1933.
Note: *Enter the Nyctalope* (translated by Brian Stableford, Black Coat Press, 2008).

X. Le Sphinx du Maroc
1. 10 July-20 October 1934. *Le Matin* (serial).
2 *Le Sphinx du Maroc.* Tallandier, 1934.

XI. La Croisière du Nyctalope (a.k.a. Wanda)
1. 16 May-10 September 1936. *Le Matin* (serial).
2 *La Croisière du Nyctalope.* Fayard, 1937.

XII. Le Maître de la Vie
1. 11 September 1938-17 January 1939. *Le Matin* (serial).
Note: *The Nyctalope and The Master of Life* (translated by Michael Shreve, Black Coat Press, 2021).

XIII. La Croix de Sang (a.k.a. Le Mystère de la Croix du Sang)
1. 8 August-3 October 1940. *Le Matin* (serial).
2. *La Croix de Sang.* R. Simon, 1941.
Note: *The Cross of Blood* (translated by Jessica Sequeira included in *The Nyctalope and The Tower of Babel*, Black Coat Press, 2018).

XIV. **Les Drames de Paris**
1. 28 January-25 May 1941. *Le Matin* (serial).

XV. Rien qu'une nuit (a.k.a. Le Roman d'une Nuit)
1. 24 August-26 October 1941. *Les Ondes* (serial)
2. *Rien qu'une nuit.* P. Trémois, 1944.
Note: *Night of the Nyctalope* (translated by Jean-Marc & Randy Lofficier, Black Coat Press, 2012).

XVI. L'Enfant Perdu
1. 3 May-12 July 1942. *Actu* (serial).
Note: *The Nyctalope Steps In* (translated by Jean-Marc & Randy Lofficier, Black Coat Press, 2011).

XVII. Le Roi de la Nuit (a.k.a. Planète sans feu)
1. 20 February-13 July 1943. *Le Matin* (serial).
2. *Le Roi de la Nuit.* Le Livre moderne, 1943.
Note: *The King of the Night* (translated by Brian Stableford included in *Return of the Nyctalope*, Black Coat Press, 2013).

XVIII. La Sorcière Nue
1. *La Sorcière Nue*. Jaeger, 1954.

XIX. L'Énigme du Squelette
1. *L'Énigme du Squelette*, Jaeger, 1955.

II. Related Works

I. Le Trésor dans l'Abîme
1 1907. *L'Echo de Paris* (serial).
2 *Le Trésor dans l'Abîme*. Boivin, 1907.
Note: First appearance of Maur Korridès from *Titania*.

II. L'Homme qui peut vivre dans l'eau
1. 26 July-28 September 1909. *Le Matin* (serial).
2. *L'Homme qui peut vivre dans l'eau*. Juven, 1910.
Note: First appearances of the Nyctalope's father, Jean, and mad scientist, Oxus, from *Le Mystère des XV*.

III. Le Corsaire Sous-Marin
1. 1912-13. Ferenczi (79 issues)
Note: Cameos by the Nyctalope and Maur Korridès.

IV. Alcantara
1. 1923. *Le Matin* (serial).
Note: The protagonist poses as Rex Sainclair, Leo's cousin. The latter, then on Mars, is contacted by the police for a denial.

V. Les Dompteurs de Forces
1 1925. *Le Matin* (serial).
2 Ferenczi, 1927.
Note : Cameo by explorer Hubert de Pibriac from *L'Amazone du Mont Everest*.

VI. Les Grandes Aventures d'un Boy-Scout
1. 1926. Ferenczi (28 issues).
Note: First appearance of Maur's brother, Prosper Korridès.

VII. Les Chasseurs de Mystères
1 1933. *Le Matin* (serial).
2 *Les Chasseurs de Mystères* + *La Mort...L'Amour...* Fayard, 1933.
Note : Cameo by the Nyctalope.

III. New Sequels by Other Authors

Tales of the Shadowmen N°2, Black Coat Press, 2005.
« Marguerite » by Jean-Marc Lofficier.

Enter the Nyctalope, Black Coat Press, 2007.
« Black and Gold » by Emmanuel Gorlier.

Tales of the Shadowmen N°5, Black Coat Press, 2008.
« The Heart of a Man » by Roman Leary.
« The English Gentleman's Ball » by Randy Lofficier.

Tales of the Shadowmen N°6, Black Coat Press, 2009.
« The Children of Heracles » by Roman Leary.
« Out of Time » by Emmanuel Gorlier.

Tales of the Shadowmen N°7, Black Coat Press, 2010.
« Fiat Lux! » by Emmanuel Gorlier.
« Death to the Heretic! » by Paul Hugli.
« The Mysterious Island of Dr. Antekirtt » by David L. Vineyard.

The Nyctalope Steps In, Black Coat Press, 2011.
« The Three Sisters » by Emmanuel Gorlier.
« The Season of the Shark » by Julien Heylbroeck.
« The Lesson of Captain Danrit » by Emmanuel Gorlier.
« The Hunters of Mars » by Matthew Dennion.
« The Nyctalope's New York Adventure » by Stuart Shiffman.
« A Present for Hitler » by Emmanuel Gorlier.
« Twilight » by Emmanuel Gorlier.
« A Moment of Perfect Happiness » by Roman Leary.

Tales of the Shadowmen N°8, Black Coat Press, 2011.
« Catspaw » by David McDonald.

Night of the Nyctalope, Black Coat Press, 2012.
« First Steps » by Travis Hiltz.
« The Dam Busters of Mars » by Martin Gately.
« The Angel and the Exorcist » by Matthew Dennion.
« Dangerous Territory » by Matthew Dennion.
« Justice and Power » by Christofer Nigro.
« The Girl from Odessa » by David McDonald.
« Una Voce Poco Fa » by Emmanuel Gorlier.

« The Hour of the Grail » by Philippe Ward.
« Blood and Weapons » by Julien Heylbroeck.
« The Road Not Taken » by Matthew Dennion.
« Requiem for a Regime » by Christofer Nigro.
« Showdown at Steam Town » by Travis Hiltz.
« Madison Square Garden » by Emmanuel Gorlier.
« The Devil You Know » by Roman Leary.
« The Algerian Dilemna » by Emmanuel Gorlier.
« The Ides of Mars » by Jean-Marc Lofficier.

Tales of the Shadowmen N°9, Black Coat Press, 2012.
« The Man With the Double Heart » Robert Darvel.
« Wolf at the Door of Time » by Martin Gately.

Tales of the Shadowmen N°10, Black Coat Press, 2013.
« The Brotherhood of Mercy » by Emmanuel Gorlier.

Return of the Nyctalope by Jean-Marc & Randy Lofficier, Black Coat Press, 2013 (novel).

Tales of the Shadowmen N°11, Black Coat Press, 2014.
« Once More, the Nyctalope! » by Emmanuel Gorlier.

Tales of the Shadowmen N°13, Black Coat Press, 2016.
« As Easy as 1, 2, 3… » by Paul Hugli.

Tales of the Shadowmen N°14, Black Coat Press, 2017.
« Tomorrow Belongs to the Nyctalope » by Nigel Malcolm.
« The Night of the Dazzling Sun » by Paul Hugli.

The Nyctalope and The Tower of Babel by Emmanuel Gorlier, Black Coat Press, 2018.(novel)

Tales of the Shadowmen N°15, Black Coat Press, 2018.
« A Waltz in Norbury » by Thierry Bosch.
« Enemies of the People » by Nigel Malcolm.
« Night of the Craven Raven » by Paul Hugli.

Tales of the Shadowmen N°16, Black Coat Press, 2019.
« Useful Idiot » by Nigel Malcolm.

Tales of the Shadowmen N°17, Black Coat Press, 2020.
« The Revolution Begins Tonight » by Nigel Malcolm.

IV. Relatives

Jean de Sainte-Claire (ancestor)
Les Trois Mignons (a.k.a. Les Mignons du Roi)
1 1913. Ferenczi. « Le Livre épatant » N°3.

Passions Ardentes
1 1919. A. Michel. « Mon Petit Roman » N°9.
Note: Features the Nyctalope's grandfather.

Vicomte Jean de Sainte-Claire (unidentified relative)
La Chair et l'Esprit (a.k.a. Le Sang des Grenades)
1 1898. Edmond Girard

L'Enfer du Soldat
1 1903. Offenstadt.

Régiment d'Irma
1 1904. Ambert et Co. Collection « Ivoire ».

Mémoires d'un Don Juan
1 1905. Librairie Universelle.

Les Vipères
1 1905. *Gil Blas* (serial)
2 1905. Bibliothèque Indépendante.

Paul de Saint-Clair (cousin)
Le Roi de la Sierra (a.k.a. Les Chemins de Santiago)
1927. Ferenczi. « Les Romans d'aventures » N°46.

THE NYCTALOPE AND THE MASTER OF LIFE

PART ONE: EIGHTEEN DEATHS

Prologue

"Very curious!" said Leo Saint-Clair.

Dumont-Warren, director of the Universal News Agency, or UNA for short, smiled and took a cigarette from the box open in front of him. He lit it and took two drags, placidly making a small, round cloud of smoke over his head.

"Yes, very curious," the Nyctalope repeated gravely. And after a moment of silence, he added: "Of course, you have a secretary or a stenographer on whom you can count for absolute discretion?"

"Indeed," Dumont-Warren said, "and, mind you, experience has proven to me that contrary to the prejudices propagated by that fable of La Fontaine, certain women are able to keep secrets better than most men."

"I agree wholeheartedly," the Nyctalope confessed. Then, in a different tone, he continued: "Would you be kind enough, my friend, to call in the secretary you're talking about? I would like to dictate the essentials of what you just told me. If I forget anything important or add anything useless, you can stop me."

"That would surprise me."

"But it's quite possible, since I have to admit that your story has stirred up a bunch of ideas in my mind that are a little confused... and emotionally charged. I'd like to get it down right away, short and sweet, but very precisely."

"I understand," the UNA director agreed. He picked up one of the telephones lined up on the left side of his huge desk and spoke quietly. "Hello, Mademoiselle Blancat? Please come into my office immediately."

Less than a minute later, a young woman entered the office through a side door. Dressed severely but elegantly in black, she was short and slim, pale, with well-defined, thin lips and magnificent, dark eyes expressing both intelligence and reserve. She was holding a notepad and two pencils in her left hand.

"Sit down, please. Monsieur Saint-Clair is going to dictate a memo. May I remind you that this is all hush-hush, including the fact that he is here. We used the private entrance."

"Certainly, Monsieur," she said flatly.

She looked in awe and almost in fear at the famous Nyctalope and bowed ever so slightly as she passed by him to reach the other side of the desk and sit at a kind of school desk, obviously reserved for stenographers.

Saint-Clair started dictating right away in a calm and steady voice:

"Monsieur Dumont-Warren, Managing Director of the Universal News Agency, makes a monthly check of all the news arranged in summary reports by a service that he created here, called the Coordinated Archives. In this manner, he can have an overview of all the categories of world events that the agency communicates to the press, and that they use to varying degrees. This UNA department is unknown to the press, unknown even to the other departments within the agency, which feed it unknowingly. It has only one employee, a young and highly qualified archivist who receives all the news every day from Monsieur Dumont-Warren personally. And this archivist, Monsieur Jean Palmade, has no contact with anyone else, except the managing director and Mademoiselle Blancat, his secretary."

When Saint-Clair paused briefly, Dumont-Warren spoke up:

"At least half of what you just said, I never told you."

"A logical deduction based on what you did tell me," the Nyctalope smiled back at him. Then he added, "I will continue. Now, some news over the past three months, January, February and March of the present year, up to April 7, the day I am dictating this memo, appear to show a strange confluence of events."

He stopped and looked at the secretary, "Mademoiselle, would you please underline the next part on the hard copy?"

"Yes, Monsieur."

A little more slowly now, Saint-Clair continued, "Here it is: *Fourteen men sentenced to death, being held in fourteen prisons spread around eight different countries in Europe and the United States, one by one, in January, February and March, died suddenly in their cells in front of their guards. There is no possibility of suicide. Moreover, the fourteen investigations and the subsequent autopsies gave the same results, reported in detail by the witnesses and doctors— results that can be summed up in the following diagnosis: sudden death due to a cerebral hemorrhage coupled with a violent, apoplectic seizure.*"

After a short pause, the Nyctalope continued, "Add this, Mademoiselle, but without underlining: No newspaper in the world seems to have noticed this mysterious oddity, the bizarre enigma of the identical circumstances in the fourteen cases, in pretty rapid succession, of victims who were all legally sentenced to death, all expiring from a violent cerebral hemorrhaging. But for anyone thinking about these fourteen different news stories, pulled out of thousands of the daily items that feed the press around the world, there is a problem that needs solving. A problem, moreover, that is likely, logically, to grow deeper, with more stories soon to occur in this gloomy, pathological and quite unusual setting."

There was a silence before Saint-Cloud concluded, "That's all, Mademoiselle. Thank you."

"I imagine you'd like a hard copy right away?" Dumont-Warren asked.

"Yes, in duplicate."

"Yes, Monsieur," said the secretary.

Ten minutes later, Mademoiselle Blancat was back and handed the Nyctalope two copies and the shorthand text.

"Perfect. Thank you."

After the secretary had left, Saint-Clair stood up, immediately imitated by Dumont-Warren. They exchanged a few pleasantries, set a date for lunch with two ministers, whom the director promised to invite, and the Nyctalope left.

On the Place de la Bourse, on this beautiful spring day, newsboys were hawking the afternoon edition of the papers. Saint-Clair bought one and froze on the sidewalk on seeing the front page.

"Ah-ha!" he said quietly with the furrowed brow and the pursed lips of a schoolboy. He was reading the headline in bold letters: *Eduardo Prin, head of the POUM, was found dead in Barcelona in his locked room from a violent cerebral hemorrhage.*

CHAPTER I
14, 15, 16...

Saint-Clair was thinking: *I knew the man. He was around forty, physically strong and morally fearless. He led the utopian Worker's Party in Spain with as much diplomacy as sound judgment. But secretly, he was as determined and ambitious as a Caesar or Napoleon. He didn't drink or smoke and led a healthy life. Yet, he died of a cerebral hemorrhage too! This is strange. I need details— very precise details.*

The Nyctalope went back into the building he had just come out of and took the private staircase up to the second floor where he knocked at the door of Dumont-Warren's office.

Leo Saint-Clair was known as the Nyctalope because his eyes, like those of some animals, had the rare ability to see in the dark almost as clearly as in daylight.

After getting back from Morocco, where he had lived through some memorable adventures, Saint-Clair had settled back down in his house at Blingy, near Versailles. His son, Pierre, had been traveling in Asia for two years making frequent visits to Japan. But Saint-Clair was not alone at Blingy because he had his dear friend Gno Mitang, a Marquis and former minister of state, personal advisor to the Emperor of Japan, staying with him.

For thirty years Saint-Clair and Gno Mitang had been bound by the kind of friendship that makes two men share one mind and one heart.

When the illustrious Japanese was staying in France, he lived at Blingy, where he had his own room on the second floor, furnished and decorated to his liking, reserved for him alone, always available and separated from Saint-Clair's by only one, very big room, the study.

The two friends were served by Vitto and Soca, the Nyctalope's two Corsican assistants, and by Yori Koto, the Marquis' secretary; and indirectly by many old and faithful domestic servants, as good as they were honest, whom one would never willingly forsake.

On this Wednesday, April 7,[7] after Saint-Clair left the office of the UNA at the Place de la Bourse for the second time, he went straight to his car, a convertible in which Soca was sitting at the wheel, and told the Corsican, "Let's get home—fast."

In one minute, the clock of the Bourse would strike noon. It was not that Saint-Clair was in a hurry for lunch, because he did not eat at Blingy until 1 or 2 p.m., but he was impatient to talk to Gno Mitang about the extraordinary series

---

[7] Which would place the story in 1937.

of fifteen identical deaths. To shed some light on his currently clouded mind, he was counting on the profound, penetrating wisdom and the vast and varied knowledge of the noble Japanese. He was a little annoyed that the strange mystery presented by Dumont-Warren, now complicated by the news of Eduardo Prim's death, created only confused and contradictory thoughts in his mind—so flimsy that they just vanished when he tried to focus and examine them.

Saint-Clair entered the study at 12:30 p.m. He had gone there directly, hoping to find Gno who could spend hours reading in his spare time. He was not disappointed. The Japanese was sitting in a leather armchair in his white flannel pajamas, half-hidden by a large folio volume standing on his lap.

"Ah, my friend!" Saint-Clair said excitedly. "What a tale I have to tell you!"

Gno Mitang was the very picture of calm, absolute calm, usually listening politely with a smile on his thin lips and a sparkle in his dark eyes. He slowly lowered the volume and looked at his friend kindly but inquisitively.

Saint-Clair had left his hat and gloves in the entrance hall on the ground floor. He plopped down on a leather footstool in front of Gno and right away started in with no warning except the single word, "Listen". He told him everything about his two conversations with Dumont-Warren. Of course, Gno listened to everything without interrupting and without changing his expression. When Saint-Clair said, "And that's it," Gno put the book on the low table and closed his eyes.

The Nyctalope was used to his friend's meditations since he never spoke impulsively, so he never disturbed these moments with a hasty word or impatient gesture. Two or three minutes went by before Gno slowly opened his eyes and spoke in a slightly hoarse but very clear and articulate voice.

"Strange indeed. But I believe that, except for mechanics and mechanical objects, nothing happens in nature that hasn't happened before, whether it be yesterday, last week, or twenty centuries ago. I was just wondering if I knew when and where... and, well, yes!"

"Yes?" Saint-Clair was on the edge of his seat.

Gno smiled. "It didn't happen yesterday or last week, but if I'm not mistaken, around the middle of the 15th century, in the year 1445 to be precise, in Tibet, around 120 miles north of Lhasa, the holy city, the secret city, right on the banks of the Tengri Nor, which is a big lake between the plains and the mountains. Of course, back then, no one knew anything about cerebral hemorrhages, but the way everyone died suddenly between the first and last day of March was more than astonishing. More than 10,000 warriors, lamas, servants, craftsmen, farmers, etc. passed away. If we were to make a modern scientific diagnosis with hindsight, using the documents in the great monastery of the Living Buddha, I would say that the way they died would be exactly the same as a violent cerebral hemorrhage."

And Gno Mitang's smile grew bigger. Saint-Clair was serious and frowned.

"Go on, Gno," he said quietly.

"Oh, just one more thing... I know very little about it—just this: in 1407, the lama Tsong Kha, a Tibetan reformer of Buddhism, founded the great monastery of Gal-Dan, four leagues east of Lhasa. He had a disciple, whom we know very little about—only that much later, it was supposed to be a female disciple who succeeded Tsong-Kha, but before she could, she had retreated to the Gobi Desert, on the shores of Lake Chong Koum."

"A woman!" Saint-Clair exclaimed.

"Yes—and what a woman! She liberated Tibet from the suzerainty of China, set herself up as Emperor and, at the same time, claimed to be the reincarnation of the Buddha... all this with great success. She was the first woman to be known as the living Buddha, who represents absolute spiritual and temporal power... Under her divinity, under her reign, which lasted 57 years..."

"57 years!" the Nyctalope muttered in awe.

"Yes, from 1417 to 1474. Under her reign, Tibet reached the height of its power, wealth, and art, with surprisingly loose morals in private life and no less surprising rectitude in public."

"Hypocrisy..."

"Hypocrisy raised to the level of state policy."

"And what was this extraordinary woman's name?"

"Her name is not very pretty to French ears, but no matter. She was Gedhun Grub."[8]

"And it was during her reign that...?"

"It was at the very start of her reign and by her will... I repeat *by her will*... that, on the shores of the Tengri Nor, more than 10,000 men died of cerebral hemorrhages, and also a few hundred nobles in the city of Lhasa. Who knows what secret she had discovered during her retreat at Lake Chong Koum—*the lake that never freezes*?"

---

[8] La Hire drew his inspiration from the historical figure of Gedun Drupa, the first Dalai Lama. Gedun Drupa (1391-1474) was born in a cow-shed in Gyurmey Rupa near Sakya in the Tsang region of central Tibet. He was raised as a shepherd until the age of seven. Later he was placed in Narthang Monastery. In 1405, he took his *śrāmaṇera* (novitiate) vows from the abbot of Narthang, Khenchen Drupa Sherap. When he was 20, in about 1411, he received the name Gedun Drupa upon taking the vows of a *bhikṣu* (monk) from the abbot of Narthang Monastery. Also at this age he became a student of the scholar and reformer Je Tsongkhapa. Around this time, he also became the first abbot of Ganden Monastery, founded by Tsongkhapa himself in 1409. By the middle of his life, Gedun Drupa had become one of the most esteemed scholar-saints in the country.

Saint-Clair was disturbed. He jumped up.

"*By her will?*" he hammered out the words. "You say that, but how can you know for sure? The microbe for a cerebral hemorrhage doesn't…"

"Who's talking about a microbe?" Gno said calmly. "Isn't the word '*will*' enough?"

"But…"

"But, my friend, you don't realize that the immaterial will can achieve real results. The whole story of God's creation of the world is nothing but a symbol of the unlimited power of the will."

After a brief silence that a contemplative Saint-Clair did not interrupt, Gno Mitang nodded and continued:

"The trick is to have enough willpower in yourself… and know how to use it. The very ancient and occult science of sorcery, which the modern world has lost, but of which that Frenchman Colonel de Rochas [9] found a few basic elements, is basically just based on the teleradiant power, so to speak, of the will."

"But then," Saint-Clair blurted out, "the cerebral hemorrhages of the fourteen dead men, as well as Eduardo Prim, would have been caused by the murderous will of a man…"

"Or a woman," Gno said. "Yes… Or a woman, indeed. Why not?"

"My friend," Saint-Clair was getting worked up, "a human being with knowledge of this power would truly be a Master of Death."

"And therefore, of Life as well."

"Exactly! If he wanted, he could be the absolute master, dictator, emperor of the world! But if he's an idiot, then…"

"That is possible," Gno nodded. "Thaumaturges have not always been shining examples of intelligence."

"Or cult leaders."

"Which would be even worse," Gno murmured.

"He could use death, or the threat of death, to cripple and enslave entire nations, devastate the world, and terrorize it."

Gno Mitang stood up and put his hands on Saint-Clair's shoulders. Very serious and gently insistent he said:

"My dear friend, if the current mystery comes from the same sources as the autocratic actions of that living female Buddha, there is reason for humanity to

---

[9] Eugène Auguste Albert de Rochas d'Aiglun (1837-1914), a leading French parapsychologist, historian, translator, writer, and military engineer. He is now best known for his extensive parapsychological research and writing, in which he attempted to explore a scientific basis for occult phenomena. His first book on the subject, *Les Forces non définies* (1887), was followed by numerous books and articles over the course of nearly thirty years, on subjects such as hypnotism, telekinesis, magnetic emanations, reincarnation, spirit photography, etc.

fear. But, first we have to find out the truth. And for that, what is the Nyctalope going to do?"

Looking into those deep, dark eyes, full of affection and intelligence, Leo Saint-Clair calmed down, cleared his mind, and got back to his usual good mood. He smiled and put his left arm in Gno's right. As they walked away, he said:

"First of all, the Nyctalope is going to have breakfast with his friend Gno Mitang. Then, after half a cigar and a cup of coffee, the Nyctalope will see."

What they saw first, or rather what they heard, after "half a cigar and a cup of coffee," enjoyed in a corner of the study between two sunlit windows, was the news over the wireless of a sixteenth strange death by cerebral hemorrhage.

The victim—since Saint-Clair and Gno were almost ready, without question, to admit that these deaths were premeditated murders—was a man of even greater importance: Lord William Stonewell, named Viceroy of India only two weeks prior. The speaker on the radio articulated clearly, and there was no interference in the mansion, so Saint-Clair and Gno heard the following:

"*The announcement was made in London of the sudden death in Calcutta of His Excellency William Stonewell, Viceroy of India. While he was calmly signing some official papers, as he did every morning at the same time, he suddenly fell over, face first on the table. The doctors were called right away and diagnosed a violent cerebral hemorrhage. An autopsy was performed immediately and gave the same results. Lord William Stonewell was 51 years-old. In good health, lean and strong, of legendary sobriety, moderate to a fault, clean of body and mind, so nothing could have signaled this threat which usually strikes men with a very different lifestyle. This is why an autopsy was performed, but no shred of doubt remains: the Viceroy died of a cerebral hemorrhage in the presence of his First Secretary and an Adjutant who were both friends as well as subordinates. Lord William Stonewell was born in Sussex...*"

Leo Saint-Clair and Gno Mitang had stopped listening. They looked at each other worriedly. Saint-Clair spoke up without hesitation:

"Gno, my friend, is it possible for you to...?"

He did not finish his sentence. He clapped his hand to his forehead. But Gno Mitang was already answering:

"Ten thousand men died like this in three weeks on the banks of the Tengri Nor because a woman desired to be Emperor and god. And I have never heard of cerebral hemorrhages becoming an epidemic."

CHAPTER II
The Deathly Call

That year, Mrs. Melody MacCross, a New York widow, was considered y the Press to be the "richest woman in the world."

Right at the beginning of April, the newspapers had announced the arrival of the wealthy American in Paris; she had moved into a luxury furnished apartment in the neighborhood of La Madeleine. Both Mrs. MacCross and Mademoiselle Florence de Salsis, her secretary and companion, had their own bedrooms and bathroom, and they shared the spacious living room, often used as private dining room.

Almost every day between 3 and 4 p.m., Mrs. MacCross and Mrs. de Salsis turned it into an office for the former to dictate her letters and go over the previous day's accounts, because a billionaire, even if she is sometimes philanthropically generous, does not throw money out the window and keeps strict account of her expenses and a close eye on her resources and revenue.

So, on April 7 at 3 p.m., Mrs. MacCross and Mrs. de Salsis were getting down to work after the cup of chamomile tea without sugar and the two nicotine-free cigarettes that were part of her healthy American diet—especially for a tall, well-built, 43-year-old woman, mostly cheerful, although sometimes a little distant and secretive, very intelligent, reasonably sociable and with good taste, but who had a deathly fear of diabetes, which her father and her husband had died of.

"Well, Flore, what about the receipt for these 15 francs?" asked Mrs. MacCross, who spoke French comfortably and correctly with only a slight American accent.

"Here it is, Madame, I found it. I'd noted it down on the corner of this envelope. It was for four stamps of the new series for your collection. The series was issued to benefit the unemployment fund for intellectuals."

"Good. Let's move on."

Suddenly, the telephone rang.

"Get that, Flore," asked Mrs. MacCross.

The phone was on the table, so Mrs. de Salsis had just to reach out with her left arm to pick it up.

"Hello... yes..." And after listening in silence for a moment: "Hold on!"

She covered the mouthpiece with her right hand and said:

"Madame, it's the doorman. He says there's a young lady asking to see you. She knows that you're looking for antique Buddha statues in gold, silver or jade, and apparently she has a huge, golden Shakyamuni,[10] very old, which has

---

[10] Another name of the Buddha.

25

been in her family for a long time, for sale. The doorman says the young lady is very well dressed, elegant, but modest."

"Well then, let's see her," Mrs. MacCross ordered without a second thought.

Florence spoke into the telephone:

"Show her up."

The young lady was indeed elegantly but modestly dressed, in a marine blue tailored suit with a small felt hat, gloves and matching shoes. Her handbag of dark blue leather with silver trim was bulging. After some small talk, she opened it and took out an object that she placed on the table. Only then did she sit down, accepting Mrs. MacCross' initial invitation.

The object was a statuette made of greenish gold, around six inches high, a Shakyamuni with simple lines, no adornments, a tiny face expressing the greatest serenity.

The American picked it up, turned it around and upside down, caressed it with desire, not trying to hide her delight.

"How much?" she inquired.

The answer was unexpected.

"To tell you its story and the price I am asking, Madame, I would like to be alone with you."

Mrs. MacCross was surprised. Only then did she take a good look at the visitor's face. Everything about it was beautiful, her lines, color, her serious, determined expression. She had a Mediterranean face with olive skin, big, dark eyes the color of roasted hazelnuts, and lips a little hard but well defined, pure, very proud. She held herself like an aristocrat, and yet very naturally, without any pretensions at all. On the sides, under her little hat, her hair was black with thick, shiny curls.

"What's your name?" Mrs. MacCross asked.

"Leone Alzac."

"Leone?" the American woman smiled. "That unusual name fits you well. Are you French?"

"Yes, Madame, but my mother was a Hindu from Calcutta."

"Well... And is your father still alive?"

"No, Madame."

"Unmarried?"

"I am a widow, Madame. For three years now."

The answers were given in a calm and clear voice, but it was obvious that the topic under discussion was not welcomed. The American saw this and blushed a little.

"Excuse me," and she motioned vaguely to her secretary, "Flore, please, leave us alone."

Without showing any offense in her pale face or in her slightly nervous gestures, Mrs. de Salsis stood up, bowed slightly to the lady of the house, even more slightly to the visitor, and turned to hurry out of the room.

When the door was closed, Mrs. MacCross smiled.

"So, we're alone now. I'm all ears."

In a steady voice, with a direct gaze, leaning forward, Leone Alzac said:

"Madame, do you still hate Reginald Strom?"

If Mrs. de Salsis had still been there, she would have been stunned because she knew almost nothing about the private life of her employer. Mrs. MacCross turned deathly pale, jumped up, stuttered and moaned, then dropped back into the armchair. She, too, leaned forward, grabbed Leone's wrists, shook them and in a voice full of both anger and confusion, said in English:

"What is this? What did you say? How do you know?"

But Leone stayed calm and did not try to pull her hands away. She answered in English:

"It doesn't matter how I know. I'll tell you later if you really want to know. But I repeat, do you still hate Reginald Strom?"

"Yes, I hate him!" Mrs. MacCross shouted. S

he dropped Leone's wrists as if she were trying to throw them to the ground and stood up, clapping her fists together. She walked to the far side of the room, came back, turned around and continued like that without saying a word.

A hoarse wheeze leaked out of her half-open mouth. Her eyes, her face, all of her body exuded fury. In this modern and socially acceptable American woman, an old savagery had come bubbling to the surface—the fierceness of her Irish ancestors, persecuted exiles who had earned their bread with rifle, pickaxe and dynamite in the Old West, then with their wits and merciless determination when building their fortunes in the brand new cities, on ruthless markets, wild speculations, riding the triumphs and disasters from the peaks and plunges of the stock market.

After pacing three, four, five times from one end of the room to the other, Mrs. MacCross finally calmed down, and stood before the mysterious young woman who had not moved from her armchair. In a wheezing voice, she asked in her New York accent:

"Do I hate Reginald Strom? Yes! Yes! But what is it to you?"

Leone Alzac's well shaped eyebrows narrowed and her face hardened as she answered in a surprisingly calm but firm voice:

"Because I can punish him and avenge you. I only have to say one word. Right now, Reginald Strom is in London at the Koh-i-Noor Hotel. You can call him, tell him that you still hate him, that you've finally found a way to get him out of your life—to get him out of everyone's life!—and you don't even have to leave Paris or ask anyone to kill him. You can tell him over the telephone that in one hour—exactly one hour—he will die a sudden and natural death and that the most meticulous and fastidious coroner in the world will authorize his burial without a moment's hesitation. That, Madame, is what I have to say to you first of all. Then... but first, you have to answer me with a simple yes or no. Do you want to make a phone call and tell Reginald Strom that he will die?"

The extraordinary speech was beyond belief. Mrs. MacCross listened with her eyes wide open, her mouth agape, leaning forward with her right hand on the back of the armchair in which the young woman was sitting. She listened. She understood, but doubted that she did correctly.

When Leone Alzac stopped talking, Melody MacCross could not say a word. Her light blue eyes stared into Leone's calm, brown eyes. She looked both skeptical and desperately inquisitive.

"Are you crazy?" she asked.

A mischievous little smile crossed Leone's lips. She shook her head very slightly and answered:

"No, not at all, I assure you."

Melody sighed. "I can't help believing you. But is it possible?"

"More than possible. As easy as just saying yes."

"How will you do it?"

"That's my secret."

"Of course!"

She shrugged, leaned forward a little more and shivered when she asked:

"Occult means?"

"Not exactly." With this, Leone Alzac stood up. "Madame, listen to me..." Now she grabbed the other's wrists and squeezed. "Listen well. I'm going to offer you a deal. First, I'll give you this statue as a gift. A simple calling card— and you know how much this Shakyamuni is worth. But I need money. Oh, don't worry about your reputation. Do I look like a blackmailer? I see what you're thinking... I need a million—enough so that my companion and I can live well for one year. One year! No more than that for my purpose. I won't waste the money; I'll use it only for our everyday's needs. Afterwards... Oh, afterwards, it will be a trifling amount to me... spare change almost! Do you hear me? Do you understand? Yes? Well, sign three checks for 335,000 francs each from three different banks. I imagine you have at least three bank accounts in France, Switzerland and Belgium? Yes? Very well. Write these checks then and give them to me. A million is nothing to you. For me and that other person, it's a year of life that is absolutely necessary. Look, it's 3:45. p.m. Reginald Strom will drop dead at exactly 4:45 p.m., no matter what he's doing or where he is. You just have to call him first, if you are truly a strong woman equal to her strong hatred. Is that a yes?"

Maybe thirty seconds of silence passed before Mrs. MacCross said coldly:

"Let me go."

When her wrists were free, with her voice still icy and firm she continued:

28

"There's only one bank where you can cash a check signed by me for a million francs without any questions—if I write a brief note also signed by me to verify the transaction. The Banque de France, the main branch, at any counter that deals with international funds."

She turned around and disappeared into the next room. When she came back, she was holding her checkbook. Two minutes later, she gave Leone Alzac a check and a piece of paper. Leone took them, read them, folded them and put them in the pocket of her jacket. Casually, she asked:

"So you do believe me?"

"Yes," the American shot back. "It all sounds as crazy as can be, but I do believe you."

"And you're right, too. As for me, I believe in your loyalty. I don't have to warn you that any indiscretion on your part would earn you the same fate as Reginald Strom in fifty minutes. Not a word about me to anyone, anywhere, at any time."

"I understand," Mrs. MacCross said quietly.

"I expected no less from your intelligence," Leone replied just as quietly.

"The deal is done," the American resumed. "We will never speak of it again. But what if I need to talk to you?"

The young woman replied gently:

"I know now that I don't have to hide from you, but I prefer to stay in the shadows. I won't give you my address because they wouldn't know a Leone Alzac. However, rest assured that I will see you again soon, Melody—and with pleasure."

"And me too, Leone, gladly because..." A brief silence, a quick hug, a peck on the cheek and in a trembling voice, she continued, "Because I owe you the true happiness of my life. Happiness that I've been waiting for for two years, because, really, it's been poisoning my life a little more every day... Till we meet again, Leone. Will you tell me how you knew that there was this disgrace, this cancer, in my life?"

"Yes, Melody, I will tell you. Good-bye."

In London, at the American bar of the Koh-i-Noor Hotel, at 3:59 p.m., on Wednesday, April 7, a bellboy came in and called out:

"Mr. Reginald Strom—telephone!"

"Yes?"

A man stood up and left the table where two other men were laughing.

"Lookie there, that must be Flossie!" he said, walking to the telephone booth and closing the door.

When he came back, he was flushed and furious. He slammed his fists on the table, shaking the glasses and ashtrays. The two other men were stunned, one frozen with a pipe in his mouth, the other with a cigar, both watching him in bewilderment. He shot them an angry, bitter look.

"You'll never guess," he growled.

"What?" one of them asked while the other shrugged.

"A silly old girl friend whom I dumped a long time ago, but who was still scared enough of me to not dare drop me. She…"

"Well? She what?" asked the man who had said "What?"

"She called me from Paris to tell me that at exactly 4:45 p.m. on the dot… get that… I will die."

"Really?"

"Damn!"

"Yes, I will die at exactly 4:45 p.m.," Reginald Strom repeated.

The others both started laughing. One of them said:

"Are you nuts? Is that why you're so upset?"

But Reginald still sounded bitter.

"I don't like it when people mock me. Tomorrow morning, I'll go to Croydon and catch a plane for Paris. I'll make her pay, that damned lunatic woman, for trying to pull one over me."

"So, may I take it that you're flush right now?" said the quiet man.

"Er… Yes."

"So you can give me what you lost last night on your word?"

"Certainly."

"Great. Shall we do it now?"

"Naturally," said Strom. "But how about another game before we settle this?"

On a signal from him, the waiter brought a felt pad and a deck of cards. The three men played in all seriousness because every hand was worth at least ten pounds—and one of them was always short of funds.

Time passed. Chance saw to it that the least talkative of the three glanced at his watch.

"Hey, Reginald, it's 4:43 p.m.," he observed.

Strom answered with a curse, which doubled as an insult. This annoyed the quiet man who was rather touchy. A minute later, he announced:

"4:44 p.m., Reggie."

The third man sneered.

"Poor old chap, you've got only one minute to live. Luckily, you're winning. Not owing us money will be a small consolation."

"Not me!" the quiet one exclaimed. "He still owes me 50 pounds from last night. If he dies in the next 50 seconds, I'll be pinched."

"You're both complete idiots," Strom groaned.

But the joker did not drop the joke. He kept looking at his watch with only one eye on the game.

"Watch out!" he shouted. "Only five seconds… three, two, one…"

And he threw his arms up in the air. The third man jumped up, knocking over his chair.

Reginald Strom had suddenly gone stiff and his mouth dropped open. His eyes rolled up in his head and he fell to the side, slowly, heavily, onto the floor.

Fifteen minutes later, a doctor certified that the man was dead. On hearing the strange story told by the two friends, the authorities ordered an autopsy. It found that Reginald Strom had died naturally of a violent cerebral hemorrhage. Naturally, the authorities did not believe a word about his death having been predicted by telephone. They thought it was a joke being played by Strom himself. Since the death was declared natural by three doctors, including the coroner, there was no investigation after the autopsy.

A few papers reported the event in three lines. The satirical *London Razzle* made a black comedy editorial out of it, which earned it a letter from a fortune teller saying, first of all, that bewitchment is not a joking matter, and secondly, death could be sent over the telephone by a competent magician. The *Razzle* announced publicly that it would pay two shillings to the fortune teller for her "copy," which would be "included in a later edition." And there was no more talk in London about the late Reginald Strom.

In Paris, however, Mrs. Melody MacCross was informed by her British lawyer that Mr. Reginald Strom had died of a cerebral hemorrhage on the afternoon of April 7.

The following week—on April 13 to be precise—two men, among other passengers, got off a plane at Croydon airport coming from Le Bourget and took a chauffeured car that had been reserved by telephone three days earlier. The two men were Leo Saint-Clair and Gno Mitang.

The Japanese subscribed to several British newspapers and magazines, including the *Razzle*. He had read about the late Reginald Strom and the macabre "jokes" made out of his death and the strange circumstances surrounding it. Saint-Clair had felt that an investigation in London was called for because Strom's case was not only part of the series of "mysterious deaths," but also had a particularly exciting new element to it.

When they got to London, Saint-Clair and Gno Mitang did not go to Scotland Yard but to the Japanese Embassy.

Two Japanese detectives, clever and informed about everything that went on in London, went to the Koh-i-Noor Hotel, and talked with the bellboys and the two gentlemen who had played cards with the deceased on April 7. Then, through an informal contact with a high-level official, the investigation continued discreetly in London's central switchboard, where one of the executives got in touch with his counterpart in Paris. It took less than a day to find out that the deathly call had come from a Parisian rental apartment located near La Madeleine.

Moreover, a detailed investigation was conducted of the comings and goings, the whys and wherefores of the somewhat adventurous life of the late Reginald Strom. They learned that he had been in Monte Carlo two years before and had had an intimate and stormy relationship with one Mrs. Melody MacCross, an American woman reputed to be the "richest woman in the world." The two had broken up, although acrimonious letters and telegrams kept being exchanged between the two.

Finally, it was confirmed that, on April 7, Mrs. MacCross was in her Paris apartment where she had placed a call to London from 4:57 p.m. to 5:04 p.m.

"It's her. It's irrefutable," said Saint-Clair.

"Indeed," Gno Mitang replied. "But I don't think Mrs. MacCross has the power to kill people at precise times by cerebral hemorrhages from as far away as Paris—even if he were a freak. I know her. I've spoken with her twice at receptions organized by the Japanese Embassy in Washington, DC. She's an Irish Yankee, sentimental and materialistic, practicing that brand of selfish philanthropy that is so common among the very rich, scheming and secretive under a friendly exterior, without many scruples behind the hypocritical façade forced upon her by her name, wealth, and social status... In the end, she's a very rich woman very much like all the other very rich women of her country. So, I don't see her as an expert in the horrific craft that our case suggests."

"I agree," Saint-Clair said. "Which leads us to make our next logical deduction, which is that this X, this Master of Death, whom we know exists somewhere, used her for his own interests."

"And that Mrs. MacCross willingly accepted his dreadful services since she's the one who told her ex-lover, Mr. Reginald Strom, that he would die suddenly at 4:45 p.m."

"We have to talk to her," Saint-Clair said.

"It probably won't come to anything," Gno mumbled skeptically.

"We'll see about that!" the Nyctalope said. And then he laughed. "All the people that X killed don't interest me. Fourteen were waiting for the guillotine, the electric chair, the noose, or the chopping block. The fifteenth was one of those revolutionary politicians whom I hate. The sixteenth could have died of anything like his predecessor in India. The seventeenth was obviously a scoundrel. That's why I'm not so sad that our path is lined with corpses. But I'm trying to think like that 'Average Frenchman' you've read so much about in the press lately."

"Oh," Gno smiled. "And how do you do that?"

"I believe that, if we told our Mr. Average Frenchman the story of the inexplicable deaths we've heard about these past ten days, he would think we were playing a bad joke, exaggerating morbidly, or were just plain crazy."

"But," Gno remarked, "if we look closely at it, three fourths of life is a crazy joke anyway. I'd tell your Average Frenchman to read and reflect on the history of humanity. What's more true, more real, than cataclysms, gullible followers, and ruthless power mongers? What could be more real? More normal? And depending on how you look at it, more insane or ludicrous? My dear friend, let's embrace life and stop judging it."

CHAPTER III
A Dead End

From the start it seemed to Leo Saint-Clair and Gno Mitang that the solution to the problem might lie with Mrs. Melody MacCross. They decided they should talk to the American woman who would likely be flattered to meet Marquis Gno Mitang. But while sitting in their suite at their London hotel, they first examined the issue in all its disturbing complexity.

It was a foggy day outside—a dark, yellow fog, so thick that in the middle of the day, the lights were on everywhere. In their overheated suite, it still felt like the depths of winter. Not yet dressed for lunch, still in their pajamas, Gno sat in an armchair with his legs crossed while Leo paced, his hands in his pockets.

"It's not so simple," said the Japanese with his usual tranquility. "For Mrs. MacCross to agree to Strom's death, and even worse, tell him that he was about to die, that woman must be hiding some ruthless cruelty deep down inside. Neither you nor I are friends of hers, although she knows me personally and you by reputation. On the other hand, she certainly admires X, the Master of Death—even fears him, perhaps. She considers him, not unreasonably, like a god. She correctly worships his power—the most powerful force in the world today. In comparison, we are nothing. If we appear to Mrs. MacCross as possible enemies, or maybe bothersome meddlers, our lives will become even more worthless in her eyes than that of Reginald Strom. She will inform the Master of Death of our visit and call for our elimination. I know it's crazy to discuss this in the middle of London, and even unbelievable, but the problem is very much real. There has been seventeen deaths; let's not become the 18th and 19th victims."

"Of course," Saint-Clair said, "that goes without saying. But every step we take now will be one step closer to death. Mrs. MacCross doesn't know and will never learn that Gno Mitang and the Nyctalope were alerted by Monsieur Dumont-Warren, who was himself alarmed by the successive deaths of fourteen prisoners. She doesn't know and will never learn that we found out about Strom's death in London. So, there's little risk of being exposed—as long as our actions remain the secret of a chosen few: Dumont-Warren and Mrs. Blancat at the UNA, your friend the Japanese Ambassador and Yori Koto. We have to work in secret, but still need to go and talk to Mrs. MacCross."

"Of course, we do," Gno said. "It should be easy. When we're back in Paris, I'll leave my card at her Parisian residence. Like most wealthy Americans, she is probably vain and like making powerful connections. I don't think I'm guilty of the sin of pride if I include myself as among them. She'll call me and invite me over because she's arrogant enough to ignore all the intermediate steps designed by the more refined civilizations of Europe and Asia. I will accept her invitation, of course, and shamelessly ask to bring my friend, the famous Leo Saint-Clair a.k.a. the Nyctalope. You are even more famous than I am. She will be in seventh heaven. And next to you, in her eyes, I'll be nothing but an ordinary diplomat, an unimportant figure on the world stage..."

Saint-Clair laughed with him.

The next day, Monday, April 19, at 5 p.m., Leo Saint-Clair and Gno Mitang were introduced by Mrs. Melody MacCross, all decked out in diamonds, into the big salon of her apartment. During the two hours of conversation that followed, ranging from one subject to another, with tea and music, the Nyctalope did not stop observing the woman and, with Gno's expert, diplomatic help, make her reveal a little of herself.

The following day, Wednesday, April 20, Mrs. Melody MacCross came to lunch at Blingy, with her secretary, Mademoiselle Florence de Salsis, whom Saint-Clair had invited to be the companion of the clever and refined Yori Koto, Gno Mitang's own secretary. And it was through Yori Koto, who had an easy time charming Mademoiselle de Salsis, that they found out this:

On April 7, at 3:15 p.m. Mrs. MacCross had a visitor, a young lady looking like such and such, dressed like such and such, called Leone Alzac. Mademoiselle Alzac claimed to have a French father and a Hindu mother from Calcutta, and to have been a widow for three years. The young lady had sold a little, solid gold Shakyamuni to the American, but had wanted to tell her story and the price in private.

Mrs. MacCross had gone on to question her, quite naturally, but the woman's attitude had put a stop to it—at least in Florence's opinion—because Mrs. MacCross had then asked her secretary to leave the room. Being curious, she had tried to listen in, but it was hard to hear through modern doors, especially when the people one is listening to are on the other side of the room and talking fast and softly.

Therefore, Mademoiselle de Salsis had heard nothing. Yet, she did know one thing: At around 4 p.m., Mrs. MacCross had called London, and after she'd gotten through, she had almost thrown Florence out and gone back to her room to make the call, so that the secretary had again heard not a word.

Having thus made his report to Gno, Yori Koto bowed deeply, took a few steps backwards, straightened up and left.

Fifteen minutes after Mrs. MacCross and her secretary had left, Saint-Clair said:

"We now have another lead—the pretty Leone Alzac. A lead of the utmost importance."

"We just have to find her," Gno said.

Saint-Clair was already on the telephone.

"Hello? Please get me Paris, TURbigo 92-00. Police Judiciaire... Extension 390, please... Thank you... Hello, is this you, Manach? Good. Listen, I need the address of a Leone Alzac. Leone, as in the feminine of Leon... Like Leon Gambetta, yes... Leone Alzac, A-L-Z-A-C... Got it? Perfect. She's a young woman, 25 or 26, pretty, brunette, with a slight Indian look in her features, impeccably dressed... No, I don't know anything else, or at least I can't tell you anything else... Why? Because it's ultra-secret! CID business... [11]We have to be careful and clever... Very urgent, yes... If you find anything before I do, I'll make a big donation to the Orphans' fund. And, of course, even if you don't find anything, I'll reimburse you for all the expenses... Very well, but above all, ultra-secret! My name should never come up, not once... OK, see you soon."

Saint-Clair hung up. Then he pressed one of the six buttons lined up on the ebony plate on the corner of his desk.

"You're calling Vitto and Soca?" Gno asked.

"Yes."

"Good idea. Call my secretary too."

The two Corsicans were no longer spring chickens, but age had not made them fat or slow. They were still athletic and in good physical shape. And still happy to be working at the service of the Nyctalope.

"My friends," Saint-Clair said to them, "you'll be working together with Yori Koto. You proceed do as you like, I'll leave the ways and means to you, but success is crucial. This is what the Marquis told Yori and what I'm telling you. Our target is a young woman, around 25, named Leone Alzac. Remember that name: Leone Alzac—although it's probably not her real name. She's beautiful, serious and determined, darkish skin with big, dark eyes, the color of hazelnuts, a full mouth, well defined, proud. She holds herself like an aristocrat, dresses well. Oh, and she has a trace of Indian blood about her. Got it?"

"Yes, Monsieur," Vitto and Soca said together.

"Our second target is Mrs. Melody MacCross, whom you just met earlier. The first place to check is her apartment near La Madeleine. You know the address. Other places—I have no idea. Keep in mind that Leone Alzac might visit Mrs. MacCross. In that case, you have to be there, you have to follow her, find out where she lives, find out as much as possible about her. As usual and if necessary, one of you can come and consult me while the other remains in place. Otherwise, in eight days, on April 27, at noon, if you're still coming up empty-handed, wrap it up and come back. Last but not least, neither Mrs. MacCross, nor Leone Alzac, nor anyone else, can know what you're doing. That's it. You can start right away."

Holding out his arm, the Nyctalope shook their hands firmly.

---

[11] *Comité d'Informations et de Défense*: a secret police force under the Nyctalope's control.

Eight days went by.

On Tuesday, April 27, at noon, Manach called from the Police. They had failed to locate a woman by the name of Leone Alzac in Paris or the surrounding area. Nothing either in the Provinces. In fact, the Police hadn't found any trace of her in any tax filings, drivers' licenses, bus passes, train tickets, passports, visas, etc. They had also searched the the birth records for the years 1911-1913, and found nothing. Basically, there was no Leone Alzac anywhere in France."

On the same day, at 1 p.m., Yori Koto, Vitto and Saco came back. Yori spoke for the trio when they reported to Saint-Clair and Gno in the library.

"Since April 19, 6 p.m., until today noon, no young brunette has visited Mrs. MacCross, or even met her elsewhere in the city. Nobody named Leone Alzac, not even with the same initials, has written to her, or received a letter from her, during these eight days. No Leone Alzac has called, nor was called, on the telephone by Mrs. MacCross. In short, neither the person nor the name has made any kind of appearance whatsoever in Mrs. MacCross's life during these past eight days."

Saint-Clair and Gno knew that, if the three men has seen and heard nothing, then there nothing to be seen or heard.

"Thank you," the two men said in unison.

The young Japanese and the two Corsicans left. After they were gone, Gno Mitang said:

"For the murder of Reginald Strom, we can assume, with some degree of certainty, that Mrs. MacCross had some personal motives. For the assassination of the Viceroy, maybe we should remember that Leone Alzac's mother was Indian. But what about the premature executions of the fourteen prisoners and the assassination of Eduardo Prim?"

Saint-Clair lit a cigarette.

"I've thought about that a lot and I think I have a theory," he said.

"Ah?"

"With the fourteen executions, X, the Master of Death, was simply practicing his power—a power bought or found or somehow received from somebody else. Executing fourteen criminals was a trial run, executed on insignificant guinea pigs As for Prim, I think it was a political assassination for hire."

"I see your point," Gno said. "But what about this Leone Alzac. Do you think she is our X? I don't have the impression that she is..."

"I know no more about it than you. Maybe Mrs. MacCross knows something more, but we can't count on it."

"You know, this is strange, but I've only just realized that our mysterious young beauty has made her first name a feminine form of yours... A strange coincidence. Is Fate playing games?"

Saint-Clair smiled.

Gno finished his thoughts.

"As for Mrs. MacCross, she talked with Leone Alzac alone for fifteen minutes. We have to find out what they said. In fact, I think that's all we can do. We've hit a dead end. Maybe there's something else somewhere we can't see, but otherwise, the trail goes back to Mrs. MacCross and no one else."

"Damn!" Saint-Clair replied.

He stood up and started pacing from one end of the room to the other, near the open window where the joyful light and scents of spring were entering.

He repeated, "Damn!" and planted himself in front of Gno. "How are we going to get her to talk without giving ourselves away and risking a sudden death? If she's the key, what can we do?"

"Let's think this through. From what we know about Leone Alzac, Melody MacCross, and her relationship with the late Reginald Strom, we can logically deduce a few things. Allow me to practice a little psychology, my friend..."

"Go right ahead."

"Her Irish ancestry probably makes Mrs. MacCross particularly susceptible to the supernatural. Plus, her grandparents founded a short-lived but very 'spiritual' church in Minnesota. She she's got secret beliefs, deeply rooted, that predispose her to accept at face value any claim to supernatural power. I'm sure she barely hesitated before believing the unimaginable proposition to kill at a distance, at a specific time, a truly contemptible and detestable man..."

"Right," Saint-Clair said.

"After Leone Alzac left, after the call to London, maybe Mrs. MacCross felt a touch of skepticism come back, perhaps because of the return to her daily routine. The money she must have given to Leone Alzac—if, as I believe, there was a financial deal struck between them—wouldn't likely matter very much. She is the wealthiest American woman in the world and can afford to throw money away for purely selfish reasons as easily as for philanthropic causes. So, the fact that Leone Alzac asked for money—which, I repeat, I have no doubt about—probably made no impact on Mrs. MacCross. Her soul must have been wavering between slight doubt and enormous hope. Then, all of the doubt was wiped out forever by her receipt of the telegram from London—which we now have a copy of—announcing Strom's death at the appointed time.

"Now, Mrs. MacCross becomes obsessed with the mysterious Leone Alzac. I suppose it's like a savage picturing a witch hiding away in some dark forest, inaccessible to all, with the power of life and death. She redirects all her efforts onto Leone Alzac. Mrs. MacCross now leads two completely different lives: one that her secretary and friends and everyone else share; the other, secretive, for herself alone, spent worshipping an all-powerful god whose priestess is Leone Alzac. Yet, there seems to be no point of contact, no exchange at all, between the two...

"In the past, a person suspected to have participated in black magic rituals would have been interrogated, tortured even, using all mental and physical means possible, but they would have suffered in silence and died without revealing anything. Mrs. MacCross would do likewise, if we had the will, the power, and the means to submit to torture with the very real threat of death. Even if we were alone with her in some far-off corner of the world, or in some deep dungeon, the most coercive and least humane means wouldn't work on her, I suspect... Besides, we're in France, hat most civilized of countries. The means we employ must respect the laws of this country with respect to individual freedoms and human life. Therefore, my friend..."

And Gno Mitang made a gesture that Saint-Clair translated into words:

"Therefore, since we've tried everything the law will allow us to use with respect to her individual freedom, but it's got us nowhere, we've hit a dead end."

"Not quite. There's still one little thing we could do..."

"I can guess what that is," the Nyctalope smiled. "Suborn the secretary. Mademoiselle Florence de Salsis."

"Indeed. Who better?" Gno smiled back.

"But I don't think she can be bought."

"She is very romantic, and I'm told she loves Japan. If she were to become the heroine in her own love story with a handsome Japanese man... such as Yori Koto... whom, I believe, can be very seductive..."

"I hope your clever Yori is up to playing Don Juan!" Saint-Clair exclaimed. "At least, his job won't be too unpleasant. Mademoiselle de Salsis is both smart and pretty."

"Yori agrees with you," Gno smiled.

CHAPTER IV
Number 18

That same day, Tuesday April 27, Saint-Clair received a telephone call. He and Gno were still in the library. The Nyctalope listened for a while and responded simply:

"Yes, with pleasure.

Then, he hung up.

"That was Dumont-Warren," he said. "He wants to talk with both of us and has kindly invited himself over for dinner. He'll be here in 45 minutes."

"Ah-ha! More news, no doubt."

"No doubt."

Using the inside phone, Saint-Clair instructed his butler, Eloi:

"Dinner at 9 p.m., three settings, champagne and mineral water."

The director of the UNA was used to drinking very dry champagne in the evening, always chased by mineral water. His friends usually badgered him about the reasons for this habit, but he never gave an explanation; he just said sometimes, "In thirty years, those of us who will still be alive will be looking at me, and we'll see who has the last laugh!" The fact was that, in 1937, Dumont-Warren was 55 years-old and did not look it.

This die-hard optimist arrived at Blingy at 8:45 p.m. Saint-Clair and Gno met him on the front steps and immediately went into the smoking room, which was separated from the dining room by the grand salon.

The UNA director did not make his friends wait. He put his hand in his right coat pocket and took out an envelope, opened it to pull out a green sheet of paper, unfolded it, and said,

"Telephone message received at 2:07 p.m. Mademoiselle Blancat was at the reception desk. She had the bright idea to intercept the shorthand message, translate it and bring it directly to me. It's from one of our most obscure correspondents. Minor new items are always ignored often because our correspondent is their only witness. Now, this particular item will be of great interest to you. I'll read it..."

This preface made the Nyctalope and Gno Mitang highly curious.

"*Saint-Honoré-Les-Bains (Nièvre), April 27,*" read Dumont-Warren. "*Car accident and lost object. On the road from Saint-Honoré-Les-Bains to Moulins-Engilbert, at 1 p.m., Lucien Rigaut was standing in front of his house, which borders the road, when he witnessed a minor traffic accident that was insignificant in itself, but had a strange outcome. A delivery truck coming from Saint-Honoré-Les-Bains, driven by a fellow who had likely drunk one too many drinks from his customers, was swerving up the hill toward Rigaut's house when its bumper scraped the left fender of a small convertible coming from Moulins-*

Engilbert. The truck driver at fault did not stop. In fact, he sped up the hill and disappeared around the bend. The convertible, on the other hand, swerved, but luckily did not go spinning off the road. A suitcase, however, did fall out of it and bounced into the ditch. The convertible stopped.

"Monsieur Rigaut ran to the car and saw a young woman get out. Without a word, she ran straight to the suitcase and saw that it had snapped open during the fall. Clothes and various objects were scattered over the grass. She ran around picking up her belongings without answering Rigaut's offer to help. When everything was stuffed back into the suitcase, she closed it and rushed back to the car. She slammed the door and took off, but not before Rigaut could see that another person, a man with yellow skin, was in the car, sitting completely still as if nothing had happened. The car had no damage except a dent in its fender.

"Monsieur Rigaut did not get the license number because the plate was covered with mud. In no time the convertible had disappeared, heading back to Saint-Honoré. But this strange story did not stop there. As Rigaut was returning to his house, he glanced at the ditch and saw an object that the woman, in her haste, had missed. He took it. It was a large notebook closed with a leather strap. When he was back inside his house, Rigaut opened the notebook but he found no information about the identity or the address of the young woman and her companion. The pages were almost all filled with newspapers clippings carefully pasted in—from French as well as many English papers and magazines.

"Monsieur Rigaut—who speaks English perfectly—was surprised to notice that the articles were filed by date and all were about the recent death of Lord William Stonewell, Viceroy of India. In the back of the notebook, after a few blank pages, he saw something else, even stranger. On the inside back cover, the word Chong Koum *was written seven times going down from the top right corner to the bottom left.*

"Monsieur Lucien Rigaut, Villa Bel Air, Saint-Honoré-Les-Bains (Nièvre), is now waiting for the owner of the notebook to contact him."

With that, Dumont-Warren looked up and held out the item to Saint-Clair whose eyes were sparkling .

"I don't think it's too hard to guess that your 'most obscure' correspondent is none other than this Lucien Rigaut?" said the Nyctalope.

"Yes," the director of the UNA replied with a smile. "He works only during the spa season and rarely reports something to our agency. He needed this strange circumstance for him to file this report himself."

The Nyctalope looked at Gno Mitang.

"What do you think? Should we enjoy the serenity of this beautiful spring evening and take an after-dinner drive for three hours over 200 miles out to Saint-Honoré-Les-Bains and visit the house of the thoughtful Monsieur Lucien Rigaut?"

"Absolutely!"

"I thought as much," Dumont-Warren said. "And that's why I invited my-self for dinner here—so you'd be near your car, ready to leave afterwards."

"I must thank you profusely," Saint-Clair said enthusiastically. "You pulled us out of a nasty dead end. We haven't seen each other since we got back from London. I must fill you in…"

Eloi the butler came in to announce that dinner was served.

It was at the dinner table that Saint-Clair brought Dumont-Warren up-to-date on the latest twists and turns of their mysterious adventure.

Because of the fast and spontaneous trips he often made, Leo Saint-Clair had a luxury 8-cylinder, supercharged, an aerodynamically designed roadster with a rear seat, a little tight but deep. It had four places: two in front for Gno (or another passenger) and for the Nyctalope, who always drove; and two in the back, usually for Soca and Vitto. The minimal baggage was put under the padded rear seat. A 40-gallon tank could go over 300 miles. In his dull gray speedster, on which nothing glimmered except the windshield and the headlights, Saint-Clair could average around 65 miles an hour, no matter the traffic jams, crossroads or obstacles he came across.

Saint-Clair and Gno decided to bring along the two Corsicans because the trip might likely make Lucien Rigaut's house only the first of many stops. After it? Who knew what track the hunters would have to follow in chasing their prey? Better to have numbers on their side and be able to split up if necessary.

Leaving nearby Versailles at 11 p.m., the Nyctalope's car—whose head-lights were unnecessary for him at night, but which he kept on for the sake of other drivers—passed through Nevers at 1:15 a.m., now on Wednesday, April 28. They went through Decize at 1:30 a.m., Saint-Honoré de Vandenesse at 1:53 a.m., and finally, at 2 a.m., they arrived on top of a hill that overlooked the spa resort of Saint-Honoré-Les-Bains, a quaint little village asleep under the stars. They stopped in front of a white, wooden fence standing before a yard in the middle of which stood a white house with a pointed roof: the Villa Bel Air.

Saint-Clair and Gno stayed in the car while Vitto and Soca jumped out. They knew what they had to do.

The white fence was around three feet high, with rose bushes growing over it in places. The gate, rising up a little higher than the fence, turned out to be locked. The two Corsicans hopped casually over the fence and stomped down the narrow gravel path to the house. Doors and windows were all shut tight. All was silent; the countryside made no sound.

Vitto spotted an electric doorbell and pressed it with this thumb. One or more windows must have been open behind the wooden shutters because even Saint-Clair and Gno, waiting in the car, could hear the bell. Lucien Rigaut would certainly have been woken up by the sound and should have come to peek through the shutters to see who was there.

More than a minute passed as the echo faded away, but there was no other noise or light.

Vitto pressed the bell again.

Another wait. Still nothing!

Was Monsieur Rigaut not at home? Did he always live alone?

"It's too early for us to go looking elsewhere for information," said Saint-Clair. "Besides, we don't have any time to waste. Let's break in and look for the notebook; it ought to be easy enough to find. We'll explain it all to Monsieur Rigaut when we see him tomorrow or the next day. And if I decide to take it with me, I'll leave a note of explanation. Do you agree?"

"I do," Gno said, adding with a smile. "I've learned all kinds of trades with you. Now I can add thief to that list. Because I'll join you."

"OK. Let's go."

Vitto and Soca were experts with locks. In their shared suitcase, they had a modern, multiuse toolkit. The door of the modest villa posed no problems.

They entered a hallway that apparently divided the ground floor into two equal parts. Soca found a light switch and a bright bulb lit up on the ceiling. There were stairs at the end of the hallway. In a loud, clear voice Saint-Clair announced:

"Monsieur Rigaut! Monsieur Rigaut!"

The house echoed, but nothing came except more silence.

"Soca, turn off the light. I'll explore the house alone in the dark."

The ground floor was done quickly. To the left was the study/living room. Saint-Clair noticed the telephone. *So,* he thought, *Rigaut must have called the UNA right after he examined the notebook.*

To the right there was a small dining room and kitchen with a French door leading out to the backyard. Nobody was there. Nothing was remarkable. Next, the Nyctalope climbed the stairs.

Upstairs were three doors on a big, rectangular landing.

The first led to a bedroom. There were blankets over the furniture, and the mattress was rolled up on the bed. *Obviously a guest room,* thought Leo.

The second door led to the bathroom and toilets—all deserted.

The third door led to the master bedroom...

"Oh my God," Saint-Clair exclaimed when he crossed the threshold. One look and he knew. He shouted, "Gno, Soca, Vitto, come up here!"

When the Japanese and the two Corsicans got to the room, the Nyctalope had turned on the light. It was brightly lit. On the bed lay a man, his head a little high on the pillow, like someone used to sleeping on his back. His left arm and hand were under the covers, but his right hand lay on the edge of the bed, cramped up. His face was frozen in that look of death—glassy eyes, wide open, turned to the right.

"Cerebral hemorrhage," Gno mumbled.

"That will be unquestionable if we don't find that notebook," replied Saint-Clair.

They did not find it.

Their thorough search left them no doubt. The notebook with its clippings and the word *Chong Koum* repeated seven times, which had fallen out of the suitcase of the woman who was certainly Leone Alzac, which had been picked up by Lucien Rigaut—the precious notebook was no longer in the possession of the dead man.

"The truth is unavoidable," Saint-Clair said, upset. "When she realized the notebook was missing, she came back. She would have seen the man who was so quick to offer his help, and easily imagined that he had stumbled across the notebook. Otherwise, she would have found it in the ditch. Since there's no other house for almost a mile, there was no other possibility... Leone Alzac was here and met Monsieur Rigaut, who had seen every page of her notebook. She would've found some rational explanation for the news clippings, then calmly left him on his doorstep—alive... His maid would corroborate it, too... For there was a maid... What I saw in the kitchen downstairs tells me so. There was a woman's apron and two letters in a drawer addressed to a Marguerite Delmas from Préporché. Préporché is less than a mile away. She must have arrived in the morning with the groceries and left in the evening. She must have seen Rigaut alive yesterday after Leone Alzac's visit. So she could be a witness if need be. Her statement would prove the woman's innocence. Then, the medical examiner would come and rule it a death by natural causes, a stroke or a cerebral hemorrhage..."

He stopped talking, simmering with rage.

"It's our 18th death," Gno said. "This man was killed to keep him from talking about something he really knew nothing about. That was overdoing it, if you want my opinion. Yes, the murderers overdid it, this time."

Leo Saint-Clair, Gno Mitang, Vitto and Soca left no trace of their presence in the villa. They spent the rest of the night in a clearing in the woods, a little outside Moulins-Engilbert, wrapped up in their coats, two in front and two in the back. Their minds and bodies were so well trained and balanced that they could all sleep anywhere.

At 8 a.m., the roadster stopped at the hotel in Saint-Honoré-Les-Bains, the only hotel that stayed open during the off-season, from October to May. After a quick breakfast, Saint-Clair and Gno told the owner that they wanted to visit some big, furnished houses to rent so they could spend the summer here with their families. The owner gave them the name of a real estate agency.

Vitto and Soca, for their part, went to a garage. They wanted to empty the tank and replace the new "premium gas" they had bought in some small town somewhere, which was just a cheap mixture of heavy gas mixed with dye.

43

At 10 a.m., Saint-Clair and Gno on the one hand, and Vitto and Soca on the other, had their full share of news and information:

First, the local MD, Honoré Garpin, was informed of Rigaut's death by a cyclist at 8:15 a.m. He went right away to the Villa Bel Air. There he found the maid, Mrs. Delmas, crying on her knees at the bedside of Monsieur Rigaut who had obviously died in the night. "A stroke or cerebral hemorrhage," concluded Dr. Garpin. The maid told Dr. Garpin that when she had left Rigaut the night before, after serving him his dinner, he had been healthy and in good spirits as always.

Second, the previous day, at 1:15 p.m., a dark blue convertible, whose license plate number the local mechanic had not bothered to note down, stopped to straighten out its bumper and "tap out' its dented fender. For the three hours it took to repair the car, its passengers—a young lady and a young man—"looking like foreigners," the ex-Navy mechanic had elaborated just walked around after making sure to lock the doors of their car—locks that were "special and particularly strong" according to the mechanic. But when they came back, the young woman opened two suitcases, apparently to repack them because one looked a lot fuller than the other, and did move some clothes and papers. Then she got antsy and wanted to leave. When the work was finally done, the convertible drove away in the same direction it had come, toward Moulins-Engilbert.

Around half-hour later, it came back, but this time it didn't stop. It went straight through town and headed off toward Luzy.

"Luzy," Saint-Clair said, "is a crossroad. To the west, towards Autun, to the south, Charolles and Lyon, then Provence and Italy, to the east, Moulins and the Massif Central, Bordeaux and Spain. If I were to alert the police, they might stop that dark blue convertible and its two passengers somewhere—but we're not going to alert the police, are we, Gno?"

"No. Besides, what excuse could you give them for stopping these two travelers? Suspected murder by cerebral hemorrhage? Unbelievable!"

At that moment, Saint-Clair and Gno Mitang, along with Vitto and Soca, stood in front of the roadster on a deserted little road that was sometimes used for the market at Saint-Honoré-Les-Bains. After a pause, Gno lowered his voice and continued:

"Finally, my friend, in this whole very strange affair, we should keep in mind, all the time, what is the most crucial…"

He paused again before resuming:

"If there is really more here than a series of macabre coincidences, if there is really a man able to kill remotely by sheer force of will, then there will be a death sentence on anyone who is a threat to the possessor this uncanny power. Whether it's the police or ourselves, whoever stop Leone Alzac and her companion are in mortal danger… Don't you agree?"

"Yes," Saint-Clair said flatly. "But you know as well as I do, Gno, that we can't stop now."

"Indeed we can't, my friend."

"Like me, you think that this mysterious Master of Death was just testing his powers on the 14 criminals; maybe avenging himself by killing Eduardo Prim and Lord Stonewell, and no doubt made a profitable business deal with Mrs. MacCross; as for Lucien Rigaut, it was certainly a mere precaution…"

"I agree."

"But you also believe that this man might have other, deadlier goals, an objective that no mad genius could resist: to rule over a nation, a continent, the entire world perhaps! Because whoever is the Master of Death is also the Master of Life!"

"I think so," Gno repeated.

"If this X who is that center of this mystery hasn't set himself this goal yet, if he hasn't visualized it, we must prevent it from ever coming into his mind. Do you agree, Gno?"

"Unquestionably."

"So, let's return to Paris. We'll discuss everything with Dumont-Warren, Mademoiselle Blancat and Yori Koto. We can take stock of what we've found out since April 7… It's been 21 days now. We can flesh out our ideas and decide on a plan of action."

"Very well."

"Great! Vitto, Soca, let's go."

Back at Blingy, Saint-Clair and Gno learned from Yori Koto that, having handled Mrs. MacCross' checkbook for a few minutes, Mademoiselle de Salsis noticed that, on April 7, the American had made out a cashier's check for one million francs. She also had not entered this million into the regular expense account that the two of them kept up-to-date. It did not take much imagination to guess that this was the payment to Leone Alzac for the death of Reginald Strom.

"That's enough for our two convertible drivers to live on for a while," Gno said.

"And work on their future plans in peace and quiet," the Nyctalope added.

"Undoubtedly."

Saint-Clair had connections. He made a phone call. An hour later, they called back to tell him that a cashier's check for one million francs had indeed been cashed at the Banque de France on April 8 at 9:10 a.m. The check came from Melody MacCross. The beneficiary was a pretty young, elegantly dressed brunette, who had put the wads of bills into an ordinary clothing box with the name of a department store from the Left Bank.

Now they were sure: the mysterious and formidable Leone Alzac, knowing the relationship between the wealthy American and the adventurer Strom, had gotten rid of him for the millionairess, earning a healthy sum of money in the process, that she and her "foreign-looking" companion would need to live on while lying in wait.

And not just to live on… The modest convertible, a few suitcases, even the relative mediocrity of the price of death—a simple little million!—showed that Leone Alzac and her companion did not have a fortune before getting the payment from Mrs. MacCross who had been careless or (possibly?) scared, keeping quiet about the transaction from fear of suffering the same fate as Strom.

As for lying in wait… Probably, but for what purpose?

"We have to get to Leone Alzac before she can get anything started," the Nyctalope said.

That night, Wednesday, April 28, Dumont-Warren, who could only come after dinner at 11 p.m., sat in the library at Blingy for a council of war.

In attendance were Leo Saint-Clair, Gno Mitang, Dumont-Warren, Fabienne Blancat and Yori Koto; Vitto and Soca were there, too, because they who would carry out orders much better if they were in on things, but needed only a minimum of instructions, either written or verbal.

Of course, only the first three debated. The assistants just listened and processed what they heard.

The meeting finished at 2:30 a.m. on Thursday, April 29.

PART TWO: THE SECRET OF CHONG KOUM

CHAPTER I
A Journey and Two Camps

"Let's wrap this up!" Saint-Clair said.

Gno Mitang, the Nyctalope and Dumont-Warren were leaning over the maps spread out on the table in the Blingy library; Vitto and Soca stood next to each other behind Yori Koto, a head shorter than the two Corsicans, all of them watching.

"Four legs of around 1200 miles each. We sleep on land, the first night in Bucharest, the second in Baku, the third in Samarkand, and the fourth as close as possible to Lake Chong Koum on the southern side of Central Asia at 3000 feet altitude on the route followed by the expedition of Gabriel Bonvalot and Prince Henri d'Orléans in 1889.[12] The name Chong Koum means 'The Lake That Never Freezes.' It's in an almost completely deserted region, rarely visited even by the Mongol nomads or Tibetan pilgrims. According to the information you got, Gno, on your trip to Tibet when you stayed in Lhasa, we should figure that

---

[12] There is a small lake named *Jong Kam* near Mae Hong Son (The City of the Three Mists), a city in northwestern Thailand, located near the Burmese border. However, it doesn't seem to quite match La Hire's description. Prince Henri d'Orléans (1867-1901), precluded by French law from serving his country as a soldier, turned towards exploration. In 1889, accompanied by the experienced traveler Gabriel Bonvalot (1853-1933), he set out from Paris to reach Indo-China overland by way of Central Asia, Tibet and western and south western China. The journey made contributions in the problems of the whereabouts of Lap Nor and the configuration of the then-unexplored northern plateau of Tibet. The party reached Indo-China in 1890. In 1895, having organized an expedition better equipped for topographical survey, Prince Henri set out from Hanoi with the intention of exploring the Mekong through the Chinese province of Yunan. After proceeding up the left bank of the Salween for a brief part of its course, and then alternating between the right and left banks of the Mekong as far up as Tzeku, the party found it advisable to enter Tibet in a north westerly direction through the province of Chamdo and crossed the south eastern extremity of the country, the Zayul, by a difficult track which led them to the country of the Hkamti Shans in present day Upper Burma, and thence to India completing a journey of 2000 miles.

there's a monastery on one shore of the lake—a secret lamasery that's deemed very holy, and known only to very few initiates.

"Tomorrow, Saturday, May 1, we'll leave from Guyancourt on my twin-engine Zig, which has been fitted out and stocked according to my instructions. You, Monsieur Dumont-Warren, will stay in Paris to run the European operations with Mademoiselle Blancat and Yori Koto, who now has some influence over the romantic, lovestruck Mademoiselle de Salsis. On board the Zig we'll have the latest radio equipment so we can keep in touch as often as necessary through the wireless in Samarkand, Baku and Bucharest. We'll be using the ingenious secret code that Gno invented. I think that's the best we can do for now."

"The best for now, yes," Dumont-Warren agreed solemnly. Then he added, "In my opinion, it's of the utmost importance that our radio communication be absolutely guaranteed. I'm counting on you having no problems with the wireless offices or their chiefs or technicians. You've got the diplomatic papers to assure this as well as enough money. Basically, you'll be geological explorers on a special mission for the UNA representing the Academy of Sciences."

"I just hope the cloistered lamas throw open their monastery doors at the sight of all these titles and papers," Saint-Clair snickered,

And he stood up, along with the others.

The next day, Saturday, May 1, at 8 a.m., the Zig took off from the private airstrip at Guyancourt. The Nyctalope's plane was a twin-engine monoplane built entirely in aluminum. It was a six-seater, supplied for a non-stop flight of a maximum of 2500 miles at an average speed of 185 miles per hour.

As (almost) always, Saint-Clair was the pilot. On this trip Gno Mitang was navigator and co-pilot while Vitto was the mechanic and Soca the radioman.

The first leg from Paris to Bucharest went smoothly. In the Romanian capital, Saint-Clair saw what he had to see, said what he had to say, and all went well.

The Bucharest-Baku trip on Sunday, April 2, also went without incident. But in the "oil city," it was Gno who did what he had to do, after which he smiled contentedly.

The flight from Baku to Samarkand, on Monday, May 3, over the Caspian Sea and the vast Karakum Desert, was more eventful because the, until now, beautiful weather went from fair to very bad with all the fog and winds and sandstorms that one could encounter along a 1200 miles journey. The Zig landed at its destination three hours late and this would have been just as well if in Samarkand...

In the spring of 1937, Samarkand, a major city in the Russian Republic of Uzbekistan, with a majority of Muslims, was in trouble with the local representatives from the Moscow government. For a month, there had been soldiers and soviet officials assassinated, and the Russians had answered with arrests and executions, which in turn caused more murders.

When the French Zig landed at the Soviet airfield, the entire city was in a state of constant rioting, uneasily controlled by martial law. The Samarkand population was made up of a mix of Tajiks, Turks, Mongols, Arabs, Persians, Indians and Chinese, all with deep roots in the region. The Russian population was mostly imported and dated back only to 1869. What the "white tsars" did until 1917, and the "red tsars" afterward, was to try to "drown" the native people under a flood of Russian newcomers. That only served to enrich the merchants who dealt with the garrisons that got fat as well and were slaughtered in turn. But nothing could strip the natives' soul of their religious piety, pride, dignity, courage and the love of independence.

Samarkand had once been the capital, the favorite city, of Tamerlane[13] and his bravest descendants. Near the port of Tashkent, they built a splendid mosque for the youngest and most beautiful of Tamerlane's 300 wives, Bibi Khanym, who was the daughter of the emperor of China, and in this building still lies the tomb of the radiant princess. Another mosque, a marvel of Persian domed architecture, contains the tomb of Tamerlane himself. In short, before the Russians flooded the region with constant waves of barbarous and ignorant soldiers and merchants, the schools in Samarkand were renowned throughout the Muslim world and rivaled those from Baghdad, Persia and North Africa.

Try as they might, however, the Russians could never fully control Samarkand unless they destroyed the entire native population, but this population was continually renewed by the settling down of nomads from all the Turko-Mongolian regions, who were impervious to the communist doctrine.

Gno Mitang, a former minister of state and personal advisor to the Japanese Emperor, did have some Chinese, Turk and Persian contacts. As a former ambassador to Moscow, he also had a few Russian ones in the higher spheres of the Soviet regime, which has quietly adopted, or maybe not fully abandoned, certain traditions of their former ruling class.

If Samarkand had truly been happy and peaceful that spring, Gno would have had as easy a time as he had had in Baku, but there had been a war, a war of spirits more than of physical weapons. Therefore, as skillful as he was in navigating the maze of a local government staffed by Russians and Tajiks, who hated each other, the subtle and powerful Japanese had trouble doing "what had to be done."

---

[13] A.k.a. Timur (1336-1405), Turco-Mongol conqueror who founded the Timurid Empire in and around modern-day Afghanistan, Iran and Central Asia. As an undefeated commander, he is widely regarded as one of the greatest military leaders and tacticians in history. He is also considered a great patron of art and architecture.

When Gno got back to the Zig late on the night on Monday 3, always escorted by Vitto and Soca, the Nyctalope was in the hangar, standing guard between two machine guns ready to fire. Gno had not a smile but a frown on his face. Saint-Clair saw it at once and inquired:

"What happened?"

"We'll probably get what we need from the local government, but we might get betrayed just as easily."

"Same odds?"

"Pretty much."

"So everything's fine. If I were fifty percent sure of our success in this mission, I'd already be calling it a victory. Do you think we can get a little sleep now?"

"Yes, but only for two hours. We'd be better leave at dawn because there's no airfield around Chong Koum waiting for us. I don't even know if it's possible to land there without crashing."

"Two hours is plenty," Saint-Clair replied. He could sleep anywhere any time. "What about the two men you wanted to bring on?"

"I brought them," Gno waved his hand.

Vitto and Soca stepped aside and Saint-Clair saw two men whom Gno introduced, first in French:

"This is Timor. He's a shepherd, gold prospector and hunter. He's lived in a caravan on the high plains to the south of the Gobi Desert. He's a Kyrgyz, speaks fluently three dialects of the Mongols and Tibetans and is 28 years-old. The Japanese consul in Samarkand guarantees his loyalty. He also understands and speaks a little French because he was taught as a child by a French missionary, a Jesuit in Tashkent who was murdered by the Bolsheviks last year."

Then switching to English: "And this is Gissa. For three years, he was an independent student in the lamasery of Lake Tengri called the Tengri Nor. For two years, he worked as a guide for the caravans and pilgrims traveling from Lhasa and southern Tibet to the ancient sanctuaries of northern Tibet. He knows the holy language of the lamas. He was recommended to me by the British consul in Samarkand for his intellectual and moral qualities. The man saved his life six months ago."

Gissa smiled at Gno's speech in English, which he understood completely.

"Excellent!" Saint-Clair said in English. "Welcome aboard, Gissa." And in French, he added: "*Bienvenue*, Timor."

Right after flying over Samarkand in the cold, gray dawn, the first complications appeared in the form of huge, steep mountains ahead. They were none other than, to the right, the Pamir, the highest peak of which reached 21,000 feet, and, to the left, the chain of Tian San, sometimes called the Mountains of Heaven, which rose up to 23,000 feet. The seam between the two ranges was made of high plains with a kind of serrated ridge, the average altitude of which was 13,000 feet.

First spiraling up to 10,000 feet, the Zig gradually rose straight up over the plateaus and, as it were, jumped over the ridge. Luckily, the air was pure, but it became so cold that the aviators had to use their electric heaters. They leveled off at around 3200 feet over the sandy desert and swamps of Takla Makran. But they had to go up again to 16,000 feet in order to get through the Cherchen Pass, the double mountain range of Altyn Tagh and Toungouz Daban.

After this difficult part, they flew along the southern chain of the mountains and, two hours later, they were in sight of the Chong Koum—the "lake that never froze."

The clock on the Zig read 16:23 p.m. on Tuesday, May 4. Gno Mitang wrote in his diary:

"The lake is below us. Its northwest end funnels though a stream, which looks pretty big, and into a swampy lake, totally frozen, which we flew over between 16:02 and 16:13 p.m. The northwest end is bordered by a plateau that we can land on."

Saint-Clair read as he wrote, nodded in agreement and began surveying the landscape before starting to land.

It was an apocalyptic panorama, an eerie lunar landscape, a dead, twisted scenery, dark and streaked with gray. Under the cold sun, in the pure air, the water of the lake looked like molten lead, with bright, shiny spots and dark lumps. There was not a tree in sight, nor the tiniest patch of grass. The plateau stretching out over the south shore of the Chong Koum, which was formed of lava streaked with strange dunes that the scattered winds spread as gray dust in the air.

To the left, the north shore shot up to 20,000, maybe 23,000, feet—the mountains were almost vertical at this point. In the distance, to the southeast, a rim of these same mountains was blocking the horizon. Lastly, the south side of the plateau was bordered by an astounding string of huge black lava cones that held together enormous dunes of gray sand among which the capricious winds seemed to come and go, stop, restart, dance and leap, kicking up clouds of sand that spread out, whirled around, gathered and dropped back down… In the hollows between the dunes, there were banks of snow.

Looking at all this, Saint-Clair, Vitto, Soca, and even Gno, felt, for the first time, that they were "out of place," as if they had landed on the surface of another world, different from Earth, a mineral world, a dead world except for the water flowing out of the seemingly still lake. But the movement the water was itself an anomaly at this altitude and in this season, when big lakes like Tengri Nor were frozen so thick that caravans of laden camels crossed them without the least incident.

Landing the Zig was easy. The lava plateau was long, wide, and in many places, smooth as a highway. Since Saint-Clair and Gno knew that they would be staying there for a while, the immediate problem was to shelter the plane from the northwest winds that blew in hard and fast, accelerated by the mountain passes; they came in from the Gobi Desert and shot out in raging gusts that swept over the barren plain.

With the engines off and the propellers still, the plane became an observatory from which the aviators studied the landscape. Gno spoke up, although he usually waited for the Nyctalope to voice his thoughts first:

"I note that these lava cones aren't in a straight line—they're staggered. It looks to me as if the passage between some of them is blocked off by the next cone, forming a cul-de-sac protected from the wind. If we park the plane in one of those closed off spaces, anchor it on all sides to the cones with iron clamps, it should be safe enough."

"Good idea," Saint-Clair said. "Let's do it!"

He turned on the engines, put it in gear, and, as slowly as possible, taxied toward the jagged line of black cones, and once there, followed the line as closely he could.

"Stop!" Gno said, raising his hand.

The six men got out and pushed the Zig back as far as it could go into the makeshift refuge. Gno was the first to try to make the plane more habitable. He heard the raging winds whirling around, but inside, they didn't affect them at all. The others anchored the plane so that it could be ready to take off again in five to ten minutes, with enough gas left for a six to seven hours flight.

Then, Vitto, Soca, Gissa and Timor set up a double-walled tent about ten feet behind the plane to serve as a kitchen and mess. In the center of it, with its pipe fixed to the central mast, was a gas stove especially designed for polar winters. A horseshoe-shaped table took up half of the space. They then unloaded and set up folding chairs, crates of supplies, gas lamps, and two buckets for the snow that would melt and be used for cooking and drinking, in case the water of the Chong Koum proved undrinkable because of too many minerals or other chemicals. Soon, the tent was furnished with all the ingenuity possible, given what the plane could carry.

The expedition's camp was protected by a group of lava cones that formed a perfect semi-circle. Considering that the lowest of the cones was over 300 feet from its base to its flattened summit, and that the natural barriers of sand, ice and snow were between 70 and 100 feet high and just as thick, they were certain that the tent and their plane were safe from everything but new snow and rainfall. As the season changed, they knew that the spring rains, which had replaced the winter snows, would eventually give way to the dryness of summer.

They could not have hoped for better conditions for their camp, which would also be safe during the night, thanks to an electric barbed wire strung between the cones that set off an alarm set up in both the plane and their tent.

The inside of the Zig had been separated into three compartments by thick canvas partitions mounted on aluminum frames attached to the walls. The one in the rear was for Gissa and Timor, the one in the middle for Vitto and Soca, and the one in the front for Saint-Clair and Gno. Each compartment had its seats that could turn into cots, and contained all the essentials. However, Gissa and Timor in the back were without weapons. There was nothing suspicious about them, but Saint-Clair thought it better to not put boundless trust in them at the start. Obviously, they could slice through the canvas and jump on Soca and Vitto while sleeping, but even this improbable eventuality had been anticipated: the two Corsicans had installed, unbeknownst to the two natives, an electric wire so that it would be impossible to cut more than eight inches of canvas without touching the wire and setting off an alarm that would wake everyone up.

Thus accommodated, sheltered, defended and encamped, the six men slept well in the total silence of the night in the valley of Chong Koum.

The next day, Wednesday, May 5, they first got busy surveying the lava plateau, which ended in a vertical cliff dropping down to the midpoint of the lake. The cones went all the way to the end, surrounded by some rocky abutments and big, steep hills. In the distance, thousands of miles to the south, were the steppes of southern Tibet with their misty lakes and swamps, riddled with dead volcanoes.

Then they examined the water of the Chong Koum. It was warm, 93 degrees in average depending on how far one was from its invisible source. It was not fit for drinking or cooking due to the high level of bicarbonate and sodium chloride, as well as iron and arsenic. The water, however, could be used for medicinal baths—none of the six men needed one.

"For cooking and drinking," Vitto said, "we have a good stock of snow barely mixed with sand between the cones to the northeast of the camp. We just have to filter it after melting it."

At the northwest end, as they had seen from the air, the lake poured through a cascading stream for a few miles, before emptying into another lake, stagnant and swampy, lying in a huge, sandy basin. The winter frost still covered both.

Finally, the main and perhaps strangest characteristic of the region was a total absence of living beings. There were no animals, birds, insects or reptiles, not even a worm! Nothing moved, except the flowing water and the blowing wind. There was not a sign of plant life either—no bush, shrub or blade of grass, not even a weed.

Whether the sky was clear and the sun bright, like during one third of the day, or covered by mists, clouds and whirlwinds of sand, which made the air unbreathable, like during the other two thirds of the day, it was a landscape of infinite desolation.

"I wouldn't want to live for too long in this paradise," Saint-Clair said, sitting in the tent for dinner.

"We just have to stay here long enough to do what we came here to do," Gno said.

"Should we start tomorrow morning?"

"I was going to suggest that."

"Perfect!"

Leo Saint-Clair, the Nyctalope, was the embodiment of the French values: he was both conservative and constructive, traditionalist and reformer, favoring evolutive progress over the blind recklessness of revolutions.

As for Gno Mitang, he knew how to uphold the noblest customs of his country, while assimilating, with moderation and discernment, the scientific discoveries of the modern world.

Both of them now considered the following phenomenon to be very real: *a human being, by merely exercising his or her will, had the power to cause the death of another person from a distance at a chosen time.*

It was an extraordinary power, certainly, but both conceivable and possible, if one admits, as any educated and reasonable mind would, that Man has, for centuries, been evolving, but with occasional relapses into the past, accompanied by the loss of collective memories, before new progress eclipses old knowledge, that becomes wiped out or partially forgotten. It is unquestionable that, in many branches of the sciences, the Chaldeans, the Egyptians and the Chinese in ancient times had knowledge that was lost but was found again, in other forms. Such knowledge that resides in certain "holy" places has been handed down orally by wise men through ancient rites, with no need for an established religion, in absolute secrecy, and without putting it to any use in the outside world.

There is a reason why these sciences are called "occult," even though no true scholar today would dare deny their existence. The fact that these sciences feed superstitions and impostors does not affect them anymore than physics and chemistry are affected by magicians and illusionists who use them in their infantile trickeries.

The sad truth is that the modern world, being directed blindly down the path of materialist discoveries and mechanical and industrial progress, has turned away from the spiritual sciences that were once highly developed in the ancient civilizations.

To kill at a distance by simply casting one's will—does it not have an equivalent in modern mechanics? And has man not been searching to rediscover this formidable power? Of course, he has! Many scientists have been trying to invent a "death ray" by projecting electromagnetic or light waves. It is but a transfer of the spiritual past into the materialistic present. And who will deny that the human will is the most powerful, most potent, and most productive of all known phenomena in nature?

Therefore, it was no surprise that such cultured minds as Leo Saint-Clair and Gno Mitang—and the very intelligent Dumont-Warren—would accept as real, and henceforth indisputable, the fact that eighteen men had died because another man (or woman?), with no personal contact or material connection, had simply willed an end to their lives.

After fourteen experimental tests, a probable vengeance against the Spanish rabble-rouser and the British Viceroy, a murder-for-hire, and the silencing of a witness, Saint-Clair, Gno Mitang and Dumont-Warren had wondered, what the Master of Death would next use his power for? If he only sought to enjoy the earthly pleasures of life, he might just keep on with the occasional scheme of blackmail or murder in order to obtain all the money he needed for his Epicurean lifestyle. But what if the Master of Death had the mindset of a Genghis Khan? A Tamerlane? An Alexander the Great, Caesar or Napoleon? Or even a Lenin? It was a truly frightening idea.

A man having the power to kill by simply willing it—as long as this will was at full strength—would be able to take over the world and force it to obey his his diabolical and capricious whims.

With these ideas in mind, how could such men as Saint-Clair, Gno Mitang and Dumont-Warren sit and wait? They saw their duty clearly—a most crucial and urgent duty. Find this potentially threatening power, unmask it, control it and, if it cannot be used for the good of humanity, destroy it quickly!

They had only two clues to guide their search for the mysterious X: firstly, Leone Alzac, and secondly, the word *Chong Koum* written seven times on an object that clearly belonged to her.

What about Leone Alzac? With the murder of Reginald Strom, she was undoubtedly either the all-powerful X herself (though Saint-Clair did not believe this) or the go-between for the Master of Death. The Nyctalope had refused to call in the police in case the information leaked, alerting the whole world, and possibly causing some cataclysmic reaction from X. They had only one point of entry in their search for the elusive Leone Alzac, Mrs. Melody MacCross. In Paris, Dumont-Warren and Yori Koto were in charge of casting a tight but invisible net around the American woman.

And what about Chong Koum? Gno Mitang had whispered it earlier in this story, even before it had been discovered by Lucien Rigaut on Leone Alzac's lost notebook. It was because the word had a precise meaning, although more legendary than historical. The word had reminded Gno (who was well versed in Asian history) of a very holy and almost unknown lamasery hidden in the volcanic mountains of a deserted region in Central Asia. It was for this very reason that, on the morning of May 6, 1937, Gno Mitang, Soca, Gissa and Timor were walking along the southern shore of Lake Chong Koum in search of a monastery that they refused to believe was just a fiction. Saint-Clair and Vitto had stayed in their refuge with the plane.

The Nyctalope and Gno had gone through every possible scenario and formed a plan of action trying to anticipate every eventuality.

We have often noticed a kind of synchronicity in the appearance of the same inventions in two or three different countries. Is it because of leaks? Blunders or betrayals? The buying and selling of information? Or is it instead because no single human mind has an exclusivity on scientific curiosity and inventiveness? Sometimes scientists, researchers and thinkers, without knowing about each other, follow a parallel path towards two identical discoveries. Their starting points are often very different, but as they progress, they get closer to each other and their goals, whether well-defined or merely suspected, merge into the same accomplishment.

It is due to this natural law of synchronicity, or, if you prefer, coincidences, that, on Wednesday, May 6, at the same time than the four explorers were setting out on their search for the lamasery, that a similar scene was taking place less than thirty miles away at the extreme southeast of the Chong Koum.

Another camp had been set up there, consisting mainly of four small tents pitched under the ledge of a huge volcanic rock on a black sand beach near the water, in front of a big hollow that served as a stable for eight saddled horses and two pack-camels.

There were eight people in that camp. One was a Chinese man called Liang Fong the Venerable, even though he was only around 40 years-old. He was one of those men still living in the Great Celestial Empire who are both scholar and soldier, administrator and priest, and who either hold the highest offices in the state or live apart from all public activity as they see fit.

Then there were two Russians. One was none other than the famous explorer Petrus Rikevitch, for whom the Gobi Desert held no more secrets, and for whom Stalin had nothing but smiles, although Rikevitch was not a registered member of the Communist Party. The other was Colonel Grigori Lazov, a close friend of Stalin, for whom he often worked as a private secretary and secret agent.

There were three other Russians, soldiers and servants, Boris and Felix, the muscle, and Manassé, a scientist.

Finally, there were two Tibetans from Tengri Nor: Chegat and Sarka, who looked like twins of indefinable age and took care of the horses and camels.

Gno and his three companions left Saint-Clair and Vitto at 6 a.m., on Thursday, May 6, to explore the lava plain bordering the midpoint of the northwest part of the warm lake. On the small beach at the southeast end of the same lake, Liang Fong and Petrus Rikevitch, along with Felix and Manassé, had left Colonel Lazov in their own camp with Boris and the two Tibetans.

The last words spoken by Rikevitch were:

"So, it's agreed, Grigori. No more than 45 hours. If we're not back by tomorrow afternoon, or if you don't see the smoke from the six flares in the sky, you come looking for us."

The Colonel had simply nodded and shook Petrus's hand firmly.

Turning their backs to the small camp, the expedition had set out on foot. Straightaway, they went along the north shore of the lake on a ledge of striped lava, a kind of natural balcony formed by the foothills of the mountains, dropping off into steep cliff—a balcony that rose gradually up the side of the mountain over the mirror of water.

From their camp, the Chinese and Russian could see through their binoculars that, farther along the lake, climbing higher and higher on a diagonal for around 10 miles, the ledge took a sharp turn to the north and away from the Chong Koum, driving straight into the mountain amidst a chaos of huge lava stones, frozen still for centuries into the dark and tortuous path of a dead planet after its apocalyptic death throes.

And it was into this frightening mystery of the mountain that the ledge led them unerringly. The scholars Liang Fong and Petrus Rikevitch, followed by the savant Manassé and the herculean Felix, walked fast but carefully, at a steady pace.

It need not be said that these men had no knowledge of the Nyctalope and his crew. Around thirty miles as the crow flew separated the two teams. And at this distance, Saint-Clair's plane had not been seen or heard.

CHAPTER II
"Stalin has the highest respect for you"

Soca was the first to see the unexpected sight.

"Ho, Monsieur Gno!" he shouted excitedly. "Over there! Men!"

He was standing on the shore looking through powerful binoculars. Behind him, squatting in front of Gno, who was sitting on a rock, Gissa and Timor were eating crackers and canned ham.

They were taking their first break, around three miles beyond the narrow cliffs where the lava plain ended to the southwest. Their watches showed 9:30 a.m. A strong breeze pushed foamed-tipped waves over the lake against the weak current. The pale blue sky was clear; there was not a cloud in sight; the sun was bright and strong, and the air cold.

At Soca's call, Gno laid down his sandwich, jumped up and ran over.

"Over there!" Soca repeated, handing him the binoculars while pointing to a spot on the mountain, high over the lake on the other bank, less than eight miles away.

"You're right!" Gno said. And very calmly, he spoke in English, which Soca and Timor understood almost as well as Gissa, "Four men. Dressed pretty much like us. One of them is definitely Chinese; another probably Russian. The last two are Russians too, or at least Eastern Europeans, I think. They're doing like us—they're eating. They're on the top of a rising ledge that stops at a huge jumble of petrified lava." After a brief pause, he went on, "Let's back up and hide. They might get the idea of using their own binoculars too."

As he spoke, he started backing away. The edge of the lake was littered with big rocks. Gno kept watching. Right away, he figured that the men must have climbed up the natural ledge, so he followed the route in reverse, going back down. As he moved the binoculars from right to left, he also turned the dial slowly to focus the view. Since their location was a rounded promontory of the lake, ,he was able to see the end of Chong Koum. And there, he discovered the four tents set up in front of a big, dark grotto on a black sandy beach. A man was standing on the beach, completely nude. Another man, also nude, was showering with a bucket that he dipped into the lake. At the entrance to the grotto, two other men appeared briefly in the sunlight, before disappearing into the shadows.

Gno described aloud to his companions what he saw. He ended with:

"No doubt about it, the four up on the ledge left that camp while the others stayed behind. We'll wait here until they get moving again. I think they'll head into the rocks where the ledge disappears. Then we'll continue on our way. But we'll have to use the terrain to stay hidden from their camp as much as possible. After half a mile or so, you can drop the packs and carry only weapons. Depending on the circumstances, I'll give the orders to enter the camp, maybe by force or with some clever trick. Do you understand?"

"*Oui, Monsieur*," Soca and Timor said.

"Yes, sir," Gissa chimed in.

"Very well."

They did not have to wait for long. Fifteen minutes later, while Gno kept the binoculars focused on the four men on the ledge, they all stood up at the same time. Two of them grabbed their backpacks off the ground and slipped the straps over their shoulders. Then, turning their backs to the lake, they all marched into the black chaos where they vanished from sight.

"Right! Let's go," Gno said. He handed the binoculars to Soca, adding: "You've already eaten, right? Neither Gissa, nor Timor, nor myself finished our breakfast. We don't know what to expect over there and we should be in top shape. So we'll finish eating while you watch their camp."

"*Oui, Monsieur*."

It took half an hour for the Japanese and his companions to get on their way. They figured that, following the lakeshore as closely as possible, the dozen miles that separated them from the four tents would take five hours maximum to cross, so they would arrive at the beginning of the afternoon, when the campers, who certainly woke up at dawn, would be tempted to nod off, it not to take a nap. At least, they would be tired. The newcomers would catch them off guard in a weakened state and overcome them without too much violence

At least, that was what Gno was hoping.

Of course, he did not imagine that the eight men might have come to the shores of the Chong Koum for the same reasons as he and the Nyctalope. But whatever their motive, they were here. At first, he considered them a mere nuisance. Maybe they were not dangerous, or stronger than them? Maybe neutrality or even an alliance between them was possible? It would be better to be calling the shots rather than be forced to accept another's commands. A simple explanation beforehand might prove misleading... And after such an explanation, what if the others took advantage of their greater number and favorable circumstances to make the Japanese and his companions their prisoners, or even just corner them and take away their weapons?

Thus, in Gno's mind, the meticulous examination of the situation and the possible outcomes produced only arguments in favor of an attack. He went through several different hypotheses, examining and restarting each one. During the whole trip, he thought of nothing else.

Thanks to the nature of the terrain on the south shore of the lake, their progress was relatively easy and fast. The different sized hills that stretched to the southern horizon left a ribbon of sloping sand between their base and the water, between ten and a hundred yards wide. This land was strewn with flat rocks that were occasionally so close to each other that the path wandered through them and kept them completely hidden from any possible sighting by the people at the other end of the lake.

Extremely alert, endowed with a keen eye, a fine sense of smell and sensitive hearing, Timor led the way, followed by Gissa, then Gno, and Soca at the rear. From time to time, Timor stopped, scrambled up on a rock and lay flat to study the path ahead. During these pauses, Soca climbed up on another rock with his binoculars, exchanged a few words with the Mongol, and relayed an account down to Gno, who was satisfied to hear every time:

"All's well. We keep going."

As their watches now showed 2:18 p.m. during one of these brief stops, the Japanese ordered quietly:

"Soca, come down. Let's take a brief pause to check our guns and get them ready. You follow me. Don't lose sight of me. Listen carefully to what I say. Depending on that, depending on my movements, my gestures, you do as I order. Be careful! If we've got no choice but to use our revolvers, try not to kill them. Try to hit their shooting arm. If there are only four of them, maybe my knowledge of *jiu-jitsu*, Soca's boxing and Gissa and Timor's fighting skills will be enough. At least, I hope so. Our goal is not to hurt them, let alone kill them, but to keep them from hurting or getting the better of us. Use your belt or the rope we've got to tie their hands and feet. I see no other choice for now. But we've still got ten minutes. Do you have any questions?"

No one did. He sat down. The other three did the same. The ten minutes passed without anyone saying a word.

"OK! Let's go," said Gno standing up. "Stay close, but nobody gets in front of me."

Dressed in warm clothes with their leather straps and high boots, they still felt lighter because they had left their packs behind—even Gno's small medical bag, which also contained flares and Bengal lights for signaling.

They started forward, full of that excitement that men of action feel when they're on the verge of an adventure. The only wind blowing was from the northwest, piling up small sand dunes between the rocks closest to the lakeshore. Their walk lasted ten minutes.

All of a sudden, the Japanese dropped down on the side of one of the dunes and crawled up to the top. There, he dug out a narrow trench for his eyes. Soca and Timor were on his left, Gissa on his right. They did the same.

From their vantage point, they saw the beach of black sand, bordered to the south by a long, bloated dune which merged with huge rock behind the mouth of the grotto. There would be about fifty feet between them and the tents, once they were at the foot of the dune. The space was clear; they saw no man or animal. Just like them, the Russians had brought no dogs. Gno and his associates could see the camels and the horses in the shadows of the grotto, but they would not give any kind of warning like a dog if a stranger approached.

Therefore, there was nothing they could see to stop them.

Just loud enough to be heard only by the others, Gno whispered:

"The four men I saw must be sleeping inside their tents. At least, they're inside because I can see the back of the grotto and there's only the two camels and the eight horses. Here's what we'll do: the tents are lined up facing us, so from left to right, Soca first, Timor second, then me, then Gissa. If your tent's empty, stand guard until you hear a call for help. Got it?"

"*Oui, Monsieur*," Soca and Timor whispered.

"Yes, sir," Gissa hissed softly.

"Good. And don't forget the advice I gave you earlier. Be careful. Now, let's go!"

Short and thin but muscular and agile, the 50 year old Japanese leaped out like a cat. Ten years younger than him, Soca was equally alert. Timor and Gissa, at respectively 28 and 32, were full of energy. They leaped over top, slided down the steep slope of the sandy dune, then the fifty feet sprint took only thirty seconds.

But halfway across the space, a cry rang out. A hoarse, savage cry. A man jumped from behind the first tent where he had obviously been on watch. He did not cry out a second time because Soca was on him and punched him in the jaw.

The shout, however, had woken up the other three men. Two huge men came running out of the first tent as Timor saw that the second was empty. As he heard Soca call for help, he rushed over to his side.

The fourth man was rubbing his eyes at the entrance of the third tent, holding open the canvas flap. He was big and tall with a weather-beaten face. Gno jumped at his chest and struck his neck on the carotid artery while driving his knee hard into his left ribs. The giant collapsed, gasping for breath. Gno had him tied up in no time.

Gissa, on the other hand, had found an empty tent too, and seeing that his boss needed no help, went to assist Timor and Soca who were fighting the two Hercules. In a few seconds, that fight, too, was over.

Inside the first tent, the four defeated henchmen now lay tied up on the ground, next to each other, on their backs. Two of them were unconscious—the first punched by Soca, the second, Gno's victim. The other two, Tibetans, bested by Soca, Timor and Gissa, were only bruised.

"Let's wake up that one," Gno pointed to one of the men. "I'll take care of the guy I knocked out. Soca, see if you can find some vodka or any alcohol in the other tents."

The big man bested by Gno's *jiu-jitsu* did not take long to come around. When he opened his eyes, and, with some help from his foes, was sitting up, his back against a saddle, Gno stood before him, leaned forward, and spoke to him in Russian.

"Sir, please, excuse me. As Fate would have it, you are obviously the leader of this camp, and therefore, it is you whom I must address. Again, I apologize for my brutality, but I had no choice. Later, if you'd like, I can explain why. In

61

the meantime, if you give me your word of honor to try nothing against us, I will untie you so we can talk together like gentlemen."

The man listened in silence to the brief, courteous speech. He answered with a short question in Russian:

"Who are you?"

"I have no reason to hide my identity," replied Gno, smiling. "I am Marquis Gno Mitang, former minister, former ambassador, and personal advisor to His Majesty, the Emperor of Japan."

The other smiled back and played his part in the strange scene.

"Very honored. I am Grigori Petrovitch Lazov, colonel in the Russian Cavalry, sent here on a geological mission."

Gno threw up his hands.

"On a geological mission! Me too, colonel! But truthfully, if your knowledge of geology is as meager as mine, I believe it is my duty to find the real reason for your presence here."

"I'd ask the same of you."

"Very well. So, will you give me your word as an officer and a gentleman that you won't try anything against us for 24 hours?"

"For only 24 hours?" Lazov asked, with a sparkle in his gray-blue eyes.

"That's all I ask," Gno said solemnly.

"Well then, Your Excellency, you have my word."

"Thank you."

Gno untied his victim and threw aside the ropes. The Russian rubbed his wrists and ankles, then from a pocket of his coat, he took out a cigarette case, a flint lighter and a wick.

"May I? And do you?"

"You may with pleasure, but I don't smoke."

Lazov lit a cigarette, took a few drags, and looked to his right at the three men tied up next to each other on the ground. He slowly brought his eyes back to the now hardened face of his adversary.

"Your Excellency, you may untie them. My word shall bind them too."

Gno nodded to Soca and said in French:

"Let them go as long as they agree to stay inside the grotto." Then to Lazov: "Colonel, would you order them to do so?"

"Gladly."

When it was done, Gno told Soca:

"Go through the grotto and the tents and take all the weapons and ammunition you find. Put everything in tent number 4. Make sure to unload all the rifles and pistols first."

Lazov frowned and said curtly: "My word of honor..."

But Gno raised his hand to interrupt and, without smiling, said:

"I take you for a man of honor and these three boys—a Russian and two Tibetans, right?—for disciplined soldiers. But your expedition has eight people, four of whom are in the mountains right now. I have to take precautions to prevent any hostile action between your men and mine. Who knows, maybe we can end up finding a peaceful agreement between us, if no bad blood makes it impossible to discuss matters reasonably."

"Ah! Japanese diplomacy;" Lazov said, shrugging.

Gno smiled faintly and responded:

"As opposed to Soviet loyalty?" After a brief silence, he added softly, "For more three years now, I've heard of the name and reputation of Colonel Grigori Petrovitch Lazov. And I know that Stalin has the highest respect for you, and total confidence." Another pause, then in a different, more blunt tone, he conclude "But enough small talk, colonel... Please do me the honor of answering frankly, even rudely if you want, as a soldier."

"I'm listening, Your Excellency," the Russian replied coldly. "I'll tell the truth—or I'll say nothing at all."

"So be it! First of all, are you the head of your joint Russian-Chinese expedition? I say Chinese, because one of your four hikers is Chinese, and from what I could see with my binoculars, he looked like a man of some importance."

"No, I'm not the head," Lazov answered directly. "His name and reputation is probably more familiar to you than mine. He is Petrus Rikevitch."

"Ah," Gno said quietly. "The explorer."

"Yes, the same."

"Good. Your expedition, then, is led by Rikevitch, assisted by a Chinese who is no doubt from the upper class, and by a valued Russian officer, a confident of Stalin himself. You understand that I don't believe a word of this geological purpose, no more than you believe in mine. Therefore, my second question is: what is the purpose of this secret expedition sent by Stalin to Chong Koum?"

Lazov flicked away the butt of his cigarette and answered simply:

"That, I can't tell you."

"But I must know it."

This time the Russian smiled and with a casual wave of his hand said:

"*Nitchevo.*"

Gno stood up.

"Colonel, all our negotiations are henceforth useless. I know your reputation, as I said. So I understand that your refusal to talk is your final word on the matter. I'm sure that when Rikevitch and the Chinese return eventually, they'll do the same. Furthermore, I'm pretty sure that your Russian soldier and the two Tibetans know nothing. So, I'll have to find out by myself. And to free you of your responsibility to Stalin later, to Rikevitch and the Chinese gentleman much sooner, and to yourself right now and until the hour of your death, Colonel Lazov, I am unfortunately forced to break our agreement. Please, do not move!"

Gno stepped back, pulled his Browning out of the holster, and called out:

"Soca!"

The Corsican came running.

"Pick up those ropes and tie up the colonel again," Gno ordered.

"*Oui, Monsieur.*"

Lazov did not budge. His rugged face was likes stone, his eyes empty. When it was done, Gno walked around to face the grotto.

"See to the three men now, Soca."

They offered no resistance. When the Russian and the two Tibetans were tied up and sitting against a wall in the grotto, Gno spoke again:

"Soca, we're almost finished. Did you get all the weapons and ammunition?"

"*Oui, Monsieur.* When you called me, Gissa and Timor were wrapping up the rifles and pistols in a tight bundle."

"Excellent," Gno nodded.

Just then, the two Mongols came from behind the first tent.

"Stay on guard between the grotto and the tents," ordered Gno. "Keep one eye on the captives and the other on the ledge going up into the mountains. Anything that happens, one of you come and tell me." And to Soca: "You and I are going to carry out a methodical search."

Meticulously, they started with the biggest tent, which belonged to the two Russian leaders; tent 2 was obviously for the Chinese. Their search was fruitful a lot sooner than Gno could have hoped for. In fact, their discovery was so fruitful, so revealing, so instructive and valuable that it thrilled him.

"Soca! Go get Timor," he said.

As soon as Gno realized the importance of the item he had found lying in a suitcase with a simple spring lock, he knew exactly what he had to do.

It was a thick notebook with good quality paper, strongly bound, kept in an airtight, metal container. He put it back in the container and tied it up in canvas. But first, he had thumbed through it and read a few pages carefully. Then, on a blank piece of paper, he wrote a note which he slipped behind the front cover:

Leo, read and decide. Come yourself or send Timor back with your decision. I'll wait here to capture the four other members of this expedition. Timor can tell you all about our wonderful excursion. – Gno

Ten minutes later, Timor was on his way, with specific instructions and carrying a backpack strapped tightly around his shoulders and waist.

Six hours later, in the twilight, Saint-Clair was sitting on a folding chair in the farthest corner of their refuge, listening to Timor standing in front of him, with Vitto at his side. He had the wrapped package on his knees.

When the Mongol had finished the story of their "wonderful excursion," as Gno had dubbed it, the Nyctalope unwrapped the box. He opened the metal container and took out the notebook, opened it, saw the note and read Gno's message.

"Timor, either you'll be going back alone with a message from me, or Vitto and I are going to join you. In either case, you should eat first. Vitto, keep him company."

Alone now, the Nyctalope stared at the first page. He read the text, written in Latin, which he translated on the spot, because, just like Gno Mitang ,he was an excellent Latinist:

NOTES
To be used as Volume II of my Memoirs
(The Secret of Chong Koum)
by Petrus Rikevitch

"Well, well," Saint-Clair said aloud.

Immediately engrossed in the notebook, he read through it. He noted that only 22 out of 100 pages (they were all numbered) were filled in on one side with small, cramped writing, all in Latin. The backs of the pages were full of notes and references, some long, some short, some only numbers or capital letters, and some memos of the scholar.

After getting the gist of the notebook, Saint-Clair went back to page 2 where the text of the "*Notes*" began. And he translated it:

Note 1: In the course of a conversation on the religions of China and Southeast Asia, Liang Fong ended up telling me about the seventh sect of the Atharva Veda whose rituals are described in the Kaucika Sutra. The most hermetic and most powerful of them is the following:

The priest accomplishes the rite of pressing the soma; *while he crushes the* soma, *if he thinks, 'let so-and-so be crushed,' his will is fulfilled and the so-and-so will fall dead, even if on the other side of the world.*

To my questions on certain details, Liang Fong said that, according to what he heard from the mouth of a very old Brahmin, the seventh sect of the Atharva Veda continues to exist today in an unknown lamasery in Western Tibet, or in the remotest regions of the great Gobi Desert.

What Liang Fong told me reminds me of a legend I heard from some of the Tcherki nomads who had agreed to accompany me in my exploration of the Gobi. The legend says that the first Living Buddha had the power to end any and all human and animal life and to wither plants and trees by the simple exercise of his will. This gift, both demonic and divine, was given to him by the invisible spirits that abound in the warm waters of the Chong Koum and often manifest themselves in the iridescent bubbles that surface on the lake.

Lastly, in the big Tibetan lamaseries, there is a tradition of dedicating two days of prayer a year (at the spring and fall equinox) to the spirits of the lamas of the seventh sect of the Atharva Veda, the priests who have been cloistered for centuries and centuries in an invisible monastery located on the shores of the Chong Koum. These are some intriguing coincidences.

"Damn right," the Nyctalope said aloud.

Under the last line was the date when this note had been written. Saint-Clair turned the page and read, again in Latin that his mind automatically translated, the following:

Note 2: I talked with Liang Fong for three hours. We delved into the problem of Chong Koum. But his vast learning could not answer the most important question: What is soma? *Yes, Liang Fong is aware that the Hindu* soma *is the sweet, intoxicating juice extracted by pressing the stalks of a fleshy plant. But what plant is it? Liang Fong assures me that his most careful research has failed to identify it. It doesn't necessarily seem to be the same as what the Brahmins get their sacred beverage from today. And the descriptions in the Veda are so full of mystic and poetic details of a highly developed imagination that you can't even make an educated guess. All we can be sure of is that the plant does not grow in India itself and the priests get it from the mountain districts in northern Tibet. (November 29, 1936)*

"Well then," Saint-Clair said. "I think I'm starting to see..." But he kept reading:

Note 3: I had to go back to Moscow suddenly. I dined with Colonel Grigori Lazov. I told him about my talks with Liang Fong (December 18, 1936)

Then:

Note 4: Stalin wanted to see me. (December 19, 1936)

And finally:

Note 5: We're leaving for Nanking where Liang Fong lives. (January 3, 1937)

The rest of the pages were nothing but descriptions, sometimes detailed, sometimes summarized, of the expedition across China to the shores of Lake Chong-Koum. The last page was dated May 8, 1937.

"Yesterday!"

Saint-Clair stood up.

Absorbed in his thoughts, he put the bound notebook back into the metal box and tucked it under his left arm. Quickly, in the cold, dark night, the Nyctalope walked to the tent where the lamp was shining through the canvas, and entered. He noticed that the wind had stopped blowing, but no star pierced the misty sky overhanging the lake and the plateau.

For the third time in this already busy day, Timor, the tireless hiker, covered the distance between the Refuge and the Four Tents Camp. But he was not as relaxed as he had been that morning, or as fast as he had been in the afternoon. Just like Saint-Clair's other companions, he had been pushed to the extremes.

With no moon or stars to brighten the nocturnal darkness, Leo Saint-Clair could still walk as if it was daytime, because he was the Nyctalope. But since he had others with him, who had to follow him, he held a rope in his left hand with rings attached every six feet that were held by his companions who could thus walk at the same pace as him, blindly but trustingly. They soon adapted to this system and rarely slowed down or stopped, even though not one of them could see the ground. Of course, the Nyctalope took care to avoid any obstacles that would be hard to get around and he signaled the others when he could not by simply tugging on the rope or, in more difficult cases, by stopping and whispering a warning down the line.

Before heading out of their refuge, Saint-Clair had taken a few precautions for the plane and the camp, which they would be leaving unattended. Three small but essential parts of the engine had been removed and well hidden, so that the Zig could not be started, even by an expert pilot or a mechanic who might have spare parts at hand. To protect the camp, the main wire of the fence had been hooked up to a swiveling machine gun so that the slightest touch would set it off fanning bullets at the intruders. Moreover, entering the camp by climbing the cones or the rock walls was neither easy nor quick, and the intruders, if successful, would still be facing the lethal booby traps. Of course, all this would have been useless for a long absence when the enemy would have had plenty of time to study and defuse said traps. But Saint-Clair was not counting on being gone for more than a day.

The other precautions taken concerned their night journey. Timor had made the trip twice during the day and, like all native nomads, had great visual memory. The Nyctalope had made a rough map of the south shore of the lake on which he drew the obstacles and traced a route to follow. He noted everything he needed to know in shorthand on the map, folded it, and put in in his pocket.

The three nocturnal explorers then set out on their march carrying nothing but weapons. The notebook of Petrus Rikevitch had remained behind, in a small safe on the plane. The important parts of his notes had been read and reread until they were engraved in Saint-Clair's memory.

The twenty or so miles between the Refuge and the Four Tents Camp took seven hours to cross. Timor had done it in five and a half hours, alone, without baggage, except for the small metal container. But here, they were looking at eight hours, with the Nyctalope leading them by the rope.

Leaving the Refuge at 10 p.m., it was not until 6 a.m. that the three men got to the foot of the long, high dune that separated them from the beach where the tents stood in front of the grotto.

Before arriving at their destination, from the moment they were in sight of the end of the lake, the Nyctalope had stopped several times to study the beach, the four tents and the grotto carved by nature out of the huge, curved rock.

"Everyone's still asleep over there," he said.

As long as it was still night, this was normal. But when the sun appeared in the east at the top of the mountains and spread its light over the lake, even though the sky remained covered by clouds, Saint-Cloud was surprised that no sign of life stirred around the camp. As they got closer, he saw that the grotto was empty.

"Timor?" he whispered.

"Sir?"

"You did tell me that yesterday, there were eight horses and two camels along with all the food and equipment in the grotto, right?"

"Yes."

"Well, now there's nothing there. No horse, no camel, nothing at all."

"I'm surprised Soca isn't up and around yet," Vitto said. "He always wakes up between 5 and 5:30 a.m. My watch says it's 5:53 a.m."

"Strange," Saint-Clair muttered.

The rope had been rolled up and hung on the Nyctalope's belt since the daybreak.

"Let's get over there on the double!"

The last pause was taken on the dune, on their bellies, on the same spot that Gno and the others had dug out their slots in the sand earlier. Timor automatically did the same, imitated by Saint-Clair and Vitto. The camp looked too empty to have people staying there. The four tents were still there, of course, closed up for the night, but there was nothing on the ground around them. And with the sun up, they were too closed, too quiet, too motionless in the still air.

"Damn," Saint-Clair murmured worriedly. "Gno must have left and took everything with him on the horses and camels. But why? If so, did he leave any-one behind? Is someone still asleep in a tent? And above all, why did take off with four prisoners, knowing that I was coming, or at least sending Timor back with an answer... No, it's not possible! Gno can't have left. So what happened?"

"I'm going to check it out," Vitto offered.

"No, not you. Timor is faster and more agile. Go, Timor, and slip in there and if anyone's on guard, I'll knock him out before you're spotted. Got it?

Yes, sir."

Swiftly and smoothly, Timor dug out a deeper and wider slot. He crawled through and slid down the sand dune, then disappeared. Saint-Clair and Vitto only saw him five minutes later as he was inching his way forward, taking a long detour to the right to stay out of sight in case anyone lifted the flap of a tent.

The Mongol slid as a snake, or rather he advanced with the sinuous movements of a big lizard stalking an insect, getting ready to attack.

When he got to the first tent, he stopped, listened, and then squatted down to lift the flap a little to peek through.

"No one in that one," Saint-Clair said.

Timor was already crawling to the next one. It was the same as the first— no one. And then the third, then the fourth... Jumping to his feet, Timor turned to the dune and shrugged.

"Let's go!" Saint-Clair said to Vitto.

In less than a minute, the Nyctalope and the Corsican stood next to the Mongol. No explanation was needed. Saint-Clair looked into every tent. Not only were there no living beings, but there was nothing at all in any of them. Not a single object remained. The same oddity—nothing—was found in the grotto. It was incomprehensible.

Left speechless, Saint-Clair had not said a word during the search, which all three of them did separately. Then all of sudden he cried out:

"Look! Look! Here and there... all over the place!"

He was pointing at the black sand from the grotto and the tents all the way to the water. There were prints of bare feet. In some spots, there were a few rare traces of boots and horseshoes, but everywhere showed the chaotic trampling of a crowd, jumping up and down here, twirling around over there, running back and forth in groups.

"I think I'm starting to understand..."

Saint-Clair hustled over to the northwest end of the beach. He ended up under a kind of wide but thin terrace. It was the start of the lava ledge that shot up over the lake more than 1500 feet before turning sharply into the mountains.

He jumped onto the ledge, turned around and surveyed the beach from one end to the other. Then he motioned to Vitto and Timor to come over. They came running and jumped up next to him.

"Look," he told them. "A set of barefoot prints there on the left. A group of men came from the ledge, ran over the beach and then spread out. Our men were overwhelmed and taken captive with their horses, camels and all the baggage. The four Russians were also taken, or maybe freed, by the attackers. Who were they? I don't know yet... There's no clue on this point... You see that second set, there, on the right? The attackers came back here and got back onto the ledge where it's lower than on the left. Why didn't they take the tents? Who were these barefoot men? They came from the mountain and they went back to the mountain by the same route..."

He paused to look at the hard lava path. Then he spoke again to his two associates as if to himself:

"There's something else I don't understand. Did these men attack before nightfall? That would explain why we didn't see them. But how could Gno, So-ca and Gissa been taken by surprise? If the men came during the night, it's easi-er to understand the surprise. But that means the attackers had no lights on their march, because if they had had lights, then we would have seen them either coming or going since we always had that camp in our sight? There are contra-dictions here... But we'll learn nothing here on this ledge. Let's go back and ex-amine that camp more closely to get a better idea of what we're up against.

"Also, we all need rest, especially Timor. We have no supplies, but we can fast for a while. Let's rest for 12 hours in that grotto, then we'll go back to our Refuge and get our strength back. After that, we'll leave by land or by air and try to find our missing friends and free them. I can't believe that... No, I refuse to think that they're still not alive! There's no sign of a bloody fight here. Noth-ing wrecked. Could the attackers have picked everything up and wiped away or covered every trace of blood? It's hardly likely. I don't see a lethal combat here. I think it was an ambush, short and fast... A barefoot horde that swarmed around our men and captured them. So they must be alive. We have to find them and free them, using tact, tricks or violence depending on the circumstances. Or all three if need be..."

He motioned to the two men and said, "Timor, Vitto, get inside the grotto."

Saint-Clair had enough self-control to keep his companions from seeing the worry and fear that was torturing him.

CHAPTER III
Earl Patrick and Leone Alzac

Meanwhile, in Paris, the clever Yori Koto had been able to use his spare time during Gno Mitang's absence to spend more time with Florence de Salsis while Mrs. MacCross was busy with her social obligations. The romantic young woman was thrilled by the thoughtful attention of her delicate and cultivated knight in shining armor. As for Yori, she was the oblivious mirror where the whole life of the Irish-American billionairess was reflected.

The whole life? Apparently, yes, all of it. But, in fact, there were "holes" in that mirror. There was one afternoon when Mrs. MacCross received a visitor without her secretary being present, and she knew nothing about it—neither the place, nor the person. As whimsical as she was, Mrs. MacCross still had her secrets. Naturally, Mademoiselle de Salsis just figured that it was a normal part of the very busy schedule of a rich socialite.

Yori Koto felt that something more important was going on, but after spending time with the French girl, he knew he would lose her trust if she suspected that he was using her as an informer.

I can use Florence forever as an innocent informer, he told himself, *but as far as her becoming a willing spy, never. Also, I would lose her completely if she had the slightest suspicions about me. But it is infuriating. Yesterday, for example, I don't know what MacCross did between 5 and 7 p.m. in that house in the 14th arrondissement where a certain Earl Patrick O'Dougal lives. I know through Florence that her boss was so preoccupied by her thoughts that she didn't say two words during their lunch together, and after that, while Florence read the papers out loud to her until 4:30 p.m., she was silently chain-smoking cigarettes, when she is usually talkative, and apparently didn't hear any of the news although she is always curious about everything. The picture is incomplete, but I can reasonably suppose that her visit to Earl O'Dougal at 5 p.m. was the cause of her introspective attitude.*

Of course, this calls for an investigation of this Earl, who is known to be an Irish separatist.[14] But it's bothersome that Florence doesn't enjoy her Mistress' total trust. It would be easier for us. Since Mrs. MacCross has an Irish background, she is certainly, or at least very likely, prepared to finance the cause of Irish independence. That might interest the Intelligence Service, but not us... Unless... hold on, now this is an interesting idea...

Yori Koto held this monologue on Saturday evening, May 8, ten days after the meeting with Saint-Clair, Gno Mitang and Dumont-Warren, at the end of

---

[14] Likely a thinly veiled reference to Peadar O'Donnell (1893-1986), one of the foremost radicals of 20th century Ireland.

which he had been tasked with the mission to learn everything he could about the day-to-day activities of Mrs. MacCross.

He was not staying in his room in Blingy, but had rented a secret apartment on May 1 for three months on Rue de Constantinople. The living room, bedroom, bathroom and tiny kitchen with electric appliances and all the other necessities allowed him to live comfortably with the occasional services of a maid, who happened to be the building's concierge. Om the private telephone he had had installed, he could call Dumont-Warren or anyone else directly. And a secure mail box at the closest UNA office protected his mail from prying eyes.

The night before, on Friday, May 7, between 5 and 7 p.m., Mrs. MacCross had indeed visited the house of the renowned Irish activist, Earl Patrick O'Dougal.

Earl Patrick was a die-hard apostle of Irish independence, including the total submission of the Protestant Ulster minority to the Catholic majority of the country, and fighting the great struggle at gunpoint. He was the inflexible author of ultimatums, the opponent of any form of independence that he termed "veiled slavery," a rebel who always chased, but never caught, a historian and lecturer, a journalist and an unflagging propagandist. Last but not least, had been sentenced to death in absentia in both Ireland and England three times, and was temporarily a political refugee in Paris.

The Irish Earl lived in the 14th arrondissement in one of those small houses that are lined up in a semi-circle at the corner of Rue Hallé with tiny front yards that the old gates and low walls divide into fairly equal parts. He had one servant, a tight-lipped, brooding, wary, old man. And there was not much to say about either of them in the neighborhood because they kept to themselves, did not talk to the shopkeepers; even their mail was unremarkable, what any old bachelor would get.

The English, Irish and French politicians and police, who knew about O'Dougal and where he lived, knew nothing about his fortune or lifestyle. They seemed modest and, as far as anyone knew, came from his translations for a big publisher on the left bank. As for his wealth, which used to be considerable, everyone knew that it had been spent between 1917 and 1930 on the generous financing of insurrections and revolts, of political and social campaigns for Ireland.

Since the militant activity of Earl O'Dougal seemed to have stopped completely after De Valera's Anglo-Irish Treaty, with the surly Irish on one side and an apparently resigned English on the other.[15], the police left the old conspirator

---

[15] Éamon de Valera (1882-1975) was a prominent Irish statesman and political leader. He served several terms as head of government and head of state, and had a leading role in introducing the Constitution of Ireland. He had been one of the leading political figures of the War of Independence. After the signing of the

alone to enjoy his exile in peace, which France has the sometimes too generous habit of granting people.

However, the police forces of three countries were making a big mistake: they believed the stormy waters were calm and quiet and had forgotten the old saying "still waters run deep." In reality, O'Dougal was more active than ever in planning a strike with sudden and violent force!

When Mrs. MacCross went to Rue Hallé, which she did at least twice a month, she got out of the taxi at the Lion of Belfort statue and walked down the Avenue du Parc Montsouris, which is never crowded and where it is easy to spot anyone following you. At the corner of the Rue Hallé and the Rue de La Tombe Issoire, she took the Rue Dareau but cut back through an alleyway that rejoined the Rue Hallé further down. These precautions were useless because she was, of course, never followed or spied on, but she never failed to take them out of prudence—not that she feared for herself or her family, but because she did not want to attract any unwanted attention on Earl O'Dougal, which might happen if people started wondering why an American billionairess was visiting a notorious Irish conspirator.

Therefore, on Tuesday, May 4, as usual, Mrs. MacCross entered the small courtyard only after zigzagging through the streets. She was sure (wrongly, this time!) that nobody had followed her. The gate was locked only at night. After crossing the courtyard, there were three front steps to climb before ringing the doorbell. She never had to wait long because she used a special ring.

Again as usual, old Michel welcomed Mrs. MacCross in the narrow hallway as soon as she had stepped inside.

"*Bonjour, Michel,*" she said in French.

"*Bonjour, Madame.* The Earl is waiting for you. If Madame would just follow me."

It was always the same conversation because O'Dougal was never away when she called. Moreover, Michel knew the reason for her visits, but he pretended not to and kept to the improvised protocol they had set during her first visit back on January 2, 1937, the day after the Earl had moved in with his four indispensable pieces of furniture.

Followed by the visitor, Michel climbed up the only stairs. He knocked gently at a door, waited for the "Come in," opened it, stepped aside, bowed and closed it behind her.

"Hello, Patrick."

"Hello, Melody."

The Earl and the woman exchanged a kiss like old friends.

The room was like a monastic cell for an intellectual hermit, without any luxuries, barely comfortable, but very clean, with a table, a chair, an old Voltaire

---

Anglo-Irish Treaty of 1921, de Valera served as the political leader of Anti-Treaty Sinn Féin until 1926, when he left the party to set up Fianna Fáil.

armchair, a couch, and many shelves full of books. The only luxury, if one could call it that, were curtains on the only window, made of very beautiful white tulle and silk, spotless, every fold perfect, without a wrinkle, as if starched and ironed in place.

The setting sun in this late afternoon bathed the room in pink light, soft but bright enough that nothing was really in shadow.

As usual, Mrs. MacCross sat in the armchair after putting her handbag on the couch, along with her gloves, hat and finally her coat—a very simple coat without fur that she always wore when she did not want to draw attention to herself. O'Dougal sat in the chair facing her.

In body type and even a little in their faces, they looked alike. Even though Patrick was ten years older than Melody, he still looked her age. He had bluer eyes and a more imperious nose, but they were obviously of the same blood, even the same family. The great grandmother of Mrs. MacCross had been an O'Dougal. (The police had missed this family connection.)

The first thing Patrick said was spoken with some worry in his voice:

"What's wrong with you today, Melody? You look upset."

"I am, Patrick, and I won't try to hide it."

They spoke in French as almost always when they were alone.

"I'm very upset about making a decision. I thought it was the good, strong side of me urging me on, but there's a weakness fighting against it, a cowardliness, Patrick, and I'm terribly ashamed that, for a month now, yes, for 26 whole days I've given in to this weakness!"

"Is that why I haven't seen you for five weeks, Melody?" O'Dougal asked softly.

"Yes."

The woman brusquely wiped off two tears that fell off her eyelids and took Patrick's hand, squeezing it.

"I'm sorry, my friend. I'm strong now. So, listen to me..."

Then, knowing she would not be interrupted, Mrs. MacCross spilled every detail about the extraordinary events that had surrounded the visit of the mysterious Leone Alzac, her outrageous offer, and the punctual death of Reginald Strom.

"That abominable man was my last sentimental mistake. It was such a terrible lapse that it was tearing me up inside with shame and despair. Leone Alzac's offer to kill him was like a gift from Heaven."

After this double confession, Mrs. MacCross stopped talking. Feeling relieved but still trembling, she stared at Patrick O'Dougal. The Irish Earl was not the type of man to lecture another on human weakness, and the morality or immorality of killing someone like Reginald Strom. To him, that was not the crux of her revelation. The key point, the only thing that really mattered, was the astounding power possessed, directly or indirectly, by this Leone Alzac.

O'Dougal had not shown the slightest disbelief at Melody's story, which might have sounded crazy to many reasonable people. He had read too much, learned too much, seen too much and thought too much to close off his mind to all kinds of phenomena. He knew that men knew little about the true nature of things. In particular, he was aware of the infinite darkness sometimes illuminated by bright flashes that lay before a man when he dared to open the book of occult sciences.

Therefore, he had quickly set his mind on a plan that required both his imagination and reason. He held her hand in his own and in a calm voice, very slowly, he said:

"Melody, I know what you're thinking right now, what you've been thinking since that irrevocable call you made to Reginald Strom in London…"

He closed his eyes, gathered his thoughts, then opened his eyes again and, staring at his guest, his friend, his "sister," he continued:

"Since the 12th century, when the Anglo-Normans, by fire, sword and gold, conquered and occupied our beloved Ireland in the name of their King, Henry II, the history of our poor country has been endless story of battles, negotiations, lies and betrayals, revolutions and sacrifices. There are still a few of us who believe in the fight, but there are many more willing to sacrifice their wealth and their life possessions for our cause! You, Melody MacCross, are one of them! And now, you are thinking that our war will be over and done quickly, ending in our victory, if this Leone Alzac agrees to kill for us… Or if, by hook or by crook, she gives us her secret, her power to kill, even for a short time."

With these terrible words spoken so matter-of-factly, Earl Patrick let go of Melody's hand. He stood up and walked to the other end of the long, narrow room, turned around, came back and sat in his chair again.

"If this Leone Alzac doesn't come back, how are you to contact her again?"

Feeling calmer now, Melody answered simply:

"She came back."

"Ah!" O'Dougal showed emotion for the first time.

"Or rather, she called me," Melody corrected.

"When?"

"Last night."

"Where?"

"I was dining at the embassy. Around 11 p.m., a young attaché who knew me personally came looking for me to tell me I was wanted on the phone. It was pretty strange… at the embassy! I thought there may be something wrong with my brother, who's in London, as you know, and might be calling me because I had spoken with him the day before and I had told him about the dinner. So, I went into attaché's office and picked up the phone—and it was her!"

"Did she say her name?"

"No. She said, 'You recognize my voice, don't you, Melody?' Of course, I recognized her at once."

"What did she want?"

"To see me."

"Why?"

"She didn't say."

"And then?"

"I made an appointment with her."

"For when?"

"Today at 6 p.m... Here."

"Here!"

Patrick got up again, but this time he jumped. He leaned over Melody who was still sitting and asked:

"What did you tell her?"

"Nothing. When she asked if I recognized her, I was so taken aback that I could only say yes. She kept talking. She said, 'I want to see you again, but not at your house, nor in a public place. Tell me where we can meet tomorrow secretly.' So, I didn't hesitate. I've thought so much about you over the past three weeks! I gave her your address. She accepted and hung up."

O'Dougal straightened up and put a friendly hand on his friend's shoulder.

"Congratulations, Melody! You did well. You'll meet Leone Alzac at the back door. If, as is always possible, a spy followed you without you knowing, he'll be hiding across from the house, waiting for you to leave. Whatever happens, you'll leave alone. If there is a spy, he'll follow you, but then, it won't matter. He won't see Leone Alzac who will go out the other door. Everything will work out."

He looked at the clock on the night table next to the couch and sat down for a third time.

"We still have ten minutes. Let's talk. What are you thinking? Will you tell her that you told me her terrible secret?"

"Yes, right after introducing you to her," Melody MacCross said fervently.

"And if she's upset with your trust in me that she might consider a betrayal?"

"We'll see. I'll explain everything. I'll persuade her that the secret is better guarded by the two of us than by me alone."

"That's right," Patrick smiled. "But still, it may be better for you to see her alone here, and for me to stay in the dining room downstairs. You can tell her about me, as you think best, but only after she's told you why she wants to see you again. Then, if you think it wise, you can also say nothing about me..."

"No! No!" Melody was getting agitated. "My gut tells me that if I lie or keep something from her, she'll see it in my eyes. I'll admit everything right away. And you should stay here with us."

"So be it, Melody, so be it. Man's reason is useless against a woman's intuition. So, I'll stay here, but you should go downstairs. We mustn't let your mysterious friend wait on the sidewalk for even a few minutes. Go!"

There was a back entrance to the house that allowed the Irishman to come in through Number 4B on Avenue du Parc Montsouris; it was known only to four people: O'Dougal, his butler Michel, Melody MacCross, and the owner of the terraced that made up a quarter of Rue Hallé. That owner used to have a nursery between the corner of Rue Hallé and the big new building at Number 4 Avenue du Parc Montsouris, so there was a ten-foot wall behind which parts of the old nursery had now turned into thick, bushy groves, paths covered with branches so thick and tangled that, even in winter, several people could pass through them without being seen from the windows facing the lot.

The little house where O'Dougal lived was the only one with a backdoor which, through a garden path, led directly to an old service gate for the nursery. That gate was numbered 4B and was never used; it was just big enough for an average sized person to fit through. When the Irishman was looking to rent the house, the owner had mentioned this particularity.

"If you want to use it, feel free. I leave the key in the gate."

"I'd like to use it, but on one condition," O'Dougal had said.

"What's that?" the owner asked.

"That you give me your word that you will never, never, tell anyone else about this backdoor."

"Oh? And why?"

"Because I'd like to keep it secret. And to give you an idea of how important this is, I'll make you an offer right away. If you give me your word, I'll sign a 10-year lease, plus… Now listen well, Monsieur… plus, I'll pay you annually and in advance twice the rent agreed upon in the lease—in cash."

Naturally, the owner had given his word. And since he was a serious-minded man—Melody had found the place and done some research on its owner—the Earl had had no doubt that he would keep it. And he had been right.

During their quick walk to the room where the Irishman had stayed, Leone Alzac and Melody MacCross didn't speak a word. Only at the gate had the latter said, "Welcome, Leone." The mysterious young woman had answered with a smile and a faint nod.

Once they were in the austere room, however, Leone saw the man staring coldly at her, In a menacing voice, she asked:

"What's the meaning of this?"

Mrs. MacCross responded with heroic simplicity:

"This is Earl Patrick O'Dougal. I believe you must know his reputation. He is more than a brother to me. We've got the same blood, the same mind and are driven by the same beliefs. I keep no secrets from him. I told him everything. If you won't talk to me in front of him, then I can't talk to you and I'll see you to the door immediately. Then you may do as you want with me… with us."

Leone Alzac's face had remained frozen without a trace of emotion during this short speech. When Melody had finished, the young woman looked at the Irishman. The blue eyes held the penetrating fire of her dark eyes. A minute passed in silence, stillness, and mutual observation.

Finally, Leone Alzac offered her right hand to the Earl after slowly taking off her glove. In a melodic voice tinged with kindly interest, she said:

"I know you of you, Monsieur, and I know your work. It doesn't take a great deal of imagination to see why Melody thought of getting me involved with your fight. In principle, I won't say no, but this is not the moment, the day or even the month, to consider the possibility. I will ask you, therefore, and you too, Melody, to hold off on this subject that I will willingly examine with you at a later date."

It was short and to the point.

A brief silence followed during which Mrs. MacCross and Earl O'Dougal looked at each other, understood, and agreed.

Patrick bowed over the long, slender hand, which he was still holding, and kissed it respectfully. He let go, straightened up, and said:

"Madame, you have our word that we will wait. For the moment, if you want to speak with Melody alone, just say the word and I shall leave."

"You can stay, Monsieur."

Then, with an enigmatic smile that contained a lot of affection and a little indignation, she addressed the billionairess:

"I'm sure you'll keep my secret better now that you can talk about it with Earl O'Dougal."

Then, becoming more serious, she continued:

"My secret is going to get bigger because I need more money. I could get it anywhere and easily, but I don't want to resort to force and thus debase this sublime power with blackmail. Mrs. MacCross agreed immediately to making a corpse out of a man who didn't deserve to live. You, Monsieur, value life, including your own, only in so far as it accomplishes your work, the triumph of the cause to which you have devoted and sacrificed your life.

"You both must understand that I don't want to kill, or even issue death threats, just for money. Besides, money itself is only good to fulfill my basic needs, with no luxuries at all except for clothes. The money is mostly used for the preparation of a superhuman work, so huge that your own work, Earl O'Dougal, is like a little city compared the vast planet Earth. I am not the creator, or even one of the architects, of this work. I'm not even one of the laborers. I am, and will remain, the *teledynamic agent* of that power, which can be deliberately impulsive, lethal, or constructive depending on the circumstances. And I am and will be *the eyes, ears and mouth* of the intelligence that possesses this power."

She stopped. She was still standing. Neither Melody nor Patrick thought of inviting her to sit down. They, too, stood, nervous and trembling, side by side, looking straight at her in her hat and coat, her small blue handbag in her left hand, which still wore a glove.

Mrs. MacCross finally spoke, very simply but hesitatingly:

"I always carry my private checkbook with me. I call it 'private' because I use it only for expenses that won't be entered in the accounts kept by my secretary. It's a special bank account whose statements are never sent to me and whose balance, therefore, is known to me alone. This account should have today around 5 or 6 million dollars." After a short pause, she added, "These funds are at your disposal."

"Thank you," the young woman replied. "I only need $50,000."

Only then did she put down her handbag and one glove on the table and started to unbutton her coat.

"Allow me," the Earl said politely.

After taking her hat and coat and the other glove, he gave them to the butler who came and went with quiet and respectful haste.

This happened in Paris, between 6 and 7 p.m., on Friday, May 7, 1937.

CHAPTER IV
Colonel Brown of the Intelligence Service

Thousands of miles away, in a section of Asia that was almost completely unknown to the western world, on that same Saturday, May 7, at 7 p.m., Leo Saint-Clair was sleeping in one of the four tents set up on the black sand beach at the southeast end of Lake Chong Koum whose warm waters were still alive at 16,000 feet of altitude amidst the dead and frozen nature.

The Nyctalope had stayed awake until noon while Timor and Vitto rested. Then the Corsican had taken his place on watch, letting the Mongol sleep since he was by far the most tired of them all.

When the sun was about to disappear completely behind the mountains that barred the horizon far to the west, Vitto woke him up. Stormy gusts of wind blew in from the northwest, and it was extremely cold under the sinister sky where big, tattered clouds raced across a star-studded dark backdrop.

Nothing had troubled their sleep or their watches during the day. However, the return to their Refuge at night proved more troublesome. Tied again to the rope, they had to fight against the headwind whose gusts were so strong and sudden that the Nyctalope and his men would have more than once fallen to their knees, if they had not taken shelter behind the big rocks.

When they finally reached their base, they were exhausted, hungry and thirsty. The wind had just died down and the dense clouds were thinning, spreading out into a low, heavy, stagnant ceiling that let only a dusky light filter through. It was a sinister start to the day!

In the tightly shut tent, in front of the stove on which they were boiling water for tea and warming up their rations, they ate biscuits with butter and drank the tea mixed with highly concentrated sweet milk. Then the three men went to get some sleep in the airplane. They were going to need all their physical and mental strength.

"As agonizing as it is for us to think about the likely situation for Gno, Soca and Gissa," Saint-Clair had said, "we can't set off on an expedition full of unknowns and plenty of danger unless we're in perfect shape ourselves. Let's get some sleep. We'll wake up, eat a light but solid meal, and only then shall we consider the situation and decide what to do and how best to do it."

It was a wise decision, especially since the Nyctalope had absolutely no idea what he was going to do. The situation presented itself as a jumble of incoherent images, with a few clear "snapshots," but truly chaotic and incomprehensible.

Let's sleep on it, he thought. Although sleep itself was not the answer, because it could also spawn nightmares and illusions and all kinds of contradictory thoughts, what was needed was rest, to get the blood flowing and the tension down, to clear the mind...

All of Saturday morning, May 8, was spent, therefore, on their mental and physical recovery by sleeping in safety and comfort, as well as by eating and drinking good rations in moderation. At 3 p.m., after smoking a pipe and mulling over the situation in the shade of a dune, watching the calm lake and the clear sky, breathing the cool, pure air that was undisturbed by any disagreeable winds, Saint-Clair stood up, went back into the Refuge and called for Vitto and Timor.

Leo Saint-Clair, the Nyctalope, was in peak physical and mental shape. Of average height, well built, slim and strong, he sported an oval face, a little bony, without a wrinkle, with dark brown hair. He was always shaved, except for a well-trimmed moustache. From the front, his thin nose looked straight, but from the side it looked more Roman. As for his eyes, normally brown, they changed color depending on his mood or the time of day, which might turn them so black that their penetrating stare could be unnerving. His eyes were unique in that they could see in the dark as in daylight, hence his nickname.

Since they had set up on the Plain of Cones on the shores of Lake Chong Koum, Saint-Clair had worn thick pants and a pea coat lined with fur, light but sturdy leather boots, and a fur-padded leather cap with earflaps and a chin strap. Gno Mitang, Vitto, Soca, Gissa and Timor were dressed in the same way and same quality of clothing.

Saint-Clair's voice was clear and resounding, pleasant to the ear. Depending on the situation, it could be commanding or comforting, warm or hard as ice. If he yelled in a certain way, his voice could carry to a great distance and thus resonate powerfully.

This was the man who spoke to Vitto that evening, a man to whom the Corsican was entirely devoted and loyal, and quite in awe of.

"My friend, there are several different and definitive reasons why you can't go with me. Since I'll be gone not for hours but for days looking for Gno and the others, someone has to stay behind to guard and take care of the plane. Timor can't do it, so it's got to be you."

The Corsican would have given anything to be with his boss, especially on such a dangerous expedition. The "someone has to stay behind" broke his heart. But he was smart and disciplined. He also spoke his mind and could therefore say:

"That's too bad, Monsieur, and I do understand why I have to stay here to guard the plane. But until when?"

"Until I return, or until Gno comes back, and his decisions will be final as if they were mine."

Vitto frowned and blinked, a nervous habit he had when trying to hide or repress his emotions.

81

"Vitto," Saint-Clair spoke quietly, gently but frankly, "fill the backpack for Timor with provisions for a fast hike that could last four days. Weapons: hunting knives, Luger and cartridges. Tools: climbing rope and pick. Got it?"

"Yes, Monsieur."

"Good. In mine, add a medical kit, flares, a dozen grenades including four smoke ones and two masks. Got it?"

"Yes, Monsieur."

"Very well. I'll take care of my own weapons. I want to leave in fifteen."

"Everything will be ready."

While they were talking, Timor was standing in the tent opening.

"Did you get all that Timor?" asked the Nyctalope.

"Yes, sir," the Mongol replied.

"I'm counting on you just like I would on Vitto if he were coming with me."

"I'm honored, sir, and I hope to prove myself worthy."

"Well thought and well said."

Saint-Clair went to the left door of the Zig and climbed inside while Vitto and Timor went back inside the tent. They filled the bags as much as they could before finishing with the supplies in the plane.

Fifteen minutes later Saint-Clair and Timor shook hands with Vitto and left the Refuge heading back towards the Four Tents camp. The leather-wrapped steel watches worn on their left wrists read 3:30 p.m.

At 10 p.m., Saint-Clair and Timor were sitting in the front of the grotto under the natural arch. Firmly anchored by the iron pegs buried deep in the black sand, their flaps tied with knotted straps, the four tents were still standing, although the wind from the northwest was blowing again, and this time in a furious storm.

"Let's take half an hour rest," Saint-Clair said. "We can eat and drink. I'll also allow us to smoke a little pipe for digestion."

"Thank you."

At 10:30 p.m., the Nyctalope stood up. The night sky was clear, swept clean, teeming with stars. The wind was still raging relentlessly and with even stronger gusts.

"I won't use the rope, Timor. Even though the darkness of the ledge, the mountain, and then the chaos of rocks we'll be entering, sucks up the little light there is from the stars, you can still follow me thanks to your keen sense of smell and hearing. As for seeing me, my gray pea coat should stand out a little from the blackness we'll be walking through. Do you agree?"

"Yes, sir."

"Then, let's go."

The ledge rose for ten miles. It took them two and a half hours to climb. Then the Nyctalope stood before the most astounding "passage" he had ever seen in all his travels across the two hemispheres.

He turned away from the gaping abyss at the bottom of which lay the Chong Koum. He thought the word "chaos" was an understatement, too common, too bland, too soft. But it did describe the natural confusion of elements and matter that preceded the first, exquisitely formed, clutter at the formation of this land.

For two hours now, the wind had slowly dragged in clouds from the northwest, swirling, tattered, dark masses separated by gashes where the stars shone forth. These clouds assaulted the mountain that stood there, cyclopean, titanic, a monumental heap of senseless, monstrous rocks, with narrow passageways and precipices, heaps of loose stones and apocalyptic towers of lava rising up or crumbling down. And this chaos looked like gigantic steps that mounted to the sky from the bottomless abyss that was Chong Koum.

Astounded and attracted by that unimaginable vision, the Nyctalope shuddered. Timor was seized by atavistic, superstitious emotions. He inched up to Saint-Clair and then, suddenly, groaned with such horror, with such profound agony, that Saint-Clair looked at him and understood. He put a friendly, protective arm around his shoulders and shouted—he had to shout because of the cacophonous racket made by the wind:

"Timor, my friend! Buck up and stay calm! All this is just rocks and the noise is nothing but the wind. We are alive, and this is nothing but lifeless lava spurted out of volcanoes centuries ago. Come on, what would Vitto and Soca say if they saw you now?"

The Mongol squeezed the nervous hand on his left shoulder in a gesture of camaraderie against the overwhelming monstrosities of nature. He replied simply:

"Thank you, boss... Thank you!"

He shook off the Nyctalope's hand, straightened up and added:

"I'm here, with all the courage and calm of your men."

"That's good, Timor. Let's get a move on."

Then Saint-Clair thought out loud and continued:

"With his binoculars, Gno spied four men walking on the ledge who disappeared into this chaos. He saw one Chinese and three Russians. Logically, the Chinese is Liang Fong, and one of the Russians must be the explorer Petrus Rikevitch, since according to your account Colonel Grigori Lazov remained behind in the Four Tents camp. We also know that this ledge was used by a barefoot horde to kidnap him and, more importantly, Gno, Soca and Gissa, with or without the knowledge and consent of Liang Fong and Rikevitch. Both parties went out in this Chaos, so it's there that we must go.

"Besides, it's easy to see, like I did this afternoon during our trip from the Refuge to Four Tents, that the only access into this mountain is to follow this ledge and go through this gorge, higher and higher between these towering cliffs and these precarious heaps of huge rocks and titanic lava. So we have no choice but to continue walking.

"That barefoot horde must live somewhere in these mountains. It's surely acting on someone's orders, probably whoever lives in the secret lamasery mentioned only in legends and traditions.

"In Leone Alzac's notebook, Chong Koum was written seven times. We're here to look for the secret of the Master of Death. My guess is that Liang Fong and Rikevitch are probably trying to learn about the 'pressing of *soma*' and the sovereign will that comes with this ritual. Therefore, both our expeditions have the same goal. We're obviously on the right track. So, let's go!"

Maybe the track was right, but it was also hard and dangerous. The Nyctalope thought:

It would be impossible for that barefoot horde to get through here without light. They might have come and gone in the night by holding hands and feeling their way along the ledge, but in this chaos? No way! I've never seen such a natural maze, rising and falling, narrowing and widening, skirting sheer drops into bottomless abysses sometimes on the right, sometimes the left...

Almost at the very start of their march, the Nyctalope had to stop and tie his rope to Timor's waist; the Mongol walked not just behind him, but right next to him on his left.

"Make sure your elbow is always touching mine. If I move away, don't make any sudden moves—you might push me over a cliff and you'll come tumbling after me. Keep your eyes and ears open!"

"Yes, sir."

They progressed at an exhausting pace, but it lasted shorter than Saint-Clair would have imagined. For two whole hours, the Nyctalope saw nothing around him but a mountain petrified in black convulsions and dark clouds speeding by with their own tortured moves. Sometimes, they caught a glimpse of the star-studded, blue-black sky.

All of a sudden, four or five minutes after he had last taken a look at his watch, which read 2:07 a.m., the Nyctalope froze. Timor could see only gray patches, darkness pierced by even darker holes that constantly shifted because of the swirling clouds. But the Nyctalope saw...

At the foot of a round of cliffs, rising up like broken organ pipes but infinitely taller, a barren space spread out, dotted with white snow and at the end of which was a kind of castle with stepped crenellations and three roofs with terraces also covered in snow.

It was a huge building with several storeys offset from each other that could accommodate an entire population. On the outside, some parts of it looked like the fortifications of the Great Wall of China. It had obviously been patiently constructed in the early days of the lamaseries, just after the monk Padma

Sambhava had brought this particular form of Buddhism from China into Tibet in the year 747.[16]

It took all the power of his uncanny eyes to make out in this darkness and at this distance (at least three miles) the details of this extraordinary castle, clearly the result of the genius of architects who had made its lines and colors fit in as naturally as possible with the turbulence of the surrounding volcanic landscape. Even in daylight, anyone finding themselves where Saint-Clair and Timor now stood, glued to the spot, would have taken a long time to see that there was a man-made building butting up against the mountain.

Obviously someone coming here, stopping to gaze, then hiking down to get a closer look, would obviously be spotted from below and ambushed, then killed or taken away, thought Saint-Clair. *Unless, of course, the Master of Death was informed and dropped him dead on the spot.*

Saint-Clair shivered, but not from the cold, which was bitter even without the wind blowing in this huge valley dug out of the mountain, but from his own thought, which was horrifying.

He shivered and felt the onset of panic. His muscles tensed. Suddenly, he stood there agape, squinting, stunned, because he'd just seen a man walking up the esplanade towards them. He was less than five hundred yards away. If he came from the indescribable lamasery, then the piles of snow had hidden him until now. He walked slowly, holding his hands out front, wagging them back and forth.

"Of course!" the Nyctalope pulled himself together. "He can't see in the darkness."

At that moment, the man stopped and a thin ray of light shot out of his right hand. It swept through the air first, then the ground. Only briefly, then the light went out.

"Oh, he's got a flashlight," said Saint-Clair. "But why doesn't he use it all the time? Maybe he's trying to escape? It's not Gno, Soca or Gissa because they're all much shorter than him. I can tell he's really tall. Maybe it's Liang Fong or Rikevitch, or even Lazov? Or someone else entirely? Let's wait and see because he'll spot us the next time he turns on his flashlight. He's walking straight towards us..."

The man kept coming. When he was ten feet away, Saint-Clair was about to call out to him, but the light flashed on. It blinded Timor, even though the Nyctalope had warned him, and he gasped loudly as he jumped back.

"Oh, by Jove!" the stranger cried out.

---

[16] Padmasambhava (meaning "Born from a Lotus"), also known as Guru Rinpoche, was an tantric Buddhist Vajra master from India who may have taught Vajrayana in Tibet circa the 8th-9th centuries. According to some early Tibetan sources, he came to Tibet in the 8th century and helped construct Samye Monastery, the first Buddhist monastery in Tibet.

Saint-Clair spoke in English:

"Turn off your light, sir. Step forward, just a few more steps. Don't worry, I see you clearly."

The other turned off the light and scurried up to them. He spoke calmly in French, with a heavy English accent, punctuating his sentences with English words:

"Ah! You see me, *naturally*... In a night as black as ink... So, sir, might you be Leo Saint-Clair, the Nyctalope?"

Saint-Clair could not help laughing, first as a nervous reaction, then because of the childishly amusing speech. And also because this unexpected Englishman looked rather funny, both his face, which belonged to an aristocratic soldier, well-groomed as if he had just stepped out of his bathroom, and also his attitude, as Soca would have said, and his clothes.

The newcomer looked like a scrawny heron, all limbs with a long body dressed in a checkered golf suit under which one could see the turned down collar of a sweater with some fancy designs. He was topped off by the strangest cap that any clubman across the Channel had ever pulled over his ears. Down below, over his wool socks with horizontal circles, he wore laced-up shoes that were bulkier than any globe-trotter had ever put on.

Saint-Clair's laughter, however, faded quickly. The expression on the Englishman's face did not allow for mockery. So he answered seriously:

"Yes, sir, I am Leo Saint-Clair, sometimes called the Nyctalope. I'm honored to be recognized in such a place by an officer of His Majesty the King of England and Emperor of India."

The Englishman switched hands holding the flashlight and, with his right hand, made a military salute. Then calmly, clearly satisfied, even smiling a little, he replied:

"I am even more honored. I am Archibald Brown."

The Nyctalope lifted his hand amiably and smiled back.

"Allow me," and in the same tone as the Englishman, he finished, "Colonel in the Intelligence Service of His Majesty, I presume?"

"Oh-ho" Archibald was delighted and showed it with that charming, childish exuberance that the British have when they are won over by flattery. "So you know me? Good evening. I'm very pleased, but not at all surprised. No more than you, I suppose. This country is so extraordinary, with its lamas and everything! The presence of the Nyctalope here is quite natural, yes, natural and logical! Because everything here, even in the middle of the day, is so obscure... But they say the Nyctalope can see as clearly as a lynx... excuse me... in the dark... where I see nothing right now and I have understood nothing for the last ten days..."

He held out his open right hand. Saint-Clair shook it. The grip was strong and true.

"Listen to me," said Saint-Clair. "Turn on your flashlight just long enough to follow me. We'll get you behind a big rock where nobody can see you, even with the light. Because we've got to have a serious talk, right?"

"Oh, certainly... but wait..."

"What is it, colonel?"

"I have to tell you... Three times already... exactly three, I've tried to leave. Getting out of that huge, old stronghold of a lamasery is easy. There are no locks. But outside, it's astounding... I walk and walk and walk... Yesterday and the day before, and before that, in the daytime, I really thought I'd gone farther than here, in this gorge that widened out behind me, in this immense, chaotic landscape... But, all of sudden, I was stopped. Stopped! Not by any physical object, or outnumbered by men, no... I was stopped by an invisible wall, a wall I could sink my hands and arms, even my whole body, into... yet without being able to pass through... I wore myself out trying to get through for at least an hour. It was like rubber, by Jove... Totally hopeless! So I went back to the lamasery, but I decided to try again tonight... That's what I'm doing, I'm trying... So far, I've met no one, seen nothing but this incomprehensible chaos.... Then, all of a sudden, I meet you! The Nyctalope! Marvelous, but natural, very natural! The extraordinary pops up in the outrageous. Most perfect, indeed! But am I going to be stopped by that invisible wall again?"

"Well," Saint-Clair spoke softly, "let's find out. I and this man, Timor, a smart and loyal Mongol, will go back. Follow us and let's see what happens."

"OK!"

"But first a question, if I may, colonel..."

"Of course!"

"I've got a friend... You've probably heard of him... At least you'll be familiar with his name and reputation—Marquis Gno Mitang..."

"Ah, yes, the famous Japanese diplomat."

"The same. He, my friend Soca and another Mongol, Gissa, were kidnapped and brought here, probably imprisoned in that lamasery... Oh, I can see it in your eyes—you know nothing about this."

"Nothing, sir, nothing at all. Neither seen nor heard, I'm sorry."

"Me, too. Let's go, then."

Saint-Clair turned around, followed by Timor, who got scared listening to every word of the conversation with this unusual Englishman.

But they had not gone a hundred feet before the shrill voice of Archibald Brown pierced the loud winds that blew and whistled and howled through the mountain.

"Saint-Clair, please, stop!"

CHAPTER V
The Nyctalope begins to understand

Saint-Clair dropped the rope that tied him to Timor and told him:

"Sit down here and don't move."

Then he turned around and faced the flashlight pointing directly in his eyes.

"Colonel, turn it off, please. You don't need to see. It's enough if I can see. Will you do what I tell you?"

"Yes."

And the flashlight was switched off.

"To your left and right, colonel, is open space, very flat for ten feet or so on either side. So, step forward, five feet over here, then try five feet over there…"

"Exactly what I did the other times."

"I can imagine. Come on."

Even for the Nyctalope, as ready as he was, it was baffling. He saw the gangly Englishman in golf clothes back up three feet, tuck his elbows against his ribs, clench his fists and push forward with all his might. He was stopped, not cleanly, like by a hard, compact surface, but like by a rope stretched to its limit that finally pulled him back when his strength gave out.

Yet, in front of Archibald, meaning between him and Saint-Clair, was a space of only fifteen feet. There was nothing else, absolutely nothing but the invisible air and the intangible wind! To the right, then the left, back and forth, the Englishman tried twenty times to pass and even remained suspended for a moment before being pulled back every time. Four times, he almost fell down on the rebound, keeping his balance thanks to his agility.

"Please, colonel, that's enough," Saint-Clair pleaded.

"Well, I say!"

Trembling, panting, Archibald Brown finally stood still.

"Turn on the flashlight," the Nyctalope told him. "Watch and follow what I do."

"Yes!"

In the narrow ray and halo of light that lit up the calm but attentive Englishman, as well as Timor, scared stiff but intensely curious, Saint-Clair walked straight toward Archibald, reached him, touched him, turned around and marched back to the Mongol. Nothing stopped him. He made the round trip four times without a problem.

"Don't be scared, but do what I did" he asked Timor. "Go to the colonel and come back to me."

Frightened but disciplined, Timor stood up and did as Saint-Clair had asked, several times.

"Perfect," Saint-Clair said. "The experiment is conclusive. It's only you, colonel, who can't get through. It doesn't affect people going to the lamasery. Let's finish the experiment. Timor and I will surround you and see what happens. To be absolutely sure, you grab a shoulder of each of us and stay very close to us, especially when you feel the invisible force pulling at you. Got it?"

"Yes."

"Good."

They huddled together as Saint-Clair had said and walked forward. All of a sudden, at exactly the same spot where the Englishman had tried to "break through," he was stopped again, even as Saint-Clair and Timor slipped away from him and left him behind, grumbling, "By Jove! Damn it!"

If Leo Saint-Clair had not been constantly thinking of the 18 deaths and especially of Gno and Soca disappearing in this infernal chaos where the monstrous lamasery brooded, he really would have burst out laughing at how ridiculous it all looked. But the ridiculous is often tragic, and in this bewildering adventure, tragedy was looming over and seeping into everything.

"Colonel," Saint-Clair said, "let's sit down by that big pile of snow and talk. It will be a screen for us. We'll be protected from the wind and from those whom I'm sure are spying on us, even though we're at least two and a half miles from that citadel. All right?"

"All right, let's," Brown sounded cheerful enough, back to his old self.

"Thank you. Come on, Timor."

When they were sitting in a triangle on the hard lava, the flashlight casting a dim light on their faces, but not able to reach the top of the snowy pyramid, and thus remaining unseen from anyone in the lamasery, the Nyctalope smiled at the Englishman.

"Colonel, first, I have to ask you a few questions."

"Certainly! And I'll answer them with all my heart, as you say in France."

"Great. First of all, why and how did you come here?"

"Very simple. I was in Moscow. I had challenged Colonel Lazov that whatever he did, I would follow him and never lose sight of him. And without trying to hide in any way—no disguises, not even changing out from my golf clothes. He laughed and took the bet. This friend and confident of Stalin knew very well that I belonged to the Intelligence Service and I was on a special mission. But he was a good sport. Obviously, he figured that he was powerful enough to lock me up and make me disappear forever if I bothered him too much. By Jove, I decided to run the risk!"

Archibald Brown snickered.

"One day, I heard that the explorer Rikevitch and a Chinese scientist named Liang Fong were leaving with Lazov on an expedition to Lake Chong Koum. The expedition was ordered by Stalin himself. Why? A very important reason no doubt. So, while the colonel and the explorer were off to Nanjing to meet Liang Fong and organize their trip, I returned to London where I took a plane with two friends. It dropped me on the shores of the lake and returned to Croydon. I looked for a campsite, found one at the southeast end of the lake in a grotto on a little, black sandy beach. I brought my supplies there and set up camp, waiting for Rikevitch expedition to show up from the west, from Nanjing. Well, one night, I was attacked by a group of barefoot men who dragged me up a ledge, then across a hellish landscape of black rocks, until they finally left me alone in the lamasery where I got absolutely no information about anything. As for Lazov's expedition, I know nothing at all. There you go! Are you satisfied?"

"I am. As for their expedition, I can tell you what happened."

"Oh, really?"

"Yes, but before I do, I have a few more questions, all right?"

"Whatever you need to know."

"What happened to you in the lamasery? What did you do? Who did you see? Did they talk to you? And what did they say?"

"Yes! I get it, you want a detailed report... Here it is, but you're going to be disappointed, my dear Nyctalope. The barefoot men who kidnapped me left me in a big, empty room that looked out on an inner courtyard. Two of them stayed with me. They took turns sleeping, tending a small fire of dried dung and, two or three times a day, going to fetch a tray full of curdled milk, hard-boiled eggs, a kind of grilled biscuit made of some unidentifiable flour and a vegetable, also unknown to me.

"For drink, I had water in a jug. For bed, twenty yak skins piled on the floor. The bathroom was a natural hot spring in the courtyard. And that's all. The men never answered my questions and I never heard them speak a word. I thought I was free to go, so I left. I got two or three miles, and then—stop! I met that empty space in front of me, absolutely impossible to get through. But you've seen this. As for the lamasery, I saw nothing but the room, the courtyard, and this view from outside. I tried to follow one of the men going for food once, but a stone door that he went through was slammed down so fast that it almost smashed my face. I tried pushing it open... impossible! That's all.... Oh, wait, no! There's a weird thing I almost forgot... At certain times of the day and night, quite unpredictably, I was struck by an irresistible urge to sleep—and I did. I couldn't help it. They had taken my weapons, but left me my toiletries and everything in my pockets, including my flashlight and pen knife. I pricked my arm hard to stay awake, but it did me no good. I felt drained and dozy. Now that's really all there is to tell. I have nothing more to say about my puzzling adventure—nothing!"

"Puzzling?" Saint-Clair repeated. "We're going to see about that together, colonel."

"Yes, I'd like to!"

"I can well imagine."

Then Leo Saint-Clair told the colonel—as only he could—the whole astonishing story of his own activities with Gno Mitang since April 7 up to the present.

Colonel Archibald Brown had fought in the Great War, had served in Arabia, Ethiopia, Ireland, Russia and South America, and was not a man to be easily amazed. But here he was, as amazed as one could be. Still, this skinny, sturdy Englishman had been born with a sense of humor, and when Saint-Clair had finished his tale, he exclaimed:

"Really, it's crazier than a Mad Hatter!"

He had no doubt about the reality, in every detail, of the ancient, mysterious power that had manifested itself in the modern world through the Eighteen dead and that was also affecting him by creating these invisible barriers to his freedom.

Twenty minutes later, Saint-Clair and Archibald Brown were walking briskly towards the lamasery:.

The Nyctalope had asked Timor to get back to the Four Tents where he would first rest, then return to their Refuge and give Vitto a letter of instructions that he had scribbled hastily. The night was so dark that, without Saint-Clair to guide him, Timor had to light his way with his own flashlight, but in the twists and turns of the chaotic landscape, the light would not likely be spotted by any lookout on the high walls of the lamasery.

The Nyctalope also had to avoid being seen. He kept twenty paces behind Brown, who was sweeping his flashlight over the ground in front of him. The night was pitch black with a single dim star in the sky because the wind had finally stopped blowing and the clouds settled in a thick fog to cover the ground and drown the mountains, leaving only the air on the esplanade of the lamasery a little clear.

This huge crater obviously had a peculiar weather pattern that created special conditions for the air, land and water because Brown had said he had seen no rain or fog before, and had felt the temperatures to be warmer than in the mountains, or even than on the shores of the Chong Koum, despite the difference in altitude of at least 3000 feet.

Of course, before leaving Timor and setting out to follow Brown back to the lamasery, Saint-Clair had not told the colonel everything he thought about what was happening and would soon come to pass, because it would have taken too long and served no practical purpose. However, he had shared his plan of action for the night and the next day.

"After that, we'll see. I'll adapt to the circumstances if I can't make the circumstances adapt to me," he had concluded.

The Nyctalope knew how to take best advantage of any situation.

It took exactly one hour to get from the edge of the Chaos to the lamasery. He had calculated the distance of his strides at the two speeds, fast and not too fast, that were both natural to him.

"An hour: three miles. That's pretty much what I'd figured. Its width ought to be a fourth less than its length. A good-sized field for the adoring crowds of the first Living Buddha, the learned Gedhun Grub... who was a woman!"

Everything had been planned by the Nyctalope and Archibald Brown, so no tactical mistake was possible. Brown went in first and Saint-Clair followed. The colonel used his flashlight and the Nyctalope his eyes. Thus they first went through an open entranceway, crossed a big courtyard that was just a section of a wide, round path between the esplanade and the inner wall. This inner wall was also entered by another entranceway that looked like the first one, but had double doors that Brown pushed open with both hands. Saint-Clair followed him in. They found themselves in a square courtyard around forty yards per side. In the back, there was a third entranceway, also closed by double doors, that the Englishman had no problem opening.

Good, Saint-Clair said to himself, *we're now in the room where the colonel was being kept by the two guards.*

He saw Archibald Brown follow his flashlight to a kind of thick couch made up of a pile of yak skins. He saw him kick off his shoes, jump on top of it and lie down as if to sleep. At the foot of the pile were two men, small but with wide shoulders and very long arms, squatting next to each other, their hands grabbing their legs and their heads resting on their knees. Obviously, they were the two men whose job was to take care of, rather than guard, the Englishman.

After seeing all this, the Nyctalope looked around the rest of the room. Since the stone floor as well as the walls were totally bare, without a scrap of furniture or the tiniest object, his eyes finally rested on the single stone door in the inner courtyard with its hidden hinges.

That's the door Brown couldn't get through because it slammed shut. One should still be able to just push it. Well, let's see if I can...

The Nyctalope went straight to the door. He tiptoed so his boots would make as little noise as possible. When he got there, he put his two hands flat on the huge stone and, with a little force, gave it a shove. The door that should have weighed several tons swung open as easily as any ordinary door.

The Nyctalope looked at his watch to know exactly how long it took to walk across the empty room. There were ramps that brought him to the next floor, then onto an outside terrace, then upstairs again, after which he went back down to the ground floor, feeling like he was going nowhere at all, haphazardly wandering through a maze. Still, he took pains to keep his sense of direction as he went. He was figuring that he had to be at the westernmost end of the lamasery when he entered a room that made him think, *Ah, this one look like it's lived in.*

In fact, his sense of smell caught it before his eyes could assess the unusual sight. The room was huge, square, almost 100 feet per side. Its ceiling formed a giant dome that looked like it had been patiently erected by generations, each one working for years on end. The top of the dome was at least fifty feet high. Its lower height compared to its length and width made it looked squashed. To the left, almost half the room was completely empty. To the right, there were piles of yak skins. And on each of these primitive beds, a man was sleeping.

Saint-Clair looked at them all, one by one. They were dressed differently and slept in different positions, but one group wore almost the same clothes. The Nyctalope counted 48 sleepers in all.

All of a sudden, his eyes stopped on one individual. He had to hold back a shout. It was Gno Mitang!

He rushed over to his friend and sat on the edge of the bed. He put a hand on his shoulder and squeezed. He leaned over and whispered repeated:

"Gno, my friend, it's me. Gno, it's me."

Gno woke up and understood right away. He did not move. He did not even open his eyes. But in a very quiet voice, he replied:

"Leo, I've been waiting for you. Sorry for falling asleep, but I really need-ed the rest. How are you?"

"I'm well," the Nyctalope answered. "I left Vitto at the Refuge. I came here with Timor, but I sent him back to Vitto with a letter. Outside, I also met an Englishman from the Intelligence Service, a Colonel Archibald Brown. Did you see him?"

"No," Gno said.

"He tried to escape three times. He always got out of the lamasery, but at a certain point, he was stopped by an invisible wall. I saw it myself and tried a few different experiments, but he couldn't go through it. Have you felt anything like that?"

"Yes," the Japanese replied. "Me and all the men here. All 48 of us. We're free to come and go as we please, out to the esplanade, but at a certain distance from the lamasery, day or night, the invisible wall pops up and we have to give up. We've given up trying."

"Very well," Saint-Clair said. "But I can get through."

"That means that, whatever power is putting up that invisible wall doesn't know about you."

"That's what I think, too," the Nyctalope agreed.

For a few minutes, the two of them remained silent. Saint-Clair finally spoke up:

"Here's what we'll do. I'll take the place of one of these men."

"I was thinking the same," Gno said. "Replace Soca. You look enough alike that the servants, who seem to be deaf and dumb, won't be able to tell the difference. Soca can hide between our beds under a few skins so he can still move freely."

"Right. I see Soca. I'll go and wake him up in a minute. Anything else to tell me?"

"Did you read Rikevitch's notebook?" the Japanese asked,

"Yes."

"Well, the Chinese-Russian expedition is here, except for the two Tibetan camel drivers. They disappeared. Maybe they joined the servants of the lamasery. There are 48 men here, including Liang Fong."

"What about Gissa?" Saint-Clair sounded worried.

"He, too, has disappeared."

There was a silence. Then, the Nyctalope spoke again:

"Have you found anything out about the lamasery?"

"No," Gno said, "nothing. I've seen no other human being, except for these strange servants. With a few other fellow captives, particularly Liang Fong, Rikevitch and Lazov, we wandered through the rooms, up and down a bunch of straight and spiral ramps… We saw nothing but servants. Obviously, a part of the lamasery, the main part, the biggest part, the only really inhabited part, is closed off. Not by locked doors but by a mysterious power of suggestion that lets us wander around freely, but keeps us from going into that part of the lamasery."

"Extraordinary," Saint-Clair mumbled.

"Indeed," Gno echoed.

"Nevertheless, I'm starting to understand," the Nyctalope said.

"Me, too, I think."

Their hands, which had been clasped together since Gno woke up, gave each other a brotherly squeeze before releasing.

CHAPTER VI
Two big blue eyes

After another moment of silence, the two friends exchanged a summary account of their adventures. Saint-Clair told Gno everything that had happened to him since he'd read Rikevitch's notebook.

For his part, Gno confirmed what Saint-Clair had guessed by telling him how the Four Tents had been attacked by a mute horde of barefoot men, and how everyone in the camp had been taken away to the lamasery where they had been thrown into this room.

"The other captives were already here," Gno went on. "You can meet them if you want. Or stay incognito, because they won't be able to tell the difference between you and Soca, whom they've barely seen. He can really only be recognized by Rikevitch and Liang Fong because we talked to them. Most of the other prisoners are Russians, groups of escapees from the USSR who were wandering around this region, robbing caravans or villages. They only came near Chong Koum by chance. They were discovered and then captured by the servants. From the little I've learned, it seems logical to assume that there's a shifting range of territory around the lake in which the mysterious lamas won't let strangers enter in case they find the lamasery."

"What do they do with the prisoners in the end?"

"I don't know. None of them have seen another prisoner disappear, no matter what their race, except on the first day for the Mongols and Tibetans. That's all I can tell you because I really don't know anything more."

"The question now is whether I should reveal myself to Rikevitch and Liang Fong—that's a crucial point."

"Let's think it out," Gno said. "In theory, we have to admit that they are our rivals in this adventure. They were obviously drawn here by the same mystery as us. Their starting point, however, was different. I don't think they know anything about the Eighteen deaths that prompted our own investigation. But like us, they're trying to unravel the mystery of the powerful will that can exert its power at a distance, either by a simple mental operation or by something more religious, which Rikevitch refers to as the 'pressing of the *soma*'."

"Yes," Saint-Clair agreed. "I'm inclined to join forces with them. It would not be in their interest to betray us. Being intelligent and reasonable, they know that the Master of Death is stronger than they are. But with me, it's a different story. I'm not known by the Master. If he reacts, it'll affect Soca just like the rest of you, but since I'm not one of you, I'm free. I alone have the possibility to overcome this unknown power and therefore save all of you. So, our rivals would do well not to betray me. Do you see any objections to this reasoning, my friend?"

"No."

"Of course," Saint-Clair continued, "when we do get out of this hornet's nest, we'll have to expect them to turn hostile, but here, on the brink of the mystery, they're in the same position as us and I think they'll be tempted to work with us to solve this mystery. However, if we're victorious in our attack, they'll try to capture the lamas and hope to get initiated into their secret science. If that happens, we'll be extra baggage, you and I, since being Japanese and French, we're enemies of the USSR and China, which has already been infected by the Communists."

"Yes," Gno said, "and it'll mean war. But an insidious, hypocritical war, even more ruthless and cruel because we'll be dealing with three men trained to use the Comintern's tactics."[17]

"Oh, they don't worry me," Saint-Clair responded calmly.

"I can see that."

There was a silence again.

Their conversation has been whispered, heard only by them in the room which was filled by a muffled but clearly audible noise—the constant snoring and heavy breathing of the 47 sleepers. It had also been held in total darkness. The Nyctalope saw Gno clearly, but the Japanese could not see his friend sitting on the edge of the thick pile of skins.

They were still clasping hands, which they always did when they needed to be of one mind, and spoke only their key thoughts, leaving out all unessential words. This time, their silence lasted a long time. Gno finally broke it.

"Leo, am I wrong or over there, along the rim of the dome, do I see sunlight starting to come through those weird arrow slits that serve as windows in this strange place?"

"No, you're not wrong. It's time to wake up Soca. I'll do it."

The Corsican was lying on his right side, all curled up, on the pile of skins, parallel to Gno, between him and the wall in a corner of the huge room. Saint-Clair climbed over the bed and went to sit on the edge of Soca's so he could wake him up in the same way as he had done with Gno. It took the Corsican longer to realize what was happening, but he had been hoping, waiting for his boss, because whenever Vitto and Soca found themselves in danger, they could always count on the Nyctalope to save them. Not once in twenty years had their hopes been dashed.

When Saint-Clair saw that Soca was fully awake and aware, he whispered, "Don't speak. Listen."

Then the Nyctalope told him enough so that the Corsican could do what he had to do to carry out his master's plan. No change of clothes was necessary.

---

[17] The Communist International (Comintern), also known as the Third International, was an international organization founded in 1919 that advocated world communism, controlled by the Soviet Union.

Except for a few tiny details, the clothes, shoes and accessories of Corsican and the Nyctalope were the same.

The hard part for Soca was that he had to stay there for hours on end without anyone seeing him, neither prisoner nor servant. It was true that the duties of the servants did not include checking or straightening the beds after the restless nights—every prisoner was responsible for keeping their pile of skins as neat or messy as they wished.

Two servants came in and left the room three times a day to give them food and water, including a little milk, a frugal meal but plenty of it and healthy. Therefore, by stretching a few skins over the ground between the two beds, they could create a kind of hiding place under them. Plus, the two beds were lucky enough to be in the corner and there was not much light that reached it. And there was one more advantage: the position of Soca's hiding place was far from where everyone walked, both prisoners and servants, to get in and out of the room.

While explaining everything to Soca, Saint-Clair was careful to add:

"Gno told me that they bring plenty of food, so we'll save some for you and you'll have enough to eat. Anyway, I hope it won't be too long and after 24 hours, I'll know enough so we can change the situation."

"Should I hide right now?" Soca asked.

"Yes, right now, before the others wake up."

"Very well, but I can't see a thing. It's still nighttime."

"Not for long," Saint-Clair said. "Feel your way around."

"Yes, Monsieur."

Five minutes later, four skins had been laid out on the oddly warm floor between their two beds. A few inches above, two more skins were stretched out and tucked into the parallel beds. It was easy to do because each bed was three feet high and had at least forty yak skins of long, gray, black and white fur, silky and very dense.

When everything was ready and Soca had disappeared, the Nyctalope climbed onto his bed while Gno lay down on his. The two friends waited for everyone to wake up.

For Saint-Clair, it was a curious sight. Gno had told him how to act, so the Nyctalope did what Soca usually did.

First of all, washing up. Individually or in pairs or small groups, the 48 men left the huge room. In a small courtyard, a hollow basin had been dug out of the ground and filled with water that gurgled up from the bottom and overflowed into a shallow channel. The water was agreeably warm. Bare-chested, the men washed their faces, necks and shoulders. They could also rinse off their feet in the channel. They dried off by doing calisthenics. Then they put their shirts back on.

Saint-Clair performed the ritual as quickly, trying to show his face as little as possible.

Then the servants brought breakfast. In dull, white, metal bowls, they served a kind of bitter milky cream that Saint-Clair found rather tasty. But the bowls were deep and heavy...

"Gno, what about this metal?" asked the Nyctalope.

"Oh," the Japanese smiled, "do you think..."

"Yes, I think it's platinum."

"It sure is," Gno agreed. "Here, we get to handle a fortune three times a day."

Saint-Clair slipped his bowl down to Soca and gave him half his portion. After the bowls were picked up and taken away by the silent servants, Saint-Clair told Gno:

"Is that Rikevitch over there staring at me?"

"Yes. And I bet he's identified you. A man like him must know of the Nyctalope, even just from photographs in the newspapers and magazines."

"Let's go talk to him," Saint-Clair jumped up.

"Gladly."

But while the two of them were making their way over to the Russian explorer, he was joined by Lazov and Liang Fong. It was Gno who nodded and motioned to them to meet outside while the other prisoners were making their beds.

They left the room, crossed the small courtyard and entered a bigger, longer one. The blue sky was clear and the sun was shining. It felt like spring.

"Gentlemen," Gno said in French, "let's take a stroll and talk of philosophy like we did yesterday." Then, less casually, "Doctor Rikevitch, you recognized Monsieur Saint-Clair, didn't you? So, I will leave it to you to introduce Mr. Liang Fong and General Lazov."

After the introductions were made, Saint-Clair spoke. Like serious students in a good prep school, the five men walked up and down, back and forth in the courtyard, talking while pretending to get some exercise.

"Gentlemen," the Nyctalope said, "I and my friend, Marquis Gno Mitang, would like to propose to you to forget about the reasons for all of us being here at Chong Koum for the time being. What do you say?"

Petrus Rikevitch did not even look at his companions. He answered with authority:

"We agree. Whatever our reasons, exposing them would only create an undesirable enmity. I say undesirable because my friends and I think like you obviously do, that together the five of us have a better chance of escaping this place or take it over."

"Six," Saint-Clair corrected, "because there's Soca."

"Seven," General Lazov added. "We could leave our two men, Felix and Boris, to their fate, but we don't want to abandon Manassé whose crafty mind might be useful in any attempt to escape or defeat our foes."

"We accept your Soca," Rikevitch said.

"And we accept your Manassé," Saint-Clair nodded.

Then Liang Fong spoke very gently:

"After escaping or capturing this place, gentlemen, we will resume our respective quests independently of each other."

"Naturally," Gno replied with Japanese courtesy to match the Chinese gentleness.

They were at one end of the long courtyard. So far, the Russian-Chinese trio had walked a few steps in front of the French-Japanese pair. They stopped now in silence. Then, they turned around and walked back without changing positions and in the same steady rhythm.

Saint-Clair said:

"I can do one thing you cannot, gentlemen—operate at night, in the dark, without the need for light. It's a big advantage. And there's something else that you're prevented from doing, but I'm not—coming and going without being stopped by the mysterious force that blocks you. Obviously, that force only works on those known to it, individuals already seen and recorded. The person known to it like all the others here is Soca, not me. Therefore, I'm not under the spell. It's another edge. You will benefit from it because we've made a pact and are now loyal allies, at least until we get out of here or get the better of them."

"Yes, loyal allies!" Rikevitch repeated emphatically.

Saint-Clair went on:

"Now that the groundwork has been laid, I think it'd be reasonable and useful if you three, like Gno Mitang, would accept that I be in charge of the operation and, if necessary, the battle to come."

"Without question," Rikevitch did not hesitate. "We will consider you our leader, Monsieur Saint-Clair."

"Very well," the Nyctalope smiled a little before continuing. "So, here's the first order I'm giving you: all day long, act as if nothing is different, as if Soca was here instead of me. And the first thing I'll tell you as an ally able to do things you can't: thanks to everything I've learned so far," (he was thinking of Archibald Brown, but had agreed with Gno not to reveal to their present allies and future enemies the existence of the Englishman) "…I think I can act tonight. But I don't think you can help me until I find a way to neutralize the mysterious force. Still, I might need your minds and muscles to overpower its master and any others like him that might exist in the lamasery. Therefore, at first, I'll have to act alone and I only ask you, in our common interest, to share with me any thoughts and observations you've got."

"Of course," Rikevitch replied.

"But for the moment…" Lazov shrugged.

"…we're all, I believe, at a loss for ideas," Liang Fong finished the thought in his gently ironic voice with an impish glimmer in his eyes.

"I'm not surprised," Gno said. "For the first six or seven hours of our stay, we learned all kinds of things just by being here and talking, watching and wandering around. Everything we found out, I've already told Leo. If we come up with anything new, you'll be here with us to share it. I say, let's just live today as if the Nyctalope wasn't among us."

It was the most reasonable conclusion. Rikevitch, Liang Fong and Lazov agreed. After a last remark by Lazov, they decided to leave their two men, Felix and Boris, in the dark about Saint-Clair replacing Soca because the two good soldiers were simple, trained peasants with little in the way of intelligence or judgment. But the others would inform their comrade Manassé, who was clever, bright and observant, and moreover had struck up a friendship with Soca the night before.

While the Franco-Japanese pair and the Sino-Russian trio were walking around and working things out, the other prisoners came out of the big room in couples or small groups, washed up in the small courtyard, and then went into the bigger one to sit or stand around the walls in the sunlight. For the most part, they looked pretty gloomy, dejected, sluggish. They did not understand their situation and they were resigned to their fate. None of them approached the group of five. From the looks of it, all the other prisoners belonged to lower social classes.

As they passed by, Lazov pointed out Boris and Felix to Saint-Clair. They were sitting next to each other against the wall in full sunlight. Manassé was not with them. It was a few minutes later, after they had talked about him, that he was identified by Rikevitch in a group he was preaching to.

"Let's go over there," the explorer said, "and pretend to listen to that windbag. When he's done, I'll call him over. We can wander off with him so it doesn't look suspicious. I'll introduce you, Saint-Clair, and give him your orders. You can count on him. He only pretends to be a blabbermouth—he will never betray an ally. He's got a really cunning mind and his almost miraculous powers of observation will make him a valuable partner. Plus, he's brave but prudent. I repeat, you count on him in any circumstance. And one more thing: he speaks as much French as the three of us."

"Good," Saint-Clair said.

Ten minutes later, no longer in the rectangular courtyard but on the vast esplanade outside, the group of now six were walking around and the man so highly praised by Rikevitch was introduced to the Nyctalope.

Manassé's dark green eyes sparkled with joy.

"Oh, Monsieur," he was controlling his sincere excitement and respect, "let me say that I've admired you for years. To meet you, talk with you and get orders from you, here, in this extraordinary situation—I'm filled with joy and pride. But I'm not surprised. It's quite logical. Chong Koum is shrouded in such dark mysteries—the Nyctalope is the only key able to crack that lock!"

He clapped his feet together, straightened up and saluted.

Saint-Clair thought, *this is no simpleton.* Then he spoke solemnly:

"Monsieur Manassé, I'll say to you what I've never said to anyone else before. I will trust you like I do Soca and Vitto. I will give you orders, put you in danger and be at your side just like them. How does that sound?"

Manassé's face was long, narrow, bony, both energetic and delicate, with magnificent green eyes, an aquiline nose, an already thinning, curly hair, thin but well-defined lips between his moustache and a short blonde beard. He was probably around 30. He was small, not too muscular, but very agile.

Saint-Clair stared at him. The big eyes did not blink. And the Nyctalope thought, *He's sincere. He'll be loyal.*

Manassé answered with a look suddenly turned very serious. So, Saint-Clair held out his hand. Breaking the military salute, Manassé shook it... then bent down and kissed it. The Nyctalope noted that this unexpected homage was too much for General Lazov who shuddered, frowned and looked grouchy.

Saint-Clair thought, *Lazov isn't stupid either. He's thinking that, after our escape or victory, Manassé might change camps. I wouldn't mind and it could be useful for us.*

The day went by with nothing new happening. In the afternoon, the hours seemed endless to the six conspirators. Luckily, the weather stayed nice, spring warm, and they could walk around the esplanade. Saint-Clair checked a few times that the occult power was still working on the others. At a certain distance from the lamasery, the human bodies were stopped and gently pushed back by an invisible, spongy, unbreachable barrier.

Saint-Clair himself, to avoid suspicion from any would-be watcher, imitated his companions, but a couple times dared to take one extra step past the limit. Thus he made sure that the mysterious barricade did not affect him. But the replacement of Soca by Saint-Clair went unnoticed by the power in control.

When night fell, all the prisoners went back into the dormitory. Dinner came like the night before. Soca ate his share in secret. Then everyone climbed onto their yak beds with nothing in mind but another night's sleep. Everyone, that is, except the six schemers and Soca in hiding.

Before going back into the room, Saint-Clair had told his companions:

"It's possible that, for what I want to try tonight, I might need to understand something being said within earshot, and even speak myself. But I know very little Tibetan. I'll be as good as deaf and dumb because I can't expect that one of the languages I do know will be spoken here. Manassé knows Tibetan, but not the local dialects. You, Rikevitch, told me you don't know that many either. That leaves Liang Fong..."

He looked at the Chinese. He was medium height, older but alert, and full of energy. He smiled at the Nyctalope's gaze and answered right off:

101

"I was expecting as much. You want me to go with you to explore the la-masery tonight?"

"I think you must."

"Well, I am at your disposal."

"I kept my weapons," the Nyctalope said. "The Browning and the hunting knife. I really hope that neither of us has to resort to using them. At most, I fig-ure we might have to tie up an enemy. For that, I've also got some rope. But what I really hope is that I'll need only my eyes and your knowledge of lan-guages." He smiled then and added, "And of course, your fine intellect and sharp wits."

The Chinese bowed.

There were a lot of mysteries still unsolved about their preposterous situa-tion. Among them these two:

After their captivity, however long it might have been, what had happened to the other prisoners? Obviously, the lamas hadn't let them go. It was certainly been not just a few years but centuries since people had been exploring around the Chong Koum and kidnapped by the servants and locked up in the lamasery. None of the myriad of prisoners had ever left. None had ever reappeared in the civilized world. Because if they had, they would have talked or written about it, and people would have known. So, what had happened to these hundreds, possi-bly thousands, of men? And more to the point, what fate was awaiting those sleeping here right now?

The second mystery was, why was the Englishman Archibald Brown held separately from the others? And why had they made sure that the prisoners not know about him? Also, why was he suddenly hit with drowsiness several times so hard that he had dozed off whenever that had happened to him?

Despite all the other puzzling questions that popped up in Saint-Clair's mind, these two remained at the forefront. He would have liked to discuss them with Gno, but not during the day when any private conversation between them might have looked suspicious to the Chinese and Russians. As for the present, it was pointless while Saint-Clair and Liang Fong were preparing for their noctur-nal adventure.

What was the Nyctalope's plan?

They had come up with hundreds of hypotheses during the day, but no def-inite plan had been drawn up because they had no idea of what they would find in the unknown areas of the lamasery. The night before, the Nyctalope had only walked straight ahead, following the corridors and rooms and courtyards that unfolded before him. This time, he had decided that he would lead Liang Fong by the hand and they'd explore the lamasery in order to find the living quarters of the enigmatic masters of this mysterious place.

The two of them left without making a sound in order not to wake the pris-oners. They did not have to worry about being seen because it was pitch black in the room. And of the 48 men, only the Nyctalope had eyes that could see in the dark.

With his left hand, he took Liang Fong's right hand as he sat on the bed waiting. The Chinese followed the Nyctalope when he pulled him up. Then they walked side by side in silence. Being barefoot had its advantages. Moreover, a strange phenomenon that also needed explaining was that the floor of black lava was warm. Therefore, they ran no risk of getting cold feet and sneezing, which would have had disastrous consequences.

Based on the brief exploration of the night before, Saint-Clair had been able to plan his initial itinerary. He remembered how he had come from the room inhabited by Brown alone into this big dormitory and he told himself:

I have to retrace part of the way, but not all the way, to Brown's prison. I'll stop on the big, semi-circular landing I saw at the top of the ramp that led up to this maze. It was from the second floor that I came back down through all those rooms and eventually found the prisoners. That landing would be odd if the only way out was where the one I took. I'm sure there are some doors that are invisible to the casual eye. If I look more closely, I should find them.

Of course, he told the others what he was thinking. Liang Fong, therefore, knew the aim of the first part of their nocturnal exploration. Blind but guided by the Nyctalope, he walked steadily toward their goal. But he did not go far. Saint-Clair had used his right hand to push open the door through which the servants passed and was stepping through when he felt some resistance from his left hand. The Chinese scholar was not following him. Saint-Clair understood right away. He stepped back and whispered:

"The invisible wall, right?"

"Yes," Liang Fong replied.

"The situation is so complex that we thought we'd considered all possibilities, but none of us remembered that the prisoners couldn't get through this door at night. Oh, well, I'll have to go alone. How very far from perfect is the human mind when none of us thought this through, even though you all experienced it."

"What a pity," Liang Fong sighed philosophically. "Go on and may your fortune tonight be favorable."

The Nyctalope let go of his hand and he felt alone.

He felt alone!

For a minute, he stood still, overwhelmed by the feeling of solitude. Alone, completely alone, against forces that might well prove to be invincible or impenetrable.

But fits of depression never lasted long with Saint-Clair. His will did not falter, only froze for a minute. In no time, he was back to himself. Once again, he pushed the door open and stepped through. He hurried through the places he remembered, from room to courtyard and courtyard to room, up and down ramps, until he got to the big landing on the second floor of the rotunda.

The ten-foot high semi-circular, concave wall looked bare and smooth to the eyes. It was a wall made of giant blocks that fit perfectly together. They were so perfectly joined, in fact, that only a close examination revealed the seams.

Very slowly, facing the wall, Saint-Clair went from left to right, not only using his sharp eyes but also his keen sense of touch. His fingers felt along the wall as he inched across it. He had noted that all the construction here, doors and windows, obeyed laws of strict symmetry, of perfectly harmonious architecture.

If there's a way in it must be in the middle of the wall, he thought.

His eyes and fingers, therefore, paid closer attention as he approached the center of the semi-circular wall. All of a sudden, he let out a sigh of relief

"That's it!"

Both his sight and touch had just noticed a little difference in the seams. He stopped and traced the more visible and slightly deeper line. To the left, over his head and to the right, it was different from a Roman or Gothic archway, but not triangular like a Greek pediment, nor square like an Egyptian temple. It was unusually formed like a stairway going down from left to right, meaning the noticeable line followed the blocks stacked on top of each other.

Here's the secret door, I'm sure of it, but how does it open?

He looked for some sign of a mechanism. He examined every inch of rock. *Nothing.*

He pondered the problem.

All the doors I've seen so far open on the left, meaning their hinges are on the right. And they all just need a simple push. Indeed, why bother with locks when the will of the master can stop anyone from going through...

Placing his hands flat against the wall where he figured the door must be, but a little to the left, he pushed. The huge mass of rocks moved without any more pressure needed. Moreover, it made no noise, not the faintest squeak, even of oil, as the tons of stone swung open.

Saint-Clair stepped through, but before he had time to turn around, the gigantic door had already closed silently behind him.

He was at the start of a long, wide corridor whose walls were of the same cyclopean construction. Of course, there was not a single opening at first sight. The corridor stretched on interrupted for at least a hundred yards.

My God, even if there's only five doors on either side and one at the end, how long will it take me to find them all and explore the rooms?

Automatically and instinctively, he walked slowly down the corridor glancing left and right. Since nothing caught his attention, he got to the end of the corridor. And it was astonishing!

The high, rectangular wall at the end of the corridor was decorated on its upper two-thirds with the sculpted image of Shakyamuni, the sacred Buddha whose right hand is half-closed in front of his belly and his left hand open and holding a plate on his knees.

The Nyctalope shuddered and thought:

I haven't seen anything like this anywhere in this crazy lamasery. Does the sacred image mark the entrance to what might be considered the tabernacle of the huge temple? The sovereign master ought to live in that tabernacle. If there's a door, I just have to push it open and go through.

Along with this thought, he made a quick search. There was, indeed, a stepped door like the last one and it opened in the same way and closed behind him without a sound.

Saint-Clair stood frozen. What he saw first was a light, a blue flame, barely flickering, looking like a votive candle with a tall wick from this distance. But there was no candle and there was no wick. No support at all, no visible source, the flame was floating in the air a few inches above a conch shell sitting on a tall, slender tripod. It was like a stationary will-o'-the-wisp, or the spontaneous combustion of a gas being spit out softly and silently from the conch shell.

But as extraordinary as this was, the flame captured his attention for only a few brief seconds because in front of the tripod was a kind of couch made of beautiful white furs, which completely covered the long, wide support beneath them. And on this gorgeous, immaculate bed a human being lay sleeping.

A light golden veil shrouded his feet and legs up to his thighs. A scarlet robe covered his body up to his neck. Lying on his back, his thin, white hands rested on his thighs. His head lay on an ebony headrest whose ends, were curved like the roof of a pagoda and jutted out on either side. There was a scarlet cap with a pointy top ending in three golden rings atop his head. And his face...

To see the face better, Saint-Clair stepped forward. Every so softly! With velvety steps! Even his body moved so smoothly that, if that blue flame had been nearer, it still would not have flickered once. Then he stopped.

The sleeper was clearly a Mongol, youth... He could have been 15, 18, 20 years-old... His face was made of refined lines and harmonious purity, and bore an expression of serenity that was truly divine. And this serenity did not come from sleep, from closed eyes, no, it was the natural, maybe the only, expression, as if this human being presenting this face to the world was divinely above and beyond it.

For a period of time that his mind could not fathom, Saint-Clair stood there, controlling his instinct to tremble, just contemplating the face in awe as he felt like he was, for the first time in his life, seeing a god incarnate.

But the Nyctalope was too much of a realist. He never cut himself off completely from time, place and action.

He had not come this far to get flustered into a kind of stupefied adoration but rather to understand, identify and defeat the power that had been exercised indirectly over the Eighteen dead men, and more directly over the prisoners of the lamasery—the power that he and Gno had set out to thwart.

Saint-Clair's mind suddenly changed his plan. *Come on!* he scolded himself. *I have to get control over this sleeper. Even if he is the powerful wielder of the will that kills, he is still, after all, only a man. A young man, alone, sleeping before me, while I am awake and standing up.*

The Nyctalope paused in his thought before continuing:

Yes, but if this man is the occult master that Gno and I have logically envisioned from the facts, all he will have to do is open his eyes, see me, think for a split second, and I will drop to the ground, perhaps alive if he is merciful, but likely unable to move my little finger, stand up, or even to close my eyes.

This last phrase stuck in his mind. He watched the august serenity of the face and saw only one thing: his eyes were closed. And he thought:

These eyes mustn't open. They mustn't see me. Either Gno and I have come up with a completely false idea of the phenomenon, or else I am outside the Master of Death's control because he doesn't know my name and hasn't seen me.

His mouth cracked a thin smile and his eyes sparkled like they always did before accomplishing a deed that he had reasoned out and had to prove reasonably be successful. Grinning, he thought:

My God, what a lot of mental effort for such a simple thing.

He wore a long, gray, silk scarf tied loosely around his neck. Slowly he took it off, folded it lengthwise to make a blindfold thick enough so that nothing could be seen through it.

If I do it fast enough he won't have time to open his eyes. But I have to get in position. Let's be careful! I mustn't wake him up before blindfolding him.

Then he thought of something else:

What if he screams? I have to gag him, too... Tie him up to keep him from moving around? No, not that. I'll sit on him, hold him down. Then I'll talk. But will he understand? Does he know any of the six living languages I do or the dead ones? He's young... Maybe he'll know Russian or English... Oh, this is complicated...

Puzzled, hesitating, the Nyctalope stood there motionless. Nevertheless, he knew the situation could not go on for long without turning mortally dangerous for him. At last, he decided to take action.

He made sure that his right coat pocket still had his handkerchief, big and strong enough to make a gag. Then, holding the scarf, he positioned himself so that he could quickly, with one swift movement, blindfold the sleeper by wrapping the scarf around his head and knotting it in front. He took a long, deep breath and leaned over...

It was fast and flawless. Before the sleeper could open his eyes or mouth, the scarf and handkerchief were in place. And Saint-Clair was sitting on his thighs, leaning on his upper arms to hold down the man's whole body.

Saint-Clair spoke in Russian first, because he knew that, for several years, Stalin had been sending emissaries into Tibet, some publicly and officially, others unofficially and secretly. So, it was possible, perhaps probable, that in the higher echelons of the lamaseries, even in this extraordinary and mysterious sanctum, enough Russian had been learned to communicate.

Slowly and clearly, he whispered:

"Listen up, whoever you are, you're in my power now. Don't worry, you won't be in any danger if you talk to me. But first, do you understand me? Answer me, please, because if you say nothing, it may cost you your life. Not just yours, but everyone else in this lamasery. If you understand me, just raise your left hand."

The Nyctalope had spoken in a slightly nervous voice. And it was with some trepidation that he turned his head to see his victim's left arm go up in the air. His anxiety was immediately replaced by relief and he thought:

He understands me, I've done it!

"Good," he kept whispering, a little more loudly. "So keep listening. My right hand is going to release you, but only to grab a knife from inside my coat, which I will then point at your heart. My left hand will take out the gag so you can talk. But I warn you: if you scream, I'll stab you. Believe me, I don't like to kill, but in the course of my dangerous life, I've had to do it many times. However, I've only done it when my own life was in danger. Like it is right now. Because I'm alone here, alone against you, against all the mysterious powers that somebody, maybe you, is using in this uncanny place. I'm alone against the hundreds of men who probably live here. I don't know exactly, but I think you are their master, the secret and supreme Living Buddha! I am absolutely convinced that if I make the slightest mistake, my life will be snuffed out in an instant. So, if you scream, I'll have to kill you."

He breathed deeply and focused his will on controlling his nerves, keeping his muscles relaxed and obedient. He did what he had said. The dagger pricked the man's skin through the silk at the same time that his mouth was freed of the gag. Then Saint-Clair spoke again:

"In theory, I don't want to hurt you, but if I'm not mistaken and you are the quasi-divine man who can, under certain conditions, by a simple act of your will, kill any living creature, then the curiosity, interest, admiration and religious respect that your power inspires is understandable, provided that you don't use it in a way that flies in the face of my morality as a civilized man. You understand Russian, but do you speak it as well?"

The Nyctalope's eyes, more than his ears, got the answer immediately. The fine, almost feminine lips, of the mysterious young man opened to pronounce one word, "*Da*", which meant, "Yes". But to his great surprise, this one word was quickly followed by others:

"You have accomplished a feat that thousands of men have tried in vain for centuries," the man said. "Most didn't get past the shores of Chong Koum. There were those who were allowed by my predecessors or by me to come here, or who were brought here, and never left. Certainly none of them understood vaguely or accurately the reality of the supreme power residing here. You, who managed to do what no other man has ever done—who are you?"

The weird voice was softly musical, but it had a penetrating force, a sovereign authority, that Saint-Clair could not dream of resisting. He answered with a modesty that was quite natural given the extraordinary circumstances:

"If you are who I think you are, you sit so high on the human hierarchy that my name should be mean nothing to you. Still, I'll obey. I am Leo Saint-Clair, called the Nyctalope."

He was surprised to see that noble, finely drawn mouth break into a smile and he heard these terrible words:

"You have named yourself. I do not need to see you anymore. I can paralyze you now, or cast death upon you, as I so choose. So, go ahead and thrust your dagger. I am waiting."

At this simple but enormous challenge Saint-Clair trembled from head to foot. His hand gripped the handle, but he suddenly fell backward, jumped a little to the side and, against his will, his arm relaxed and threw the dagger, which went clattering over the stones.

At the same time, the young man in the scarlet robe sat up on his bed of white furs and untied his blindfold. His two, big, bright eyes stared at the Nyctalope. They were unbelievably blue.

PART THREE: THE MYSTERY OF THE ROSE GARDEN

CHAPTER I
A Strange Journey

Meanwhile, in Paris, Yori Koto, Gno Mitang's astute and active secretary, had kept up-to-date on the expedition through the radio.

The last message, dated Thursday, May 6, had informed him that the expedition was on the shores of Lake Chong Koum. On Saturday, May 8, Yori Koto went to the office of Dumont-Warren at the UNA to report on Melody MacCross and the famous Irish revolutionary, Earl Patrick O'Dougal.

"In a charming conversation with which Mademoiselle de Salsis," he said, "I was fortunate enough to learn that Mrs. MacCross has a private account at the branch of the Banque de France located in the 7th arrondissement. Mademoiselle de Salsis knows nothing about the activity on this account, but she happened to learn that a transfer of $50,000 was made by a large American bank into this private account on May 7.

"Now, through an English friend we have in the Intelligence Service, I also found out yesterday, Friday, that the little house on Rue Hallé where Earl O'Dougal lives was visited by two women. They weren't identified, but thanks to a happy coincidence, my friend saw them coming out of a back entrance located on Avenue du Parc Montsouris.

"We know that Mrs. MacCross has been colluding with the mysterious Leone Alzac since the beginning of April. Therefore it is logical to suppose that she and Madame Alzac are the two women who met Earl O'Dougal. And we then would be correct in assuming that this money transfer was a result of this new meeting."

Yori Koto had spoken without stopping, but here, he paused to give Dumont-Warren time to answer. But the director did so curtly. Although interested, all he said was:

"Yes, of course."

Yori cracked a smile, stood up and concluded:

"It's 8:30 a.m. The bank opens at 9 a.m. I'll head over there right away. We have a clear enough description of Leone Alzac for me to recognize her because I'm sure she'll be the one who'll go there to cash the check—if it is a check. Also, we haven't found the slightest trace of an accomplice. Plus, we know that her mysterious male companion never shows himself. Finally, if the amount is large enough, which we can legitimately suppose, the beneficiary of the check will have to cash it in person.

"Therefore, Monsieur, I bid you farewell. If things proceed as I imagine they will, and if I see Leone Alzac, I'll stay on her. I'll have my car there. If she leaves on foot, I'll trail her on foot, but my driver will follow us. If she has a car or if she takes a taxi or a bus, I'll stay in my car and follow her that way. Where she will lead me and for how long, I have no clue.

"So, Monsieur, I shall see you late—or it is goodbye. However, as long as I'm alive, I'll get you news one way or another. My chauffeur, Isha, will stay in Paris and act as my liaison. He has detailed instructions. I've seen to everything, even the possibility of my own death."

"Very well," is all Dumont-Warren replied.

He stood up, too, and the two men shook hands. Then Yori Koto left.

At 9 a.m. sharp, a uniformed employee opened the doors of the Banque de France in the 7th arrondissement. Several people were already waiting. Yori Koto was the second person to enter.

Among the clients, he had seen no woman, even down the street, who fit the description of Leone Alzac. He went to stand between two teller windows so that he could see the entrance without being obvious. He took some paper and a pen and jotted down a few numbers as if calculating a sum.

He did not have time to lose patience because, within minutes, he saw a young woman enter who was, without a doubt, Leone Alzac.

She must feel very self-confident, he thought. *She's dressed exactly like on her first visit to Mrs. MacCross when she was scrutinized by Mademoiselle de Salsis. No make-up to change her appearance. Yes, she must feel very sure of herself! It's true she might think that nobody would be spying on her because none of the papers mentioned anything unusual about the Eighteen deaths. This bodes well for my trailing her...*

Pretending to look for a specific form, Yori went from window to window until he was near her. She did not have to wait this early in the morning. She handed the teller a check.

From his clever vantage point ,Yori could see everything. He saw the teller raise his eyebrows and get up. When he returned with the check, he leaned over and said:

"Madame, will you please wait just a minute?"

It was spoken in a whisper so that Yori guessed more than heard what was being said. The Japanese had a good five minutes to observe the young woman. He did so with as much caution as eagerness. On the outside, she looked like nothing special, even a little banal. She was leaning on the counter, gazing at a notice that described the advantages of the latest Government Bond. She did not look nervous, quite simply waiting for whatever would happen.

Yori, therefore, could make all the mental notes that a smart, observant detective would make. Almost to the exact inch, he could now confirm that Leone Alzac was 5'2" bare feet, petite, size 5 shoe, size 6 gloves, with long, slender fingers. Of course, he also examined her face, every feature—size, form and symmetry.

I think that in the future, even disguised, I'll recognize her. And I heard her voice, simple, without a trace of emotion, her everyday voice, her natural voice. If she loses me today, nothing will keep me from identifying her if I see or hear her again.

At this point, Yori smiled inside. He was laughing at himself because, until now, he had not noticed what should have been the first thing to catch his eye: her patent leather bag sitting on the counter in front of the thick glass. It would have been necessary for travel, but was not a proper handbag for the city. It was equipped with a whole system of metal buckles and zippers. Two thick straps wrapped around it were used as handles.

My word, if all she's got in there is a handful of calling cards and some make-up, then there's plenty of room for a hundred stacks of bank notes—even a million or two. But would they disburse such a large sum at the window? No. They'll ask her to step into the manager's office.

He was right. The teller came back with a gray-haired gentleman whose classically elegant coat bore the rosette of the Legion of Honor. He spoke confidentially.

"Madame, if you would be so kind as to come with me into my office, I will provide..."

He did not finish. He motioned across the room for the client to follow him.

"With pleasure," the young woman replied, smiling at him.

Yori watched her disappear behind a door that opened as if by itself before she reached it—a door which read *No Entry*.

Ten minutes later, Yori Koto left the bank following Leone Alzac. Under her left arm she carried the patent leather bag like a lawyer protecting a big, heavy briefcase full of important documents.

A plain, slim convertible, but likely equipped with a powerful engine, was waiting for her. First, she put the bag on the passenger seat, then she climbed behind the wheel. The door slammed shut and the car took off.

It passed by a roadster with its soft-top up. This second car started off right away, driven by Yori Koto, leaving a short Japanese man on the sidewalk, dressed in his formal but sober chauffeur's uniform.

Taking Boulevard Raspail and Avenue d'Orléans, the dark blue convertible left Paris. At the intersection of La Croix-de-Berny, it turned left and got on the highway from Versailles to Choisy-le-Roi. But at the Belle-Epine intersection, it turned right and headed toward Fontainebleau.

The weather on this fine morning of May 8 was typical for spring. In the clear blue sky, pretty wisps of cloud drifted according to the northeast wind. The landscape radiated light. For Yori, who had not been out of the city in a long time, this pursuit in the open air was a real physical pleasure.

However, the Japanese quickly realized that the chase was also testing his driving skills and his prowess as an amateur detective. In fact, he had to keep speeding up in order not to lose his target. On the other hand, by keeping the convertible in view, he was risking discovery if Leone Alzac noticed the same car in her rearview mirror at always the same distance behind her. And it was of the utmost importance that she should not notice him, nor think she was being followed.

A tough problem to solve. Up to Fontainebleau, I can handle it. On this beautiful spring day, a lot of people wants to drive there or to Barbizon to have a nice lunch in a good restaurant. But after that? There are so many intersections leading off in different directions... Highway 7 goes to Nevers, Moulins and Lyon, or to Clermont-Ferrand and all the cities in the Massif Central. Highways 5 and 6 go to Dijon and Switzerland. And what about all the others! If she sees my car behind her town after town, she's first going to think, "Well, there's a car going in the same direction as I am," and then, right after that, she'll say to herself, "That's strange!" And her first reflex will be to stop somewhere to let me pass. She'll get back on the road fifteen minutes later, but if she passes my car pulled over to the side or puttering along, and then sees me behind her again at every turn, she'll know for sure she's being followed...

His reasoning was simple logic. No less logical was his conclusion. The Japanese had to find another way to find out where Leone Alzac is going. When he left Paris, he had nothing in mind but trailing her. Now this notion had become secondary because trailing her required a new plan. It took a few minutes to think about it.

I have to wait to be in a relatively deserted area. Then, I'll speed up and pass her. A little farther down, I'll park my car across the road and get into a fight with her. Yes, it'll be risky on several levels, but it could work if she behaves like an ordinary woman. However, if she's the one with the power to kill by simply willing it, then for sure, she'll kill me. I'll be victim number 19 and that's all.

He shrugged and concluded:

Either my pursuit will fail because Leone Alzac notices me and finds a way to shake me loose, or I have to risk being struck down by her lethal will. This is serious! I should think about it some more...

The needle on the speedometer wavered between 60 and 70 mph. The blue convertible barely slowed down in the Forest of Fontainebleau when it took Highway 7 at the La Fourche intersection and then stayed on it at the Obélisque.

Montargis, Nevers, Moulins, Yori thought. *Good! But then will she head toward the Auvergne and the Massif Central? Or toward Lyon and the Côte d'Azur? Unless we're not going that far... I've never been so uncertain!*

Ten minutes later, something happened that cleared everything up. He saw the convertible slow down and stop almost immediately, on the right side of the road. Then he saw Leone Alzac get out of the car and plant herself in front of the hood, to the left. By her attitude and the direction of her gaze, she was obviously upset that someone might be following her and she was waiting for them to pass.

So, Yori made a quick decision, at the risk of his life. Slowing down enough to pull over and stop without having to slam on his brakes, he parked ten feet behind the convertible.

He then jumped out and made sure his gloved hands could be seen carrying no weapon as he marched up to the young woman. With a quick glance around, he noticed that the fields were deserted and no car was in sight. Then, all of a sudden, like a hungry tiger pouncing on its prey, he dove at her.

If she fights back, it'll be because she doesn't have the occult power. Then I only have to hope no other car comes along.

Remaining calm, Yori was as composed as he was swift and skillful, despite the fact that he was half expecting his life to be snuffed out at the very instant that Leone Alzac would understand what he was doing. And he could not hold back a cry of joy when he felt not only the blood still rushing through his veins but the young woman struggling in his grasp. As she cried out, he thought:

She's not the killer, so I have a chance of success.

His first assumption was correct, but not the other. It took less than a minute for Leone Alzac to get the better of her opponent. With strength and agility that the Japanese had not anticipated, the young woman jerked, jiggled and jolted her flexible body, raised her arms and slithered out of his strong hold.

Then, going on offense, she threw a right hook into his jaw that sent him reeling back. Before he knew what had happened, she hit him again on both side of his head. He was knocked out and fell to the ground.

Yori opened his eyes fifteen minutes later. He realized that his legs and wrists were tied up, and his arms were strapped to his sides. He heard a clear, musical voice speak calmly:

"I advise you not to move. You'll force me to be more brutal."

He did not answer. He did not move. He was sitting to the right of Leone Alzac whose gloved hands were on the steering wheel. He turned his head a little to the side and saw her tranquil, beautiful profile. For a couple of minutes, he contemplated it. Then he spoke as if they were holding a normal conversation.

"Would you mind if I said something?"

"What?" she raised her eyebrows without turning her head.

"To ask you to be kind enough to answer a few questions that spring to mind."

"Why not. But I won't promise to answer all of them."

"Thank you. First of all, what did you do with my car?"

A faint smile crossed the young woman's lips.

"I left it on the side of the road. But since I've got a wrench and a screw-driver, I took off the license plates. I also made sure to take out all the papers, maps, guides and anything else that might identify its owner. So, abandoned in the middle of the French countryside, I'm afraid your pretty car is now com-pletely anonymous and contains nothing to alert the police."

"Congratulations, Mademoiselle," Yori said without any bitterness. "Well done."

"Coming from you," she replied seriously, "that's a real compliment."

"Thank you. Another question: what are you going to do with me?"

Leone Alzac laughed a little and shot a sideways glance at the Japanese.

"Oh, my, you've caught me off guard. I haven't thought about it yet. What am I going to do with you? Let's think about it. All I know from the papers I took off you and your car is that you're Yori Koto from Tokyo, living at the moment in Paris. And I'm wondering why a Japanese without a job, hence inde-pendently wealthy, I presume, would be interested in me. Now, it's my turn for questions. Why were you following me? Why did you attack me? Is it because you saw me come out of a bank with a bag full of money? I consider myself a good judge of faces. I've studied yours and I don't think you're a thief. Am I right?"

"Absolutely right," Yori answered. "The contents of your bag, which I see and feel at my feet, is of little importance to me."

"So?"

After considering the question for a few seconds, Yori answered:

"Well, Mademoiselle, excuse me for not answering right away. Maybe lat-er, maybe soon; it will depend on the circumstances, what you do with me and how I feel. Because, and please excuse for reminding you of this, but you still haven't answered my most urgent question—what are you going to do with me?"

"My God," the young lady stuck out her lower lip a little, "I'm going to keep you. In a few hours, we'll get to a house that is one of my current hideouts. If you give me your word of honor to try nothing against me, not to escape but to be a well-behaved prisoner, I'll stop the car and untie you. Then, when we arrive, you can have your own room and eat with me if you'd like. I'll let you walk in the garden because the house is surrounded by an old, high wall. In short, life won't be so bad there. The garden is big and beautiful, the house is well furnished, and there's a vast library. You'll remain there for a few days, or weeks, or maybe months. Of course, only if you give me your word of honor. You'll be free to break the promise if you feel your captivity is too much for you and you start dreaming of escape. But I warn you, the minute you tell me you can't keep your word, you will no longer be free. You'll be locked up in a room of about fifteen square feet, which is the size of your bedroom if I remember correctly."

"Thank you," the Japanese said. He sat up and turned to look directly at Leone Alzac as he went on: "Mademoiselle, I give you my word of honor not to escape or try to attack you again."

"Very well," the young woman said solemnly.

Five minutes later, after a quick stop, the dark blue convertible was cruising down the highway again at a good pace. But Yori Koto had his legs crossed and was lighting a cigarette with his free hands after asking the driver if she did not mind him smoking.

"By the way," she said gravely, "Y\you keep calling me 'Mademoiselle,' but I might be married, so 'Madame' would be more appropriate."

"I saw your bare hands at the bank. You do not wear a wedding ring."

"Well, well, so Mademoiselle it is. But do you know my name?"

Yori did not hesitate to lie/

"Not at all."

"Hum... I don't believe you. You're lying, right?"

"Maybe," he replied.

"Anyway, it doesn't matter now," her voice had become cold. "My name's Leone Alzac."

"Thank you," he bowed his head.

Then the two passengers, brought together so unexpectedly, fell into a long silence. Yori was asking himself all kinds of questions. But the main one was this:

Should I tell her what we know about her? Common sense says no. The hard part is getting information from her, without telling her the truth about me. She's probably asking herself why did this Japanese man attack me and what does he know about me?

The car passed Montargis without a single word being spoken. After two cigarettes, Yori stopped smoking. He appeared to become interested in the countryside. The young woman seemed to be concentrating on driving, which she did well. Since she was cruising at a steady 60 to 70 mph, except when the traffic forced her to slow down, her full attention to the road was natural.

At Briare, Yori Koto turned to her and said very politely:

"May I ask you, Mademoiselle, where we are going... the name of the place where I will be your prisoner?"

She smirked and replied casually"

"My God, yes. And I will even answer you. We're going through Nevers to a thermal resort with medicinal waters called Saint-Honoré-les-Bains. I have a villa there that a whimsical architect built in the Norman style, which fits pretty well into the landscape. It sits on the edge of a big meadow that slopes down from it and it backs up against a forest. You can see the whole valley from its windows, all the way to the hill where there's the spa and the village of Saint-Honoré.

"It's peaceful and I'm left alone. Only one private road, of more than a half a mile, connects my villa to the highway from Saint-Honoré to Luzy. The forest belongs to an old, retired military man who's kind of a misanthrope. His chateau is on the other side of the wooded mountain, three miles from my place. In the summer, in the high season, tourists coming to the spa will stroll through the forest, but very few of them and very rarely. Anyway, my whole estate is surrounded by an old wall, 13 feet high, which I've restored. I really feel at home there."

She stopped talking. Two or three minutes passed in silence again. Then Yori said simply:

"That means that my imprisonment, as far as my strolls on the grounds, will be a secret to the neighbors and to the tourists if it lasts until summer."

"That's right," Leone Alzac nodded her head.

Cosnes and La Charité went by without the young lady showing any interest in stopping for lunch. Yori blurted out:

"Are we eating in Nevers?"

"Oh, Monsieur," she said, "you can, like me, I imagine, wait for us to arrive at my villa to eat and drink. Didn't I tell you it was given a rather ordinary name by its previous owner—the *Rose Garden*?"

"Ordinary, sure," Yori smiled, "but is it, at least, descriptive of its reality?"

"Yes. The whole front of the house, across the edge of the meadow, is a garden of roses. They bloom all year long, really, because there are spring roses, summer roses, autumn roses, and even a big greenhouse exposed to the sun with a modern heating system so we can have flowers even in the winter."

"It must be beautiful," Yori said politely.

"Very beautiful!" Leone Alzac corrected him.

And silence again. Yori lit a cigarette. Before he even offered the open case to the driver, she shook her head.

They went around Nevers through the suburbs. A few miles past it, Leone Alzac stopped the car for a moment where the road stretched out, straight and long, completely deserted. She pulled her hat down over her eyebrows, put on huge glasses with yellow lenses and wrapped a big scarf around her neck that covered the bottom of her face.

"Oh," Yori observed, "you're hiding your face."

The young woman laughed and got back on the road. They followed the scenic route to Chateau-Chinon, but turned off a few miles before the city to take a road leading directly to Saint-Honoré-les-Bains.

The convertible only went through part of the city. Shortly, it turned onto a narrow dirt road, barely drivable, which ended in front of a huge wooden gate inside a massive stone archway built into a high wall.

"One minute, Monsieur," the young woman said.

She got out of the car and went to the gate. She took out a long, thin key, put it in the lock and turned it counter-clockwise several times while pushing it farther in at different points.

Strong secret lock, the Japanese thought as he looked on.

With her hands flat against the huge gate, Leone Alzac pushed and opened the way. Then Yori saw her staring at him, smiling, and heard:

"Since you know how to drive, Monsieur, get behind the wheel and come through."

He obeyed. Once through the gate he stopped the car and Leone Alzac got back into the driver's seat. She drove along the wall down a driveway that must have been very old since it was made of wide paving stones. Yori could see the Rose Garden and the roses: a big, beautiful mansion whose grounds disappeared behind a curtain of poplars on the left. To the right, the tall windows of the greenhouse sparkled.

"It really is very beautiful," Yori said sincerely.

"Yes, but I had nothing to do with it. It was like this when I got it a few months ago. Its owner, a wealthy South American, spent two months a year here, but half a dozen servants kept it up all year round in case he came. The staff are long-standing, tried and true, loyal, paid handsomely and have no relations with the people around. They consist of two families bound by marriage. I've kept them all. They are and will be, I know, as devoted to me as they were to their Brazilian master."

With that mischievous smile he had seen a few times already, she added:

"If ever you decide to take back your promise not to escape, Monsieur, don't count on any help. You could be a billionaire and offer them millions, nobody in my service would even be tempted. Of course, the slightest attempt at bribery will be reported to me immediately."

"I've no doubt."

She slammed on the brakes, swung around and looked him straight in the face.

"You sound so innocent. I'm sure you know more about me than is wise to know. I will let you decide when you want to talk to me openly, but I warn you, don't make me wait too long."

As she spoke, her dark eyes drilled into him. Then she turned her pretty, spirited face away and got the car moving again.

Fifteen minutes later, Yori was alone in a bedroom that had a door leading to its own bathroom. Before handing him over to a young servant, who looked relaxed but whose face was cold, and emotionless, Leone Alzac had said:

"Please join me for a meal that will be lunch, snack and dinner all at the same time. It will be served in an hour, which gives you time to rest a little. You must have seen that one of my servants has taken care of your bags. I took them out of your car and put them in my trunk."

"Mademoiselle," the Japanese replied, "I gladly accept your invitation."

"Until then," she said.

Then, she left.

Yori Koto spent twenty minutes in the warm bath, not to relax or to wash himself, which he did not need, but to focus his thoughts by forgetting his body.

I'm done playing around. When I went after Leone Alzac, it wasn't to capture her, because what would have I done with her if I couldn't get her to open up. I let myself be taken by her when I could've stopped her with a simple jiu-jitsu move. I hope she's proud of her victory and still believes it. I wanted her to beat me, to take me, to bring me with her. And it worked.

I gave my word of honor not to escape or try anything against her so I wouldn't be locked up or kept from doing what I need to do. So I'm a willing prisoner, but up to a point! I can't jump the wall or fight her, but I can go wherever they let me, look and listen, and ask question whenever I can. Maybe I'll get nowhere, but maybe, knowing what I know, I might find out more and shed a light on the mystery of the Eighteen deaths and on Leone Alzac.

It would've been easier to follow the MacCross trail, but I'm sure that she would've done nothing more than what she's been doing so far. The Irish business is a matter for the Intelligence Service and my friend there will take care of it. If he finds anything puzzling, he'll tell me. And if it relates to the Eighteen deaths and Leone Alzac, I'll use it when I'm free again... if I ever am!

So, after all, I think I was right to do what I did and I should be glad to be in the same place as Leone Alzac.

After analyzing his situation, the clever Yori Koto immediately asked himself some questions:

With Leone Alzac was spotted at Saint-Honoré-les-Bains on Wednesday, April 28, she was with a man whom the local car mechanic had described as looking Asian. It's now obvious that she and that man were coming here on that day. The mechanic obviously didn't know it, because otherwise he would have said so. Therefore, in Saint-Honoré they don't know that the Rose Garden villa is being rented by the same man and woman who had their car repaired on April 28. That seems strange! In the countryside, in a small rural community like this one, they usually know everything about everyone. So, the servants here must be discreet to a fault. And Leone Alzac and her companion must have taken precautions to keep their presence a secret. I wonder if I will be meeting this mysterious Asian man and, more to the point, is he the one with the power to kill at a distance?

It's all so fascinating! I've really ended up where I ought to be. But how will I get out? I still haven't thought of a plan to do that. Whether I find out anything or not, my being here, willingly or not, will do nobody any good if I can't get out.

Yori was still deep in thought when he followed the butler who had come and announced very formally:

118

"The meal is served. If Monsieur would allow me to show you to the dining room."

The Japanese kept his thoughts to himself—nothing showed on his face or in his attitude, not the slightest hint of mental turmoil, when he entered the dining room and saw, right away, standing with his hands on the back of a chair, a man of average height, probably around thirty, dressed well but simply in a light gray suit. His face matched the brief description given by the mechanic.

That's him! He looks like a Tibetan. I certainly can picture him dressed all in red, leading the lamas in some kind of Buddhist ceremony.

With these thoughts, the Japanese bowed deeply to Leone Alzac, who was also dressed simply in a close-fitting, gray silk dress and standing in almost the same position as the man, but on the other side of the table.

Yori stood up straight and faced the Tibetan. The young woman spoke in a calm voice:

"My dear friend, let me introduce Yori Koto, whom I told you about."

She immediately turned to the Japanese and gestured to the man who nodded his head.

"This is Brahmin Oryas Zabad Khan, who is doing me the great honor of being my guest here."

Yori said nothing but he greeted the Brahmin with Japanese reverence. Then Leone Alzac sat down, imitated by her "guest," and then by Yori.

The table was set and served with elegant and expensive simplicity. Hors-d'oeuvres, cold cuts, vegetable salads, cheese, fruit, purées and jams, all nicely laid out. But there was no wine, only cold milk and water, lightly flavored with oranges.

The big bay windows looked out onto the rose garden. The setting sun bathed everything in a soft light that harmonized beautifully with the somber gold of the wallpaper above the light mahogany wainscoting. Four paintings decorated the panels between the furniture, still-lifes, rather modern. There were no flower vases or cut flowers on the table.

For a few minutes none of the three talked. Then Leone Alzac looked at Oryas Zabad Khan and said:

"My dear friend, did I tell you that Monsieur Koto is staying longer with us even after he deciphers the document we couldn't read? In fact, he's agreed to give me Japanese lessons and he won't leave until I'm able to continue studying on my own."

The Brahmin smiled at the Japanese:

"Monsieur Koto, if Madame Alzac allows it, and if you'll accept a second student, I'd love to sharpen my skills in your beautiful language of which I know only the basics."

Yori noticed at once that the Brahmin had said "Madame" Alzac and not "Mademoiselle." Then, he understood that she had told the mysterious Brahmin the truth about him, but they had agreed on this ploy to make their lives together not just manageable but comfortable, maybe even, intellectually speaking, pleasant.

Does this document really exist? he thought. *A document they would need me to translate? Or is that just another conversational ploy? Let's see!*

He responded to Zabad Khan with a kind of natural respect in case the Tibetan really was a Brahmin:

"Master, I hope I prove worthy enough to be your instructor." Then, turning to Leone Alzac: "And let me say that I'm anxious to see this document that you only described vaguely when you asked me to come here from Paris."

"Are you in the habit of sleeping early?" she asked.

"No, even if I go to bed early, I read or work until midnight," said Yori. "I get up early, though. My constitution needs five to six hours of sleep every night."

"Well, that's just fine," she sounded delighted. "I'll give you the document tonight and you can begin studying it."

"Thank you."

Silence fell over them again. The three of them were, of course, hungry and thoroughly enjoyed the dishes brought by the white-gloved butler who presented them quietly and very ceremoniously.

Yori Koto had plenty of opportunities to observe the picture-perfect butler. And he wondered:

Is he French, English or German? He looks Nordic. The masters in this house are mysterious, but their servants might be stranger still. What does this man know about Leone Alzac and the brahmin? What does he think? Why is she so absolutely sure of their discretion and loyalty? He does his job and nothing else, like a perfect machine. So, who is he? And who are the other servants of 'Madame' Leone Alzac? This is all fascinating!

The young woman broke the silence when she happened to glance out at the rose garden. She talked about flowers, bragged about their variegated beauty, the care that the gardener took to make sure none of them withered on their stems. Oryas Zabad Khan also talked about roses. Yori showed interest in the flowers, their varieties. He found out that they never cut them while budding or blooming to put them in vases inside the house. The flowers lived their whole life as plants, and only when they were past dying, actually withering on the stalk, did the gardener cut them.

"We burn them," Leone Alzac said. "We burn them right away. They go from plant to fire."

"That's good," Yori replied. "There's nothing sadder than wilting flowers wasting away in neglect."

Thus the meal ended on this floral note, a subject that the two hosts seemed passionate about, and in which Yori, being Japanese, had a sincere interest as well. When they stood up, Leone Alzac proposed a stroll in the meadow.

Before leaving the dining room she offered cigarettes and took one herself. While walking beside the rose garden, the three of them continued talking about flowers, but other than roses. Yori displayed his keen and learned mind.

Anyone hearing them talking so calmly would never have believed that it was all just a façade hiding past tragedies and more to come. And what tragedies! Eighteen deaths was a staggering problem; the fate of the Nyctalope, that of Marquis Gno Mitang and their companions, of Yori Koto, and maybe beyond them, that of all humanity, were at stake!

After half an hour of walking, Yori felt that he had had enough of the charade. When they were back at the main entrance, he broke the awkward silence that had settled over them for a few minutes.

"Madame," he bowed to her, "please allow me to go to my room." He smiled and added, "Taking with me the document, of course, which you would like me to examine with my modest knowledge of ancient Japanese idioms."

"Certainly," she said.

With a few flowery expressions of politeness Yori and Oryas Zabad Khan parted and the Japanese followed the young woman into the villa while the Brahmin went smoking down a path in the rose garden.

Leone brought Yori into a room set up as a library. She opened a desk and took a piece of paper out of the drawer. The Japanese noticed that it was blank. He watched her sit down, picked up a pencil and started writing. Standing too far to read, Yori just waited.

After writing for a little while she stood up, faced her willing prisoner, looked him straight in the eye and spoke softly:

"Take this paper, Monsieur. In your room you can read what I have just written."

She folded the paper and handed it to him. He took it and bowed. Then before her deep gaze, he left the library and went to the staircase that led to the upper floors. Yori's "prison" was on the third floor. He slowly climbed the steps and, only after closing the door to his room, did he unfold the paper. He read:

I imagine you're smart enough to know that I wasn't fooled by your apparent physical weakness that let me, a woman of average strength, beat you with a couple of jabs, you, a man from the country that invented jiu-jitsu,. Therefore, I imagine that you know that I know that you willingly became my prisoner. You might have thought that being attacked by you and beating you, I couldn't run away because, sooner or later, you'd find me again and the same thing would happen. So, you achieved your primary goal, which was to find out where I live, even temporarily. You must also know that you will learn nothing more. But did you really want to learn this? Why did you follow and attack me? How much do you really know about me, and how much do you really want to know?

I will tell you this: One, we shall exchange only small talk until you decide to answer all my questions. Two, you have entered a circle of forces far beyond your ken and which, if I deem it necessary, will kill you without any possible de-fense from you. Three, I feel no need to hide the fact that, if you don't talk, your captivity will last until mid-September and end, inevitably, with your death.

Therefore, it's up to you. Either you confess until I believe you have noth-ing more to hide, or you wait and die. Leone Alzac.

Yori furrowed his brow. Still holding the note, he went to sit down in the armchair near the window and then reread the dire message more slowly.

"If I don't talk, if I don't confess, as she says," he murmured, "I'll live here until September basically translating documents and giving Japanese lessons. I can look forward to some good reads, because I saw the library is filled with in-teresting books, exquisite food, philosophical discussions, speeches on the beau-ty and scents of flowers and on the changing weather, and all kinds of conversa-tions, mostly intellectual. That's what awaits me in my daily life with the enig-matic Leone Alzac and the mysterious Oryas Zabad Khan. Then—death! That's very clear..."

Silence. Reflection. Then more murmuring:

"But if I confess, if I talk, if I tell them everything—because I'll have to—about the Nyctalope, Gno Mitang and myself, about the Eighteen deaths, what will happen? Won't I be found even guiltier? Won't I be sentencing to death my dear master, the great Monsieur Saint-Clair, his loyal companions, and of course Monsieur Dumont-Warren and maybe others as well?"

Silence, followed by a third reading of the note, then a long, deep thought in total stillness, eyes closed, face pale and placid meditation that lasted more than an hour.

When Yori opened his eyes, the cool night had crept into his room. He shivered, stood up, closed the window and looked out of the frame at the rectan-gle of starry sky on this beautiful spring evening. Feeling around in the dark, he found the bedside lamp and pressed the button. The light filtered through the pale green silk lampshade.

Automatically, he looked at the note again, which he still held in his left hand. He was astonished. He leaned over to look at it closer under the light—but now, it was blank! The writing had disappeared! He turned it over. It was blank, front and back. In fact, which was the front and which the back? There was not a single line of writing, not a word, not a letter!

Calm and collected, he concluded:

"Very well. Even with the super-human powers these people believe they have, they feel they must nevertheless remain careful about the little things, such as protecting themselves from future accusations. Leone Alzac wrote with a pencil made of something that evaporates with time. So, their powers aren't un-limited. If they were, they wouldn't need to resort to such tricks. Good. My mind is made up: *I'm not going to talk.* And my stay here doesn't necessarily have to end in death as Leone Alzac claimed with her vanishing ink!"

Half an hour later, with the room dark again, Yori, relaxed and peaceful, was asleep in the bed. His last thoughts had not been about Leone Alzac and her Brahmin, but about Flore de Salsis.

CHAPTER II
A Young Woman in Love

Yori Koto's quick mind had been quick to grasp the potential use of a human resource that had not yet been exhausted. This resource was none other than Florence de Salsis, whom he called Flore privately.

For the young lady, their intimacy had not gone far enough when Yori had last visited her in his quiet apartment on Rue de Constantinople. She would have been happier to go farther then, because she was ready, deep down inside, to give all of herself to him. It was a very serious and precious gift because it was the first time in her 22 years of life that she had imagined agreeing to such a thing, with nervous excitement, of course, but also with determination.

As for Yori, he was subtle and skillful in faking a love that he did not feel, and expressed it so cautiously that it could also be construed as a manifestation of great respect. The fiery Florence loved him, with all her heart, but her natural modesty and social restraint kept her in a state of waiting, which had begun recently enough that she was not suffering from it yet.

That a French girl from a noble but impoverished family had been reduced to find work as a lady's companion and secretary—a well paid task, certainly, and in no way humiliating—and then, fall in love with a foreigner was unusual, but not so much if one considered that Yori also came from a noble family, was physically and exotically attractive, well educated, spiritual, thoughtful, and that his job with His Excellency the Marquis Gno Mitang was somewhat identical to hers with the wealthy Mrs. MacCross. Finally, Yori had been the first young man with whom fate had allowed Florence to spend some time as equals.

But when all is said and done, love needs no reasons, motives or goals. Love is, or is not. It was not in Yori for Florence, but it was in Florence for Yori.

The last meeting between the two had taken place on Thursday, May 6, at the Rue de Constantinople for five o'clock tea. Chit-chat that sounded casual but was less free and cheerful than it seemed, tinged at times with timid sentimental hints, broken by dreamy lulls, had ensued. But where Florence's dreams were of love, Yori's were of secret police and diplomacy.

When it was time to part, the young man staying there and the girl getting ready to leave, Florence had had a sudden premonition of an ominous future, a dark and dire day to come, vague but sorrowful. As she was giving him her right hand to kiss, before putting on her glove, she blurted out:

"When shall I see you again, Yori?"

The young man had barely been paying attention to her, whose soft, delicately perfumed hand he had touched with his lips. He heard the words, but did not hear the anguish in her voice. He smiled a little indifferently and answered

"Whenever you want, Flore. But not tomorrow or the next day—I'm busy then. But after that, yes. I'll call you tomorrow at noon if you'd like?"

"Yes, please, call me."

If Yori had looked at her in a certain way at this moment, and if he had opened his arms, she would have thrown herself in them and babbled words that she had been choking back for days and that she had never uttered before: "I love you! I love you!" But the Japanese had stepped back, bowed formally and then opened the door. Mademoiselle de Salsis had almost fled.

Naturally, on Sunday, May 9, at noon, Mrs. MacCross was still in her bathroom dressing for lunch. Florence was in her own room, waiting for a phone call. But the minutes passed, then half an hour, then an hour... The call still had not come when she had to go down to the dining room.

During the meal, while answering Mrs. MacCross appropriately with the few snippets of conversation she threw out, Florence was thinking hazily:

My intuition yesterday was not wrong. Yori has never failed to keep his word. Why hasn't he called?

At 2 p.m., leaving MacCross to read her newspaper in one of the big rooms, Florence went back to her room, shut the door and asked for a line to Blingy. She knew that Yori often stayed at the Versailles home of Monsieur Saint-Clair with his employer, Marquis Gno Mitang, until at least 3 p.m. when he returned to Paris. Several times, she had called him there in the morning, and he always had answered.

As usual, the butler picked up the phone, but this time, he did not say, "Yes, mademoiselle, I'll get him for you." Instead she heard, "Monsieur Koto has not returned since yesterday, Mademoiselle. He called to inform me that he and Isha would stay in Paris. I'm terribly sorry but I know nothing further."

"Thank you," she replied, panting, and she heard, "You're very welcome."

She hung up, waited two minutes in a state of dizzy confusion... and then abruptly decided to call the house on Rue de Constantinople.

Florence knew the voice of Isha, Yori's chauffeur. She recognized it at once. And right away, she shuddered and her hands started trembling when she heard:

"Oh, Mademoiselle! I was just about to call you. I'm very worried. I've just read something in *Le Journal de Midi*, something..."

"What? What is it?" she asked nervously.

He answered immediately and she could hear the emotion in his polite voice:

"Mademoiselle, I think it'd be better if you came here. The morning before yesterday, Monsieur Koto gave me certain instructions that concern you in case of an unexpected event. I feat that unexpected event has occurred... but really so unexpectedly that... Please, Mademoiselle, come right away. Or tell me where I can come to meet you and talk freely... secretly."

"Secretly!" she burst out.

This word! What menace did it contain about the "unexpected event"? This word made up her mind. Her voice was determined when she replied:

"Don't move, Isha, I'm coming right away!"

Florence looked frail; she was one of those small, thin blondes whom love has not yet brought out of their shell, but who have a strong personality and a lively spirit capable of reacting to anything.

Small, thin, messy blonde hair and naïve eyes—that was how Florence usually looked. But this outward appearance hid a strong soul and a tireless body. Mrs. MacCross and Yori Koto both had always seen the first side of her, but only twice the second, when the innocent blue eyes glared coldly like blinding light off a steel blade.

Isha was a stocky Japanese with a gaunt face, always clean-shaven. The chauffeur and trusted servant of Yori Koto met Mademoiselle de Salsis in the entranceway of the ground floor apartment on Rue de Constantinople. He bowed and asked her respectively to enter. He skipped the small talk and directly handed her the newspaper pointing to the article. Flore read:

An automobile without identification was found on the highway near Nemours (Seine-et-Marne).

This afternoon, five miles north of Nemours, on the route to Fontainebleau, two policemen on motorcycles came across a gray, luxury roadster parked on the side of the highway. What made them stop was that there were no license plates on the car. No other car was in sight. After carefully examining the interior of the vehicle, the policemen became convinced that it had been abandoned on purpose, after being completely stripped of anything that might have identify its owner or driver. No sign of violence was found. One of the officers stayed with the car while the other went to Nemours to get someone to drive it back to the police impound yard...

Florence stopped there when Isha, who had been staring at her, shot out:

"The rest is just a description of the car. I'm absolutely sure that it's his roadster."

She put the newspaper on the table and looked worriedly, confusedly at Isha. He understood.

"Mademoiselle, I don't know what to think. If Monsieur had abandoned his car willingly after taking the license plates, his luggage and his papers, he would've called me from a nearby town, or written to me. But I've heard nothing. I just talked to the butler at Blingy. There's been no mail, no phone calls. I don't know what to think."

"Come on," Florence forced herself to stay calm. "When did he leave?"

"The morning before yesterday, we left from Versailles a little before 8 a.m. I drove Monsieur to the UNA office, then to the branch of the Banque de France at the corner of Boulevard Raspail and Rue de Sèvres. Around 9:15 a.m., he came out and told me: 'Return to Rue de Constantinople. Wait for me to contact you. If you hear nothing from me in 48 hours, tell Mademoiselle de Salsis that I'm on the trail of Leone Alzac.'"

"Leone Alzac!" Florence yelped.

Her keen memory pictured the strange woman who had met privately with Mrs. MacCross three or four weeks ago.

"Yes, I'm sure of the name," Isha went on. "Leone Alzac. And Monsieur finished by saying, 'You'll take Mademoiselle de Salsis to see Monsieur Dumont-Warren, whom you will also tell that I'm on the trail of Leone Alzac. The two of them will make a decision and you'll do as they say.'"

After a brief pause Isha wrapped up with:

"That's all, Mademoiselle."

Florence did not hesitate. She went to the telephone and quickly found Dumont-Warren's home number. She thought that, at this hour, if the head of the UNA was not eating breakfast out, he would probably be at home. But at the other end of the line, she got a secretary who told her to call the Agency because the director was having his breakfast in his office that morning, as he often did. There, too, she talked to another secretary who said that he had just gone out, but would probably be back soon.

"Isha, let's go now," said Florence. "If Monsieur Dumont-Warren isn't back when we get there, we'll wait."

At the Agency, Mademoiselle de Salsis and Isha were taken directly to Dumont-Warren's office since he had just returned. Seeing her face and hearing the first words out of her mouth, the Director understood that Yori Koto had not wrong and that this woman loved him deeply.

He also understood that this little blonde girl with various shades of blue in her eyes, her tense body, but a clear and determined voice, was spunky and clever. After a few questions and answers to frame the problem, Dumont-Warren thought about it for a moment and then looked gravely at the girl.

"Mademoiselle, could you get a few days off from Mrs. MacCross? Find some excuse, a family matter or helping a sick friend or something?"

"Yes, Monsieur," Flore replied calmly. "I have an old aunt in Clermont-Ferrand. I can say she called me because she fell ill all of a sudden. I know Mrs. MacCross has no plans to leave Paris before the middle of June, so she could very well spend a few days without me."

"Good," Dumont-Warren said. "So, here's what I suggest: Go looking for Yori Koto because knowing what I know, I think he might be in some very serious danger right now. Yori expected that one day it might be good for him—and for you too—to tell you all about certain things—very extraordinary things. Before I give you a message written by Yori, I must ask you to swear on whatever is dearest to you to destroy this message after you've read it and never tell anyone anything about what you have learned. Will you swear?"

"Of course! I swear on my life that this secret—since it is a secret—will never escape my lips."

"Very well, Mademoiselle. Now, let's not waste any more time. First, get some time off from Mrs. MacCross, then go to the Gare de Lyon, as if you were taking a train to Clermont-Ferrand. Isha will be waiting for you there. He won't be alone. I'm sending a young man, whom I consider to be the best of my investigative reporters. His name is Jacques Fitou. He'll be your partner and, when needed, your protector. I'll let you use one of my cars—the fastest and the most comfortable, an 8-cylinder convertible. Can you drive?"

"Yes."

"Very well. Fitou can drive too, naturally. With Isha, there will be three of you to take the wheel. You'll go to Nemours first. Fitou has a special card from me that will give him some authority with the police. You'll need money. Fitou will have cash for all three of you to split up in case you get separated. Finally, Mademoiselle, here's the message written by Yori Koto for you..."

Dumont-Warren stood up, opened a small safe that looked like a file cabinet and took out an envelope that he handed to the young woman.

"You can read it in the taxi on your way home. Then reread it on the way to the Gare de Lyon. Do you think that after a second reading, you can memorize and destroy it?"

"I'm sure of it. My memory is good and accurate."

"Very well. Naturally, Jacques Fitou will have read it too, because I've got a copy to give him. As for Isha, you can tell him as much as you want, when you want, as you see fit."

So far Dumont-Warren had spoken without showing any emotion. He was less self-controlled when he took her hand and held it in his for a moment, looking very paternal with all his concern. His voice was tender when he wrapped up:

"I see in you courage, but also prudence. I also see your intimate feelings. I have great confidence in you as you enter upon this... extravagant adventure. Take advantage of Isha. He's smart, brave and trustworthy. And count on Fitou, whose personality and virtues you will appreciate. He will give you and Isha any information I get and can contact me anytime. But first of all, learn Yori's message by heart. Now, go, Mademoiselle. In an hour Fitou and Isha will be waiting for you at the Gare with the 8-cylinder."

He gently raised the girl's trembling hand to his lips, kissed it and then let it fall.

"Thank you, Monsieur," she replied.

An investigative journalist ready to travel anywhere for a story, an outstanding detective in the best sense of the word, Jacques Fitou, whom Dumont-Warren highly respected, was around 30 years-old, thin and brown-haired, of medium build, clean-shaven, with sharp features, a hooked nose and dark eyes that were sometimes alert, sometimes dreamy, and sometimes absolutely expressionless.

He smiled at Flore de Salsis, whom Isha had no need to point out, when she got out of the taxi at the curb in front of one of the big entrances of the Gare de Lyon.

"Mademoiselle de Salsis? I'm Jacques Fitou. I'm at your service."

Florence looked very pale and grave. After reading Yori's alarming note three times, she had just torn up into a thousand pieces and scattered them in the wind. Her whole being was seized by an emotion that was hard to control.

"Thank you," she whispered. "But let's not waste any time. Let's go to Nemours."

"Right away. If you don't mind, I'll drive. I know the way better than Isha and maybe better than you."

"That will be fine, Monsieur."

Florence got into the car next to Fitou while Isha sat with the three small suitcases in the backseat. The weather on this May afternoon was beautiful and dry so the top had been left down.

As they were leaving Paris by Avenue d'Italie, Florence spoke calmly to Fitou:

"What do you think of what Yori said in his message?"

With the same calm but with a little more energy, he answered

"Astounding! Really astounding! And I'm not exaggerating. Just imagine if... astounding, yes..."

Then, sounding a little flippant and sarcastic, which was not rare with him, and was done on purpose, he added:

"If the famous Nyctalope and his friend, Marquis Gno Mitang, get hold of this stupendous power in Asia, I can see the two of them setting themselves up as dictators, and establishing the reign of common sense throughout the world. The Earth will see the first empire of fraternity, prosperity and peace. Absolutely! But if the mysterious power falls into the hands of a fanatic, or an idiot, or a man who's both at the same time, as often happens, what a heinous tyranny is in store for all us, poor humans."

And then in a different tone of voice:

"Sorry for joking, Mademoiselle, I do that sometimes, especially when things get dire, but I take things very seriously and I'm sure of one thing right now: our only goal is to find and save Yori Koto. That's our mission—that and nothing else."

"Yes, Monsieur—that and nothing else," repeated Florence.

Having left Paris at 4 p.m., the 8-cylinder entered Nemours at 4:50 p.m. and pulled up on Avenue Carnot to talk to the first pedestrian Fitou saw so that he could get directions to the police station. There, he showed the sergeant his UNA ID card with four lines written on the back, followed by a prestigious signature and an official stamp.

The anonymous gray roadster was in the impound lot of the station, i.e. in the back of their yard. Florence and Isha recognized it at once, but did not show it, except to give a discreet nod to Fitou.

The reporter questioned the sergeant who was cautious but disciplined enough to answer candidly:

"An investigation?" he said. "Sure, we did, but it produced nothing. We found no witnesses, so we don't know what happened, or when, or why all the identifying papers were removed. I put in the official report that I'm waiting for orders."

"May I examine the vehicle?" Fitou asked.

"Go ahead. I've already gone through it with a fine-toothed comb. There's nothing. No sign of a struggle, no drops of blood, or anything of the sort. Just empty and anonymous, that's all."

Fifteen minutes later, the reporter told the sergeant:

"You were right. Nothing. Empty and anonymous—I like your phrase. Thank you for your help. There's nothing more for us to do here."

The 8-cylinder left Nemours heading for Montargis because the plan of action they came up with was to use a piece of information contained in Yori's message: they knew about the Eighteen deaths and Leone Alzac being spotted in Saint-Honoré-les-Bains, and having had her car's bumper repaired there. Now, to get from Paris to Saint-Honoré-les-Bains, one would normally pass through Nemours and Montargis. So wasn't it logical to think that Leone Alzac, followed by Yori Koto, might have been returning to Saint-Honoré-les-Bains?

Therefore, on this day, right around 8 p.m., Jacques Fitou stopped the car in front of the garage that had performed the repair. He filled up with gas and water, chatted with the mechanic, got information on the hotels open during this season, and finally asked about a green roadster passing through.

"Could be. So many cars go through here," the mechanic was friendly and polite.

They offered him a drink at the nearby café. They sat down. More small talk ensued, mostly gossip, stories from the job and mention of local crimes. Finally, Fitou got to ask about the repair of the little car driven by a young woman with an Asian-looking passenger.

"The lady looked foreign, like a Hindu temple dancer, and the guy like Clemenceau, but without a moustache, and Asian," the mechanic expanded on the description that he had given Yori.

Gently urged on by Fitou, he provided a crucial new detail:

"They couldn't have gone far. The gas gauge I saw was down under one gallon. I offered to fill it up, but the girl got behind the wheel and told me 'No need.' Then they took off. I figure they must've been staying at the Hotel Europe, the only one open then..."

This new and important detail had not been given to Saint-Clair and the others on April 28. Maybe something had cut their conversation short, or the mechanic had been distracted and forgot? Whatever the reason, Fitou did not care. He knew this was important.

First to himself, then to Florence de Salsis and Isha, he concluded:

"The mysterious Leone Alzac and her no less mysterious companion must have a house in the area. With less than a gallon of gas, the car could not have gone far."

They got rooms at the Hotel Europe. While filling in the registration card, Florence and Jacques claimed to be engaged to be married, and traveling with their driver-mechanic. Florence explained to the hotel manager, a friendly but nosy old lady, that they had come to Saint-Honoré to look for a villa to rent for the summer. This would explain them staying there for a few days and give an innocent excuse for asking about the local houses and villas and their inhabitants—who lived there year-round and who only seasonally.

Fitou quickly found out that, on April 27, Leone Alzac and her companion had not stopped at the Hotel Europe after refusing the offer to fill the tank of their car, as the mechanic had supposed.

"Did they get gas somewhere else?" Fitou wondered aloud. "Hard to know after three weeks, in a region where a lot of cars come through. Let's drop that for now. Instead, let's suppose that she didn't go farther than 15 miles around Saint-Honoré..."

The entire next day was spent searching. Isha stayed near the hotel and the car. He washed and polished it, tuned the engine, then had an aperitif, meal and another drink with the only male worker at the hotel, who talked. He was from Saint-Honoré and knew everything about the town and its inhabitants.

Florence and Jacques started with the two real estate agencies in town. They visited some available houses and villas, got a list of all the others, discreetly got information about many of the inhabitants in the commune of Saint-Honoré-les-Bains, got names and stories, gossip. And in the evening, after an early dinner, since the end of the day had been bright and the twilight was long, the two "fiancés" decided to take a stroll to the Lac des Chèvres, two or three miles away. It was an excuse to be alone so they could talk freely without anyone eavesdropping.

At the lake, on a path that was completely deserted in this season and at this hour, the three investigators could speak openly and honestly. And one fact came to the fore as obvious, undeniable, and particularly intriguing: among all the hundred or so houses, villas and chateaux in the area, empty, rented or sold, there was only one property that had recently become unavailable, and nothing was known about its occupants—the Rose Garden Villa, also known as the Norman Villa.

There was no doubt. All the other properties were either rented or for rent. They had been, or would be, occupied by such-and-such a couple, family or single occupant. Everything was known about them, nothing hidden or suspicious. Except the Rose Garden Villa.

"Let's sum it up," Florence said. "This beautiful country house that we can't see, except from a distance, was built in 1925 by an architect from Nevers, now deceased, for a rich Brazilian, Senhor Armando Golves. He spent two or three months there in the summer. He maintained it all year round with half a dozen servants. In 1936, he stopped coming and the villa was put up for sale.

"So far, everything is clear. One strange thing, though, which obviously has to do with the servants' family situation—they live together, but alone, never associating with anyone else, neither locals, nor tourists, in any season. There's only one butler, always the same, known as Monsieur Alfred, who comes into town for food, although rarely because the villa gets its supplies by van from markets and warehouses and various shops in Nevers, the biggest city in this department. I said strange, which might be an exaggeration for life at the Rose Garden up to November 1936, but after that…"

Florence de Salsis took a deep breath before continuing her report:

"After November 1936, the word strange is not strong enough. We know the Villa was purchased, but by whom? Nobody in Saint-Honoré knows the name of its new owners. Nobody has ever met them. In the past, Monsieur Alfred would sometimes be accompanied on his trips into town by another male or female servant. But since November 1936, only he has been seen, always alone. When asked about the new owners, he just says, 'Oh, they're good people, but they don't come here often.' That's all, nothing more. By chance, a few townspeople, maybe two or three times, saw a car on the dirt road leading to the Villa. The road comes out at an old intersection that's hidden from sight. Rumors abound about who's in the car, but all agree that the driver is always wearing a hat pulled down low and big sunglasses and he or she is wrapped in a scarf to completely hide their face…"

Jacques Fitou raised his hand.

"What is it?" Florence asked

"Just a second. I think…"

"Wait. I'm almost done," Florence cut him off. "And I know what you think. You think that, on April 27, after the Eighteen deaths, Leone Alzac passed through Saint-Honoré, stopped at the garage to fix her car, strolled around with her companion without either of them bothering to hide their faces, and you think that this was probably more clever than keeping to their habit, that people would think they're just tourists and nobody would suspect them of being the new owners of the Norman Villa."

"Yes!" Fitou agreed. "It was a blunder by Leone Alzac when she said 'No need' to the mechanic to fill up her car. She was already behind the wheel and anxious to get home, maybe thinking about the Eighteen deaths. Anyway, she slipped up there, but it's only this one mistake that makes me sure it's her. Right, Mademoiselle? Right, Isha? Do we all agree that Leone Alzac and her companion are the new owners of the Rose Garden?"

It was Florence's turn to blurt out:

"Yes!" but she immediately corrected him. "Sorry, but this 'No Need' business isn't a real proof. What makes me sure is the very mystery, the deep, dark mystery, surrounding the ownership of the Rose Garden."

"If you say so, but this mystery wouldn't have come to our attention without the mechanic telling us about the gas."

"I agree."

One thing led to another, and Florence de Salsis, Jacques Fitou and humble Isha succeeded where the Nyctalope, Gno Mitang, Soca and Vitto had failed!

The next morning, Isha got some upsetting information from the young baker who came to deliver the bread to the hotel. He had to share it right away with Fitou, who immediately went to knock on Florence's door.

In the afternoon of Saturday, May 8, the day when Yori Koto had left Paris chasing after Leone Alzac, the baker had been lounging in the doorway of his bakery when he had seen a car slowing down almost to a stop because the bakery van was coming out of the driveway and blocking part of the road. Inside the blue convertible he had seen two people very clearly: the driver was wearing big sunglasses and a scarf hiding the bottom of his face. "He must've had a helluva cold," the baker had said, "because it was hot out." As for the passenger, he was "A Japanese like you, I swear," and had been smoking a cigarette.

Isha was sure of one thing: the car that had left Paris from the Banque de France and that Yori Koto had followed had been indeed a blue convertible!

Now Florence, Fitou and Isha were certain sure that Leone Alzac was the owner of the Norman Villa and that, at least on May 8, she had gone there with Yori Koto.

"A Japanese next to Leone Alzac!" Florence raised her voice. "In plain sight and normal as could be, at least to this baker on his break. So, Yori was alive, awake... and free, since he was smoking."

"He might only have looked free," Jacques Fitou said. "From the start of this mysterious adventure, who can tell what's real and what's fiction?"

"In any case," Florence shot back, "there's a high probability that Yori is at the Rose Garden."

"I agree," Jacques replied gravely.

He was thinking that love, so obvious in this nervous and passionate but smart and clever girl, could be used for a lot more than just saving Yori Koto. For Jacques Fitou was putting his heart and soul into this dangerous game. And from now on, Yori Koto was less interesting to him than Leone Alzac and the mystery of the Eighteen deaths.

Thus, circumstances had conspired to bring together a determined journalist, a bold young woman in love, and a devoted servant to solve a mystery that had caused the Nyctalope's and Rikevitch's expeditions to risk their lives in the distant region of Chong Koum.

CHAPTER III
A Basket of Goat Cheese

Both Florence de Salsis and Jacques Fitou thought that the presence of Isha in Saint-Honoré might actually be dangerous. If Leone Alzac and her mysterious companion really did live at the Rose Garden Villa, if they really were holding Yori Koto prisoner, and if, finally, they had half a dozen servants obeying their orders, then it was likely that they kept some kind of watch over the area. And the presence of another Japanese in Saint-Honoré might look suspicious. At least, it would put them on alert. That other Japanese would be investigated and they would soon be informed of the young man and woman accompanying him. Could Leone Alzac somehow see Florence? And would she then recognize Mrs. MacCross' secretary?

"It's unlikely," Florence said. "When she went to see Mrs. MacCross, she didn't really even look at me. Still, it's possible she might recognize me if she sees me here. And it's certain that she'll be wary of us by the sole fact that we're with a fellow countryman of Yori. We should let Isha go."

"No," Fitou nodded, "I think all three of us should disappear."

"What do you mean?"

"I'm going to tell the hotel manager that we didn't find anything in Saint-Honoré for the summer. We'll pack up as if we were returning to Paris, but in reality, we'll only go to Decize, which is about 20 miles from here. It's a small industrial town where the servants of the villa, from what I've gathered, never go. They get their supplies from Nevers. Anyway, I'll pose as an engineer and journalist researching a story on the various industries in and around Decize. You'll be my sister and Isha our driver. We'll set up in a hotel and every day travel around, but without Isha. We'll leave the car in a garage in the tiny village of Seu, on the other side of the forest from the Villa, two or three miles away depending on which road you take. The two of us will figure out how to get a look inside the walls of this Rose Garden. Then we'll get in there ourselves, probably sneaking in rather than forcing our way. What do you think?"

"I like it."

"Then, pack your things. You and Isha bring around the car while I pay the bill. We'll leave in fifteen minutes."

Twenty miles south of Nevers, between the Loire and the Aron rivers, near the canal, Decize was a town divided into three parts connected by the Pont-de-Loire and the Pont-Neuf. It had a population of 7000. Foundries and glassworks, coal mining, plaster, lumber and charcoal were thriving industries, providing jobs for a lot of workers, many of whom were foreigners.

There was, therefore, no surprise at the local hotel when at 12:15 p.m. on Wednesday, May 12, a new couple sat down in the dining room while their chauffeur, said to be Chinese, sat with the servants in the pantry. In the afternoon, the engineer from Paris and his sister went to visit the glassworks. The car stayed at the hotel garage with the chauffeur.

The next day, Thursday, May 13, the three visitors left in their car right after a quick breakfast at 7 a.m. They brought with them three cold lunches because they planned to visit the area and would not be back until dinner, probably very late. But a few miles outside of Decize, near a village by a small river, the car stopped. Isha got out carrying his lunch and some basic material for fishing, which they had bought in Decize. The sky was clear and bright with a breeze from the northeast. It would stay nice all day long. Isha could enjoy his time fishing and lazing about.

Florence de Salsis and Jacques Fitou got back on the road. About fifteen miles further on, they parked at an unassuming garage. They were in the village of Seu, whose country houses were built around the edge of the lake by the same name. Much of the countryside was the property of the Marquis d'Espeuilles.

If one walked around the lake, through the fields and the woods, one ended up on a wooded hill, which belonged to the Marquis, but was surrounded by a forest that was open to the public. After climbing the hill and crossing the forest to the east, one came down on the north side onto a beautiful view: a succession of natural prairies mingled with woods and the small town of Saint-Honoré in the distance, arranged in a semi-circle around another hill with thousand-year old trees. Farther off were the rolling forests of the Morvan.

Closer up, to the right was a big, rounded stone wall enclosing a vast domain of natural prairies, also spotted with woods, where, at the highest point, stood the Rose Garden villa.

When Florence and Fitou walked out of the forest, they stood still for a few minutes at the top of the hill. From there, they could see the huge old wall stretching out from left to right, and the roof and tall chimneys of the Rose Garden villa.

"Can you climb trees?" asked Florence all of a sudden.

"My God, yes, when it's necessary," replied Fitou, smiling. "Even if I ruin my nice golf pants."

"Well, I think you need to climb that tree over there and plant yourself in the high branches. But first, you must give me a boost so I can reach that low branch, and I'll climb up before you. I'm light and agile and strong enough to lift myself with only my arms if I need to. I climb well. You want to see?"

"Very much, Mademoiselle. At this hour and at this time of the year, there's little chance that a hiker or woodcutter or a game warden is going to wander off the paths. Let's climb up, and when we come back down, we can fix the branches so that nobody will suspect we've been here."

"Right you are!"

Ten minutes later, and without Florence's simple, sturdy dress or Jacques' golf outfit suffering any tears or snags, the two were sitting over sixty feet off the ground in the leafy branches of a beech tree. The branches and leaves hid them completely, but when they moved, they could see the whole front of the villa, its paths and blooming flowerbeds, and the vast, sloping prairie dotted with groves and bounded by the big wall.

They took it all in at a glance and paid no attention to details because they immediately spotted an open window from which a song came lilting through the air all the way to their ears. A song without words, a light melody sung with "ou" and "a" and "i", stopping and starting again as if the singer were moving from one room to another, busy with trivial chores that did not stop him from singing, but interrupted his distracted, unconscious tune. It could have been a man getting ready, going back and forth from and to the bathroom. And this man was...

Florence grabbed Jacques' arm. Her voice hushed but hoarse, she whispered:

"I know that song. I heard it at Rue de Constantinople. It's Yori's. He is in that room with that open window on the first floor!"

"Stay calm," Jacques whispered back, gently tapping the nervous fingers gripping his upper arm. "Let's see if he sticks his head out, which is likely on such a beautiful morning."

No sooner said than done! In a bright red, silk kimono embroidered with dark blue motifs, Yori Koto showed up at the window filing his nails. He looked up at the sky and smiled at the fine spring weather. He whistled like a cheerful thrush, turned around and went away.

"I'll be...!" Jacques muttered. "He sounds happy enough. At least being imprisoned at the Rose Garden doesn't seem to be too painful."

"All the better," said Florence, obviously delighted. Then, sounding less emotional, she added: "Let's stay here and watch what they do. We can stay until nightfall if nothing happens. You have the bag of food so we can just get comfortable and wait, you on that forked branch there, and me on his one, a little higher. OK?"

"Yes, Mademoiselle. You're incredible. I see, I listen, and I obey."

During the next twelve hours, until sunset, Florence and Jacques sat unseen, watching the daily life of the Norman Villa unfold. It looked exactly like what it was: a daily routine. They saw a few men and women coming and going around the grounds. They saw Leone Alzac, whom Florence recognized right away, walking in the Rose Garden with the Asian man and Yori Koto. They saw Yori sit alone in the shade of an oak tree in a lounge chair brought by a servant and spend two hours reading and smoking. They saw him go back inside and appear briefly at the still open window of his room. And finally, at end of the afternoon, they saw something unexpected, which struck Florence like a pebble tossed into a lake causing ripples through the water.

That something happened at dusk, when one of the bay windows on the ground floor suddenly lit up. Florence and Jacques saw clearly into the dining room. Two human shadows were bustling about.

"The servants are setting the table for dinner," Florence whispered.

That was when a small bell rang, the rusty bell of a field gate. Its sound, the first of its kind all day long, jolted the already alert attention of the two watchers. They saw an old woman open a small door in the wall that ran behind the property and let out into the forest. Another woman appeared in the opening. She was thin and blonde and held a basket in her hand, which she gave to the old woman after she closed the gate. While the old servant scurried off toward another building and disappeared, the girl started walking casually over to the edge of the rose garden, bordered on that side by a simple, low-cut hedge that the girl hopped over easily. And quickly, she picked two roses that she hid under her apron. Then she went back and waited, walking in circles around the courtyard.

Now, in all this Florence noticed one detail that took on some great importance for her. She whispered excitedly:

"Monsieur Fitou, that girl went by directly under Yori's window. My God, I've got an idea! Let's go. The trees will hide us. Let's get down... without a sound... so we can see where that girl goes. Quick!"

Ever being careful to avoid making too much noise, they got down as fast they could. They then took a path they had seen leading to that small gate in the wall while taking care to remain behind bushes or hiding behind trees. Soon, they spotted the peasant girl returning. She was walking fast, swinging her empty basket.

Florence and Jacques had no problem following her from far enough away to not be heard, but still close enough to not lose her at the forks and crossroads that wound through the tangled forest in the fading light. They saw her go into a clearing lit red by the setting sun. It widened in the back where the buildings of a modest country farm sat. In the distance, the sky was clear between the trees as the forest thinned out. There must have been some fields back there, with a few crops, some cows and a barn that Florence and Jacques could smell from their hiding place.

"We have to go inside that house since the girl went in there," said Florence.

Fitou put a calm hand on her trembling arm and said:

"Don't you think it'd be better if we found out the lay of the land first?"

"Yes, but listen..."

She did not have to say much before he interrupted her:

"Right, I got it. But please let me do the talking. I know country folk. My mother and father are both from the Yonne. We're neighbors. I know how you have to talk. Plus, I'm calm whereas you're not—at least not enough."

"You're right," Florence said. "Say whatever you want. I'll just back you up with a word here or there when it seems natural."

"Perfect."

They went through the open gate and crossed the yard; they heard a chained dog barking. In the doorway of the old, humble abode, already darkened by the approaching night, a man appeared, standing with his hands in his pockets. Quickening his pace ahead of his companion, Fitou tipped his hat and spoke in a friendly voice, using his regional accent:

"Good evening, Monsieur. Excuse my sister and I for bothering you. We're not quite lost, but we're still pretty far from Vandenesse, where we're staying with some friends. It got cold and we're tired. Might we get a cup of warm milk while we take a fifteen minute rest here? We would be much obliged."

The farmers on the borders of the spa resorts are used to accepting money from tourists and hikers in need of "a cup of warm milk," or, as often happens despite official health warnings, a cup of raw milk.

The young man and his "sister," therefore, were welcomed. There was electricity in the front room. On the table, the farmer's wife laid out a clean tablecloth smelling of lavender. She said:

"Well then, milk is fine for young ladies, but you, Monsieur, should drink a glass or two of our local wine."

Jacques Fitou laughed his approval before she disappeared into another room. As for the young farm girl with blonde hair whom they had followed, and she was there, wearing an apron. She started heating up the milk, which she had ladled from a big, tin churn containing the day's milking. The farmer's wife came back carrying two bottles.

"Oh, my!" Fitou exclaimed. "I'd love some cheese, if you have any, and a slice of bread. And I bet my sister would, too."

"Yes, indeed."

Florence smiled at the farm girl who was watching her.

The farmer was won over by the young man's casual warmth and his sister's kindness, and maybe figured that these "tourists" would be just as generous.

"Well then, my wife was going to serve the soup," he said. "If you want, we won't wait and you can eat with us. The night will be clear and the road to Vandenesse is a short way from here, if you go through Saint-Honoré. We'll show you the way with the lantern. You'll spot it easy enough."

Fitou smiled at Florence and asked:

"Is that OK with you, sis?"

"Yes, that would be wonderful!" she replied, visibly delighted.

"So, the milk, Mademoiselle, do you still want some?" asked the farmer. "You know, the soup and the mushroom omelet deserve better 'cause my wife's a fine cook... and our wine comes from a sunny little hillside on my father's land near Semelay."

"So let's go for soup, omelet and wine!" said Florence, smiling back.

An hour later, the farmer, his wife and daughter were all charmed by Jacques and his "sister." Their last name was Charbonneau, the farmer being Révérien, the mother Jeanne, and their daughter Jeannette.

About the Rose Garden Villa and its occupants, they knew only that there were a lot of servants, a "not very talkative bunch," and few owners whom one never saw. One day, about six months ago, the head servant, Monsieur Alfred, had come to ask if the Charbonneaus would make daily deliveries of ten liters of milk every morning at daybreak.

"I couldn't turn that down, 'specially when he offered to pay the same price as in a big city!" said the farmer. "They didn't need no eggs, however. At the Rose Garden, they've got first-rate chickens, choice hens as they say. But cheese, yes! On his first visit to our farm, Monsieur Alfred leered at the cheese Jeanne was making. It was *fromageon*, a special goat cheese they make in the Midi where Jeanne was a cook before coming back home to marry me. Monsieur Alfred tasted the cheese, liked it, and now every evening, Jeannette brings some for him and the other servants."

That's what Florence and Jacques learned from Charbonneaus. And here's what they told Charbonneau about the "real reason" for them being in the area:

"I have to tell you the truth," the young man declared at the end of the meal, when he felt he could trust the farmers. "We need your help."

"Our help?" Charbonneau laughed while his wife and daughter narrowed their eyes curiously.

Florence played her role, smiling and blushing.

"Yes. You know the Rose Garden has a new guest now?"

"Yes, I saw him yesterday," Jeannette blurted out. "He's Chinese."

"Actually, he's Japanese. He works at the Japanese embassy in Paris. He's on holidays right now. He's my sister's fiancé, and she has something very important to tell him. But she can't go to the Rose Garden Villa because our family is caught in a dispute with the new owners. And yet, my sister has to talk to her fiancé tomorrow at the latest. She can't wait for him outside the villa because it's too risky and could take too long. We were already waiting all day today in a tree. Then we saw Mademoiselle Jeannette come out, and we had an idea. It seems simple enough now that you've told us about the goat cheese. With a little makeup, my sister could easily pass for Jeannette, especially in the evening... do you get it?"

Tapping his knees, Charbonneau smiled at them. He had drunk plenty, spoken plenty, and was in a good mood. His wife was less enthusiastic, puckering her lips and furrowing her brow. But Jeannette was a romantic and tickled pink. She clapped her hands and cried out:

"Yes, that's a lovely idea!"

"By God, let's do it," Charbonneau announced.

"And of course, we'll be very generous," Florence looked gravely at the mother whom she guessed was greedier than her husband or daughter.

The farmer's wife smiled. What did those foreigners in the Rose Garden Villa matter to them anyway? If this young man and his sister paid well, a few minutes of passive cooperation would earn more than a year of goat cheese deliveries. Her eager eyes shifted to Jacques Fitou; she nodded and pronounced slowly:

"That's fine by me, too."

"Bravo!" Fitou exclaimed.

"Oh, thank you," Flore murmured, sincerely pleased, and her slender hands held the rough, dry fingers of Mrs. Charbonneau.

Afterward they'd all agreed, they quickly worked out how they would do it.

"The business will take place tomorrow evening," concluded the farmer.

They shook one another's hand vigorously and said good night.

In Seu, Jacques and Florence picked up their car and then fetched Isha who was starting to worry. The three of them then drove back to Decize together.

The next day, Friday, May 14, at 6 p.m., Jacques and Florence returned to the Charbonneau farm. This time, they did not leave their car in Seu. They took a narrow but drivable dirt road up to the farm.

It took an hour in Jeannette's small bedroom for Florence to get dressed, do her hair and make herself up to look like the farm girl. Luckily, the sky was gray. The evening would be dark and cold, so it would be normal for the girl delivering cheese to be wrapped in a scarf and even a hooded cloak. As for her voice, Jeannette had only said "hello" and "goodbye" to a couple of different servants. Florence listened carefully to her accent and imitated it back to the great amusement of the farm girl.

In the front room downstairs, Jacques and the Charbonneaus formed a jury that judged the lookalike to be as perfect an imitation as could be.

When came the time to leave, Florence threw the cloak around her shoulders, pulled down the hood, and wrapped a big scarf around her neck. Then, she grabbed the basket of cheese and headed into the woods for the Norman Villa. As a precaution, in case of an unexpected encounter, Fitou followed her discreetly at a distance.

When she got to the small gate, Jacques flattened himself against the wall a little ways away. Like Jeannette did every day, Florence pulled the rusty chain hanging there with a big metal ring. The bell rang. Soon shoes were clopping across the courtyard. Two big bolts slid noisily open. The gate swung on its hinges and she said, "Hello."

"Good evening," growled the servant as she closed the gate behind her.

Florence held out the basket, which the servant took and carried away toward another building where she disappeared.

Just as casually as Jeannette had done, Florence wandered over to the rose garden. Under the window where Yori had appeared, she stopped. Despite the cool air, the window was wide open, but because of the darkness, the room was lit up. Inside, someone was humming a tune, the melody stopped and resumed as the singer went about his business.

Like yesterday, exactly like yesterday, Florence thought.

Her heart was racing. Her face and neck were covered with sweat. But what she had to do was simple and she was determined. Her movements were calm and precise.

First, she checked to see that the doorway where the servant had disappeared was still clear; then, her eye measured the distance and her arm made a sweeping movement upwards. From her hand an object flew out and soared through the open window. Inside the room, the brief sound of broken glass was barely audible.

Just then, the old servant came through the doorway. Florence went to her, took back the empty basket, and followed her back to the gate. Bolts were pulled and it opened.

"Goodbye. Til tomorrow."

"Good night."

On the path in the woods, Florence was joined by Jacques, who had been waiting anxiously and impatiently.

"Well?"

Florence giggled nervously. "Everything's fine. He was singing like yesterday."

"I heard. And also, a faint sound of broken glass."

"Yes. My stone must have hit a glass or something. But that's good because Yori will know it came from outside."

"A note tied to a stone… perfect! We'll see how he responds tomorrow."

"Yes," Florence sighed. "Oh, God, I wish it were tomorrow already!"

He laughed, which relaxed her and she joined in.

The next day, Saturday, May 15, it was not the cheese girl who threw a stone but Yori Koto himself. He was at the window, which had stayed dark this time, just long enough to toss a stone at Florence's feet. She picked it up and buried it inside her cloak. She could feel the paper folded against it and a thin tissue covering it, all tied with a thread. With her right hand, she took her basket back from the servant.

"Goodbye. Til tomorrow."

"Good night."

But in the woods, off the path, between two stacks of freshly cut logs, Florence was the first to read Yori's message. Jacques lit it up with his flashlight.

"So? What did he say?" he asked as his patience was running thin.

"Read the whole thing," she replied, handing him the note. "Yesterday, in my note, I wrote nothing romantic. So why would he in his?"

Her voice was a little emotional.

"A touch of bitterness, my friend?" Jacques mumbled as he took the paper.

"No, but I'm a little worried. I'm starting to realize that, in this mysterious and obviously dangerous affair, the two of us don't count for much. The love I feel for Yori, and maybe the one he feels for me, are but tiny sparks in a giant fire!"

"That's not a pretty picture," the reporter said, trying to console her, "not at all. But let's talk about it later. First, let me read Yori's reply..."

And he read the following:

For an unspecified time that depends solely on me, I've given my word of honor to not try to escape and attempt anything against Leone Alzac. I'm voluntarily sentenced to stay here, where she resides. You two must do nothing to attract the slightest attention. Arrange it with the Charbonneaus for their daughter to keep coming every night. The day I renounce my promise, I'll send a message that Jeannette will bring you. Figure out a way to be informed quickly. Because I am begging you, even ordering you—as I have the right—to return to Paris. I'm sure there are spies around. Your being here, your visits, your stunts will eventually be found out. And that will mean instant death *for both of you and probably me as well. Go back to Paris tonight and wait to hear from Jeannette one of these evenings. But tell M. D.-W. everything so he can inform my master and his friend, if possible. Thank you both. –Yori Koto.*

After reading this, Jacques Fitou turned off his flashlight. In the woods, the dying daylight was not enough to read by, but one could still see someone's face. Florence was watching his. His eyes stared off distractedly, pensively. She waited. The wait lasted a good, long five minutes. Then the reporter burst out:

"I've reached a decision!"

Since he said nothing more, Florence asked:

"What is it?"

"I'm staying, but you're going back to Paris."

"Why?"

"Listen to me, Florence, my friend..."

He had put the note in his pocket with the flashlight. He took her hands in his and looked into her eyes, bringing his face close to hers.

"You have to go back to Mrs. MacCross where you can look and listen. That's your job. Go see my boss, Dumont-Warren, and tell him everything, show him Yori's message that is decisive and logical. Meanwhile, I'll stay here ready to receive any message from Jeannette that Yori might throw out of his window. I'm from the country and I can fit in without any problem. I'll be Charbonneau's nephew—that's it his nephew from the city! You do understand and agree, right?"

"Yes," she sighed.

"And don't worry! When Yori decides to break his oath, I'll be here to help him—in earshot and even in sight. He doesn't know that I can pass for a local, but if he did, I bet he'd be the first to suggest it. He'd say, 'Flore, you go back to Paris and Fitou, you stay at the farm.' Whenever he finds out, he'll be glad I did. I'm right, aren't I, Florence?"

"Yes, my dear friend."

"Bravo! Let me kiss you, on both cheeks. There… now, let's go!"

Two hours later Florence de Salsis was riding next to Isha in the car back to Paris. At the Charbonneau farm, their new "nephew," Jacques, a farm worker, was getting set up in the attic in a room next to his "cousin," Jeannette.

CHAPTER IV
The Brahmin and the Samurai

Yori Koto had not been overly surprised when the relatively heavy stone had come flying through his window. By chance, the Japanese had been facing the window. He saw it curving through the air, land on the middle of the table and break a small crystal bowl. After it rolled onto the carpet, he picked it up. It was a roughly rectangular rock with a folded piece of paper tied to it. He recognized the handwriting as soon as he saw it.

"Flore de Salsis," he muttered. "I figured as much."

He read and reread it. Then he threw the rock as far as he could beyond the rose garden. As for the note, he burned it in the bathroom and flushed the ashes down the toilet.

"I have 24 hours to think up an answer," he told himself. "Plenty of time."

That evening and the next day passed pretty much the same as the other days for the voluntary prisoner. With Leone Alzac, or in a trio with Oryas Zabad Khan, he talked politely about all kinds of things or he stayed alone and thought. The former was just to pass the time, but during the latter, he came up with an answer to Florence de Salsis that could be summarized as "*Go away!*"

Yori had no doubt that he would be obeyed. But the next day, Sunday, at precisely 7:38 a.m., he realized his instructions had only been halfway followed.

He was dressed up for dinner when another stone flew through the window and, like the previous evening, landed on the table. The real Jeannette had followed Florence's instructions. The crystal bowl had been replaced by a silver one and was not hit. But the thud of the rock was loud enough for him to hear. He turned around, went to the table, picked up the rock, took off the paper and read the note:

She left but I'm staying. I'm now the "cousin" of the messenger. I make a very genuine farmer, above suspicion. And I'm at your service. –Jacques Fitou

"Ah-ha, that's good," Yori muttered. "Even better, yes... but only if Leone Alzac doesn't get wind of the Japanese driver and the young woman whose identity she will recognize if given a good description of her. Because Mrs. MacCross could very well have told her about her tea with the Nyctalope and that she lunched at Blingy. I'm Japanese, Gno Mitang is Japanese and this new chauffeur is also Japanese. As for the young blonde, Mademoiselle de Salsis, I think a woman like Leone Alzac or her mysterious friend will soon realize that she is none other than the American woman's secretary. But it doesn't matter! None of this changes anything and this Jacques Fitou might come in handy if or when I decide to break my word of honor."

That night, Yori watched Leone Alzac a little more closely and listened for hidden meanings that might reveal that something was up, but nothing came of it. The same went for the next day, Monday, May 17. There were only small talk, quiet walks on the grounds, eating together, language lessons—nothing out of the ordinary, as far as ordinary went for them.

"She knows nothing," the Japanese told himself.

The next day, Tuesday, on the breakfast tray always brought to his bedroom by the same silent, diligent butler, Yori saw an envelope with his name on it. He opened it, took out the card and read:

Madame Leone Alzac will see Monsieur Yori Koto in the study at 10 o'clock.

"Ah-ha! There's something new. If everything was normal, she wouldn't call on me like this when every other morning was spent in the rose garden or near the woods, or she would come and get me while I'm reading the morning paper. So, there's obviously some news. But what?"

The study was a beautiful corner room with four windows. Books on open shelves or in display cases covered almost all the walls. Only over the double doors and the monumental fireplace were rather light paintings in panels giving a cheerful note to the generally dark furniture. It was a comfortable room with thick carpets, low tables that could be moved around, a big worktable, rolling stepladders, and leather armchairs with velvet cushions. Light came in through four windows, arranged in pairs, and the room stayed warm in the winter from the radiators and especially the wood fire built in the wide, deep fireplace. This was Yori's favorite room.

At 10 a.m., he met a somber Leone Alzac, who nevertheless seemed more relaxed and informal than usual. Straight away she invited him to sit in an armchair while she took another across from him. Without preamble, she started talking calmly and confidently:

"Monsieur, I must first remind you of what we said and of what I wrote for you on Saturday, ten days ago. It feels like yesterday. I will remind you word for word—you can judge for yourself. First of all, in my car before Montargis, I asked you why you were following me, why you attacked me? And you replied, 'Well, Mademoiselle, excuse me for not answering right now. Maybe later, maybe soon, it depends on the circumstances, on what you do with me and how I feel.' That's what you said, was it not?"

Yori was very curious but showed no emotion.

"Yes, that's right," he replied.

"Good. Now, secondly, but still in my car on the road, I asked you, 'Do you know my name?' And you answered, 'Not at all.' I replied, 'I don't believe you. You're lying, right?' You simply answered, 'Maybe.' Do you remember this?"

"Exactly so, Madame," Yori responded quickly.

"I'll continue. A little later, when we got to this house, I said, 'I'm sure you know more about me than is wise to know. I will let you decide when you want to talk to me openly, but I warn you, don't make me wait too long.' And that night, in the letter I gave you, I added, 'I feel no need to hide the fact that, if you don't talk, your captivity will last until mid-September and end, inevitably, with your death.' The writing faded away, but you haven't forgotten this phrase, have you?"

"No, I haven't forgotten."

"Very well."

Leone Alzac waved her hand to indicate she was finished recalling the past. Without transition and in the same tone of voice she went on:

"Are you ready to talk today?"

"Today?" he repeated, raising his eyebrows. "Why? It's not September yet."

"No," she shot back with a spark in her beautiful dark eyes. "It's still May. I ask you because firstly, something new has come up, and secondly, your answer will decide what I'm going to do with you."

Her response was both mysterious and direct, but the Japanese could also play rough. He snapped back:

"Logically, in order for me to decide whether to answer or not, I need full knowledge of the facts, and you should tell me the news."

"OK," she shot back. "That's why I called you in here anyway, but I needed to clear the ground first. With what I've just reminded you of, you will appreciate how serious these new developments are... Serious for you, I mean."

Her last words came out cold, menacing and hostile, but Yori did not react. He said nothing. He stared glassy-eyed into the sparkling gaze of the extraordinary woman and waited. When she saw his mute resolve, she started talking, still calm but not so polite as before, her voice sometimes struggling to stay under control.

"Monsieur, you must have known that I wouldn't just leave it at holding you here in a cushy confinement. You shouldn't be surprised to learn that, in Paris and elsewhere, I have a pretty well organized secret information network. And you certainly won't need to ask me any details about my investigation of the first two facts I learned about you: the license plate number of your car, which I abandoned on the highway, and its registration and your personal papers, which I took. What I've found out about them is what I want to talk about..."

"OK," said Yori. "I'm listening."

"Good," Leone Alzac replied in all seriousness. And she went on: "From one, we came up with the name of the car's owner, His Excellency Marquis Gno Mitang, currently residing at Blingy, the private residence of Monsieur Leo Saint-Clair, the famous Nyctalope. From the other, we found a small apartment located on Rue de Constantinople rented by one Yori Koto, the Marquis' secretary and personal assistant. My men were there at that apartment to spot Mademoiselle Florence de Salsis coming out with ha man we identified as the Marquis' driver, Isha. They followed her to the office of Monsieur Dumont-Warren, the head of the UNA and a close friend of the Nyctalope and Gno Mitang. We asked Mrs. MacCross, whom Mademoiselle de Salsis works for, and she did not hide the fact that she had had tea recently at Blingy. Further, we found out that Mademoiselle Florence de Salsis, a UNA reporter named Jacques Fitou, and Isha subsequently traveled all the way to Saint-Honoré and Decize, and in fact made contact at the Charbonneau farm…"

Leone Alzac stopped. She had to take a breath because she had rattled all this off rather quickly.

At first, Yori was shaken up, but nothing in his face or hands or motionless body betrayed his inner turmoil. He waited, silent and still, for the rest. It did not take long.

"Mademoiselle de Salsis and Isha have returned back to Paris, probably on your orders. Monsieur Fitou has stayed on and has certainly contacted you by a message tied to a stone that little Jeanette threw up to you. We also learned that Saint-Clair and Gno Mitang, along with Vitto and Soca, their tough and clever helping hands, left Guyancourt by plane for an unknown destination. Do I need to add that everyone in Paris is under constant surveillance and followed everywhere they go at all times? Here, Jacques Fitou can't take a step or say a word without me knowing. As for you…"

There was cruelty now in her voice. She stood up, took a few steps forward and passed by Yori who stayed seated. She went around the armchair and put her hands on the back. In a terribly sharp and icy voice, she continued:

"…Because of all this, you are now going to tell me the reason, the ugly reason, for your being here, for all this hostile action against me, which all seems to come down from the Nyctalope. You're going to talk right now; otherwise, I'll revoke your word of honor and act most harshly against you. There you go. I'll wait for exactly three minutes."

Her finger pointed at the grandfather clock that ticked softly in a dark mahogany niche between two rows of books.

Only then did Yori stand up. He stepped forward and spoke calmly:

"I will talk, Madame, but only after you revoke my word of honor."

"No problem, consider it done!"

"Thank you. Then I'll talk."

He stepped forward again, slowly, casually, and pronounced every syllable:

"Make me your nineteenth death!"

An irresistible intuition? A crazy gamble? An attempt to shock her, to get a reaction that he could read in her face? In any case, these words could have been fatal for him. But a second after saying them, he was still alive. And a second after that… still alive!

Standing before him, Leone Alzac was pale, but her eyes were ablaze. Her whole body was tense. She raised her arms to let out a deep breath and in a hushed voice said:

"Oh, you know about that..." And then, with something like pity, she added: "Poor things."

Yori replied curtly:

"So, there's more?" And, sounding surprised, "Aren't you going to kill me? Then you mustn't be the one with that dreadful power... If so, I've got you!"

And he jumped. He pounced like a tiger on its prey. He flew over the back of the chair in pursuit of Leone Alzac, who turned and ran screaming to the far end of the long table where there was an ebony board with six ivory buttons used to call different servants. But she did not make it. Two hands landed on her shoulders and pulled her back. Then they grabbed her throat.

He gave her a jiu-jitsu chop placed expertly on both the larynx and the external carotid that knocked her out instantly. The blackout would not last long since he did not hit her harder.

However, before passing out, Leone Alzac had had time to scream. Yori wondered if anyone had had heard her as he deposited her limp body in the armchair. Thick, heavy, velvet coverings hung over the doors. Books crowded the walls. The room next door was the sitting room, certain to be deserted at this hour. But there was still the entry hall where maybe a maid was dusting or mopping. Over the ceiling was, Yori just realized, Leone's bedroom and bathroom. He thought of all of this quickly and told himself:

They didn't hear anything.

In fact, for one nervous minute, he waited but the door did not open.

Good. Even though she's most likely not the possessor of the deadly power, she was still sure of herself because she took no precautions. I'd bet she didn't even tell Zabad Khan about our little get-together. I think that, for now and inside this room, I have control of the situation.

Leaning on the arms of the chair, he bent over so that his face was right in front of hers. She just sat there with her head thrown back and her arms limp beside her. Her pale skin and frozen face proved she had really passed out.

Gently but steadily, Yori blew on her closed eyelids and pale lips. Almost right away, her face showed the first signs of coming out of her faint. Color returned to her cheeks, her eyelids twitched, her neck muscles softened up. In less than a minute, life had returned, but sluggishly.

"Madame... Madame Alzac!" said Yori, his voice calm but firm.

Her eyes opened slowly. At first, her gaze looked hazy and confused, even though she was staring at the Japanese. But she came around quickly and her beautiful eyes regained their spark of intelligence.

The Japanese did not wait.

"I swear on my ancestors that I'll strangle you if you scream. When I jumped at you, I thought I'd be struck dead, but I still attacked. Now you know me and understand who I am. I want an immediate decision from you. It's your turn to give me your word of honor. But I only want it for 24 hours. Swear that, until tomorrow noon, you will say nothing and do nothing to harm me. Until tomorrow noon, I'll be free to come and go around the Rose Garden without you sending the servants or Zabad Khan against me."

He stopped there, a little out of breath. Her eyes beheld him, questioned him, calmly, profoundly. Her lips had their color back, were soft again. They opened slowly and she murmured:

"Why noon?"

"Because that's all the time I need. Or rather, because that's the deadline I've set myself to solve a problem entrusted to me by Marquis Gno Mitang and the Nyctalope. I think the problem regarding you is solved, but I have an idea about Zabad Khan."

"Can I hear it?"

"No!"

"What if I refuse to swear?"

"Feel my hands around your throat. See my determination! This is a fight to the death between the forces that I represent and those that you and Zabad Khan control. If you refuse, I'll choke you to death."

"A promise forced out of someone under threat of violence is worthless."

"Was I free when I gave you my word of honor on the highway, Madame Alzac?"

"Nicely played, Monsieur Koto."

After a moment's reflection, she added:

"Until tomorrow noon, I will say and do nothing against you and you will be free to come and go around the Rose Garden without me sending the servants or Zabad Khan against you. I give you my word of honor."

"Very good."

And his two hands released the warm neck they were holding gently but could have snapped in a second. Yori stood up, but stayed planted in front of the young lady.

She was half lying in the armchair. She sat up and automatically straightened her curls while speaking calmly.

"But you've taken back your word not to do anything against me?"

"I'm generous," he smiled. "I'll give it back to you until noon tomorrow. But watch out, it's only for you. Just like yours is only for me."

"What do you mean?" she was puzzled.

"Zabad Khan is outside our pact."

She suddenly tensed up.

"Watch yourself! Zabad Khan is... Oh!"

Her right hand shot up to cover her mouth to keep her from finishing her thought. Yori chuckled silently and briefly. Then, with a little humor and unexpected familiarity, he said:

"No, Leone, I don't think you're so worried about me that you need to cover your mouth like a child. You left the threat hanging, like the famous

'*Quos ego*' that Virgil put in the mouth of Neptune.[18] Yes, although I'm Japanese, I do know the classics. As for Zabad Khan, either he does have the power to kill with a simple thought, in which case I'll be risking the same by attacking him as I did when I jumped at you, or else he is as powerless as you are, and I will only become sure of it by attacking him. Right now, I'd doubt the truth of anything you might tell me or anything he might say if I decided to talk to him. Direct action is the only way to know the truth. Therefore, I'm going to take direct action."

He had stepped back while talking and Leone Alzac had stood up. They were facing each other now, and her eyes blazed as she said:

"You're crazy!"

He smiled back at her.

"No, I'm logical."

But deep down, he was surprised because he now saw her in a new light, as a girl seething with emotion. Her eyes were wide with fear like a scared animal. He heard her panting as she mumbled:

"You're crazy... crazy..."

Then he grabbed her arms and pulled her close, in total control.

"Leone, why do you think so? I see that you really believe it, but why do you think I'm crazy? And why do you tell me that now, as if to put me on guard instead of letting me face my destiny?"

"Because this is all bigger than us, unfortunately, bigger than you or me. Because any action you take will be useless, whether you kill Zabad Khan or, somehow, beyond the realm of possibility, make him talk. You, me, Gno Mitang, his friend the Nyctalope, even Zabad Khan himself... Oh, gods! You don't know..."

Tears filled her eyes and she sobbed. As if the physical expression of her emotions had cleared her mind and invigorated her spirit, she suddenly shook her head, narrowed her eyes, now looking resolved and stubborn. Her voice was hoarse, and strangely gloomy.

"Oh, will I never be able to completely tame the beast in me?" Her eyes turned blank and her voice ice-cold. "Let me go, Monsieur, and you, as you said, may face your destiny."

This abrupt reversal worried Yori, but only for a few seconds. He accepted it, without fully understanding it, without even trying to understand it. He released her, stepped back and said simply:

"I'll go now."

---

[18] Latin, literally "Whom I," are the words, in Virgil's *Aeneid* (I, 135), uttered by Neptune, the Roman god of the Sea, in threat to the disobedient and rebellious winds. Neptune is angry with the winds, whom Juno released to start a storm and harass the Trojans. He berates the winds for causing a storm without his approval, but breaks himself off mid-threat.

Every morning, between 10 and 11 a.m., whatever the weather, the brahmin Oryas Zabad Khan did his exercises, some very simple, others curiously complicated and especially *internal*, meaning affecting the organs inside the body—muscles, nerves, veins, arteries and organs, all at the same time. His rigorous daily workout had its "temple," so to speak, in the unused greenhouse, sometimes with the bay windows open, sometimes closed. The greenhouse was specially fitted with carpets and hard cushions, a pommel horse, parallel bars, high bars and stairs. Well-situated, facing the south, it was built against the surrounding wall to the right of the villa, opposite the courtyard and the outbuildings.

It was toward this makeshift gymnasium, therefore, that Yori Koto was walking after making up his mind once and for all to sacrifice his life, if necessary. As he was leaving the study, he had heard Leone Alzac say:

"I'll go with you, but you have my word that I'll do nothing to interfere."

He had just nodded without turning around.

After a few steps out of the house, he did stop and turn around. He went up to the young woman who had stopped behind him, and said:

"Madame, in my car, there was a Browning pistol. Did you bring it here with everything else?"

She hesitated for an instant, surprised, but finally answered:

"Yes." And right away, she added: "Why?"

"Not to shoot Zabad Khan!" he shrugged. "And I'd be just as ashamed if I'd thought of using it against you. No, it's just to keep the servants at a safe distance if he calls them."

"He won't call anyone," she said curtly and proudly.

Yori knew from her voice that she was back to normal, having "tamed the beast" in her. He smiled and bowed.

"Very well. I believe you," he said.

Turning around, he started off again toward the greenhouse gym.

On this Tuesday, May 18, all over the Morvan, there was a wispy fog low to the ground, while thick clouds over almost the entire sky drifted northwest, casting the mountains in shadows and the woods in darkness. The pale, haloed sun peeked out only occasionally. The air was cold and humid. It was a bad weather for the nerves and for arthritis. Leone Alzac, with her nervous temperament, was undoubtedly a total wreck. But Yori Koto was not on edge, or afflicted with arthritis. By nature, he was muscular, but intellectually refined and morally principled, well balanced on the whole, even when in the eyes of common sense, he might look crazy. He was calm, both physically and mentally, when he stopped at the wide open door, the only door to the greenhouse where Oryas Zabad Khan was doing his exercises.

The Brahmin had a marvelous body, like the living statue of a young god, one of the fabled immortals of Indochinese legends. The proportions and lines of his muscles, the golden-brown hue of his skin, the harmony and balance, the grace and subtle strength, everything about him was perfect.

Standing still before this body, which was at the moment on tiptoes stretching out its arms to the side, Yori Koto stared in admiration. Before so much strong and beguiling virile beauty, whose small loincloth barely covered its nudity, he could not help but stand still in awe. Not for the first time, he wondered what was the relation between this glorious young man and the gorgeous Leone Alzac?

A kind of instinctive and obvious answer popped up in his mind, then faded away. Right after it came another thought, freely, boldly, a crucial one at this time.

"Oryas Zabad Khan!" said Yori, speaking loud and clear.

The brahmin now stood flat on his feet; his expressive eyes, slightly slanted, looked attentive and questioningly at the Japanese. Yori repeated:

"Oryas Zabad Khan! I am here because of the deaths of fourteen men sentenced to death, because of the death of Eduardo Prim, the Spanish revolutionary, the death of Lord William Stonewell, Viceroy of India, of Reginald Strom, the socialite, and of Lucien Rigaut, a middle-class Frenchman. I am here because of these eighteen mysterious deaths. I am here, alive and breathing."

Speaking thus with a kind of cold frenzy, Yori was ready for anything—except what happened.

After this verbal attack, he looked stupid. Yes, stupid, because the expression on Zabad Khan's face was one of pure stupor. Seeing the astonished eyes, the open, speechless mouth, the suddenly limp body of the young brahmin, Yori was first just as stupefied, then confused. He thought he had braved death by using all his strength to break down a door that hid a mystery, but he was just a man who'd crashed through paper scenery and found an innocent and comfortable couch in a quiet room with a stranger who was not only astounded but offended.

He heard the usual gentle voice of Zabad Khan speak with baffled caution:

"What's gotten into you, Monsieur Koto? What are all those names?"

Yori was Asian. He was aware of facing another Asian. Suddenly, the brahmin's game became clear to him. Was he, a Japanese, going to lose face before the Indochinese? No! What was the point of a violent physical attack? And what good would come of it? He did not have to strangle Zabad Khan. He just had to win this round and show him he was not fooled. But what a pitiful peace after so much heroism!

Yori turned around. He saw Leone Alzac a few feet behind him. She was smiling a little sarcastically.

She's back to herself alright, he thought.

And he spoke casually:

"Don't think that I hold it against you, Madame, for not acting against me on the highway in such a nice and simple way as Zabad Khan has just used, disarming me, at least in this first duel. You're a spirited young woman and a westerner. You kidnapped me without being fooled by me. You imprisoned me so you could do away with me if I became too much trouble. It all fits in with your vivid imagination, the fire in your blood, the latent violence in your character. Plus, in this battle, you have great advantages over me, because you succeeded in learning about my humble origins, the no less humble origins of Mademoiselle de Salsis and Monsieur Fitou, and those who dispatched us, Marquis Gno Mitang, the Nyctalope and the head of the UNA. So, you've scored some points. But I did too by the sole fact that I spent ten days, with my eyes and ears open, with you and Zabad Khan. I can, therefore, reasonably and honorably, congratulate you.

"But this young brahmin is so much better than you! He just has to look like he doesn't understand anything I said, and my words are stripped of their meaning, and anything I might do is useless. With you, I really thought I was in danger and, sooner or later, that I might die if it were just the two of us battling it out in the Rose Garden. But with him, I've already lost the first round. Because what can I say or do now?"

The few words spoken by Zabad Khan meant, as clear as day, *Eighteen deaths? What are you talking about? Are you joking or have you gone mad? And what do these deaths have to do with me anyway? I'm an honorable foreigner. I'm a wise and well-behaved brahmin studying the western world. I have my passport and my visa. All my papers are in order. Just like those of Leone Alzac. Didn't you follow her of your own free will after abandoning your car so ludicrously on the highway? A modern roadside love affair, Monsieur! And aren't you free here? Are you locked up? Tied up? If our friendly smiles irritate your sudden and quite inexplicable paranoia, what's stopping you from packing your bags and going away? Go ahead, leave! We're not going to stop you. We will regret, however, losing a guest at this charming time of the year.*

After speaking to Leone Alzac, Yori bowed deeply before the cold and stone-faced woman. Then, he turned to face the enemy, the true enemy. And he spoke very softly:

"Zabad Khan, I'm not beaten yet, because I have figured you out. But if you killed eighteen others, which I have no proof of, and which I can hardly imagine given this current dilemma, but if you did kill these eighteen men by simply willing it, then you can make me the 19th corpse whenever you want. Please, let me beg you one favor from you, O brahmin whose nature and purpose is a mystery to me. It is this: Spare Mademoiselle Florence de Salsis. She's young and loves life. And she loves being in love. There are so many other young men in the world besides me."

He took three steps back and bowed proudly and respectfully as befits a noble Japanese. Then he straightened up and looked Zabad Khan in the eye:

"I salute you, O brahmin."

Zabad Khan remained aloof and responded softly:

"I salute you, samurai."

Half an hour later, without anyone or anything stopping him, Yori Koto left the Norman villa through the gate leading into the crescent-shaped clearing where a large path led through the forest to the spas of Saint-Honoré. He had not seen Zabad Khan or Leone Alzac again. He was accompanied by Alfred who carried his suitcase and told him:

"The path to the Charbonneau farm crosses this one twenty yards down from here. I am honored to carry your suitcase to the farm, but Madame also asked me to tell you that if you and your friend, Monsieur Fitou, would like to take the train to Paris, one of the cars from the Rose Garden is at your disposal to drop you at the nearest station. You just have to send Jeannette back to tell us."

That evening, Yori Koto and Jacques Fitou did indeed take the train to Paris. Neither of them could say if the Charbonneau family, being rather greedy, had been loyal and honest, or if the whole family was in the service of the Rose Garden.

CHAPTER V
"Let's take stock!"

The next day, Wednesday, May 19, at 3 p.m., in the director's office of the UNA, Dumont-Warren welcomed Yori Koto, Florence de Salsis and Jacques Fitou. On one side of the big table the four of them were sitting around with Mademoiselle Fabienne Blancat, his trusted secretary, ready to record everything they said. She was an expert in shorthand and could write down every word, no matter how fast it was spoken.

She had already noted as a kind of prologue the fact that Florence de Salsis had been let go by Mrs. MacCross. The Irish-American had told the young lady:

"My child, I've just learned that you are working with the honorable Yori Koto on something that could someday do irreparable damage to something I'm working on. Therefore, it's better if we part. I have been satisfied with your work. Please accept this check that should cover your monthly salary plus three more months as compensation for the abrupt dismissal. No, please, don't say anything. Good-bye, Mademoiselle de Salsis."

The young woman had taken only thirty minutes to pack her bags with all her possessions. Before noon, she had found a boarding house, comfortable and modern, on Rue d'Assas. She had then called Dumont-Warren immediately. He had had already had a brief conversation with Yori and Jacques, who had arrived in Paris the night before. A meeting had been set for 3 p.m. at the UNA office.

Dumont-Warren was serious; Yori worried; Florence disturbed and confused; Jacques Fitou excited. The director had given orders that he was not to be disturbed so the meeting would not be interrupted. He was to receive no phone calls, telegrams or visitors for an hour. He started things off:

"Monsieur Koto, tell us what happened."

Without leaving anything out, but briefly and clearly, the Japanese related the unforgettable phase of his life from entering the Banque de France on May 7 at 9 a.m. to leaving the Rose Garden on May 18 at 11 a.m.

After Yori had finished, Dumont-Warren said, "Very well," and asked his stenographer, "Did you everything, Mademoiselle Blancat?"

"Yes, Monsieur."

Dumont-Warren then looked at Fitou and said:

"Your turn, my friend."

In graphic but precise descriptions, Jacques rattled off what he and Florence had lived through after leaving with Isha on May 10, until May 18, when Yori had showed up with Monsieur Alfred at the Charbonneau farm.

"OK," Dumont-Warren said after Jacques had wrapped up his story. The he asked Florence: "Mademoiselle, did he leave anything out?"

"Not a thing," she replied.

"Do you have anything to add? Theories, clarifications, details?"

"No, nothing. I agree with everything Monsieur Fitou said, conclusions and all."

"Perfect. And the stenography is all right?"

"Yes, Monsieur," confirmed Mademoiselle Blancat

Dumont-Warren crossed his arms over his chest, leaned back in his chair, threw back his head and stared at the ceiling. He stayed like that for three minutes. The young woman and the two young men watched him in silence. Mademoiselle Blancat was looking down, sharpening her pencils without a sound.

All of sudden, jerking forward and dropping his elbows on the table, Dumont-Warren glanced at the two others and then looked at Yori Koto. He spoke in the calm and serious voice that he used in board meetings at the UNA.

"Well, my friends, let's take stock. It's a mental exercise I'm used to. I'll be brief and, I hope, thorough. Then, when we're sure of what we know, we can discuss our options calmly. I dare say, I believe we'll make the right decisions. Do you agree?"

All three nodded.

"Good. Here are the facts. My attention was drawn and my professional curiosity piqued by the series of deaths of the condemned prisoners. They were all in different jails, spread out over ten different nations. One after another in January, February and March, fourteen men sentenced to death died suddenly in their cells in front of the guards. There was no possibility of suicide. Moreover, the autopsies showed the same results, corroborated by doctors and witnesses: sudden death by cerebral hemorrhaging coupled with a violent, apoplectic seizure. I was intrigued and told my friend Monsieur Saint-Clair about it. The Nyctalope listened to me, thought about it, and concluded that it deserved investigation. That was the first stage of this affair."

He made a small gesture with his hands, took a deep breath, and continued:

"The second stage happened in several steps. One, Eduardo Prim, a political agitator and Spanish revolutionary, was found dead in Barcelona in his room locked from the inside—cerebral hemorrhage. Two, we learned of the sudden death in Calcutta of His Excellency the Viceroy William Stonewell. He was in perfect health. He took care of himself, inside and out. Nevertheless, he died suddenly. Diagnosis: cerebral hemorrhage. Three, in London, a socialite called Reginald Strom died suddenly with the extraordinary fact that it was announced to him by telephone from Paris an hour before it happened—also, cerebral hemorrhage. Four, in Saint-Honoré-les-Bains, Lucien Rigaut was found dead in his room the day after another story we'll get back to—cerebral hemorrhage. Fourteen plus four more equals Eighteen 18 deaths. This wraps up the second stage of the affair. Are you still with me?"

The three heads nodded in unison without saying a word. Dumont-Warren went on, still serious but a little more excited:

"Now, after the first fifteen deaths and while the sixteenth was happening, the Nyctalope explained the problem to his friend, the great Japanese diplomat and scholar Gno Mitang, who reminded him of the true history of the Empress of Tibet, the quasi-divine Gedhun Grub. She established and maintained her power by the restrained exercise of an extraordinary mental faculty: by merely willing it, this woman, who was the first Living Buddha, could kill any number of healthy men at a distance. The diagnosis back in the 15th century would correspond to what today we would call a cerebral hemorrhage. Saint-Clair and Gno Mitang were thinking long and hard about this when they happened to see an English paper that mentioned the death of the socialite Strom under mysterious circumstances. The two of them went to London, investigated, learned of the macabre telephone warning from Paris, from such and such number and such and such person—who was identified as the Irish American Melody MacCross, the richest woman in the world, one of Reginald Strom's past lovers whom he had blackmailed emotionally and financially in the past. And so ends the third stage of the affair."

Dumont-Warren straightened up, put his hands flat on the table and went on controlling his rising passion:

"And now, we enter the fourth stage. The Nyctalope follows the clues. They bring him to Melody MacCross who, as Mademoiselle Florence de Salsis revealed to Yori Koto, had a strange meeting with a Madame Leone Alzac prior to the fatal telephone call. The Nyctalope goes looking for her and finds her, thanks to a new death by cerebral hemorrhage of Lucien Rigaut, victim number 18. Why do we consider him a victim? Because Leone Alzac had been there—and not alone. She was with an as yet unidentified Asian male. And also because Leone Alzac lost a notebook that was picked up by Rigaut, which she recovered from him before sentencing him to eternal silence. The pages of this notebook were almost all filled with news clippings from French and English papers, all related to the recent death of Lord William Stonewell. On the inside cover was the word *Chong Koum* written a number of times in a configuration the hermetic significance of which was recognized by Gno Mitang: seven times going down in steps from the top right corner to the bottom left. This is of the utmost importance! First, on the shores of Lake Chong Koum there was and probably still is, the secret temple of Empress Gedhun Grub. Also, the number seven is the number of letters in the first part of her name. The Marquis explained that the stepped arrangement is the ritual sign of the lamas of their supreme rite, which renews itself perpetually and eternally from the summit of wisdom down to death and reincarnation.

"Consequences: On the one hand, on Saturday May 1, the Nyctalope and Marquis Gno Mitang, accompanied by Vitto and Soca, flew out of Guyancourt heading for Lake Chong Koum. On the other, I, myself, using the resources of the UNA, and Yori Koto, with the unknowing assistance of Mademoiselle de Salsis, kept up the investigation here focused on Mrs. MacCross at her Parisian residence, and on Leone Alzac and her Asian companion in the department of the Nièvre. May 1 marks the end of the fourth stage. There we are! As for the fifth stage... Do you want to take it from here, Yori?"

"Gladly," the Japanese jumped right in. "The fifth and final stage is the shortest and, above all, the most dangerous after a turn of events for which, I believe, I'm responsible. We lost more than we gained, and it's led us into a dead-end rife with threats and dark with mystery."

Yori's emotions must have been very deeply felt for him to talk like this since both in word and deed, he always tried to be clear and precise, direct and down-to-earth, even analytical. Florence, who knew very well the man she loved, was troubled by his emotional reaction. Dumont-Warren saw her turning pale, but the Japanese went on:

"Why waste time going over this fifth stage again? Monsieur Fitou and I just told you in detail the two different sides of it. I'll just mention one key point about the threat, the dark mystery. We can file it at the end of this 'let's take stock' moment. Would you like me to elucidate?"

"Please do," Dumont-Warren urged.

"First of all, let's forget for the moment about the expedition to Tibet, since we only know by radio that our friends arrived safe and sound at the site, which my master believes is the occult center, the power source of the murdering will. Let's put that aside because, for now, there's nothing we can do for them. Instead, let's look at the question of whether they, if they found out about us, could help. Isn't that what you were thinking, Monsieur?"

"Yes!" Dumont-Warren shot back.

"What do you think, Flore?"

"Fine by me."

"Monsieur Fitou?"

"Me, too."

"Very well. In theory, and despite the clever and adamant denial of Zabad Khan, I firmly believe that he and Leone Alzac, together or alone, directly or by delegation, are responsible for the deaths of Reginald Strom, who was a thorn in Mrs. MacCross' side, and also of Lucien Rigaut, who had picked up the notebook. Do you agree?"

The three heads eagerly nodded yes. Yori continued.

"I believe that Zabad Khan is perhaps from Indochina, but more likely from Tibet, which lies at the Indian border of the English Empire. Lord Stonewell was allegedly thinking about exploring, even occupying, southern Tibet. Therefore, we could logically assume that, until proven otherwise, Zabad Khan had motives for killing the Viceroy. Do you agree?"

Three nods again.

"You may also remember that Leone Alzac looks like a Southerner; her name certainly is characteristic of Southern France, maybe the Pyrenees region?

Is this enough to blame her for the death of a Spanish revolutionary, the anarchist Eduardo Prim? We can't rule it out."

"I agree," Dumont-Warren said.

"Me, too," Florence and Fitou pronounced together.

"There remain the fourteen prisoners. Don't forget they were all sentenced to death and their names, faces and crimes were all published in the papers. Their sudden death was just an execution being carried out a few days earlier. Monsieur Saint-Clair and Marquis Gno Mitang saw it as an *experimental exercise* of the occult power, a kind of practice run so to speak, a *moral* way to work out the technique of the murderous will. Isn't it logical to suppose that Zabad Khan and Leone Alzac, whether they inherited or stole that secret, might have wanted to try it out on specific, but deserving targets?"

"Clearly," Dumont-Warren exclaimed.

"Go on," Fitou panted.

"Yes, yes," Florence was almost quivering.

Yori also shuddered. He became self-conscious. The enthusiastic approval affected his natural modesty, his culture of restraint, calm and outer coolness. More slowly, he continued:

"The experiment was carried out, the victims targeted, and killed. Two were probably selected out of hate, vengeance, religious faith or patriotism—the Viceroy and the Spanish anarchist, who were killed only a few hours apart. But their overriding goal seems to have been to get money—lots of money. Where does Leone Alzac come from? Where and how did she grow up? Her papers, probably forged or stolen, say she's 26, but that doesn't mean she didn't know the handsome socialite Reginald Strom and his relationship with Melody MacCross, the richest woman in the world. An offer made and accepted—Strom died, and we know without the shadow of a doubt that she was responsible. Leone Alzac got a lot of money from Mrs. MacCross. Obviously, they want to leave no visible traces of their activities. After a stupid car accident, a notebook fell out of her suitcase; she noticed the loss; she went back to look for it, but in the meantime, it had been found and read by the poor Lucien Rigaut who, inevitably, became their 18th victim."

With these final words, Yori Koto raised his hand as if to highlight them, which was certainly not necessary. Then, with deliberate detachment, although emphasizing certain words, he went on:

"Now, what *surprises* me is that this series of sudden deaths was continuous enough to form, in time and reasoning, a *series*. Why wasn't I number 19? And you, Flore, and you, Jacques, numbers 20 and 21? We, much more than Lucien Rigaut, who couldn't have understood anything of what he read, are a real threat to Leone Alzac and Zabad Khan. *Because we know!* And it's my fault that they now know that we know. Logically, all four of us here should be dead. But we're not! We should be under the threat of sudden death every second. So why are we still alive? Why did Zabad Khan pretend to be ignorant of the Eighteen deaths I mentioned when, only minutes before, Leone Alzac, hearing the same reference, cried out: 'Oh, you know about that… Poor things," then said, 'this is all bigger than us, unfortunately, bigger than you or me,' and added, 'any action you take will be useless, whether you kill Zabad Khan or, somehow, beyond the realm of possibility, make him talk. You, me, Gno Mitang, his friend the Nyctalope, even Zabad Khan himself… Oh, gods! You don't know,' concluding with: 'You may face your destiny.'"

Yori took a breath before continuing with unexpected gentleness in his voice:

"I ran to face my destiny. I made accusations, stuck between Leone Alzac, who denied nothing, and Zabad Khan, who completely threw me off balance with his 'What's gotten into you? What are all those names?'"

The Japanese took another deep breath and smiled. Then he was back to the cold, serious Yori.

"Taking stock, my friends, is easy. Now, if you'd like, let's see how this adds up. On the one hand, the Nyctalope and my master are at Lake Chong Koum, convinced that they'll find the source of the occult power. On the other hand, we are convinced that the source, or at least its lethal reflection, is with Leone Alzac and Zabad Khan, right now at the Rose Garden. Then, finally, as a side issue, we're also certain that Mrs. MacCross has joined forces with Leone Alzac and, on her order, fired Flore this morning. Do you have anything to add to this?"

Dumont-Warren thought for a moment before answering:

"Not a thing."

"Another thing that we are certain of is that we can't provide a shred of evidence about all this. We haven't got the slightest proof. Therefore, calling in the police and the justice system is out of the question. Besides, I'm sure that an investigation of the Rose Garden would turn up nothing. So, legally, we're powerless. However, what could spell a death sentence for all of us is the fact that Leone Alzac and Zabad Khan know that we know the who, how and why of the murders. Anything else to add?"

After thinking again, Dumont-Warren answered calmly as the circumstances called for

"No, but I must reluctantly note that our liabilities are far more important and far deadlier than our assets."

Florence and Jacques were both pale. They nodded without turning their intense gaze away from Yori's impassive face.

Dumont-Warren added:

"What are your proposals?"

"They consist of one possible plan, easy enough to fulfill, and two questions, which are perhaps unanswerable."

"Let's hear the plan first," Dumont-Warren suggested.

"Very simple: send a message to the Zig telling my master and the Nyctalope the state of affairs here in France."

"Very simple indeed. Fitou will write it up and we can add whatever we feel is necessary. And the questions?"

"First, does this power to kill have any limitations, any restrictions that might make it intermittent? Or fragmentary? If we're all alive in eight days, I'd say yes, and make it a priority to find out how it works."

"Ah," Dumont-Warren said excitedly. "Yes, indeed, we should look into that. And the second?"

"The second question, if we can answer it soon, will help us solve the first. How can we, obviously risking our lives in the process, capture Leone Alzac and Zabad Khan at the Rose Garden while neutralizing their servants?"

"At last!" Fitou could not hold back any longer. "We've come to the point at last." He jumped up, walked quickly around the table and grabbed Dumont-Warren's right hand, shaking it wildly. "Boss, that's the only thing I've thought about since Mademoiselle de Salsis and I first sat in that tree outside the Rose Garden. How to capture it... Well, I think I've found a way! A way that, in my opinion, won't be too risky if we stick to my plan. Yes, I know the threat of that mysterious death is looming over us every second, but doing what I propose won't set it off or target us..."

"Fitou, enough with the comments!" Dumont-Warren almost shouted. "What's this plan of yours?"

Visibly excited, the reporter went straight to Fabienne Blancat and the others looked at her as she stood up, pale, trembling, her eyes filling with tears as the young man marched over to her. Until now, she had been nothing but a stenographic machine. All of a sudden, she was revealed as a real, thinking woman, ready to do what Fitou asked of her. And although this was surprising to Florence and Yori, it was absolutely astonishing to Dumont-Warren who stood up and stared in wonder at his private secretary and his star reporter.

Jacques Fitou took her hand and turned around to face Dumont-Warren. As casual as could be he said:

"I have the pleasure to announce that in two weeks, Mademoiselle Blancat and I will be married. We were waiting to tell you until we set the date, and she thought of asking you to do us the honor of being her witness. So, this morning, before starting work, she and I decided to tell you today because if you agree to put my plan in action, she would like to take the same risks as the rest of you. And since she has an important role to play, I think it's only fair to tell you this now, for the success of the plan... and our love. There you have it, boss. First of all, will you give your blessing to our marriage?"

He was charming. Despite the gravity of the situation, they could not help smiling tenderly at the young couple. Dumont-Warren said warmly:

"I'm delighted, Fitou. Congratulations to both of you. And of course, I'll be a witness at the ceremony. But..." he changed his tone before going on: "Regarding Mademoiselle Blancat's participation in an action against the Rose Garden and its inhabitants, and therefore in our general activities against these lethal foes, it's not a question of sentiment, respect or friendship, but of work. I won't permit her to switch jobs, even temporarily, until I know what you have in mind. That's all I have to say. Now, Mademoiselle, sit back down. Let's all sit back down. And you, Fitou, explain."

The reporter started talking. He spoke slowly, calmly, describing and developing his idea, explaining his plan with as much logic and common sense as imagination. His explanation, comments and conclusions took fifteen minutes. They listened with bated breath. Not once was he interrupted.

CHAPTER VI
The Assault

The next day, Thursday, May 20, Monsieur Dumont-Warren and Jacques Fitou spent the day in conversation, visiting two specialized factories and making various purchases. Following their detailed plan, they were accompanied at certain steps not only by Yori Koto, Florence de Salsis, Isha and Mademoiselle Blancat, but also by two new recruits, Pierre Daloz, the Dumont-Warren's driver, and André Black, a UNA investigator. The former was a tall, sturdy 25 years-old and a former certified mechanic from the military; the latter was 34 years-old, and was famous for having been the head of a team which had conducted a major investigation across Central Africa.

The "troops" which Fitou was going to command, therefore, numbered seven: five men and two women. Everything they bought was delivered to four different addresses, and, on Thursday night, was moved again and packed into a van that had also been bought and parked in a garage on Boulevard Brune near a big intersection to the south of Paris at the Porte d'Orléans.

During all these preparations, each of the seven was careful to cover their tracks in case they were being followed. They used all the tricks available to anyone suspecting he or she was being spied on and wanted to lose their tail.

On Thursday night, none of the seven spent the night at their regular home. Mademoiselle de Salsis did not show up at her boarding house on Rue d'Assas; instead, she telephoned to tell the lady in charge that one of her relatives in Roubaix had been taken ill, and that she might be gone for weeks. But she left her belongings in the room and paid a month's rent in advance. The other six all did pretty much the same thing.

On Friday morning, May 21, at 6 a.m., the aforementioned van pulled out of the garage, driven by Pierre Daloz, dressed as a mover. Sitting next to him was André Black, also dressed as a mover. On their way from Paris to Orléans, the two men took side roads to make sure that they were not being followed.

After Orléans, they headed for Vierzon; from there, they went through Bourges and Saint-Pierre-le-Moutier and on to Moulins. After that, on the road to Autun, they stopped at Luzy, a big town around twelve miles southeast of Saint-Honoré-les-Bains. There, they stayed in a truckers' inn that was always busy at an intersection where half a dozen routes crossed.

For their part, on the same morning, Florence de Salsis and Fabienne Blancat arrived separately at the Gare de Lyon. They met in a 2nd class compartment at 7:30 a.m. on the train for Nevers, scheduled to arrive at 12:30 p.m. Together, they stepped onto the platform, both carrying a small suitcase, and walked down to a café where they ate a light breakfast at a corner table from where they could see the entire room. They were dressed the same, like nuns visiting from Annecy: black coat, dress and veil, white guimpes; most of their faces, including their forehead, were covered up and a big silver cross hung on their chest. The two pale nuns with their eyes humbly lowered looked nothing like the elegant, spirited Parisians whose makeup was always stylish.

On the platform, then at the café, and finally at the railway station in Nevers, the two young "nuns" made sure that they were not being followed or spied on. At 1:42 p.m., they climbed into the 2nd class car of a local train pulling out of Nevers. They got off at Avrée. At the station, an old carriage yoked to a horse was waiting for them. It was the only vehicle going to Chantal Manor, located near Highway 127, less than a mile south of where it connected to the highway going from Luzy to Saint-Honoré.

For fifteen years, Chantal Manor had been a convalescent home of the Visitation Order, also called the Visitandines, founded in 1610 at Annecy in Savoie by Saint Francis de Sales[19] and the pious Baroness de Chantal. In 1937, the Mother Superior was Mother Calixte, formerly known as Jacqueline Dumont-Warren, who had stayed in constant and affectionate contact with her brother, the director of the UNA.

On Wednesday, May 19, late in the afternoon, the brother and sister had had a long conversation on the phone. To call to Chantal Manor, the Parisian had used a phone booth located in the lobby of their branch office Rue Dupin, so he would not be traced or spied on without his knowledge. Thus, Dumont-Warren could speak safely to his sister, trusting that their enemies would know nothing of their conversation. And he got what he wanted from his sister since, on Friday, May 21, at 4 p.m., Florence de Salsis and Fabienne Blancat walked into Chantal Manor.

The two young women were now only ten miles Saint-Honoré-les-Bains.

Jacques Fitou, on the other hand, dressed like a camper, left Paris on a motorcycle that same Friday morning by the Porte de Saint-Cloud. On the back of his motorbike, he carried all his camping equipment. He passed through Versailles, then Chartres, from where he veered off toward Orléans, Nevers and Decize. It was easy for him to check periodically that he was not being followed on the highway.

At Decize, he took the road that went through Fours to Luzy. At Luzy, at a gas station, he exchanged a fleeting glance with Black and Daloz, who were having a drink on the terrace of the inn across the road. He then took off and headed for Saint-Honoré.

---

[19] François de Sales (1567-1622), Bishop of Geneva revered for his deep faith and his gentle approach to the religious divisions resulting from the Protestant Reformation. In 1604, Jeanne-Françoise Frémyot, Baroness of Chantal, a young widow of 28 years and the mother of four children, met in Dijon with François de Sales. Between them, a great spiritual friendship was born, which convinced her to settle near Annecy and found the order of the Visitation of Sainte-Marie.

Half an hour later, having selected his campsite, he set himself up. It was just outside a village called La Vieille Montagne, in the mountains, from where he could look to the southeast over the high slopes rising out of Luzy and to the northwest over the jumble of paths winding off toward Saint-Honoré only three miles away.

Finally, there were Yori Koto and Isha. Their Japanese faces forced the two of them to adopt a more radical method for hiding their identities. On Thursday afternoon, they did not take part in any of the activities organized by Dumont-Warren. Instead, they hired the services of a filmmaker and a dozen technicians, and rented two special trailers and all the necessary equipment for filming outside. They spared no expense and the cost was substantial. Above all, they made sure to cover their tracks.

On Friday at 8 a.m., what appeared to be a legitimate film crew embarking on an ordinary production left Joinville. They drove non-stop (breakfast was available in the trailers) until nightfall, making sure they were not followed, when they arrived at their destination, a town called Semelay, located five miles south of Saint-Honoré. It was a picturesque village, famous for its church and bell tower built in the beautiful Romanesque style of the 12th century. It was also famous also for its Butte de Montécot, a rocky outcrop that overhung the shores of a charming little river, the Alène, half a mile from the village. On its summit were the ruins of a Roman *castrum*—a fortified camp. There was enough there to justify the arrival of a small documentary film crew, and they registered at the only inn, telling the innkeeper that they would be staying for "approximately three days." Meanwhile, Yori and Isha remained carefully hidden inside the trailers.

Therefore, on Friday evening, the seven associates were spread out between Luzy, the Chantal Manor, the pass at La Vieille Montagne and Semelay, over an area that stretched southeast to northwest, just over a mile wide at most (from Semelay to La Vieille Montagne) and thirteen miles long (from Luzy to Saint-Honoré).

Saturday was a day of rest because the operation was not scheduled to go into effect until after sunset, at 8 p.m.

At 7:30 p.m., the investigator Andre Black and the chauffeur Pierre Daloz left Luzy in their van. They headed for Saint-Honoré.

At the intersection of the road to Avrée, two "nuns" climbed into their van through the back doors, which Black had opened for them.

At the La Vieille-Montagne intersection, they stopped again. This time, Jacques Fitou joined Mesdemoiselles de Salsis and Blancat inside the van. He told them right away:

"Everything's fine. I was able to see Jeannette Charbonneau and talk to her in secret. I convinced her easily. She'll do what I asked. So, our plan won't change."

Where the road from Semelay met the highway, they pulled over and added Yori and Isha to their cargo.

The van started descending along the winding road. After passing the village of Seu, it went on toward Saint-Honoré-les-Bains. But around a mile from the town, it turned off the highway and took a small dirt road through the forest. The van had a new but broken-in engine, which made no sound. Its body was new, too, and did not squeak or grind. The muffled purr of the exhaust made barely a noise, like the quiet hum of flying insects in the silence of the forest as night fell.

Thus crawling through the woods in total solitude, the van entered a clearing surrounded by tall bushes beyond which a circle of trees stood tightly packed. The Rose Garden Villa was farther below, around five hundred yards from the clearing. No path led to it.

The seven climbed out of the van, which was left unguarded, and walked in single file toward the villa. When they came out of the clearing, Jacques Fitou veered off to the right and disappeared. They others went on their way toward their goal.

A peasant who might have happened to cross their paths then would have turned tail and run screaming in fear. But at this hour, in this neck of the woods, nobody was wandering about; and it wasn't yet the season when oddballs and poets would have been compelled to wander through the woods.

All of them—Yori Koto, Isha, André Black, Pierre Daloz, Florence de Salsis and Fabienne Blancat—were dressed very bizarrely: their heads were covered in tall hats that dropped below their necks behind, and in the front formed a metal snout with two windows for the eyes—the latest model of gas masks, effective and simple. Furthermore, Black, Daloz, Koto and Isha were carrying on their backs devices that looked like sulfur sprayers for vines. Connected to their belts were long tubes that ended in nozzles.

Florence and Fabienne carried nothing. They did not have belts on their robes so their bare hands were free. However, since they had left the van, they kept their fists clenched because their palms were coated with some kind of phosphorescent product. The light would be bright but short-lived, and only begun when their hands were open, exposed to the air. In Jacques' plan, these glowing hands would play a brief role at the beginning.

Everything had been meticulously organized. Individually and together, they operated like a well-rehearsed dance troupe executing a choreography that alternated between simple and complicated movements.

Until the final line of trees, just at the edge of the Rose Garden, the march lasted around ten minutes because it was cautious and slow. Then they lined up behind the crowded trunks.

In the last light of the day, the surrounding wall was gray, shadowed by the upper stories and roof of the villa to the right, and the roofs of the outbuildings to the left. In that wall, carved in black, was the gate through which Florence de

Salsis had entered disguised as Jeannette Charbonneau with her basket of goat cheese.

For the seven, it was time for a pause, for watching—and waiting for Jacques Fitou. They did not have to wait for long. When he showed up, he was not alone. A girl was with him—Jeannette with her left arm swinging the cheese basket. Fitou was also wearing a gas mask, but carried nothing on his back. From his belt hung a line of cords fixed so that he could just yank them off. There were ribbons of black cloth snapped on, strips of absorbent cotton attached with tiny hooks and, lastly, a small metal gourd with a button on its side.

Since everything was going according to plan, Florence and Fabienne were the first to leave the woods with Jeannette Charbonneau between them. The three of them walked straight to the gate. There, Jeannette pulled the little chain. The rusty bell tinkled. The five men were already sneaking across the path and flattening against the wall on either side of the gate.

They heard footsteps. Then a voice groaned:

"Is that you, Jeanette?"

"Yes, Madame Sidonie," the country girl answered coolly. "I'm a little late because of one of the cows got the dropsy."

"That's fine, that's fine," Sidonie grumbled as she unlocked the gate.

The door opened and Jeannette went through.

But when the old servant was about to close the gate behind her as usual, something happened that froze her to the spot, sent shivers down her spine, and struck fear in heart as her mouth dropped open, speechless.

In front of her, in the door frame, stood two strange figures with shining hands spread open, giving off the stench of sulfur. Evil-looking snouts stuck out over their high collars and big silver crosses.

Sidonie's mouth did not close, nor did her goggling eyes. A third satanic form appeared that pointed a nozzle and sprayed something on her. Breathing in the vapor, the stunned woman immediately passed out.

Then Jacques Fitou jumped forward, caught the unconscious body and laid it on the ground, covering her mouth with a cloth soaked in chloroform from his gourd.

The well-organized action did not stop there.

Jeannette marched straight to the servant's entrance that stood wide open. She went into the room lit by a bright bulb on the ceiling and said:

"Good evening people."

Then, she turned around and flipped the light switch. Everything was drowned in darkness. And she walked out, stepping aside to stand by the rose bushes.

In her place appeared the two "nuns" who waved their glowing hands around their nightmarish heads. Black and Daloz opened their nozzles and let loose the sleeping gas that made anyone breathing it pass out instantly.

A second jet sprayed on the victims in a small room would have affected their lungs and put their lives in danger. A third and final dose would have killed them on the spot. Obviously, they were not prepared to do this, hence the chloroform cloths.

The common room, with its open door, got only one spray from the canisters. According to Yori, at this time of the day, except for Sidonie, there would only be five servants there.

When the light was back on, Yori's information was confirmed: two men and three women, one of whom was very young and prettily dressed as an elegant maid, were lying on the ground or slumped in a chair. Jacques Fitou rapidly put the chloroformed cloth over all their mouths.

Then he hurried back to Yori, Black and Daloz who were waiting under a bower of roses with the patient but puzzled and always wary Jeannette Charbonneau.

As for Florence and Fabienne, they brought Sidonie into the room and then tied up the others, hand and foot, with anything they could find lying around. All six servants were now helpless.

According to Yori's information, every day at this time, Zabad Khan and Leone Alzac were in the dining room being served by Monsieur Alfred and his wife, Louise. They ate a modest meal, but did it slowly because they talked a lot about their philosophical or historical interests. Their temperance did not keep them from enjoying good food since the vegetables from the garden and the fruit jams were delicious. Adelaide, the chef, was first-class.

Therefore, between 8 and 9 p.m. every evening in the villa, the four of them were in the dining room, while in the basement kitchen, connected by an electric dumbwaiter, Adelaide stood alone.

Now, on this beautiful May night, the big bay window of the dining room was opened wide. It faced a ten-foot wide walkway separating the house from the hedges behind which stretched the rose garden with its bower, its bushes and its artistically arranged flower beds. The front of the villa was too far from the courtyard and service entrance for anyone to have heard the little noise caused by the attack of the seven.

Signaling to his four companions and Jeannette not to move, clearly seen even in the bower from the light filtering out of the house, Jacques Fitou went to get a good look at the room from a distance through the window on a balcony with a low railing.

He saw Zabad Khan and Leone Alzac, whom Yori had described in detail. He also saw the butler, Alfred, and his wife, Louise, the former standing at the back of the room next to a buffet, the latter holding a dish out for Leone Alzac.

"Good," the reporter whispered to himself. "No changes to make."

He went back to the others, signaled for them to follow him. They hunched over and snuck out of the bower onto the path, and slowly, silently, over to the balcony.

All of a sudden, four of them stood up, grabbed the balcony and leapt over. They were such an unexpected monstrous sight that Alfred, who was the first to see them, stood petrified, speechless. Leone Alzac and Zabad Khan turned toward the intruders almost at the same time, only to receive a shot of gas full in the face.

The whole affair had lasted only three minutes.

Black and Daloz dealt with Alfred and Louise while Yori and Isha left the dining room to go the kitchen and take care of the cook, Adelaide. Jacques blindfolded Zabad Khan with one of the black cloths hanging from his belt. Then he tied his ankles and wrists and bound him tightly to the back of the chair. Swiftly he did the same to Leone Alzac.

All the open doors and windows were letting in the cool evening air that dissipated the gas. When they could take off their masks, Fitou looked at his watch and triumphantly declared:

"8:15 p.m.! It only took 15 minutes!"

He laughed contently at Black and Daloz who were shrugging off their gas canisters. The UNA investigator took some cords from the reporter's belt and tied up Alfred and Louise, lying next to each other on the rug between the buffet and the table. Then Yori and Isha reappeared, also free of their accoutrements. Yori went over to Fitou and said:

"My friend, I congratulate you. Such an easy victory is all thanks to your perfect plan."

"Thanks," the reporter replied. "But my role as leader is finished. Now let's leave reality and enter the mystery. It's your turn to take over."

The Japanese nodded and spoke slowly:

"I hope it will be simple, but I'm not so sure about that. First, we have to wait for Zabad Khan and Leone Alzac to wake up." After a short pause he went on: "Isha, pick up Zabad Khan's chair and put it next to Leone so I can see their two faces at the same time. Good. Push them back from the table. Yes, against the wall. We'll stand up by the edge of the table facing them. We, meaning me, you, Isha, and Jacques."

He looked at Black and Daloz. Everything had been prearranged for them too. The two men picked up their gas cans and masks and hurried outside, jumped over the balcony and disappeared. Then Yori waved over at Alfred and Louise:

"No need for them to hear what I have to say when they wake up. Take them away, Isha. Where? Into the room with the other servants. Might as well grab the cook and put her there with the rest of them. When you're done, come back here."

The chauffeur, a champion of Japanese wrestling, had herculean strength. He lifted Alfred's limp body, though tall and heavy, without effort. Then he came back and carried away Louise's small, light, thin body. He came back for the last time and stood to the right of Yori with Jacques Fitou on the other side.

Leaning their thighs on the edge of the big, heavy table with its tablecloth still full of silverware, crystal, porcelain and plates of endive and beet salad—their meal so bizarrely interrupted—the three men waited for the enigmatic brahmin Oryas Zabad Khan and the no less mysterious Leone Alzac to show some sign of life.

Leone Alzac was the first to come around. Color rushed back into her face and her parted lips started breathing heavily while her breasts heaved...

Suddenly her whole body jerked.

Calmly, softly Yori said:

"Do you recognize my voice, Leone? Take a minute. Clear your mind. I won't say anything until the brahmin is awake. Oh, here he is..."

Barely a minute later he continued:

"My dear Oryas, if you've really got the power to kill simply by willing it, I know you won't use it on me before hearing me out. And I believe you won't use it afterward either. You'll see why. So, first, please, tell me, do you understand?"

"Yes," the brahmin responded immediately.

"And you, Leone?"

"Yes," the young woman sighed.

Yori was about to talk but Zabad Khan broke in:

"Koto, why did you blindfold me, and I imagine Leone, too?"

"So that you won't know who is with me. You can identify me by my voice, so I'm taking the risk to be killed by you, but if you do, my partners will splatter your brains."

In a voice that sounded surprised Zabad-Khan replied:

"I don't understand."

Yori kept calm:

"Come on, cards on the table. Listen up, I'll be brief and everything will be clear. After the Eighteen deaths, my master, Marquis Gno Mitang, who knows many things, was determined to find the truth about what he defined like this: find the heir or heirs of the occult power of Gedhun Grub, who centuries ago, was the first Living Buddha of the Tibetan brahmins and lamas, who reputedly had this power to kill at a distance by simply willing it. Given this mission, step by step, I arrived at you, for I think it's you who, directly or not, is the Master of Death here in Europe. But certain clues, like the fact that Mademoiselle de Salsis, Monsieur Fitou and I are still alive, make me think that this power is somewhat limited. For example, you can't kill people you don't know, or if you don't where they are when you aim your invisible, lethal will. Still, your power may be used on the spot against a stranger if you can see them.

"There are several of us here. If I hadn't blindfolded you, you'd have been able to strike down everyone—if you do have this power. With the blindfold, I'm the only one risking death, since you already know my voice. And since I don't know if Madame Alzac also has some, or all, of the same power, I took the precaution of blindfolding her too. Finally, I repeat, now as an ultimatum, that if I die, you and Leone both will be shot to death. Coming here, we all swore to see this through to end.

"Do you still say you don't understand? Are you still going to say to me, like the last time I mentioned the Eighteen deaths, 'What are all those names?' If you deny everything, if you don't come clean now, you'll stay tied up and blindfolded, and your life will answer for mine and all those working with Gno Mitang and Monsieur Saint-Clair to elucidate this dreadful mystery. Because I'm sure you can do nothing by chance. You can do nothing against people you can't name, locate, or see. Now, in this villa, right now, are three people whom you probably don't know even exist. These three are the saviors of the others. If one of us dies, they will take revenge immediately. And they will take it first on Madame Alzac, then you, Zabad Khan.

"Have I explained things clearly enough? You can talk now."

In the same surprised tone, the brahmin said:

"Yori Koto, I assure you that I don't understand what you are talking about. You talk about eighteen dead men; last Tuesday, you said their names. You talk about a lethal power, a deadly will, occult mysteries—I know nothing about any of that. You mentioned the holy name of Gedhun Grub. Of course, I know that this extraordinary woman was the first Living Buddha, but thousands of legends have distorted her history. And it's a legend that her very real victories were won by using her willpower to kill people. I assure you one last time: I do not understand! Leone Alzac and I are victims of your master's vivid imagination—the illustrious Gno Mitang."

This time, the Japanese could not completely control his anger. He shouted:

"Go on, then, tell me what Leone Alzac meant by what she told me so ardently the first time I mentioned the Eighteen deaths?"

"What did she say?" Oryas asked.

"Ah!" Yori snickered. "So she didn't tell you about our conversation? Well, either you're lying again, or things are not so open between you and your companion as you think. OK, here's what we said—I swear I'm not making anything up and I'm not distorting anything…"

Stripping down the conversation to the basics, he calmly, objectively, dryly recounted their previous conversation in the library.

The clever Japanese, however, was careful not to say that, after that exchange, Leone Alzac's eyes had welled up with tears and she had sobbed. He also did not say that this physical expression of her emotions had seemed to clear her mind, give her more strength, that she had shaken her head wildly, narrowed her eyes, and then had suddenly looked determined.

He did not mention her saying, "*Will I never be able to completely tame the beast in me?*"

171

Yes, clever Yori kept all this to himself because he knew that Leone Alzac would thank him afterward for his silence.

Another pause ensued, followed by a more direct question:

"So, Oryas Zabad Khan, mysterious brahmin or Tibetan lama, there are seven of us here, men and women, ready to go as far as necessary. And we're still alive! If one of us loses his or her life, so will you. Now I'm done and you will respond."

Without the slightest hesitation, the inscrutable brahmin spoke as serenely as ever:

"My final response will be the same as it was last Tuesday and just now. Yori Koto, what does all this mean? I swear, I do not understand." Silence. Then: "As for what Leone said to you—what you just told me, what I've just heard for the first time—I don't understand her either."

It was, indeed, final, at least as long as new facts and other measures could not produce a fuller, more conclusive result. Jacques Fitou and Isha saw this as clearly as Yori. During the duel between the Japanese and the Brahmin, the reporter and the chauffeur had stood still and silent. But with Zabad Khan's last words, Yori signaled that he considered the battle over. Fitou then touched his arm and, with his other hand, pointed to Leone Alzac. The Japanese understood.

"No," he said aloud. "Look at her face, at least what we can see of it around the blindfold. It's stone, a little pale maybe from her emotions because she's got a nervous temperament. When she was caught off guard the other day, it got loose. She won't let that happen again. She'll just tell us now that she doesn't understand either, so it's up to us to find out by ourselves without counting on any help from these two. But we've considered all this. Let's stick to the plan. Wait for me. I think I'll find what we need in no time."

What they needed was a room where they could put Leone Alzac and Zabad Khan in the meantime. Yori wanted it both comfortable and easy to lock up and watch. In the villa, he knew only about his bedroom, the study, the living and dining rooms, and the big entry hall. He went upstairs first and did not have to search long. The second room he entered was obviously a guest room. There were two twin beds and only one window looking out on the front steps. On one side was a bathroom with a toilet, bathtub and all the modern conveniences.

"This'll do," Yori said. "We'll just have to put something to bar the window. We can do that tomorrow. Either the servants can do it or Isha and Daloz can go into Nevers to get the materials. And we'll switch the locks on the door so they're on the outside. Perfect. Tonight, Fitou, Isha and I will stand guard in shifts."

He went back down to the dining room.

"Oryas, Leone, we're going to take off your blindfolds and untie you. It doesn't matter if you see your guards, Jacques Fitou, Isha and me. If you have the power to kill, you'll be using it at the price of your own life because the others whom you do not know will remain unseen, watching us... especially you."

He waved to Fitou and Isha to free the two prisoners. The three men saw only quiet tranquility in their eyes.

"Please follow me.," said Yori.

They climbed the stairs and Yori stood before the open door of the bedroom.

"You can get undressed in the bathroom, if you want, put on your pajamas and then go to bed. We'll be taking turns watching you until tomorrow night. Mademoiselle de Salsis, who is known to you, will bring your things from your own rooms in a few minutes. Of course, she'll let you tell her what you need. In the meantime, I'll leave you with Monsieur Fitou and Isha because I have other things to take care of with your servants."

Awake and sitting on the chairs under the surveillance of Black and Daloz holding their Brownings, the servants had been waiting.

Jeanette Charbonneau had returned home and Fitou was absolutely sure she could be trusted.

Florence de Salsis and Fabienne Blancat were pacing in the rose garden, which was lit enough from the glow of the dining room lights. It was to them that Yori Koto went first. He sent Florence upstairs with specific instructions, and to Fabienne he said:

"Will you come with me until Jacques is free to join us? I'm going to take over for him with Zabad Khan and Leone after I'm done with the servants."

There were eight servants: Alfred; his wife Louise; their daughter Paulette, who was Leone's maid; the gardener Lucas; his wife Sidonie; Adelaide the cook; Antonio, the driver/mechanic; and Bertha, his wife, who was in charge of the chickens and the laundry. During his own captivity, Yori had seen them all and Leone Alzac had not kept their family ties a secret when asked. They all knew their masters' Japanese "guest" quite well.

Florence de Salsis had taken off their blindfolds and gags. All of them were completely stunned on waking up. Black and Daloz kept their guns trained on them to be safe.

"For tonight," Yori told them, "you'll stay here in this room. I'll let Lucas and Antonio go get mattresses, pillows and blankets so you can bed down and sleep comfortably. You'll be constantly watched in shifts. If you try anything, the punishment will be death. If you can't sleep, think about your situation. Tomorrow, I will explain everything and give you a choice individually and together. Got it? Very well."

To Black, he said:

"Go with these two to the bedrooms and make sure they don't split up and run away."

To Daloz, he said:

"Keep a close eye on them here until I return."

Finally to Adelaide, he said:

"You and this lady who is armed (he gestured to Fabienne) and watching closely will go back to the kitchen. You'll make coffee for seven people, plenty of it. Don't get smart and drop poison into it because you'll be taking the first sip. Get up and go."

Less than an hour later, the Rose Garden Villa was all quiet again.

Leone Alzac and Zabad Khan in the their pajamas lay in the twin beds being watched by Yori, Fitou and Isha who took turns sleeping in comfortable armchairs.

André Black was next door in Leone Alzac's bedroom. Fabienne Blancat was next in Zabad Khan's room. And finally, Florence was in the room that Yori had used during his stay.

All the doors, which connected all the rooms, including the toilets, bathrooms and even linen closets, were left open. Taking their turn in two-hour shifts, Fabienne Blancat and André Black stayed outside the prison-room, but were able to see the guard inside—sometimes Yori, sometimes Jacques, and sometimes Isha. For it was crucial that the life of the guards be constantly observed as well. If by some extraordinary circumstances, as Yori had put it, their lives ended, Black, either seeing it or being told by Fabienne, would immediately, without even entering the room, empty his gun into Zabad Khan and Leone Alzac. Moreover, Fabienne was also armed with a Browning and, although not as skilled as Black, she, too, would fire at the prisoners kept visible in the light of a lamp purposely set up over the door to shine on them/

The brahmin and his alluring companion had free use of their arms and legs, but only on the bed, because among all the gear brought in the van, there were shackles and chains designed by Yori who had gotten them made in Paris on Wednesday night, by a skilled metalworker friend of his. That night, May 22, Zabad Khan and Leone Alzac had a bracelet on their left ankles linked to a twenty-inch chain securely fastened to the left leg of the bed. So the murderous will power might kill, but the wielder of that power could not leave the cone of light shining on the twin beds without becoming a target.

As for the eight servants lying on mattresses on the floor, sleeping or thinking, they were under the surveillance of Pierre Daloz alone, who had been supplied with half a pot of coffee and had sworn not to close his eyes all night long as long as he could smoke his pipe. Naturally, no one complained about the pipe smoke.

The next morning, Sunday, May 23, was a busy day at the Rose Garden Villa.

Without having to go to Nevers, just with what could be found at the villa, and thanks to the ingenuity and handiwork of Daloz and Isha, the windows of the prison-room and its bathroom were barred off with grills made from the iron usually used to fashion the bowers. And the door locks were switched to the outside.

Leone Alzac and Zabad Khan listened to Yori Koto tell them:

"Now we won't put chains on you at night anymore. Other measures have been taken. If one of the four of us whom you already know happens to die suspiciously, you will both be suffocated, strangled and then buried under the bushes of your charming villa. Got it? We're living in a state beyond the reach of the law. We won't kill unless you kill first, but if you do, we will kill you without mercy."

Meanwhile, the status of the servants was settled to everyone's satisfaction. Given the basics about the routine of what amounted to a "state of siege" in the villa, with his masters being held prisoner, Alfred spoke on behalf of the staff, of whom he was the boss, and stated:

"We shall follow the orders of Monsieur Koto and Mademoiselle de Salsis. I swear, we all swear, obedience and loyalty."

"We're counting on that," the Japanese replied curtly. "And don't forget that if anyone betrays the others, we'll take hostages. All of you are husbands, wives, parents, children... Understood? Besides, you know that if a traitor gets in touch with the police, he will be the first one locked up and sentenced as an accomplice to murder, blackmail and thievery. I already explained why, so you understand. Now, get back to work. The lady of the house is Mademoiselle de Salsis. There will be five place settings at the table instead of two. Your former masters will be eating in their room, served by Isha, Monsieur Fitou or myself. Lastly, you will add two chairs to the staff's table for Monsieur Daloz and Isha. But these two are in no way your fellow servants—treat them as your bosses."

Alfred bowed like a good butler.

He and the staff were used to it. After the Brazilian Fernando Golves had brought them all together at the Rose Garden and ruled them with an iron fist, though well paid, they then had had Leone Alzac and Zabad Khan, who paid better but were even more severely disciplined. Now, they had Florence de Salsis and Yori Koto paying even better! So they would obey, and their obedience would be docile thinking that, one of these days, they would be free again. They would then enjoy to the full the fortune earned during their service, strange and suspicious as it may have been, but in many ways generous and rewarding.

Throughout the afternoon, Yori and Florence, Jacques and Fabienne, and André Black, had divided the inside of the villa into sections and were making a methodical, meticulous search. Every wall was probed, every piece of furniture scoured, every book rifled through, every letter opened and read.

At 9 p.m., Yori called Dumont-Warren on the phone. After a succinct but thorough description of the "occupation" of the Rose Garden Villa, the Japanese finished with:

"We're in control of the house and its occupants. But the brahmin is guarding his secret and the villa its mystery."

CHAPTER VII
The Power of the Kingo

Endowed with an exceptional work ethic, Monsieur Dumont-Warren was not content with running the many services of the UNA with intelligence, skill and authority. Well known in Paris and no longer worried about his reputation for going out into the world, tired of the theater and other outings over his twenty-one years of life in Paris, needed by the official spheres more than he had need of them, he rarely ate out and almost never went out at night.

Usually at 8 p.m., he left his office and went directly to his home on Rue de la Faisanderie, where he owned a little house. A widower, the father of a girl married to a governor in the colonies who had been following her husband on a fact-finding mission across the British Empire, he lived alone with three carefully selected servants and his chauffeur, Pierre Daloz, who had been replaced by a new driver highly recommended by a friend.

In the evening, Dumont-Warren did not eat a fancy meal. After taking a bath and putting on his pajamas, he drank a bowl of milk or cold broth and ate some fruits. Then, smoking a short, thick pipe, he sat in his study until 11 p.m. or midnight, reading new books or rereading old ones. It was there, jealously protected against any outside interference, that he found his real daily rest and his main pleasure in life. He only broke his routine for his rare friends, among whom Leo Saint-Clair was his closest.

On this Sunday, May 23, Dumont-Warren had spent the morning at the UNA. Then he had stayed home all afternoon waiting for the prescheduled call from Yori Koto. He took time, as always on Sunday, to catch up on writing personal letters, which he never dictated and always wrote by hand. The director of the UNA was very modern in his management of the company he had founded, but in his private life, he held to certain traditions.

He was pleased to hear of the victory of his seven agents, but was also worried.

During his bath and frugal dinner, he kept thinking, imaging, hoping… applying his mind and memory to the full. While preparing his nightly pipe, he suddenly cried out:

"Oh, but… yes!"

Very methodical and organized, never giving in to impulses, he kept packing down the tobacco until it was ready for the slow match. With his "puffer" between his teeth, he went straight to the shelf where he kept the new books he had liked enough to want to read them again.

The book he pulled out was titled *The Country of Kingo*, a first edition in English written by the famous American naturalist Y. H. Garnoch.

Now, as the title and subject flashed in this memory, Dumont-Warren recalled having read two days ago in one of the UNA reports that Garnoch was in Paris and had two lectures scheduled on Tuesday 25, one at the Geographic Society at 11 a.m., and the other at the Academy of Medicine in the afternoon.

He thumbed through the book standing up, reread an entire chapter and then a few pages here and there.

"Good! Good! Good!" he said as his pipe puffed smoke into the air.

Twenty minutes of reading was enough to find out everything.

"Damn, if all this is true, which is likely, and if Garnoch has a suitcase full of samples from his collection, success just might be possible. But will Garnoch even see me? Of course, if his book is a reflection of the man... They must bear a resemblance."

He remembered the name of the hotel where the American was staying. With his pipe in his left hand, he used his right to dial a number. Soon, he was connected:

"Hello, Mademoiselle, is Monsieur Garnoch in? This is Monsieur Dumont-Warren, director of the UNA... Very well. Thank you."

And he waited. Then suddenly, he spoke in English:

"Hello, Monsieur Garnoch? Yes, Dumont-Warren here. Good evening. Please excuse me for calling you at this hour... and on a Sunday! But I hope you will judge for yourself that this is exceptionally important... Yes, exceptionally... I'd like to talk to you confidentially as soon as possible... Tonight? Yes, I'd be most grateful. Have you eaten? Good... I can come over there... Oh, you'd rather go out for a walk? Along the Seine... Just as well then, because the easiest place to meet would be my study here at home. Would you like me to send a car for you?... It'll wait for you in front of the Chambre des Députés... I myself will be... Oh, fear not, I'll recognize you, I've seen photographs of you... Yes, well, as you prefer... Then, take a taxi and I'll be waiting. The address is 43bis Rue de la Faisanderie... Yes, 43*bis*... Thank you very much. See you soon."

He hung up and mumbled contentedly to himself:

"He did seem to be like in his book. In that case, I'll tell him everything. As long as his Kingo isn't totally imaginary or exaggerated..."

Continuing to smoke because one's evening pipe was sacred, Dumont-Warren went to change out of his pajamas into a suit. Then he rang for a cart of alcohol, cigars and cigarettes to be brought into his study.

Greeted by Dumont-Warren in the long, wide entranceway, then hastily led into the study, the famous naturalist answered the thanks and the praise with a big smile and said warmly that the UNA and its director were well known to him, adding that he did not drink or smoke. He sat down in the armchair and went on:

"Tell me, Monsieur Dumont-Warren, what is this all about? We can speak in English, can't we? I'm more comfortable with it than with French. And I could tell over the phone that you are quite at ease in my language. So, what is this all about?"

Dumont-Warren looked at his guest. He had good feelings about the man. After the welcoming smiles, he turned serious and spoke gravely:

"Excuse me for what I'm about to ask you, but it's only a precaution. I am working on a very important, very urgent matter…"

"Of course! I'm listening."

"I want to ask you to give me your word of honor that, under no circumstances, you will reveal the subject of our conversation, now or in the future, to anyone, and also to promise to not write about it, even in your private journal if you keep one. Everything said here, especially what I'm about to reveal to you, must be kept strictly confidential."

He had spoken so earnestly, stared so firmly, that the American naturalist and explorer was moved. But he did not balk. Just as gravely, he replied very slowly:

"Monsieur Dumont-Warren, I give you my word of honor that neither in speech or writing will I ever repeat anything I hear or say here tonight. Unless, of course, you explicitly release me of this oath someday."

Dumont-Warren almost shouted, "Excellent!", then he lowered his voice:

"Listen and believe me—this is no fiction, no game, but a series of incontrovertible facts that have forced some people to take action, which I will now tell you all about…"

And he told him everything, from his meeting with the Nyctalope on April 7, the reports about the first 14, then 18, deaths up to the phone call he had just received at 8 p.m. this May 23 from Yori Koto at the Rose Garden Villa.

Garnoch did not interrupt him once.

When the director had finished, the American sat still and quiet, his eyes half-closed, his face tense. Then he clapped his hands, brought them up to his chin and spoke:

"A man with such power! The mind boggles! Such a man would, of course, want to stay anonymous, hide in some secret place… Such a man could rule the world, if he wanted! With a mere thought, he could bring down kings and dictators, leaders and rebels… By simply threatening death, he could make men do as he wanted. If this man were a man of peace and kindness… but he might be a warlord and a demon from Hell! Everything you have just told me is almost unbelievable…"

"And yet, it's true," Dumont-Warren replied.

"And yet, it's true," the naturalist repeated. "I don't doubt it. Therefore, I must ask you, straight to the point, why have you told me this?"

"Because in your last book, I read and reread what you wrote about Kingo."

"Oh, now I get it," Garnoch said.

Then he sat in silence for a long minute with a friendly smile on his face.

"Kingo, yes... In Africa, on the shores of Lake Tanganyika, in the middle of a vast and still wild region, there is a cult of snake-men. They're called that because they can heal the bites of reptiles and they themselves are immune to them. Their priests are said to be the keepers of ancient secrets that combine wild superstitions with genuine science."

Dumont-Warren broke in:

"And you are the only white man who managed to be accepted among these snake-men?"

"Yes. Thanks to my knowledge of ointments that protect against the worst bites, powders that stifle pain, herbs and flowers whose scent can cause either dementia or death... All these plants and products are being studied in my labs right now."

"Can you tell me more about Kingo?"

"I can, indeed, and shall do so at once, Monsieur. On the top of a wild mountain, completely isolated, far from any village, grows a weird bush that's unknown to modern botany. Only the Snake Emperor, the high priest of the cult, has the right to pick this shrub and, after a complex ritual, extract its extraordinary, terrifying poison—the Kingo. The effects of this liquid or powder—it can be made in either form—are similar to those of the mysterious concoction called 'Colombo,' according to the most arcane books of magic."

"Colombo! That's it!"

"Whoever ingests Kingo loses all self-control, all willpower, all control over his thoughts, speech and actions. He becomes the prey of whoever holds his hands, looks him in the eyes and speaks with authority. Then, one of two things happens. Either the patient drones out all his inner thoughts, his secrets, his desires, memories, and even dreams; or else, under orders from the manipulator, he says what he is told to say when prompted."

"Well, well... Don't they say that, in Russia, there's Stalin can get generals, diplomats and politicians to confess to the most abominable and odious crimes before a tribunal..."

"Perhaps. That would explain a lot. But I haven't finished. I witnessed the Kingo in action on several men whom I had picked out from the tribe, and not haphazardly but selected for being the healthiest, smartest and most energetic of them. The Kingo worked wonders! But I wasn't satisfied. I wanted to be absolutely certain, to be able to record and remember the feelings and sensations myself. So, I took a little dose of Kingo at home in my office..."

"Your book says..."

"Allow me to recite a page from my book: *Sitting back in my armchair in front of a mirror and a stopwatch, with pen and paper at hand, I took the carefully prepared potion. When I felt the first signs of change, I started writing. But all of a sudden, the pen slipped from my fingers, which became weak and out of my control, although I was fully aware of it happening, very quickly, to the point of losing all my willpower. I was unable to move any part of my body. I was hypnotized by my own dilated eyes staring at me from the mirror. And I know very well that this was the effect of the Kingo because, right after the fit, I took great pains to remember all the phases, one by one... I know perfectly well that the drug had transformed the natural state of my brain somehow, and I was no longer thinking as myself. I was incapable of forming an idea, let alone putting two and two together. Moreover, I experienced no mental or physical hallucinations, like with opium or cocaine or other drugs of that type. I was myself, fully awake and healthy, but without having any power over myself.*

"*For precisely two hours and four minutes, I stayed in the armchair staring at my pale face without blinking. I heard the tick-tock of the stopwatch but if a fire had erupted around me, I would have sat there, frozen stiff, and would have burned to a crisp without being able to move a finger. Initiative, will, energy, self-control, all of it was gone.*

"*Finally...* Listen well to this, Monsieur... *I had only one single, strange desire growing stronger by the minute, an agonizing desire for someone to talk to me. Thus, I started repeating to myself madly that I wanted someone to look at me so that I might be able to think through him. I had a burning need to think, to speak. And I was also aware that, by staring by myself like this, I would never think and never talk again!*

"*But you might object that that was, indeed, a thought. Yes, I had only that single thought and no other. I was tortured by the anguish, the dread of being alone, seeing myself staring wide-eyes and agape, but totally mute.*

"*Then, just as suddenly as I had fallen into this trance state, I came out of it. I was astonishingly, blissfully, gratefully aware that my mind was back to normal! I had a brief, harmless nervous fit, followed by tears. And then, it was over—completely. My experiment on myself had no disagreeable side effects. The Kingo affected only the vital centers that are the sources of our willpower, giving it control over it. It attacked no other organs. But the organ it did seize, it held under its control tightly. As it does so, it transfers the will of one person over to another person, the manipulator who knows how to use and control the dangerous effects of the Kingo.*"

With that, Garnoch paused, shook his head and, as if with boundless regret, added:

"I never tried it again."

"On you?" asked Dumont-Warren.

"On me."

"What about others?"

After a second of hesitation, Garnoch answered:

"On others, yes. But with their consent and sworn to professional secrecy. My guinea pigs were three of my students."

"What were the results?"

"Convincing. Conclusive. They told me their most intimate thoughts and then repeated my suggestions, what I was thinking... in silence."

Dumont-Warren spoke more soberly now:

"So, you're an expert on using the Kingo now... To manipulate people under its influence?"

"Yes."

Dumont-Warren excitedly stood up and started pacing. Then he came back and stood in front of Garnoch, who had also gotten up.

"Do you think," said the UNA director, sounding emotional, "that you could go to the Rose Garden Villa on Wednesday morning and... I assume you brought some Kingo with you, right?"

Garnoch was no less emotional and did not try to hide it when he replied slowly but firmly:

"Why wait until Wednesday? Why not go tomorrow?"

With a big smile and tears in his eyes, Dumont-Warren grabbed the American's shoulders and shook him with joyful abandon:

"Oh, thank you, thank you! My dear friend! That's wonderful! But you forget about your two conferences on Tuesday that were the purpose of your trip to France."

"Oh my, that's right," Garnoch replied, laughing. But right away, he turned serious again. "This is no laughing matter. I know it's only nervous laughter, but I really must learn to control my nerves. Clearing up the mystery of the Eighteen deaths and preventing new ones is serious business... Tell me, my friend, is your whiskey first rate, as I presume?"

"Yes, but..."

"I know, I never drink. But today, however..."

Going to the cart and taking a bottle, the naturalist filled a glass and gulped it down.

At the Geographic Society as well as at the Academy of Medicine, the bold explorer and learned naturalist held his two conferences with great success. But unlike his original intention, he did not talk about the Kingo or make the slightest reference to it.

As for Dumont-Warren, he called Saint-Honoré and immediately recognized the voice on the other end of the line.

"Anything to report, Fitou?"

"No, nothing, boss."

"Well, I've got some news—big news! But I can't say more on the telephone."

"What is it?"

"A big surprise. On Wednesday, be in Luzy with your motorcycle. At noon, at the Hotel des Sapins. No, you won't be eating lunch there. You'll just wait for me. I'm coming by car and I won't be alone. I'll have someone with me who should be able to do a lot for us... A lot! You'll be leading us back to the Villa on the quietest roads. Then we can all eat together at 1 p.m."

Dumont-Warren smiled when he heard:

"I say, boss, for you to leave Paris in this busy season, this must be really..."

"It's serious, my boy, very serious. But enough of that for today. Go tell Yori Koto right away to keep a lid on things until I get there. A tight lid, understand?"

"Yes, boss, but if I may..."

"What?"

"Our enemy's organization must be a little confused at not hearing from the Rose Garden. We know nothing about their organization. We don't know if they're connected to Mrs. MacCross or that Irish Earl... You get it, boss, it's really important for you to cover your tracks well so that..."

"I've thought of that already. Don't worry. See you Wednesday."

On Monday and Tuesday, Dumont-Warren prepared everything at the UNA for his absence.

"I might not come back for three or four days," he told his second in command. "I'll call you every day at 9 a.m., noon and 8 p.m."

On Wednesday, May 26, at 7:20 a.m., a fast, two-seater convertible left Paris through the Porte Dauphine with Dumont-Warren at the wheel. Next to him sat Mr. Garnoch, chewing gum, his arms crossed.

During the previous night, the American had left his hotel through a service door leading to an alley. First, he'd done a little walking to check that he wasn't being followed. Then he had proceeded to a rendezvous at a building located on the Avenue de la Grande-Armée where Dumont-Warren, unknown to anyone but the owner, who lived in the same building, rented an apartment and a garage. The owner had fixed up two rooms for the night and agreed to lend them his own car, the convertible. He had also picked up their bags in total secrecy and packed them in the trunk.

Dumont-Warren had joined Garnoch at the Apartment at midnight. It was not unusual for him to leave Paris for a few days. As for Garnoch, the newspapers had announced that he was going to Le Havre. Besides, it was unlikely that the evil "organization" would be much interested in the American naturalist, even if they had caught him visiting Dumont-Warren on Sunday night, since famous travelers met with the UNA director all the time.

Still, Dumont-Warren had required that such precautions be taken that night because he was nagging at himself for his mistake—"let's hope it's harmless," he told himself—seeing Garnoch on Sunday without trying to keep it secret.

It was noon sharp when the convertible arrived at the Hotel des Sapins in Luzy. It did not stop. It just slowed down a little as it passed Fitou on his motorcycle with one foot on the sidewalk.

When the reporter saw his boss through the windshield, he lifted his left arm, kicked down on the starter, and the bike pulled out. The car just had to follow it until they entered the Rose Garden Villa at 12:30 p.m. through the back road without encountering any other vehicle outside the town.

Before lunch, which had been scheduled for 1 p.m., Dumont-Warren introduced his seven agents to Garnoch, who recognized them all from the descriptions he had gotten during their trip from Paris. Then the two arrivals got a tour of the villa and the property. Lastly, they met the eight servants.

Leone Alzac and Zabad Khan were not included in the tour because when Yori Koto had shaken Dumont-Warren's hand, he had said:

"The two prisoners after lunch, please."

During the meal, they avoided talking about the situation. The food was tasty and there was plenty of it. Afterwards, they paid honor to the coffee with cigarettes and cigars. Then, since the weather was nice, they strolled around the grounds. It was important that they faced their mysterious captives—how dangerous were they?—only after they had digested their food, their bodies alert and their minds clear.

Therefore, it was almost 4 p.m. when Yori led the two newcomers upstairs with Fitou behind them. Today, it was Isha who had been watching the maid Paulette—the daughter of Alfred and Louise—cleaning up the bathroom and making up the two beds.

Why had Yori decided to not separate the brahmin and the young woman and put them in the same room together? When asked that on the first night by Fitou, he had answered:

"I don't know. I'm not too clear about it myself. I'm following my instinct."

Trusting in the clever Japanese the reporter had dropped the issue.

After taking their lunch and their customary mint tea, Leone Alzac and Zabad-Khan had been sitting reading in two armchairs away from each other when the door flew open and several men appeared on the threshold. The brahmin closed his book and tossed it on the bed. The young woman dropped her cigarette in the ashtray. Neither of them got up.

Yori came in first and stepped aside. Two strangers entered after him, followed by Fitou who closed the door and leaned back against it.

Yori waved his hand at the two prisoners staring at him and introduced the newcomers:

"This is Monsieur Dumont-Warren, director of the UNA, and Monsieur Garnoch, explorer and naturalist whose work I'm sure you don't know."

Neither of them had wanted to stay anonymous to the captives. Leone Alzac voiced her thoughts right away. Scornfully, in her cold voice, she said:

"What's the point of this? Are we exotic animals in a zoo, or a spectacle for the music hall?"

"It seems so, my dear friend," Zabad Khan added, reaching out to get his book, a big edition of Montaigne, which he laid on his knees before starting to read again.

Leone Alzac took another cigarette from the box on the low table and lit it.

Dumont-Warren spoke quietly and politely:

"Madame, Monsieur, you insult us if you think we came here just to satisfy our vulgar curiosity. Monsieur Garnoch is not such a trifling man. Neither am I, especially in such a grave situation as this. You both know why you are prisoners here, closely guarded in your own house…"

He was surprised to feel a hand on his left arm. He turned to see Garnoch smiling at him and saying:

"My friend, excuse me for interrupting, but I think it's better if I speak first because I can contribute a new element to the story of the presumed guilt, direct or indirect, of Madame Alzac in the matter of the Eighteen dead."

Dumont-Warren raised his eyebrows at these unexpected words. Yori looked at the naturalist with excitement. Fitou was intrigued and stepped closer. Leone Alzac's dark eyes were riveted onto the American. Zabad Khan also deigned to glance up at him.

"What do you mean?" asked Dumont-Warren.

"Well," Garnoch was still smiling as he said: "It happens that I know Madame Alzac."

"What?" Fitou barked out.

Yori and Dumont-Warren looked amazed. The American went on:

"Leone Alzac is the real name of this young lady, but I knew her first as Lady Leone Medwin." He turned to face her directly. "Madame, I first saw you in Bombay in April 1935 at a reception in honor of Lord William Stonewell. Your beauty was remarkable, truly beyond compare. You were the wife of an English lieutenant, George Medwin. Your husband was more interested in scientific matters than military ones. I wasn't formally introduced to you at that time, but soon after, I went with your husband on a scheduled punitive expedition. We left Bombay the day after that evening. I spent three weeks with your husband, which is how I learned that you were the daughter of Baron Louis Alzac, a Frenchman from Gascony, and Señora Mercedes Comtal, a Spanish noble woman from Seville.

"Lieutenant Medwin was a fascinating character and passionate about science, so we kept in touch. You loved each other, but you kept it quiet, discreet, within the bounds of a loving marriage. It remained quite separate from his military existence. When he wrote to me , he usually told me everything, as it often happens between two men bound by the same intellectual interests. So, I learned about his disgrace, his being sent far away on a dangerous mission during which he was killed. His last letter had foretold it, and afterward, I received a telegram from one of his friends.

184

"Therefore, Madame, I understand you had your reasons—and were probably right—to blame his disgrace and inevitable death on the inexplicable enmity of Lord Stonewell. It was only natural for you to hate that man..."

Garnoch paused, leaned forward and said slowly:

"A hatred that was no doubt the cause of his death when, somehow, you acquired the power to kill by thought."

What emotion! Leone Alzac sat rigidly in her chair, deathly pale, her big black eyes glaring at the man who was stirring up a marvelous past that had ended in tragic mourning. Dumont-Warren, Yori and Jacques, looked back and forth at the two of them. Zabad Khan had closed his book and his aloofness had turned to eager curiosity.

Garnoch very calmly continued solemnly:

"That explains the death of Lord Stonewell, the murderer of your beloved husband. But there's Eduardo Prim. That, I can only guess at..."

He stopped and was obviously having trouble containing his emotions. He breathed and got control of himself before going on:

"Everything that has happened since the discovery of the first fourteen deaths, and in which I am now inextricably involved by an unbreakable bond, isn't just a wild nightmare acted out in some form of collective madness... Madame Alzac, I am reasonably certain of being able to accuse you of the death of Eduardo Prim..."

He took a breath and stuttered a little as he went on:

"There was a military insurrection in Spain in July 1936, ten months ago During it, the Dowager Baroness Alzac, daughter of Mercedes Comtal, and her youngest sister, Marie Conception, were in Seville. An anarchist by the name of Eduardo Prim tried to organize a popular uprising against the army. At the same time, with a gang made up of villains, he raped and pillaged, killed and burned the rich neighborhoods in the city which he was temporarily controlled. Mercedes Comtal and her daughter were taken, tortured and killed. I read this awful story in a newspaper in New York. Mercedes Comtal? I remembered my conversations with Lieutenant Medwin. You correctly blamed Eduardo Prim for the deaths of your mother and sister. When you found the power to kill at a distance, you executed him."

The emotions in the room grew stronger. The ensuing silence lasted for several minutes, an emotional silence, full of memories, admiration mixed with pity. Everyone, even Zabad Khan who was gripping his book in his long, nervous fingers, had their eyes and thoughts focused on Leone Alzac, the widow of Lieutenant Medwin, the daughter of Mercedes Comtal, the sister of Marie Conception.

Her chest straight and stiff, her fingers laced under her chin, her head lowered and leaning on them, her eyes closed with her long lashes fluttering, Leone Alzac cried. There was no sobbing, no noise, no wincing face or shuddering body. Just tears—glittering tears that fell on her fingers, flowed through and ran down her bare arms.

After a short while, the young woman unlaced her fingers, took the white handkerchief sticking out of the pocket of her black dress, and dried her eyes, cheeks and hands. She looked up and turned to look at Zabad Khan. The brahmin met her eyes, understood, responded with a look, but said not a word.

Then Leone Alzac faced Garnoch and spoke wearily but still with a firm will and determination:

"You said what you know and what you believe. I don't have to confirm or deny it. I'll keep my mouth shut. Always."

Then her dark eyes passed from one to the other of the four anxious men standing before her.

"You put us in prison, now leave me in peace."

Garnoch was the first to bow politely, turn around and march out. Dumont-Warren, Yori and Jacques followed suit.

After they left, Isha closed the door.

That night, in the mint tea that was being served to Leone Alzac and Zabad Khan after their frugal dinner of cooked vegetables and cold fruit, Garnoch dissolved a tiny dose of the Kingo powder, barely tainting the golden liquid, making it undetectable.

Through a small peephole that had been secretly bored into the door on the first night, the naturalist watched the two prisoners. He saw them drink their tea totally unaware of the terrible but justified attack against their formidable secret.

With a watch in hand, Garnoch kept his eye on the spy hole. Behind him in the hallway all the others waited. Fabienne Blancat had brought a notebook and a pencil.

Minute by minute, a quarter of an hour ticked off, then another, then a third. And they all felt the fourth would never end when Garnoch raised a hand.

"They are in the inhibition stage that lasts until the end of the intoxication. Don't forget my warnings to stay quiet and still. And you, Mademoiselle Blancat, please keep your notebook hidden and don't rustle the paper... Isha, you may open the door—quietly."

Leone Alzac and Zabad Khan were sitting in their armchairs next to each other in front of the window. The purple and pink glow of twilight was the only light in the room. Garnoch went to shut the window and close the shutters. He untied and pulled the curtains as well. Then he turned on the two lamps that had a pretty Empire clock in their base.

He pushed the armchairs closer together with their backs to the light. He took another chair and sat in front of them, so close that his knees were touching theirs. His smooth, bony face was in full light, softened by the lampshades.

At the other end of the room, near the door, the others huddled together, except for Fabienne Blancat who was leaning against a little corner table hidden from sight, but not far enough that the weak light wouldn't reached her. All these preparations were made as quietly as possible.

The two prisoners were sunk down in their chairs, arms hanging at their sides, their hands limp on the thighs for the man, and on the belly for the woman. Their dilated eyes stared blankly, expressionless—the eyes of tranquil visions.

At first, nobody, not even Garnoch, made a move. There was total silence. Then he leaned forward, reached out and put his hand on Leone's crossed hands. He laid the other on the left palm and wrist of Zabad Khan. His bright, piercing, commanding eyes stared into the pupils of one, and then the other, and back again. He went through this hypnotic game for two or three minutes. Then he said in a loud, deep, slow voice:

"Oryas Zabad Khan, Leone Alzac Medwin, you see me. You hear me. I am your master. Do you see me? Do you hear me? I order you to answer me!"

Leone Alzac was the first to show a sign that she was affected. The corners of her eyes twitched. Then her lips parted and, after a little sigh, she answered:

"Y-yes."

It was not a prompt, open, strong yes. She was struggling against obedience with her still intact inner strength.

Garnoch frowned, pressed harder on the brahmin's palm and stared hard into his eyes. His voice, too, came out hard:

"Zabad Khan, do you see me? Do you hear me? I order you to answer me!"

The brahmin's dilated eyes had a glint of fear. His mouth opened. First came a raspy wheeze; then, suddenly, he shouted:

"Yes!"

That was obedience, but full of hatred and inner revolt.

Garnoch recognized the effect. He had seen it in himself, and during his experiments in America with his favorite students. That experiment had ended up with the Kingo winning and the student answering the agreed-upon question despite all his resistance: "Where did you put your sun glasses?"

Now, faced with the reluctant yes of Leone Alzac and the defiant yes of Zabad Khan, Garnoch remembered these experiments and knew he had succeeded. He mustered all his inner strength so that it would show in his eyes and voice and flow through his hands, which were the vehicle for the vital fluid— and started with the woman first, who appeared to be the weaker of the two:

"Leone Alzac Medwin, I order you to answer my questions. I demand that you respond quickly and clearly. First of all, this...." Here, he marked a brief pause, then hammering out each syllable, asked: "Who in this world has the power to kill at a distance by simply willing it?"

Oh, how those eyes burned in that room as they converged on the face of Leone Alzac. What power of natural suggestion emanated from them adding to the force of the manipulator! Dumont-Warren, Florence, Yori, Fitou and Fabienne, all were drilling their optical "beams" into the young woman and these "beams" were loaded with their wills, their expectations, their feverish anxiety.

"Speak! Speak!" they all cried out silently through bated breath.

Leone Alzac trembled from head to toe. Her whole body shook. Her eyelids fluttered, then stuck. Her face seemed to shrink, to petrify. Her lips twisted, then parted over her shiny teeth. A shout sprang out:

"No!"

A raspy wheeze. Then the shout was repeated:

"No! No! No!"

Her hands slipped out of Garnoch's grip. Her whole body tensed up and she leaped forward at Garnoch. Her stiff fingers and sharp nails scratched and dug into his forehead as she kept howling and shrieking:

"No! No! No! No!"

The counterattack was instant. Dumont-Warren grabbed her under her arms, lifted her up and carried her away. He threw her face down on the bed with one hand on her neck and the other on the small of back, holding her down as she writhed like a snake trapped under the fork of a hunter.

Instinctively, Yori Koto and Jacques Fitou had run over to Zabad Khan. They stopped in front of him but did not touch him because he had not budged. He was sitting completely still in his armchair. But his eyes were already starting to show signs of normality as his body relaxed. His hands slowly raised to the level of the velvet arms of the chair.

As for Florence and Fabienne, they were nervous and confused as they watched Garnoch patting his bloody forehead with a handkerchief.

In the next fifteen minutes, everyone did what was expected. Florence went to the bathroom to get some hydrogen peroxide. Fabienne found what she needed in a dresser to make a bandage. Garnoch's brow was duly cleaned, sterilized and bandaged.

Dumont-Warren kept Leone Alzac on the bed until her fit wore itself out. He took care not to hold her too tightly so that, when he felt her body go limp, shaken only by sobs, he let her go and whispered in her ear:

"Madame, stay calm." Then in a louder voice: "Mademoiselle de Salsis and Fabienne, would you please take care of Madame Alzac and get whatever she needs?"

After this, he went to Yori and Fitou standing in front of Zabad Khan. Garnoch joined the worried and curious group and the four of them could think of nothing better to do than observe the brahmin.

Soon, he was back to himself, gradually regaining the use of his limbs. He just sat there relaxed, his face calm, his eyes clear and expressive, a little smile on his lips—one that lingered, but with no sparkle in his eyes. His eyes looked grim. It was, therefore, only a smile of contempt, which was translated into words as he spoke, his voice as calm as ever:

"Monsieur Garnoch, I read your latest book. I was in Lhasa, and one of my men had brought it from Bombay. I admit, however, that when you were introduced to me, I had forgotten about your travels in Africa and your experiments with the Kingo. I had other, more important matters on my mind. So, it was just as if I knew nothing about you and the Kingo. Madame Alzac and I drank the tea without suspecting a thing, like every evening. I suppose the Kingo was in the tea, wasn't it?"

The smile vanished from his face. His eyes bored into the American becoming even grimmer, heavier. But still in a quiet voice, he went on:

"You would have thought that she and I were endowed with wills stronger than any man's power of suggestion, even when drugged with Kingo. You would have believed this, and rightly so, given the conclusions you made about one or both of us—that we had this great power to cast death by simply willing it."

There was a brief pause, then he added simply:

"You are a scientist and I didn't know it, but now, I know that you are not a logical scientist."

Dumont-Warren spoke up with the same attitude:

"Monsieur Zabad Khan, don't forget that even the greatest of scientists don't always act in a purely logical manner. But I'm a businessman and I make it a point to always be logical. Everything we've seen and heard in this room has definitely changed what I believed."

When it was obvious that Dumont-Warren had finished talking, Zabad Khan was polite enough to ask

"And what did you believe?"

The answer was direct.

"That you, Madame Alzac and you, or just you, are the original or the reflecting mirror of the murderous will that has already killed eighteen times. This power exists, and you have used it! You can deny it, or say nothing, but our belief will not be dismissed or even weakened because of it. In fact, that will only feed it, make it stronger and clearer, and force us into more drastic action. And our first victory is to have you in our power physically."

Yori Koto cut in here, speaking softly:

"Our second victory—by the same logic—from everything I've seen and heard since I first accosted Leone Alzac on the highway up to this very minute, makes me believe that neither she, nor you, can wield this deadly power all the time."

"Well reasoned!" a voice rang out.

Leone Alzac slipped past Dumont-Warren to come and sit in the armchair next to the brahmin. She smiled at Oryas, then turned her beautiful, velvety eyes towards Yori.

"Well reasoned, but now, Messieurs, it's my turn to use logic. And I say that knowing what we know, Zabad Khan and I, about your activities, as well as

189

those of your friends Saint-Clair and Gno Mitang, admitting that we have this power ourselves, or from another, and that it is not permanent, as Yori Koto just said, would be a mistake, since by the same logic, some day, some hour, some minute will come when it is given back..."

She almost giggled and her eyes sparkled.

"So, Messieurs and Mesdemoiselles, what will then become of Saint-Clair and Gno Mitang when that happens? What will become of you all? Corpses! Stiff corpses in a split second!"

Silence loomed over the room for a moment.

Leone narrowed her eyes and said coldly:

"By the same logic, that fateful day might very well be today; the hour, the one we are living through; and the minute could be any passing by. Are you prepared? Can you protect yourselves? Are you ready to kill us both, if we can kill you in seconds?"

It was both undeniable and unacceptable, reasonable and insane. All the madness of the adventure—unfortunately all too real—unveiled itself in the minds of the six people standing before their two mysterious and terrifying prisoners, both sitting casually in their comfortable armchairs.

It was an alarming dilemma: either kill this strong and healthy young woman and man, right here, in cold blood, or live with the constant threat of sudden death at any time and any place. Was this real? Was it even believable?

Yes, it was, said the Eighteen deaths, the "Poor things" of Leone Alzac, the story of George Medwin by Garnoch, the emotion and tears of his widow, also a bereaved daughter and sister; but also the resistance of Leone and Oryas to the powerful Kingo, their whole attitude and everything she had just said...

Yes, of course, the situation was very real. Either Leone and the brahmin would be killed or many people, from Saint-Clair to humble Isha, would live in continual danger of being suddenly struck down.

Then, there was an idea too dizzying just to imagine: the notion that a human being or two, or even a small group, could reduce the entire human race to slavery after making a show of purging or punishing a dozen dictators, kings, generals and ringleaders...

There was a long silence weighed down by dark thoughts with flashes of illumination. But in the end, common sense prevailed. The typically French common sense, elegance and courage! It was Dumont-Warren who spoke first:

"Before leaving Paris, I paid a visit to a man who none of you know. I handed him a notebook. This notebook is my diary of the year. Day by day, I wrote down all the details of the case of the Eighteen deaths. Day by day, up to last night; yesterday was my last entry, about Mr. Garnoch and I coming here, the whys and wherefores... Listen up, Madame Alzac, and you, Monsieur Zabad Khan, I will return to Paris tomorrow morning and every evening, I will continue writing my diary, and those pages, in a secret but guaranteed way, will join the others in that bound notebook. When I die, if my death is in the least suspect…"

Here he stopped and a smile crossed his lips. With a casual wave of his hand, he continued:

"I've said enough."

Then with a kind of detached skepticism he went on:

"Madame, that you avenged your husband against Lord Stonewell and your mother and sister against Eduardo Prim is between you and your conscience. But, Monsieur, that you tried out your power to execute fourteen prisoners, that, for money, you got rid of Mrs. MacCross' bothersome gigolo, and finally that you murdered a poor, innocent man just to escape detection… All that shall end up in the French courts."

He stopped again and made an unexpected move. He grabbed Florence de Salsis around the waist and kept her on his left while his right hand reached out and pulled Fabienne Blancat closer. He embraced the two girls like a father and spoke forcefully but gently at the same time:

"But when it comes to these two young ladies, both of them in love and looking forward to a bright future, and also these two young men, who love life, on whom life is smiling, and finally this globetrotting scientist who, like me, is enjoying the fruits of a healthy, active life, an honorable and honored life… Well, the six of us here, only one of whom can shoot you with a Browning, we, by unspoken agreement, will let you live. And we, too, will live with this threat of sudden death that your own continued existence presents to us… All six of us."

Suddenly he pushed the girls away, stepped forward and his voice turned hard:

"But watch out! If Monsieur Saint-Clair or Marquis Gno Mitang were to die suspiciously… or if any great and useful Frenchman dies… or if an influential Englishman promoting our alliance dies… or if… but you get my meaning, Monsieur Zabad Khan. Right now, I'm talking only to you. If anyone who should live dies, you, Zabad Khan, will be struck down by a hand you do not know, have never seen, and can never locate. And Madame Alzac, by logical extension, will be brought down with you. Now, I'm sure I've said all that needs to be said. But you two, do you have anything else to say?"

Leone Alzac and Zabad Khan had listened attentively, with obvious, perhaps *lively* interest, and did not hide their feelings behind an impassive façade, which would have fooled nobody. However strong their mind and occult powers were, she was a woman and he a man, and not some alien creatures made from some unknown, inhuman substance.

When Dumont-Warren had finished talking and asked that question, Leone and Oryas did not need to look at each other—they were immediately and tacitly in perfect agreement. Both of them, at the same time and in the same tone of voice, answered coldly:

"No."

"As you wish," Dumont-Warren spat out.

He made a gesture that everyone understood and they left the room, which Isha locked behind them.

They went downstairs and when they entered the study, Jacques Fitou sounded surprisingly like a young kid when he said:

"You were great, boss! But I think it doesn't matter that the Kingo was basically a flop. Don't forget what Yori Koto told you on the phone on Sunday: the brahmin and his partner are guarding their secret *and the villa its mystery*."

PART FOUR: THE LIVING BUDDHAS

CHAPTER I
The Three Conspirators

The Pope is the spiritual ruler over 450 million Catholics. Under his supreme authority, the administrative and diplomatic services of the Vatican govern a powerful hierarchy of regular and secular priests. Everyone knows or can find out the details of the machinery of this administration, the means and goals of the diplomacy. Books, newspaper articles and even the movies have popularized, or at least spread, this information, and continue to do so every day. The secrets of the Church, when it has secrets, do not remain secret for long from the lay states, although the secular governments do not see much interest in understanding the plans, or following the intrigues, of the Vatican.

The Dalai Lama reigns over 486 million Buddhists. He also holds great prestige among 140 million worshippers of Brahma throughout India. But the administrative and diplomatic services of the Dalai Lama are erratic. The hierarchy is weak and shifting. The secrets, however—and there are secrets aplenty—are totally unknown in the official spheres around the world. The people, even in Asia, venerate only the old, obscure and terrifying legends, or more recent rumors.

Only those hiking boldly and with astounding endurance over the steep mountains of Tibet and across the high plains of Koko Nor, through the endless swampy flatlands of Tsaidam, only those rare, adventurous explorers have known one or two of the secrets of the hermetically sealed world where the true Buddha lives.

The *true* Living Buddha—because there are false ones. Since the death of Gedhun Grub in 1474, there have always been false ones. The Russian Bolsheviks were ignorant and arrogant for thinking that they were dealing with the real Dalai Lama when they entered Outer Mongolia. But many of these alleged "Living Buddhas" do not exploit their temporary power—this illusory, deceptive, fraudulent power is bestowed on them by a special delegation from the true Dalai Lama.

Around two centuries before the establishment of Dalai Lamaism by Gedhun Grub, the explorer Marco Polo was undoubtedly informed of some of the secrets that the great priestess/empress would later claim, and maybe even use in her quest for power. For, during his extraordinary exploration of Asia, Marco Polo had been welcomed honorably by the great Khan of the Mongols,

Kublai Khan, where he stayed for many years performing various important services. Over the centuries, other travelers have seen or glimpsed the quasi-divine light of Dalai Lamaism. When they spoke of it, it was only with a kind of holy fear and very vaguely, often unreliably.

The latest of our age is Ferdinand Ossendowski.[20] On May 17, 1920, he was allowed to talk with the powerful Lama who wrote out the story of a vision that the Living Buddha had had that same day in his private sanctuary and that he had deigned to tell his most intimate lamas. During his travels, Ossendowski was apparently aware of what he called the "mystery of mysteries," and known about or at least suspected the existence of a mysterious, fearfully obscure being whom he dubbed the "King of the World."

Meanwhile, at this moment, during the night of May 10, in a sacred chamber, a noble mouth smiling kindly was saying to the Nyctalope:

"You have named yourself. I do not need to see you anymore. I can paralyze you now, or cast death upon you, as I so choose. So, go ahead and thrust your dagger. I am waiting."

Two big, bright eyes, extraordinarily blue, stared at Leo Saint-Clair, filling him with an emotion he had never felt before. He threw his weapon off to the side.

In another room of the mysterious lamasery of Chong Koum, three other men were sitting like Buddhists in three corners of an equilateral triangle, each side about six feet long, drawn in a mosaic by embedded bars of what looked like slightly tarnished silver. One of the men had a red cushion under him; he was called Alin Sikha, and was a Mongol from Urga; another sat on a yellow cushion and was called Hai Feu, a Chinese from Shanghai; the third sat on a green cushion and was called Om Jahan, a lama from Tengri Nor.

The room was small and round with a low, vaulted ceiling. Magnificent but dark-colored carpets covered the walls all around, from the narrow molding all the way down to the mosaic floor. There was no visible door or window. From the top of the vault hung a chain from which hung a metal cup in which a liquid burned, spreading a soft white light without smoke or scent.

The middle of the triangle was directly under the strange lamp. A big, round platter lay on the floor there. It was full of flasks and urns, apparently of silver, and porcelain cups containing tea leaves, mint and white, red and green

---

[20] Ferdinand Antoni Ossendowski (1876-1945) was a Polish writer, explorer, university professor, and anticommunist political activist. He is best known for his 1921 book, *Beasts, Men and Gods*, the description of his travels in Central Asia. Ossendowski had tried to escape from communist-controlled Siberia by going to India through Mongolia, China and Tibet. While in Mongolia, he met and worked as political advisor for Baron Ungern von Sternberg, a mystic fascinated by the local beliefs. Ossendowski left for Japan and then the US in 1920.

powders. In the very center of the platter was a tripod holding an urn bigger than the others over a small, blue flame.

The three men had been there for hours. They did not speak. They did not take a break to smoke. From time to time, one of them leaned forward, reached out and prepared a cup of mint tea that he sprinkled with various powders. And slowly, taking very small sips, he drank. The rest of the time, he put his hands flat on his thighs, lowered his eyelids and sat perfectly still. When all were sitting like this, they looked like three Buddha statues dressed alike in a kind of white wool robe that left their necks, shoulders, arms and legs bare.

All of a sudden, from an unidentifiable point in the round room, in the air saturated with the scents of mint and tea, there was a sound that lasted a few seconds, then faded away, like the vibration of crystal being struck by a felt hammer.

The man on the red cushion, Alin Sikha, the Mongol from Urga, opened his mouth and spoke quietly, without moving:

"What do we have to fear more? Russian madness or cold, greedy Japanese ambition? We of Mongolia know the Bear from inside out. It thinks it scares us and tames us when it says it is freeing us, but it only makes us smile. If Mongolia shakes its shoulders just once, the Bear will fall down, struggle to get back up, and then run away trembling in fear."

His right hand rose, then fell again, and slapped his bare thigh.

The man on the green cushion, Om Jahan, the lama from Tengri Nor, in a lowered voice, very calm, said slowly:

"As long as the Hindus accept their fate, as long as we give England an ironclad guarantee that our hordes will go by Upper Burma, Bengal and the Punjab without entering their Empire, as long as we ignore the fate of Afghanistan that London wants to annex, the British won't get involved and won't help the Russians."

And with his left hand Om Jahan slapped his thigh.

Then the man on the yellow cushion, Hai Feu, the Chinese from Shanghai, in a soothing voice, said:

"The Japanese dream of enslaving Asia with their cruel modernism. They are now preparing to take over all of China. And their success in Manchukuo[21] turns their hopes into certainties."

He paused, lowered his head, thought for a moment, then lifted his intelligent face that was always mellowed by a courteous smile and continued:

---

[21] Manchukuo, officially the State of Manchuria prior to 1934 and the Empire of (Great) Manchuria after 1934, was a puppet state of the Empire of Japan in Northeast China and Inner Mongolia from 1932 until 1945. It was founded as a republic in 1932 after the Japanese invasion of Manchuria, and in 1934 it became a constitutional monarchy under the de facto control of Japan. It had limited international recognition.

"Japan , therefore, is the only country that can really go to war with China. Alin Sikha, dear brother, you ask what is to be feared more, Russian madness or Japanese ambition? You answered your question yourself. Om Jahan, venerable uncle, you say the British won't get involved and won't help the Russians. It appears that we agree. Japan is the only enemy of China like the tiger is the enemy of all the animals in the forest. Therefore, the strike must be aimed at Japan."

And his two hands rose slowly, fell and slapped his thighs together.

A long silence followed. One, two, three cups of mint tea lightly powdered with white, red and green were poured. One heard small, tasty sips.

When the three transparent cups were finally put down on their transparent saucers, the old lama of Tengri Nor, the "venerable uncle," pronounced the formidable words that the others were expecting.

"We are not unenlightened barbarians. Even less are we civilized people for whom war is but the scientific achievement of mass slaughter, with fire, ruin and cataclysm. To rule over men, we do not need to kill millions of them, pillage their fields, raze their cities to the ground. The people are led by chiefs and they obey whatever these chiefs tell them to do. I am the Master of Death and therefore of Life. It is I who commands from now on. Obey!"

His long, ascetic face was still tense. His eyes sparkled. He nodded. And in a less solemn voice, as if he were speaking kindly of simple, everyday matters, he added:

"The Emperor of Japan, three of his ministers, thirty-four generals and admirals, three presidents of patriotic organizations, two heads of unions, a communist agitator, the secret representative of the Third International—these are the men sentenced to death. After..."

He made a sign with his right hand.

"After we talk with Chiang Kai-shek and his wife," Hai Feu declared.

"After I go to Stalin with my ultimatum," Alin Sikha added with cheerful irony.

There was more silence and more mint tea. Then, finally, they came to the crux of the matter. It was Hai Feu, with a meaningful glance to Alin Sikha, who leaned to the side of Om Jahan and asked the question:

"Venerable uncle, holy lama, all these things we just said as final, after having said them for years less definitively, all these things... Does Jing Pusa know about them?"

The lama nodded and brought his hands to this chest.

"Jing Pusa, the Divine Virgin, the Living Buddha of our age, knows all these things... all... and even more than us, because I told her, and other lamas said the same, adding things, showing her other things over the past year, when they returned from Paris, London, Berlin, Moscow, Nanjing, Beijing, Tokyo..."

Hai Feu pressed harder:

"So, Venerable uncle, what decision has Jing Pusa made?"

This time the answer took some time coming. The lama was hunched over, head lowered, his hands flat on his thighs. The Mongol and the Chinese watched him with intense curiosity, with the kind of patience that would not be satisfied with an evasive response.

And Om Jahan, who was wise, understood this. Suddenly, severely, he spoke:

"The Divine Virgin has made no decision."

Cruel disappointment consumed and darkened the faces of Hai Feu and Alin Sikha. The latter was more a warrior than a diplomat and dared to grumble:

"But it's time, by Krishna!"

Hai Feu, more prudent, said:

"Alin, do not blaspheme!"

Right away, the Mongol got hold of himself, brought his hands to his forehead, bowed deeply and murmured:

"Forgive me, Venerable uncle. It's so hard to forget, for us who are suffering in Urga, how heavy the paw of the Bear is upon us."

"Alin, my friend, it's not a matter of forgetting," said Om Jahan. "And I understand your bitterness."

The lama's voice was so different from the expected scolding that the two others raised their eyebrows, leaned forward and stared at the Tibetan with as much curiosity as surprise. Hai Feu had the feeling that everything said that night was nothing, or rather that it was all just a prelude, a preamble, a game whose goal was to ask the right question. But what question?

The diplomatic Chinese and the Mongol general knew that the Tibetan lama was ambitious and crafty, that throughout all the temples in Asia, he had a reputation for great holiness and deep intellectual and moral power. In fact, he had the title and responsibilities of being the Grand Lama of Tibet, but he never used the title and delegated the responsibilities to a small group of administrators. He professed humility.

As a wandering lama, he had traveled the land for twenty years and, despite appearances, despite looking like an old man, he was only 40 years-old. From the banks of the Manchurian Amur to the estuary of the Ganges, from the mountains of Salansk, which are Russian to the west and Chinese to the east, to the shores of the three seas of China, all the temples, whatever their shapes and sizes, worshipping the trinity of Brahma-Vishnu-Shiva or the multi-ritual unity of Buddha, welcomed him as the holiest of priests, the highest delegate of the Living Buddha who, for the past twenty years, had been Jing Pusa, the Divine Virgin.

What was this formidable man thinking and planning when, instead of scolding the blasphemer, he had said, "I understand your bitterness"? Four little words, but how full of hidden meaning they were! Astonishing words after which he could no longer conceal his thoughts, to himself or to the others.

Quivering but controlling their curiosity and impatience, Alin Sikha and Hai Feu waited for more words to pour out of Om Jahan, eagerly watching his long, hard, bony face with its wide, intelligent brow. They did not see his eyes, which stayed closed.

And more time passed, but none of them made a move to drink more tea. Over their stillness, the pot breathed its round, calm flame. There was absolute silence.

The grand lama raised his right hand just a little, holding it in the air briefly, then putting it quietly back on his thigh.

"Master, O Master, we are listening to you."

And Om Jahan spoke. His voice was low and slow, giving life to words only after considering, weighing and repeating them over and over to himself alone. He said:

"The Divine Virgin has found the secret that no Living Buddha since Gedhun Grub has discovered. Jing Pusa, a woman, is the Master of Death, just like the first female Living Buddha. She has the power to paralyze every living, breathing creature, man and animal. Yes, I see what you're thinking: We know this. But what you don't know is that Jing Pusa doesn't want to be the Master of Death. She's refusing to use the supreme power. She's afraid of regenerating the world. She's so afraid that she won't act. Worse, she's preparing for the Night of Oblivion."

"Ah!" the Mongol and Chinese exclaimed together, horrified and fuming.

Silence fell over them again. However, Om Jahan had not expressed all his deep thoughts. His friends were sure of this. They waited for the lama to continue. Shortly he did.

"The secret was rediscovered by Jing Pusa in the 77th book of the Rig Veda. She hid it in the third sanctuary of the underground world. This world, as you know, is guarded by the 333 cohorts of Servants under the command of the 33 Brahmins of the Sacrifice. And only the Living Buddha, who in this age is the Divine Virgin, can enter its sanctuaries... Only the Living Buddha, accompanied by a lama if he's too young or too sick to walk, can go there. Now, I repeat, Jing Pusa has clearly refused in my presence to use this extraordinary power to regenerate the world. She has even threatened, if I press her too hard, to sink our shrine into the the Night of Oblivion. Therefore, we can't count on the supreme weapon to give us the universal victory we've been dreaming of... I can tell you with a sickened heart, my brothers, that we have to give up the plans for our domination of the world."

He stopped talking. His dilated eyes caught the fervent looks in the Mongol and Chinese. Then, quietly, very quietly, he added:

"Unless..."

With sweat glistening on his forehead, leaning forward, Alin Sikha panted: "Unless...?"

More silence, in which these words of Hai Feu, barely audible, seemed to sizzle.

"Master, tell us, is there the seed of a Living Buddha in Lhasa?"

The Grand Lama answered in the same tone:>

"Better than a seed."

"Oh, a sprout?"

"Better than a sprout!"

"What then?"

Leaning forward so close to the tripod that their pale, sweating foreheads were almost touching it, communicating in thoughts more than words, speaking with their eyes more than their mouths, all three of them trembled. And their nervous hands clutched their thighs, dug their nails into the flesh.

"What then?" the Chinese repeated.

"A child?" the Mongol panted.

Om Jahan raised his arms, put his left hand on Alin Sikha's shoulder and his right on Hai Feu's long neck, and barked:

"Yes!"

The excitement had climaxed. Abruptly, they simmered down. The lama's hands fell away and he straightened up on the green cushion. Hai Feu and Alin Sikha on the yellow and red cushions went back into their former calm and balanced position. Soon their hands reached out for the mint tea. One, two, three cups.

After they had drunk, put the cups back on their saucers and their hands were back on their thighs, the three conspirators looked at each another. Now their faces were back to normal without the forced indifference. Om Jahan looked pitilessly determined; Hai Feu, the diplomat, was pensive and shrewd; Alin Sikha, the Mongol general, showed impatience.

Alin spoke first in a sharp voice, loud and harsh, which was normal for him:

"Enough with the cautious words. Nobody in the world knows that we're here together. No eye can see us. No ear can hear us. And each of us knows that we all want the same thing. So, let's be clear. What do we want? We want this: to replace Jing Pusa with the child. Isn't that right?"

"Yes," Om Jahan answered without hesitation.

"That's it exactly," Hai Feu said clearly.

"So," Alin Sikha went on, "what is the best way? Poison?"

"No!" the lama protested. "Everything the Divine Virgin eats and drinks is prepared privately by the priests of the first sanctuary."

"Are they incorruptible?" the Chinese wondered aloud.

"They are," the lama replied.

"So, no poison in the food," Hai Feu proposed, "but what about the air she breathes?"

"No. She doesn't leave the Temple of Sleep and entry is forbidden to all, including me, by her paralyzing power. Only someone whose presence in the region is unknown to her could breach the impassable barrier. But what man coming from afar could avoid the watchers and the guards, the secret spies and the prowling servants, and all the lamas roaming all over the three sanctuaries? How would we choose a man to make him into the assassin of a girl who is more ravishing than the goddess Kali in her youth? No, this won't work..."

"The sword!" Alin Sikha growled. "The sword, I tell you!"

"How? When?" the lama asked.

"Jing Pusa will be seeing us on the day of the seventh star, exactly sixteen days from tomorrow. It's a ritual which can't be cancelled or postponed for anything, even if the Divine Virgin herself were in the throes of death. I say we can do it during the ritual. Yes, I know, there'll be seven priests watching, but who cares! We'll ask the Divine Virgin to finally become the Living Buddha, the incarnation of Krishna who ought to awaken the true nature of the divinity by dominating all of humanity. You have already asked this, Om Jahan. Jing Pusa will reject it. You'll stand up and accuse her of being unworthy of the mission imposed on the Living Buddha of this age. However she reacts, Hai Feu will back you up and then—the sword!"

A heavy silence followed. Then Om Jahan asked:

"Who will strike?"

"Me!" Alin Sikha said, shaking as he pounded his chest with his fists.

"Before you can pull your weapon, the Divine Virgin will kill you," said Om Jahan.

"No," the Mongol shot back.

"Why not?"

"You, venerable uncle, but also Hai Feu, will keep her busy talking. You can pace around so that she'll be looking to her right. In the meantime, I, the dumb soldier who hasn't said a word, shall proceed in the opposite direction as if to get away from the terrible argument. And when the Divine Virgin isn't looking, I'll jump on her, from her left side, and thrust the sword. I know how to use a sword. I've never missed the heart and I won't miss this one."

The warrior was quiet and Hai Feu spoke softly:

"The simplest acts are often best and most effective. My brother Alin Sikha speaks wisely, even in anger. Our disagreement can set up a situation favorable to an attack that will basically be an act of justice since the Divine Virgin will be punished for refusing to do her duty as the Master of Death. The seven priests will be confused and upset by your arguments and my logical explanations of the present state of the powerful organizations and nations of the earth. Before they can sound the alarm, if they think of it, won't your own lamas come rushing in? Because, with Jing Pusa dead, the supreme will that kills and paralyzes won't be working."

The Chinese stopped talking. Neither of his accomplices objected. Their simple plan was therefore feasible. Feeling confident about this, Hai Feu went on in the same gentle voice:

"Then there are the 33 brahmins of the sacrifice and the 333 cohorts of servants. What do you think about them, venerable uncle?"

"The servants are stupid slaves who obey whoever is their master," Om Jahan replied.

"Yes, but the master right now is the chief, and the chiefs of each cohorts obey the Daï Brahmin, who receives orders directly from the Living Buddha. So, if she died—was killed—what would the Daï Brahmin do? Is he a friend of yours, Om Jahan?"

"No," the grand lama answered darkly.

"So?"

"I've thought of that, Hai Feu."

"What have you come up with, venerable uncle?"

"Yes!" Alin Sikha bellowed in support.

But Om Jahan was in no hurry to satisfy their curiosity. He took his time purely as a display of that supreme authority that he was hoping to use soon in the name of the new baby Dalai Lama. A minute of silence passed before he answered:

"I'll give the Daï Brahmin a poison that will kill him without fail within an hour. So, before seeing the ritual tomorrow, I'll have the first meal of the day with him."

"Vishnu be praised!" howled the Mongol general whose feverish excitement was burning brighter.

But Hai Feu was not forgetting any detail.

"What about the child who's supposed to be proclaimed the Living Buddha when the news of Jing Pusa's death is announced, for official recognition of this child's divinity, will the Daï Lama of Lhasa agree to it? You know that, according to the rites…"

Om Jahan raised his hand to interrupt the Chinese diplomat. Letting a smile cross his lips for the first time the grand lama replied:

"The Daï Lama is the child's father. Since the premature death of the Living Buddha is always planned for, just like any possible eventuality, the Daï Lama, following the rites, has named me as the child's guardian until he comes of age."

"Ah-ha!" Alin Sikha was no longer trying to control himself. "You hadn't told us!"

Hai Feu was more subtle.

"All things at the right time. Since the time has come, venerable uncle, you have spoken. Thank you. And so, you will be the child's guardian and…" he paused before pronouncing very emphatically, "…the new Master of Death!"

"Yes!" the grand lama said majestically. "With the baby Living Buddha in my arms, I'll cross the three sacred thresholds. Escorted by the new Daï Brahmin, whom I shall appoint according to the rites, I'll greet the 33 brahmins of the sacrifice. Carrying the infant, I'll walk over the flowers scattered by the virgin girls of the servants. And I'll go into the underground world. Then, I alone, with the child in my arms, will enter the three arcane sanctuaries, the last of which holds the 77th book of the Rig Veda that contains the secret—the formula of death and paralysis!

"We have lots of time to prepare for the ritual, which will be Jing Pusa's last, starting in sixteen days. Of course, without saying anything that might give us away, we'll work on the minds of my lamas and their novices, on your Mongol soldiers, Alin Sikha, and on your Chinese emissaries, Hai Feu, so that the room will be opened when one of us cries out 'The living soul has departed the body of Jing Pusa'..."

Om Jahan was panting a little as he said this. What silence now fell over the three men dizzy with omnipotence! One of them, however, never strayed far from practical realities. When he figured that the silence had lasted long enough, he dared speak, but in more humble tones:

"Om Jahan, venerable uncle, master... For centuries and in the hands of several Dalai Lamas who, I imagine, read and reread the 77th book of the Rig Veda, it did not give up its secret until it was rediscovered by Gedhun Grub. The new Living Buddha has to be a woman for the secret to be revealed. Is this just a legend? Is it true that the secret can only be mastered by a woman? And you..."

The lama raised his hand and stopped the Chinese from finishing his thought. Then Hai Feu the diplomat and Alin Sikha the soldier were witness to a miracle—a miracle that had nothing supernatural or divine about it.

"I?" Om Jahan exclaimed. "Watch!"

What a voice! These three words came out in a voice that was not the lama's usual hoarse, hushed murmurs, but in a higher, clear, almost melodic tone.

And Om Jahan jumped up and undressed! His robe, a big, white, woolen toga that covered his whole body, was unhooked and unwrapped and fell from his body. He stood there proudly, completely naked.

The body of a woman—slender and strong, tall and muscular, but voluptuously curvy with delicately brown skin that the suspended flame turned golden, while shining on her shapely hips, her rounded breasts, and the charming slope of her shoulders. But the face and neck, the arms and hands, the legs and feet looked weirdly masculine and mature.

Om Jahan simply bent forward, took the jug of warm water and, on the mosaic tiles, washed her limbs, rubbed them with her robe and a kind of yellowish film peeled off her skin, falling in pieces to reveal the woman beneath.

Om Jahan was a woman around 25 years-old, well bred, intensely, fiercely beautiful, imperious and imperial!

With modesty in her noble eyes, her face, and the sculptural nudity of her body, she spoke softly but firmly:

"Don't you believe, Hai Feu, that a third woman will find what two other women found?"

Together, the Chinese and the Mongol bowed down with their faces in their open palms between their knees. Maybe in the rush of emotions they did not hear well when Om Jahan went on:

"The venerable uncle died two years ago in Nanjing. I am his daughter. I went with him everywhere among his disciples. He himself was preparing for the future. He was wise and learned. He made me look like him, taught me to speak like him, imitate his gestures. He told me, 'If Jing Pusa obeys you, you will rule over the world in her name. If she doesn't, you will replace her with a boy who will one day become the Dalai Lama. Carrying the infant Living Buddha, because Om Jahan is appointed to do so, you will enter the third sanctuary.' That is what my father said. Now, I'll remain Om Jahan, the holy protector, and I shall be the third woman to decipher the mysteries of the 77th book of the Rig Veda!"

CHAPTER II
A Sleeping Man

The true Living Buddha does not die. This means that his soul is always the same. Sometimes it passes into the body of a newborn infant or else it takes the place of a soul in someone already born, male or female. The reincarnation of the soul is proclaimed in the grand monastery of Lhasa by the Tashi Lama, or the Dai Lama sent from Chong Koum when the Dalai Lama is physically dead. The probable receptacles of the liberated soul are children always numbering 77 and less than 17 years-old. There are 76 boys and one girl. It is by the inspiration of the Brahma-Buddhist trinity and during a seven-hour meditation session that the high priest, called the Tashi Lama, and the Dai Lama *see* the child chosen for the incarnation of the immortal soul of the Living Buddha.

Such is the dogma behind the many rites, some secret, others public and formal. But like all dogmas, this one was created by men and in particular circumstances. The unchangeable rites were often used to hide the fact that the divine inspiration has been replaced by intrigue ruled by human passions.

Now, Leo Saint-Clair knew all this. He was not too surprised, therefore, to see not a man a woman standing before him, tattooed between her eyebrows with the thrice holy sign of the Living Buddha—the symbolic lotus in the middle of a seven-pointed star.

After Saint-Clair had jumped back and to the side while his right arm had sent the sword clattering over the paving stones, the "young man" in the crimson robe kept sitting there and staring at the Nyctalope with two big, bright eyes that were extraordinarily blue...

Then, this "young man" finally stood up and took three slow steps forward, and Saint-Clair could finally see that the robe was tighter around the breasts and hips of a woman. Moreover, now that the beautiful face had been fully awakened from sleep, there was no longer any doubt about it: the Living Buddha was a woman—a young woman.

The Nyctalope quickly got over his surprise. Still, he was so deeply affected by the revelation that he did not hear himself muttering:

"A young woman!"

But other surprises and other emotions lay in wait. The first was that this strange, tattooed creature answered him in French while her lovely, noble lips kept a charming smile:

"Yes, a young woman. The Living Buddha is a young woman. I am aware that you know many things, Monsieur Saint-Clair, because your reputation has reached my ears. But you did not know this. And you do not know my name, the name of the true Living Buddha. Only the lamas initiated into the seventh degree know it. But you can learn it from me—my name is Jing Pusa."

"Oh," Saint-Clair let slip out, "the Divine Virgin..."

"How do you know that?" she said with amused surprise. "So, you did know the name."

"My friend Gno Mitang..." he murmured. "He believes in an old legend..."

"That dates back to Gedhun Grub. She had a daughter called that, and I am her reincarnation," Jing Pusa said, solemnly this time.

Saint-Clair did not respond.

In the magnificent chamber, the mysterious blue flame flickered in the air a few inches above the conch sitting on a slender, tall tripod. It lit up three quarters of the scarlet robe, the bare face and the narrow scarlet cap topped by three golden rings on top of each another.

The Nyctalope felt his whole being filled with an immense, powerful joy that would have been blissful if he could have kept a cool head, a clear mind and his usual self-control. But of course, only the most banal, commonplace ideas came to mind, the kind that any man would have about any woman who suddenly started speaking his language. With a polite smile and in a casual voice he simply asked:

"How do you know French?"

He was pleased to hear the young woman laugh—the warm, open laugh of an amused girl—a laugh that was followed by an answer as simple as the question:

"Of course, you noticed. It's not a mystery, and my knowledge of other languages has nothing very original or exciting about it. Besides Chinese and the Tibetan dialects, I speak French, English and Russian. Until I was 14, I was raised in the grand monastery in Lhasa. The main languages of the world are taught there. There are teachers and many students. Most teachers, lamas of various ranks, have resided in the countries of which they teach the language. The the lama teacher of French, Louis de Favart, was born in Angoulême of Lutheran parents. He has a PhD from the Sorbonne University. During a research trip in India, he met one of our grand lamas. They conversed for weeks. And he agreed to join the grand monastery at Lhasa where he still lives as a lama of the seventh degree. You know, Monsieur, that we share a gift for languages. Doesn't your friend Gno Mitang speak close to a dozen? Oh, there you are surprised again. Don't be. How could I not know the reputation of Marquis Gno Mitang, advisor to the Emperor of Japan. A Japan that... but no! No politics. I won't say a word. Haven't I said enough already? I'm a chatterbox, aren't I? Chatty like a giddy French schoolgirl!"

Again, he heard that warm and cheery laugh, so sweet and musical and full of joy. Trying to keep his mind focused, the Nyctalope was astonished. And he thought:

The Living Buddha, the most tremendous and precious power of our age, the Master of Death, the keeper of the occult power that is the greatest power ever held by man is a young woman, a delightful girl who speaks my language with a funny accent, who laughs and makes jokes!

But his eyes, the eyes of a man waiting and watching for the battle, examined the strange room in all its luxurious magnificence with its wall hangings, mosaics, carpets, cushions, furs, and the single tripod under the waving blue flame, the only source of light but that filled the whole, vast, domed space.

They also saw an ordinary woman despite the appearance of holiness created by her robe and hat with its tiara of three golden rings, and an ordinary human face, despite its stamp of sanctity that turned hermetic and distant when her mouth closed in silence.

After some puzzlement, the Nyctalope clasped a trembling hand to his forehead and spoke more to himself than to the unsettling person before him:

"So, it's all possible, my God!"

Suddenly, he felt exhausted. The great joy, the feeling of power, the male pride in coming face to face with the mystery incarnate—all this just vanished. He was aware of nothing but his mental confusion, his nervous exhaustion, his physical weakness. There had been so many days of constant action and nights of deep reflection! The mental and physical efforts he had been subjected to during the past 48 hours now piled up... For the first time in his life, Saint-Clair did not resist that sinking feeling of depression. Moreover, he had the strong impression that, if he did not give in, something in his body would break and make him go crazy—or die. So he gave in...

He took two hesitant steps forward and dropped to his knees on the pile of white furs. Then he fell on his elbows, his chest, and buried his face in his hands, weeping and trembling.

This was how Jing Pusa, the Living Buddha and Divine Virgin, first saw a man agree on his own to be nothing but a man before her.

After his fit of depression, Saint-Clair wiped away his tears, took deep breaths and stood up. He faced Jing Pusa who was standing up, watching him without moving or saying a word. With all his experience, he guessed some of what she was thinking and he spoke gravely but gently:

"After your childhood, you have surely known only worshipful priests, flattering advisors, devout disciples, and slaves. You see in me a man suffering a moment of exhaustion, giving in to his emotions, but who has now calmed down, and is already feeling stronger and ready to keep moving forward... Jing Pusa, I have no doubt that you are the true Living Buddha. From the moment I saw you sleeping here, I've known it, but that miraculous power that is said to reside within you—is it real?"

She did not balk or avoid the question. With the same gentle gravity, she relied:

"In Lhasa, Louis de Favart often quoted the great English chemist Michael Faraday, which your own Villiers de l'Isle-Adam used in one of his stories...[22] You're smiling? I think I know why. Being who I am in a lamasery in Chong Koum, quoting Villiers..."

"That's right," Saint-Clair broke in. "It is unexpected, to say the least."

"Oh, I have plenty more surprises in store for you. What caused this one is really just a trifle. Anyway, Faraday said: *Nothing is too wonderful to be true, if it be consistent with the laws of nature, and in such things as these, experiment is the best test of such consistency.*[23] *But one must know ALL the laws of nature to determine whether or not the phenomenon is consistent. And only with the natural laws that men are ignorant of, could one create a universe.* In theory, therefore, let's say that I, the heir of two thousand years of occult knowledge, know some laws of nature that humanity still does not..."

"I'll do more than say it," Saint-Clair said, "I accept it and..."

"No!" Jing Pusa cut him off. "No, don't say anything else. We have plenty of time and I need to think in silence. If I'm a wonder to you, you are also a wonder to me. You, the first man... alone, coming here, this far, all the way to me... Your coming here, working against me, the fact that you're still alive, that I'm listening and talking to you—aren't all these strange and unheard of things miracles? I need to think in silence, I tell you. And you, human that you are, you need to sleep. I could order you to. I wouldn't even have to will it. I could just say, 'Saint-Clair, please, lie down and go to sleep.'"

She had a lovely, almost shy smile.

She pointed to the luscious bed of white furs. Saint-Clair had the audacity to put three fingers under that long, slender hand and raise it to his lips, which leaned forward to kiss it lightly. But then the mysterious will obviously entered him because he staggered and then dropped onto the furs. And then, he was nothing but a sleeping man.

---

[22] *L'Eve Future* [Future Eve] (1886).
[23] In his diary, March 1849. The rest of the quote appears to be made up.

CHAPTER III
The Message from Paris

Meanwhile, under the star-studded sky shining fantastically upon the earth, in the glacial cold that he fought off by walking as fast as possible, the Mongol Timor was struggling out of the chaos of rocks and heading down the long ledge toward Lake Chong Koum.

As Saint-Clair had ordered before marching down to the lamasery with Archibald Brown, he was supposed to go to the Four Tent and there have a rest. Then he would return to the refuge and give Vitto the letter that his boss had written for him.

While making his way through the dark chaos, Timor lit his route with his flashlight. In the gullies and alleys of the mountain, it posed no risk of being seen by any would-be sentinel on the walls of the lamasery.

When he arrived on the ledge, out of the shadows, the light from the stars was enough, so he legged it like a long-distance runner. At the beach of the Four Tents, he went to the back of the grotto, made a fire with dried yak dung, of which there was plenty, and lied down under the blanket he had carried rolled up. At daybreak, he ate the rest of his provisions, drank some cold coffee and got back on the road.

That same evening, tired but content, he arrived at the refuge and shouted before the security barrier. Vitto was in the plane and came running out. The two men hugged like brothers. Right away, without any further explanations, the Mongol gave the Corsican the Nyctalope's letter. It was short and to the point. Vitto read it, first to himself, then aloud:

Vitto, my friend, get Timor to tell you everything he saw. Wait for 15 days for word from either Gno Mitang, I, Soca or Gissa. If nothing comes, that will mean that we're dead or being held prisoner. In this case, return to Paris and contact M. Dumont-Warren and ask him to do everything possible for the governments of France and Japan to open diplomatic channels in an attempt to find us.

There is another possibility: you may receive a very important radio message from Paris. If you judge it necessary for me know about it, fly over the lamasery for 15 minutes as low as possible and drop the message inside a metal container on the esplanade. The drop point will have to be within 500 yards of the big archway in the outer wall. Then fly around at 1500 feet. If you see someone crouch down to read the message, you can land on said esplanade as close as possible to him. If the person reading the message stays standing up, you should keep flying around. If you don't see anyone you recognize after 15 minutes, return to Paris.

I won't hide the fact that, as soon as the plane is in sight of the lamasery, your and Timor's lives will be in danger. But you're used to danger and I think Timor will be just as hardy. Vitto, my friend, good luck. Saint-Clair.

"Very well," Vitto folded up the paper. He turned to Timor and said: "You're tired. Go drink some hot chocolate. I made some for myself but I can make another. Right after that, naptime. Tomorrow, you'll be rested and clear-headed and you can tell me all about your adventures."

"I'm not tired..." the brave Mongol wanted to protest.

"No, no, not a word. Go inside the plane. In ten minutes or so, I want to see you sleeping."

The next day, after Timor had told him about their encounter with Archibald Brown and all the strange things that had followed, Vitto responded with a few chosen cuss words and curses. After letting loose like that, he could speak more calmly because he was naturally soft-spoken.

"Well, that's a story anyone would find hard to believe. But since it's true, I must believe it! The Nyctalope has seen things like this before—not as... extraordinary, perhaps, but just as dangerous. Yet, he's pulled through every time, and us with him. So, my good man, we shall follow his instructions. First, since he asked us to wait, we'll wait. But I hope we'll see the boss or get some news from him or a radio message from Paris before the fifteen days are up."

With respect to a radio message, everything had been arranged on Thursday, April 29, during a meeting at Blingy with Dumont-Warren. An ingenious code had been agreed upon, along with strict procedures.

The crucial point was that any messages from Paris would be sent between noon and 1 p.m. on any day, and from the expedition between 9 and 10 a.m. Every message from Paris would start with a special code so the receiver could identify it without fail. The expedition on board the Zig would only listen during the first two hours of the afternoon because it took time for a normal radio message to travel halfway around the world. If Paris got no answer the next morning, the message would be sent again.

The daily watch had been kept in the Zig rather liberally, meaning the radio was on every day through the whole afternoon. But no message had come through so far.

Beginning on May 10 at nightfall, the wait in the refuge, monotonous but patient, was organized by Vitto and Timor along a schedule that left no room for laziness, no possibility of boredom. The roster of tasks included: meticulous maintenance of the airplane and all the machines; preparing meals; hunting yaks, which were the antelopes of Tibet, or birds, mostly larks, which came out in flocks with the sun when the winds died down; listening duty on the radio, always by the Corsican; alternating sleep time so that one of them would always be on watch; keeping the fire lit in the back of the tent to save fuel... Their time was spent full of activities, busy but calm.

Ten days went by like this.

That the two men's anxiety grew daily was natural, but neither of them said a word or gave the slightest hint of it. And yet, the fifteen-days deadline was already two-thirds gone.

Being more aggressive and less prone to silent fatalism than Timor, on the morning of May 20, Vitto felt that swearing out loud and kicking things around was no longer enough to relieve his anxiety. Pretending to be in a good mood was a role he could not play. So, on that morning, in order to swear and complain and hit whatever he wanted, he decided to go hunting. He got back to the refuge at noon without a catch. He had emptied his gun shooting furiously at all kinds of things, but had hit nothing.

Timor understood and just smiled. With his usual serenity, he served the lunch he had prepared. Then it was time to turn to the radio—their mess hall was also the radio room in the plane.

Sounds constantly came through the headphones from the nearest station at Lan Chou, the busiest relay between Calcutta and all of Eastern China and Japan. It also served Irkutsk and Lahore. Vitto listened gloomily, silently, eating slowly though he was barely hungry, even after all his physical activity.

Then, all of a sudden, he threw out a fist and spit out his food, shouting:

"Timor! The call!" He started laughing heartily. "Finally, the message from Paris!"

Entirely immersed in his duty, passionately but with perfect clarity, Vitto started recording the message. It took some minutes. When he was finished, his forehead and nose were dripping with sweat.

"A glass of water," he yelled, impatient to know what it said.

It was his duty to understand the importance of the message that would determine their action, but it was in code, so first he had to translate it into clear French!

Using Hebrew, Greek and Latin characters, the code was simple for anyone in possession of the key created by Dumont-Warren in the quiet solitude of his study. Timor had learned it from Saint-Clair and could use it as easily as Vitto. The two men worked together and the words were deciphered, eagerly at first, soon joyously, and at the end, with clapping, hooting and bravos!

Letter by letter in the three languages, the code revealed its secret. Here is what Vitto and Timor scratched on their piece of paper:

Are certain Leone Alzac and Oryas Zabad Khan guilty. We attack their hideout after tomorrow. Sure to capture them. Stay on radio. D-W.

They read these lines over and over again. The Mongol was smiling and calm:

"Vitto, what do you think?" he asked.

210

"We wait, damn it! If this message is only number 1, then number 2 should be coming soon, certainly before our deadline is up. So, we wait for message number 2 and then will fly off to the lamasery."

"Unless the boss sends news and new orders," Timor added.

"Yes, that's possible."

The notion that Saint-Clair and Gno Mitang were free and could, even should, send news and instructions before the deadline had gotten stuck in Vitto's mind. It was so firmly embedded that, on May 20, the Corsican said

"It's weird that in ten days the boss hasn't sent a messenger yet."

"It really is," said the Mongol who also thought that the delay was worrisome. But as they did not expect a second radio message before May 24, they spent their days thinking about Saint-Clair and Gno Mitang, while keeping to their radio duty faithfully. However, twenty times a day, one or the other of them climbed up the rocks to the west and glued the binoculars to their eyes, scrutinizing the distance. Nothing appeared in the desert except thick clouds being chased by the glacial, northeasterly winds.

On the evening of May 23, Vitto said:

"Timor, I'm scared."

"Why?"

But the Mongol knew the answer, which he felt too. Still, he asked the question because his partner had been quieter than usual and needed some relief by talking.

"Because I know the boss!" the Corsican barked.

"And?"

"And, my friend, for the Nyctalope and the others not to have found a way to send us some kind of message means there's something wrong."

"You don't know that. The lamasery is not like anywhere else. Life obeys different laws there, different ways and means than any other places in the world. Let's not give up on them yet, Vitto."

"I'm not giving up. I'm scared for him. He's brilliant and strong, sure, but after all, he's just a man."

"Come on, Vitto!" the Mongol sounded friendly but firm. "You think bad thoughts and you talk too much. Go lie down and get some sleep."

The next day, May 24, at 1:17 p.m., another message came through the radio. The decoding was handled calmly by the two men who were so different but, at that moment, a perfect match. It read:

The culprits have been captured and are prisoners in their villa at Saint-Honoré. They seem incapable of doing further harm but are not admitting to anything. Wait for further developments. D-W.

This, which explained nothing, did not please Vitto. The Corsican swore as always when he was suffering either morally or physically.

"May 27! May 27! The deadline set by the boss is in two days!"

"Our duty, however, is to extend it by 48 hours," Timor said. "From what I've heard you say since I joined this expedition, Monsieur Dumont-Warren isn't someone to do or say anything for no good reason. Radio message #3 might be crucial. We can't go flying over the lamasery before getting it, otherwise the first two may not mean much."

"You're right," Vitto grumbled. "We'll wait."

May 24 and 25 went by in the refuge without receiving the anxiously awaited message. The two men now felt anxious, Timor as much as Vitto.

May 25 was the last day before their new deadline. Was the Nyctalope and his companions dead or dying, or utterly unable to get news to them? This question was understandably very important to Vitto and Timor.

That night, neither of them could sleep. They spent the whole next day waiting in front of the radio, but trying not to place too much hope in it. The next night, they were exhausted and dropped off into a deep sleep.

The following day, they waited for message #3 impatiently, almost in anger, both of them trembling with fever. At least, they had not lost their common sense and took a strong dose of quinine.

The message finally came at the appointed time. It read:

Impossible to get confession or any useful information from the culprits. They are imprisoned and watched around the clock. Can't do anything more. What news at your end? We are worried. D-W.

"It's true," Vitto groaned. "I haven't sent a message for 20 days! Let's get to work. Then we'll decide what to do."

"Very well," Timor agreed.

With the help of the code, they encrypted a message first composed in French, a short but thorough summary of the situation including the mystery surrounding everything about Chong Koum. According to the rules, a radio message from the Zig could only be sent to the UNA director between 9 and 10 a.m. Written and coded, the message would have to wait until the next day, May 28.

So far, Vitto and Timor had enough to do to stay busy except for the few hours reserved for a necessary rest. So, under the present circumstances, their decision was made rather quickly. Vitto declared:

"Even though it's three days past the deadline set by the boss, tomorrow we'll act as if it was May 25, meaning that we we'll follow the instructions you brought point by point."

"I agree," the Mongol shot back.

"OK," replied Vitto, about to jump out of the plane, "let's get to work, pal. We have to clear the path in front of the plane so we've got a smooth runway along the lake."

"Right."

"Then we'll run maintenance and get every last drop of gas that's in the tents. Lastly, we'll stick the messages from Paris in a tube, stick that in a bigger tube fitted with a parachute that we'll have to make because we never figured on dropping a message from the Zig."

"Very well, but you forgot something."

"What?"

"The machine gun."

"Oh yeah. One never knows. Maybe a bunch of slugs in the right place at the right time could serve us well. We'll bring it along."

For a couple of minutes, the two men stood facing each other in silence, thinking.

"I think that should do it," Timor said.

"Me too," Vitto replied.

One after the other, they jumped to the ground. They worked calmly. They slept little but well.

On the morning of May 28, they ate a hearty breakfast. Then they made the final preparations for the flight before Vitto sent the message off to Dumont-Warren.

Under the gray clouds bunched together high up in the sky, in the quiet air without a breath of wind, the plane rolled past the cliffs and soared up over the lake. It rose and rose, veered around, and finally shot off to the southeast.

CHAPTER IV
The Messenger of Fate

In the meantime, what had been happening in the lamasery that had kept Vitto and Timor from getting the message that they rightfully should have received?

What had been the actions and reactions of the men and women, individually and together, who were tossed by fate at the same time onto paths that either brought them closer together, or pitted them furiously, lethally, against each other?

Finally, what events had taken place since that night of May 10 when the Nyctalope had succumbed to fatigue, obeying the dictatorial desire of Jing Pusa and fell asleep? While, in another part of the huge lamasery, the fiendish Om Jahan, the wicked Hai Feu and the violent Alin Sikha were plotting the death of the Living Buddha, and already bequeathing her legacy to an unwitting child whom they would use as a weapon, both offensive and defensive, all-powerful in both cases, to accomplish the secret frenzy of their mad desires?

The Nyctalope had slept.

Sitting on the edge of the couch made of thick, white furs, Jing Pusa had watched him sleep, that extraordinary man, the first to have reached her by braving death, the first to consent to be nothing but a man before her, with both his strength, which he did not exploit, and his weakness, which he did not hide.

For a long time, the young woman had watched the man sleeping. She was barely 20 years-old, but she had 2000 years of quasi-divine knowledge.

As for the Nyctalope, he may have been in his 50ies, but he was still young in spirit and healthy of body and mind, active and cultivated, well balanced—youth remained in him. And here, stretched out, having succumbed to the guileless truth of a deep, quiet sleep, his arms not quite touching his body, his head leaning a little on his left shoulder, she could see his long, muscular neck, his virile, harmonious face, and his noble and robust body. His eyes were closed so it was his lips that gave expression to his face, pure in shape and color, lips that smiled slightly... Blessed in rest... Serenity...

"Yes, serenity," Jing Pusa told herself. "But with what dreams? Did this man leave behind a beloved woman in France?"

For Jing Pusa, the Living Buddha, the mysterious and formidable incarnation of an occult divinity, was still a woman, a young woman, a virgin. And watching this man sleeping, she was thinking of love.

No matter how he slept, Saint-Clair was always wide awake, right away, when he woke up. Coming out of his long rest and before opening his eyes, before budging an inch, he knew where he was and remembered why and how he had come here, and how he had fallen asleep. On his right side, between his shoulder and his chest, he felt a light weight. He turned his head and opened his eyes. Jing Pusa was snuggled up against him, also sleeping. He contemplated the beautiful face of the young woman, and he smiled seeing that his coat had been unbuttoned and opened by her so she could put her cheek against the soft fabric of his flannel shirt.

Back to his usual self-control, the Nyctalope enjoyed the moment, the outrageous contrast of the childish abandon and the dangerous personality of the sleeper. But he was also greatly moved by the total trust this showed. And again he got to thinking: *Is it only trust in my sense of honor?*

Leo Saint-Clair had not an ounce of pretentiousness and was less of a Don Juan than anyone, but he was a red-blooded man and he knew by experience that in the mental and physical surrender of a young woman sleeping nearly in the arms of a man, especially a mature man, there is always an element, be it unconscious, of sensuality. So, he felt flooded by her alluring distress, but was able to control it.

He thought, *I could wake her up with a kiss. She is at my mercy.*

But he did not obey this tempting thought. On the contrary! Very gently, he pushed her off, broke the enchanting contact that was so full of unimaginable danger. He managed to free himself without waking the sleeper. He stood up, buttoned up his pea coat and looked around. Nothing had changed in the weird, sumptuous room still lit by the strange soft light of the floating flame.

How long did I sleep? he wondered. *Hours, obviously. It must be daytime, but the light doesn't enter here. The air I'm breathing is pure, though. Their invisible ventilation system is perfect. Yes, I must've been asleep for a long time because I'm thirsty and hungry...*

Another thought crossed his mind and made him laugh:

I'd love to take a bath before breakfast. How weird to think like this, of normal, everyday things in the middle of such an unbelievable situation. No! All the better! It proves that I'm back to myself.

He felt now the very strong and not unreasonable desire for a warm bath followed by a cold shower, then a good rubdown and a little exercise as was usual for him, no matter where he was staying. Automatically he buttoned up his coat and walked up to the circular wall while wondering:

Why wouldn't Jing Pusa have a bathroom here, close to where she sleeps? It'd be logical. Baths and ablutions are regular parts of rituals. And I've seen enough to know that she takes care of herself. Her quasi-divinity would never allow her to neglect her mortal coil. Let's just look around...

All around the room, from the edge of the dome down to the mosaic floor, the wall was covered by dark red curtains with heavy folds. Some of the folds might be hiding an exit. Saint-Clair went slowly around the room feeling the curtains.

Suddenly he found what he was looking for: the fabric separated. The two sides parted, but did not reveal a door.

Saint-Clair now had a very precise idea of the strangeness of the lamasery. He stepped through the curtains, which closed behind him. He put his hand on the wall and pushed. It opened onto darkness.

But for the Nyctalope, there was no night, just as for certain special animals like the lynx and some species of cats. The medical books say that nyctalopy, also called hemeralopia, is a sickness because it is relative, never giving total night vision and diminishing the ability to see in the light. However, in Saint-Clair, because of a congenital phenomenon of his whole visual organ, his nyctalopy was not an infirmity but a normal state that gave him perfect vision in the day and more than enough sight at night.[24]

One can imagine how daring this made Saint-Clair feel. And it is understandable how often this faculty got him out of dangerous scrapes when anyone else would have perished.

Therefore, in the darkness of this new place, Saint-Clair moved forward. He found himself in a kind of rectangular vestibule with four walls. In the four corners were metal poles topped by cups, but no mysterious flames floated above them. From one end of the room to the other was not a plush, woolen rug but a "path" of flexible slats stretched between two long boards.

"Bravo!" he whispered contentedly. "But you only walk over this barefoot."

While he was taking off his shoes, he felt the temperature here was higher than in the "bedroom." He did not think twice. He got completely undressed, laid his clothes on the warm tile in a corner and walked over the slats.

At the end, he pushed the wall, part of which opened like a normal door on hinges, and he stepped through the new threshold.

There still were no lights, but to his great satisfaction, the Nyctalope saw a huge room with three successive vaulted ceilings in the middle of which, between two rows of columns, was a round swimming pool, stirred by a gentle jet of water. The walls, made of subtly faded colored tiles, were furnished with a few big mirrors between which stood the bathroom furniture full of golden instruments, crystal bottles and boxes of precious stones.

---

[24] Nyctalopia and hemeralopia are the rare examples of words that may lead to a good deal of controversy and confusion among doctors of different linguistic backgrounds, because of different definitions and meanings. Nyctalopia is a word from the Greek medical antiquity, defined as "night blindness" or defective dark adaptation. Hemeralopia is a word that originated in the 18th century, which means "day blindness" or visual defect characterized by the inability to see as clearly in bright light as in dim light. Standard English dictionaries also conform with the meanings of nyctalopia and hemeralopia as night blindness and day blindness, respectively. However, the words have been used in an opposite sense by many non-English-speaking doctors.

"Damn," the Nyctalope said aloud after a few minutes of closer examination. "Asian splendor blended with smart and tasteful modernism. Congratulations to the person who designed the vestibule as a dryer and this bathroom-cum-exercise room for a mythologically ancient but pretty modern Venus."

He laughed and plunged into the huge pool that he could see was deep enough on one end to dive headfirst.

An hour later, refreshed and full of energy, even a little perfumed from the pool water, and fully dressed again, Leo Saint-Clair went back to Jing Pusa's bedroom. He was welcomed by a teasing laugh.

"Good morning, Monsieur Saint-Clair. I see from the look on your face that you liked my bathroom. But it's my turn now, isn't it?"

He stood there frozen, stupefied at what was so different from he was expecting to see.

First of all, the light in the room looked so strangely intimate after the bathroom. The flames no longer floated in the air. Instead, daylight filtered in from the domed ceiling, gently spreading through the whole space.

Then he saw the furniture that he had not noticed before: a sculpted, polished chest made of lovely, golden-pink wood, two armchairs of the same wood, low to the ground and piled with cushions, then a low table built of the pretty wood with baskets full of bread, cakes and all kinds of fruit, pots of jam, jugs of wine and liqueur, a crystal pitcher with what was probably water, cups, plates, various utensils, napkins folded into triangles... And finally, Jing Pusa herself!

She was no longer the high priestess dressed in a flowing scarlet robe and a tiara, which had been set aside when she slept next to him. She was no longer the Living Buddha with the face of a beautiful idol...

Now she was a young girl with eyes as blue as seaweed, dressed in light, silk, white pajamas with big red flowers—a beautiful girl who laughed candidly and said playfully:

"It's my turn now, isn't it?"

Then parted the curtain, turned around and before leaving told him:

"You must be dying of hunger. Eat. Don't wait for me. I'll eat when you tell my about your life... Oh, just the last few days since you started on the path that led you here."

The curtain fell back behind her. Saint-Clair thought:

It's true, I didn't tell her anything yesterday. How and why I came here. She didn't ask. Was she just having fun with me? Can she also read minds? Open people's memories like a book? She didn't ask me anything yesterday. She talked about herself a little, but if she didn't read my mind, didn't see my memories, she ought to be very curious to know what I've been doing these last few days. She won't take long to wash up so I'll wait and we can eat together.

But another thought flashed through his mind and he muttered:

"If I wanted to take a stroll, could I? Am I free to leave?"

He thought of Archibald Brown bumping into the invisible wall and heard Gno Mitang describing the same feeling of the obstruction. And he wondered:

Am I still free?

He remembered that, on entering the room the night before, he had seen the flame right in front of him and a little to the left at around a 25-degree angle from the long, high couch of white furs. He got his bearings and pointed.

So, the door I came through is over there.

He went to the section and opened the curtain.

When I pushed open the door, it lifted the curtain with it and that's why nothing stopped me. But I don't see a handle to pull it this way. So, this part of the wall must open both ways by merely pushing.

He put his hands on the wall and pushed. The door opened onto the long, wide, high hallway that he remembered clearly. But when he tried to step through, the same phenomenon occurred which he had been expecting. He could not take another step. An invisible barrier was blocking his whole body and pushing him back, gently but irresistibly.

Twice more he tried to pass through, not hoping to succeed but just to feel that weird sensation that had only been described to him before.

It's like the air is forming an invisible, elastic wall in front of me...

After the third try, he gave up. He stepped back into the room and saw the door close at the same time as the curtain fell back into place. He muttered again:

"Another experiment is needed."

He went to where he had gone looking for a bathroom an hour ago, where Jing Pusa had gone through. She was certainly in the bath now. Was it still open for him?

Again Saint-Clair put his hands on the wall and pushed. The door opened again. But like with the other door, he could not step through. Access to where the girl was bathing was now forbidden.

Knowing what he wanted to know and still set on waiting for Jing Pusa to eat and drink, he went to sit in one of the two armchairs. He started thinking about his situation, and also of Gno Mitang, Soca, Archibald Brown and the Russian Rikevitch and his companions. Of course, he also thought of Vitto and the Zig that Timor would be reaching this very same day. And he made plans and certain decisions.

He was so absorbed that he did not know how long he had waited when Jing Pusa suddenly showed up.

"You waited for me?" her sweet, young voice said. "How heroic!"

Standing before him was the astonishing girl in white pajamas with red flowers, her short, black hair now let loose and curly, with her extraordinary blue eyes, slightly slanted, with her delicate, not too round face, her light golden skin... She stood there smiling.

He stood up.

"Mademoiselle, I…"

Right away, he corrected himself.

"I feel silly saying 'Mademoiselle' to Jing Pusa, the Living Buddha."

"Oh, here with you alone, I'm not the Living Buddha," she laughed.

He dared to interrupt her:

"No, with me alone and here, you're still the Living Buddha, since your strange power is keeping me from leaving."

Jing Pusa's face turned serious and her eyes hardened when she spoke, now without any humor in her voice:

"So, I was right to suppose you would try to take a stroll outside. I wasn't trying to keep you prisoner, I was only trying to keep you safe, to save your life. Beyond the sacred vestibule where no human being can be found without my express authorization, you would have have been able to get to an outside terrace. But as a sacrilege and obviously thinking it was without my knowledge, the servants would have have killed you on the spot. Do you understand?"

"I understand," he nodded. Then, he put a smile on his face and changed his tone, "I still feel silly calling you 'Mademoiselle.'"

They looked at each other. He was almost sure that the golden-brown face blushed and the big, blue eyes were less cold. A little mischievousness sparkled when a smile replaced the worry in her beautiful lips. And her voice changed a little, maybe became a little more hesitant, when next she spoke:

"My name is Jing Pusa… officially. But often, when I talk to myself in the secret recesses of my heart, I don't use this name. I have another, a kind of first name which was once used in China by the queen who gave a thousand virgins to the thousand brahmins of the The Tai monastery in Beijing. This queen was smart and generous. She was called Li…"

Saint-Clair could not help smiling even though he was also deeply moved:

"Well then, I'll call you Li. But I can't forget…"

With a youthful passion that flared up on this spring morning to free her from her countless chains, she said:

"Forget! Yes, forget! In no time at all we'll be called back to our pressing duties, to the struggle of certain feelings against these duties, to the scheming that needs to be rooted out and destroyed, to a weakness that is already precious to me and that I'll have to protect against, to a power that I possess but that I hate to use, to… No, enough! Forget it all, I say! Let's forget!"

What passion! What new beauty, so touching, in this young, troubling girl! Saint-Clair shivered but he was not troubled. Nothing in the world could trouble him now—ever. He pulled himself together, bowed and spoke softly.

"So, I'll forget everything… except that you put your head on my chest to sleep and that I can call you Li."

He did not straighten up until he heard her say with playful formality:

"Would you be kind enough, Monsieur, to sit and eat with me?"

He did not blink but there was a smile in his voice when he replied:

"Oh no, not 'Monsieur,' that's almost as ridiculous as 'Mademoiselle.' I have a first name too."

She blushed and her eyes twitched. But she lowered her eyelids right away. There was a moment of silence. At last, her young voice, a little forced to be fully cheerful, said:

"Well, Leo, sit down and let's have breakfast."

Leo Saint-Clair held back a sigh. He was scared. He was too happy.

The meal was eaten almost completely in silence. One reason was because both of them were very hungry. But also, they were absorbed in their unspoken thoughts and personal feelings that they did not want to reveal or to hide under a façade of small talk. Jing Pusa and Saint-Clair said only a few words about the food, the tasty jams and beautiful pastries. The fruits came from the lamasery greenhouses, she explained. The rest out of kitchen storehouses located in the underground world and used only for her needs.

"The underground world?" Saint-Clair wondered aloud.

"Later! Later!" Jing Pusa replied. "But it's unlikely you'll ever see it. The wines, the liqueurs, the mint tea, even the sugar, everything comes from the lamasery. We have a little universe here that's separate from the rest of the world. It's completely independent... except that machines are excluded, at least those insane ones that are mostly just used to kill—the pride of the West that are sadly being exploited in the East now, Leo... But that's politics, and we're supposed to forget all about it. Let's forget! Try this peach. Tell me if it's as good as your French peaches from Roussillon?"

"Good God, Li, you're so cultured!"

"I've read a lot, Leo. And you forget that my favorite teacher was Monsieur de Favart from the Angoumois."

"That's right."

And he bit into the magnificent, juicy fruit offered by Li. But no peace lasts forever. This one finished when the two of them had had their fill. There was no room even for the wine or liqueur.

"Full?" Li smiled at him.

"Full," Leo smiled back.

She said and did nothing, but at that very moment, the curtain moved aside in a part of the room that the Nyctalope had not been through yet. Two female servants came in, half-dressed in long, pearl-gray scarves worn from shoulder to thigh. They were Hindu from the Southern Deccan plateau where Saint-Clair had once admired the sculptural beauty of the women. Without seeming to see either Jing Pusa or Saint-Clair, they lifted the table and carried it away. One of them came back to take a kind of metal basket from the carpet where it had been tossed, empty, at some point, along with the dirty napkins. Then the two girls came back together with a deep bowl, a tall jug and new towels to wash their hands.

When they had gone for good, Jing Pusa stood up, walked over to the big couch made of the pile of white furs and lay down with her chest and head supported upright by the cushions she arranged for her comfort. Very casually but no longer with the voice or eyes of Li, she spoke softly:

"Leo, sit wherever you'd like, in that armchair which you can bring over here, or on the furs by me. And let's talk. Tell Jing Pusa what she needs to know, meaning what's happened to you, what you've thought and done since you first set out on the path that led you here, where no man has ever set foot before without first falling on their knees and putting their face to the floor in front of me."

Saint-Clair had brought over the armchair that he placed so that he could sit facing Jing Pusa while she had to only turn a little to the left to look at him directly. After sitting down, he started talking.

Without neglecting to name the day and time when necessary, he told her the main points about what had happened, alone or with his friends and others, since that first morning in April when Dumont-Warren had presented the mystery of the first Fourteen deaths, up to last night, May 10, when he had grabbed that mysterious, powerful, magnificent "reclining young man."

After telling her everything, with these last three words, Saint-Clair fell quiet. During his story, which was exciting, even without all the details, he kept his eyes on Jing Pusa. Her body did not move and her face remained unexpressive, supremely calm, gravely attentive. Not once did she blink, but her eyelids were a little less open, a little more slanted around those clear blue eyes that were not cold or empty, but both friendly and inscrutable. As for her beautiful, red lips, full and proud, not once did they part.

Nevertheless, her hands had "answered," so to speak, the extraordinary and emotional tale. In a casual way, which must have been normal in this solitude and idleness, Jing Pusa had first kept her hands crossed just above her firm, round breasts. But as the story had unfolded, her hands would separate, cross again, sometimes stiff, sometimes limp and relaxed, hovering... When Saint-Clair had finished, they laced their fingers together and were again held on her chest.

Her eyes closed, her brow furrowed, and her face became meditative. The Nyctalope waited and watched. It felt like a long time. Finally, she opened her eyes, stared grimly at Saint-Clair, and spoke:

"Leo, I knew nothing of what you just told me. I didn't even know the name of this woman, Leone Alzac, but her companion, I can identify him. He's Oryas Zabad Khan, a brahmin from Benares. He lived here for the past three years and was initiated in the Seventh Degree. The first day of the January moon, he left on a mission to Lhasa. After a while, I found out that he never showed up there. Nobody has seen or heard from him since then. Listen, Leo, to what happened the night before he left, which had been decided the day before."

She paused to consider carefully what to say. Then she went on:

"All the initiates of the Seventh Degree know that I, the second female Living Buddha, rediscovered the divine secret of the will that can stop, paralyze and kill, the secret that no one since Gedhun Grub has been able to discover. I found it in the 77th book of the Rig Veda. I hid that book in the third sanctuary of the underground world. Following the rites, I revealed both the discovery and the book's hiding place to the Dai Lama in Lhasa, who, in turn, told the initiates of the Seventh Degree. Now, Leo, understand that the third sanctuary is guarded by the 333 cohorts of servants under the command of the 33 brahmins of the sacrifice. Only the Living Buddha, alone, can enter the third sanctuary in the underground world..."

There was another pause, a brief silence, and then with slow, dramatic emphasis, she continued:

"Alone—or if he or she is too young or too weak to walk, with a lama to carry him or her."

She made a gesture with her right hand, and a bitter smile, full of pity, crossed her beautiful lips then disappeared.

"Leo, here's what happened the night before Oryas Zabad Khan left on his mission. I wanted to give him a document requested by the Dai Lama of Lhasa. The manuscript was stored, like many others, in one of the chests in the library that makes up part of the first sanctuary. Oryas went with me into the section of the underground world which he was permitted to enter. Before entering the sanctuary, he was supposed to wait for me while I went alone to fetch the document. Now, I'm a woman. Although I'm in perfect health, I'm not exempt from particular frailties inherent to women. Before crossing the sacred threshold, I got dizzy. Until now, I thought it was because of my physical changes after puberty. But while you were talking just now, I changed my mind. Whatever it was, I fainted. When I woke up, the first thing I noticed was that I was in the arms of Oryas Zabad Khan, who was carrying me into the first sanctuary. Using the sacred law, he had been able to enter the forbidden area because of my fainting. By carrying me, he could pass through and neither the lamas nor the servants on guard, nor my own will, could stop him..."

Once again, Jing Pusa paused. Her face was full of emotion; her eyes flashed with anger; her voice shook when she resumed heatedly:

"But, Leo, when you told your story, I remembered everything. There was one thing I noticed instinctively but that had become immediately buried in my subconscious. I noticed that, while carrying me, Oryas was not going toward the back of the first sanctuary but was coming back from it. Now I know, and you also know, because you've gathered all the elements of the truth, that, by popular belief, the secret of the murderous will can only be understood by a woman This is based on the fact that no male Living Buddha has ever seemed to possess such power. Now, we know that the legend is wrong since Oryas does have it. I never worried about his intrusion in the first sanctuary, which we know now reached all the way to the third sanctuary, to the contents of the 77th book of the Veda, because of such belief."

She scooted up to the edge of the couch, her knees touching Saint-Clair's and she leaned forward, holding out her hands, which he took in his.

"Tell me what you think happened!"

"Taking advantage of your fainting fit," he said excitedly, "which lasted longer than you thought, Oryas carried you into the third sanctuary. No one had the right to follow you. No one could watch over you. He went to the secret book, laid you on the carpet, if there is one there..."

"Yes, there is," the girl sighed.

"...Then he picked you up again, still passed out, and went back to the first sanctuary where he had not yet had time to leave before you woke up. But he had had time to read the 77th book of the Rig Veda and the formula of the dreadful secret."

Saint-Clair was surprised to see that Jing Pusa was smiling, not bitterly but almost cheerfully, mischievously. And her eyes no longer looked angry but amused. The Nyctalope also changed his expression.

"Li, why are you smiling like that?"

"Because your logic, so wise at first, is now flawed."

"What do you mean?"

"If Oryas Zabad Khan had found the formula, or rather formulas, of the terrible secret, you wouldn't be here, Leo, or any of your friends, or even me. Especially me. I would have been the first death! If Oryas killed eighteen men, he wouldn't have hesitated to use the full extent of his power on me. If he had killed me, he could have easily succeeded me. I think he read the formulas, but didn't understand them all. Maybe as I was unconscious, I sighed or groaned, or just moved, and he got scared of being caught and struck down on the spot if I woke up. Of course, I would've killed him without the slightest hesitation. So, he hurried to get me back to the first sanctuary. And the next day, he left on his mission but he didn't go to Lhasa. Instead, he vanished. Since then, nobody here or in Lhasa has been able to find out what became of him. But you described him accurately... Oryas has tried to use the power he stole in the third sanctuary, but he has only a precarious, fragmentary, incomplete power that rebels against certain uses since..."

She jumped up and raised her arms. Then her voice turned almost joyous, with a touch of defiance, as she exclaimed:

"...Since I'm still alive, Leo!"

The Nyctalope leaped to his feet, too. They stood face to face. They took each other's hands again. By reflex he drew her to him. Her warm breasts heaved against his hard chest. She repeated in a whisper:

"I'm still alive, Leo!"

Giving in to his embrace, she looked up at the face leaning over her. And she offered her lips to his, the first man obviously sent to her by fate.

CHAPTER V
The Sword of Alin Sikha

Meanwhile, anxiety was growing heavier among the group of friends and allies of Saint-Clair.

First of all, in the middle of the night, right after the Nyctalope had left, Gno Mitang, Rikevitch and Lazov had been approached by Liang Fong who was making sure he had the right man and subsequently alerted them quietly:

"The invisible wall worked on me and I couldn't leave the room. Saint-Clair went alone."

In the morning, just before daybreak, Gno remembered to wake Soca and get him out of his hiding place in case a servant decided to count the captives, which happened sometimes, so no one would be missing.

When they met outside as usual, after the morning meal, Gno and Soca, Rikevitch, Lazov, Liang Fong and Manassé walked around together. The Chinese knew only one thing, which he repeated in detail: he had been stopped but Saint-Clair had gone through freely.

Gno and Soca, who knew the Nyctalope well and believed that he could handle any situation, had faith, even though they could not dispel the increasing anxiety gnawing away at the Russians and Chinese as the morning wore on, and nothing hinted at what might have happened to Saint-Clair in the perilous recesses of the impenetrable lamasery.

That day, over the mountains of Chong Koum, the sky was clear, the sun shone and the air was fresh. All the prisoners, as usual, in groups or pairs or all alone, stayed on the esplanade until the bell rang calling them to lunch. But then, something different happened, something unexpected. Gno and Soca and their allies were set on seeing Saint-Clair in person, but this event at least got their minds off their present worries.

As Gno Mitang went first into the room, he was surprised to see a man standing before him, apparently one of the lamas whom they had glimpsed briefly sometimes on the terraces overlooking the courtyard. He was dressed in a big, brown robe tied with a belt, wore a white, felt hat in the shape of a pagoda roof and had on soft shoes, black with white stripes. His face was gaunt, dry and ageless, but his eyes were astonishingly young and his smile was charming when he showed it after taking a deep bow. He spoke softly in Japanese.

"Is it really the famous Marquis Gno Mitang whom I have the honor of addressing?"

"Yes, brother," Gno replied after bowing like the startling lama.

"My famous brother is invited humbly to follow me on the way I have been instructed to show His Great Wisdom."

Friendly and formal at the same time Gno replied:

"May I kindly ask my holy brother…"

He interrupted his politeness because he did not want to keep talking in formalities.

"All questions are allowed to His Wisdom," said the other. "But all answers are forbidden to my humbleness."

Following tradition, Gno bowed deeply again and the lama did the same. Then, turning to the group of friends behind him, Gno said in French:

"I am summoned. I will obey. For you, the orders are to wait."

"It's not like we have anything else to do," Lazov grumbled sarcastically.

The lama started walking across the courtyard toward a porch on the side that nobody had been able to enter. Gno smiled at Soca; then he followed.

The extraordinary incident had other witnesses besides their group of friends. Many of the prisoners heading back towards their room had seen and heard. Some understood Japanese, others French. When Gno had turned his head, he had realized that all the groups were getting excited. But he did not care much. He was thinking only of the lama in front of him and the path the holy man was opening before him.

"Opening" was the right word, because down corridors, up stairways, through vast, bare halls, many doors were opened by the lama simply pushing his hand flat against the walls. They all closed by themselves, silently, after Gno had passed through.

All of a sudden, after going through a new doorway, the lama stepped aside, bowed and, still leaning over, said slowly:

"His Wisdom will permit me to withdraw since my mission is accomplished."

"Go in peace, brother," Gno said, knowing the formalities.

The lama backed out and the door closed, leaving Gno alone. He found himself in a square room hung with carpets and piled with cushions. There were no furniture except a big, low table full of crystal, silver, porcelain and three stacks of tiny napkins, containers of all shapes and sizes full of meat, fruit, pastries, jams and drinks. The cheerful, warm light of the sun poured in through a big window opening onto a blooming terrace that formed a hanging garden.

Well, well! the contented Japanese thought, *this is all very nice.*

He took a few steps toward the table, but a muffled sound stopped him. He turned to the left.

Saint-Clair was there, next to a young woman with a beautiful face, short, black, gorgeously wavy hair, and extraordinarily blue eyes. She was bareheaded but dressed in a scarlet robe with a high collar and narrow sleeves that hung down below her wrists and she wore buskins with heels. But what Gno Mitang noticed most of all was that Saint-Clair was smiling and so was the young woman.

In his mind Gno cried out, *We've done it!* But his face expressed only the simple, affectionate joy at seeing his friend, then admiration, both quietly surprised and deeply respectful, as he bowed before the unexpected woman.

He straightened up, smiled back at them and waited.

He needed all his strength of character, all his self-control, not to show his astonishment when he heard Saint-Clair speak solemnly, with authority but also casually, as he gestured quickly with his left hand to the young woman:

"My good friend Gno, in your presence, I want to thank, with infinite gratitude, my noble friend Li Jing Pusa, the Living Buddha, the incarnation of the Divine Trinity. I want to thank her for inviting you to eat at this table today, which she will honor with her inestimable presence."

The Living Buddha—this girl? This young woman who, right now, was blushing! Any other man would have been rattled, but Gno Mitang was a samurai, and he knew the Nyctalope, for whom nothing was impossible, as they often said.

The Japanese diplomat took three respectful steps backward, bowed, stepped forward and bowed again. After a third show of respect, he was very close to Jing Pusa who, still blushing, spoke in French:

"For one or two hours, please forget about the Living Buddha, Marquis, and see me only as the happy friend of your friend, Leo Saint-Clair."

Imperial and royal courts have never lacked in conspirators and schemers. Hidden, aggressive, fierce ambitions thrive, even at the Vatican where the earthly sport of human passions should be at its minimum. Popes, emperors and kings were almost always blind and deaf to what was afoot around them, often against them. How could the Living Buddha in her fortress-palace, the temple of Chong Koum, not also be blind and deaf? And a young woman now possessed by love? Naturally endowed with omnipotence, paying little attention to the soon-to-be-forgotten incident involving Oryas Zabad Khan, Jing Pusa had not the least suspicion that she had been spied on for the last few hours and during her whole meal with Saint-Clair and Gno Mitang by prying eyes who were watching, pricked up ears who were listening, and a sharp mind who was analyzing.

These eyes, ears and mind belonged to Hai Feu, the Chinese from Shanghai, co-conspirator of Om Jahan, the female lama from Tengri Nor, and General Alin Sikha, the Mongol from Urga.

These three and their respective retinues, together comprising thousands of devoted, determined followers, had their own building in the lamasery reserved for high-ranking pilgrims and noble guests. Climbing down the various terraces, one could get to the hanging garden next to the living quarters of the Living Buddha, which were located on the same floor as the holy rooms that no one can enter save by the express permission of Jing Pusa.

Early in the morning, after their scheming the night before, Om Jahan, Hai Feu and Alin Sikha had been anxious to organize a spy network in all the services that, directly or indirectly, were in daily contact with the servants, both male and female, who worked for the young brahmins and lamas, the priests in various functions who made up the staff in immediate contact with the Divine Virgin.

Every fifteen minutes, they were told what these spies found out about what was happening around Jing Pusa and what she herself was doing. When they heard that one of the 33 lamas of the sacrifice had talked to one of the prisoners, a Japanese, and he had led the man to the room where Jing Pusa had her lunch on nice days, always alone, looking out on the flowers of the hanging gardens, they were flabbergasted.

"What does this mean?" Om Jahan asked. "It's unheard of."

Indeed, it was unheard of. The Living Buddha had never invited another human being to eat with her, even the Dai Lama of Lhasa.

The act seemed so serious, and rightly so, to the three plotters that they agreed without delay on the need to know more, and that this important mission should not be left to a subordinate.

"I'll go," Hai Feu said. "I know nine languages including Japanese and all the languages Jing Pusa knows. I'm small, agile and light. I know how to get down there without being seen. Let's just hope that Jing Pusa won't have thought of putting up an invisible wall to bar access to her."

He took off his shoes, tightened the belt on his robe and left.

Like every day, as distinguished guests in the lamasery, Om Jahan and Alin Sikha ate breakfast in a small room that also opened onto a terrace warmed by the sun. But that day, they were not joined by Hai Feu. They were served by their own slaves, who got the dishes from another room, rather far away, handed to them by servants used to pilgrims and illustrious guest staying for any amount of time.

Lost in their own thoughts, the two of them did not say a word during the meal or after while smoking the opiate tobacco and drinking many cups of mint tea. They smoked for a long time, waiting for Hai Feu to return. Several hours passed...

The sun was already halfway down the western sky. Worry was making them shudder. Their minds were contemplating the worst possible scenarios. Would Hai Feu ever come back?

Suddenly Hai Feu showed up, a dark shadow against the light in the corner of the doorway leading to the terrace. He came in and sat down. His whole body was trembling. His face was a wreck, his eyes wild.

"Quick, some strong tea!" he exclaimed in a broken voice that terrified his companions.

Nonetheless, the two of them hurried to serve Hai Feu who sipped this tea slowly. As he drank the strong, burning hot beverage dosed with soothing powders, he calmed down and regained his usual, placid, spiritual composure.

Om Jahan could not wait any longer. He demanded:

227

"Hai Feu, talk! Tell us right now!"

"Yes," the other replied. "Now I can speak. But don't expect me to give you a detailed report, my friends. I'll give you the gist of it first. Then we'll go over it and make up our minds about what to do."

"Enough! Speak!" Om Jahan barked.

"Jing Pusa was with two men," the Chinese rattled off. "A Japanese who is the famous Marquis Gno Mitang, secret advisor to the Emperor. The second is a Frenchman, Leo Saint-Clair, known as the Nyctalope!"

Just like Hai Feu, Om Jahan and Alin Sikha would not have been who they were if they had not known by reputation these two men. The female lama and the Mongol general were speechless. Hai Feu continued:

"It's nothing. Listen up. Believe me. Don't think I'm crazy. I saw their faces and heard their voices, all in secret." He leaned forward, started shaking all over again and went on. "Saint-Clair spent the night in Jing Pusa's bed. And she's… no longer… the Divine Virgin! No more! The Living Buddha is the love slave of that westerner, that Frenchman!"

Now, this was an idea so inconceivable, a deed so outrageous, that it went beyond the tragic. For Hai Feu, who had said it aloud, and for Alin Sikha, who had heard it, it was at first incomprehensible. But quickly, it took on its full meaning and turned farcical. Nervously, Hai Feu could not help laughing. Alin Sikha followed suit. For a couple of minutes, the two men were cracking up.

But Om Jahan did not laugh. She was a woman. She understood it and did not consider it outrageous. Moreover, she had met the Nyctalope before in Beijing in circumstances that had been dangerous for the Frenchman. As if merely amusing himself, he had gotten out of the danger without weapons, without a fight, just thanks to his keen mind and a few simple, clear, well-chosen words that had rendered his enemies—quite a few of them and angry to boot—harmless.

It was the Nyctalope who had attempted the colonization of Mars, and had defeated the awesome powers of Lucifer and the malevolent schemes of Leonid Zattan and Titania. When the other two conspirators' laughter had died down, Om Jahan spoke coldly:

"Pull yourselves together! The problem of arranging for the Living Buddha's death and her succession has just changed. Not by the fact that Jing Pusa, true or false, may have given herself to a man, but by the fact that Leo Saint-Clair is here, free to act. He was not here yesterday. I'm sure that Jing Pusa was alone in her rooms. But now, the Nyctalope is here, and as you, Hai Feu, bore witness, he has transformed the Divine Virgin into his love slave. Moreover, the Nyctalope has freed Gno Mitang, who is eating with the Living Buddha as if he were her friend. Just these two facts should give you an idea of Saint-Clair's power. Yes, our problem has changed and become more complicated. The solution, *our* solution, will be hard. But it doesn't matter! Personally, I won't give up trying to find one. What about you two?"

Om Jahan spoke these last three words as a harsh, dogmatic demand. Hai Feu and Alin Sikha pulled themselves together. They did not even look at each other like they so often did. The impulsive Mongol answered first, with conviction:

"I'm not giving up, Om Jahan."

"Me neither, dear friend," the Chinese said more softly.

"Well, then," Om Jahan went on. "Hai Feu, tell us now in detail everything you saw and heard while you were hiding in the flowers near Jing Pusa and her guests."

From that day, Tuesday, May 11, many things happened in the lamasery as well as around the lake, some because of Saint-Clair, others because of the three co-conspirators. But whereas the actions caused by the Nyctalope were (unbeknownst to Jing Pusa, Saint-Clair or Gno Mitang) immediately revealed to Om Jahan and the two others, the deeds of the traitors remained unknown to Jing Pusa and her new friends.

According to the conspirators' plan, their plot was supposed to come to fruition during the Living Buddha's public ritual set for the day of the "Seventh Star," i.e.: May 28.

On May 11, before the evening meal, Soca was approached by a lama who told him in perfect French:

"Friend, please follow me. Messieurs Saint-Clair and Gno Mitang are awaiting you."

On the same day, Gissa was pulled out of the group of lowly slaves he had been assigned to and reunited with Soca, Saint-Clair and Gno.

On May 12, in the morning, Archibald Brown was approached in the same manner by the same lama who spoke excellent English and gave him the same invitation.

On May 13, another lama, who spoke Russian very well, called together Rikevitch, Lazov, Liang Fong and Manassé, along with the soldiers Boris and Felix, and told them:

"Don't worry about Saint-Clair, Gno Mitang or Soca. They're in no danger. As for you six, nothing will change for you. Live in peace and be patient."

When Rikevitch asked for specific information, the lama just smiled, shrugged, turned around and left.

On May 14, a lama and three armed servants left the lamasery, crossed the esplanade, entered the chaos of rocks, then went down the ledge to the black sand beach where the Rikevitch expedition had camped for a few days. But on the beach, they were ambushed by twenty Mongols who had been hiding in the grotto. The fight lasted less than five minutes. Surprised and outnumbered, the lama and the servants were killed. The Mongol chief searched the lama and found a leather satchel containing a folded piece of paper. The four corpses were then weighed down by heavy stones tied around their waists and thrown into the deep lake.

The next night, Om Jahan came into possession of the satchel and its contents. The paper was a letter written in French to someone named Vitto. Om Jahan had learned French in Saigon. She read the note and translated it for Alin Sikha, who knew no western languages except Russian.

It was short. In it, Saint-Clair was giving Vitto orders to stay at the Refuge until he received a radio message from Paris, which would decide matters one way or another. Then, he could take off and come to the lamasery where he would land normally, following the instructions of the lama messenger. Vitto and Timor were asked to treat the lama as an honored guest. He and the servants would stay at the Refuge and come back to the lamasery in the plane with them. Finally, Saint-Clair added that he and Gno, as well as Archibald Brown and Soca and Gissa, were all in good health and in no danger. They were preparing "something wonderful."

"We've also got something wonderful in the works," Om Jahan grumbled.

"And we're not sending letters to inform our enemies of them," Hai Feu mumbled with a smile.

Alin Sikha just snickered. He was happy. Not a day passed that he did not polish his sword.

But from May 15 to 28, nothing was done by the Nyctalope that came to the ears of the three traitors. The reports they got from their spies became less and less informative. The three of them knew that the westerners were living as honored guests in one of the buildings closer to the "central bloc" of the Living Buddha and her court of brahmins and lamas of the Seventh Observance. Under this central bloc was the entrance to the mysterious, formidable underground world.

During the afternoon, Saint-Clair, Gno and Archibald Brown had a secret meeting with Jing Pusa. Since the meeting was held in one of the strictly private rooms of the Living Buddha, it was impossible for the conspirators to know what was discussed.

At night, the Nyctalope was not with his friends. Sometimes he was with them again at daybreak. There was no way for the spies to see him come and go. Of course, the conspirators were sure that Saint-Clair was spending the nocturnal hours alone with Jing Pusa.

And the days lumbered on, slowly, too slowly for the likes of the traitors.

But they were calm now in their decision to assassinate and replace Jing Pusa. With Om Jahan alive and her dead, the conspirators were planning every last detail so that nothing would be left to chance.

Of course, Saint-Clair, Gno Mitang and Archibald Brown would be sentenced to die within five minutes of Jing Pusa's death. Soca and Gissa would also be murdered, as would be—good riddance!—all the prisoners in the big room.

As for Vitto and Timor, who were still with the plane on the shores of the Chong Koum, they would send out, under cover of night, a horde of servants to kill them as soon as the new Living Buddha was proclaimed. Their orders would be obeyed by the 333 cohorts of the underground world. The plane would be attacked, torn to pieces and sunk in the lake.

Thus the lamasery and the Chong Koum would be cleared of all the foreigners. After this, Om Jahan would enter the third sanctuary and come out again as Empress-Queen of the World! Hai Feu in the East, and Alin Sikha in the West, would be her viceroys.

Like all the big public rituals every three months, always following tradition, the ritual on May 28, 1937, the day of the Seventh Star, was to be performed by the Living Buddha in the temple of the Veda Buddha, the protector deity of the monasteries.

In the lamasery of Chong Koum, this temple was located in the middle of a terrace that overlooked all the others, except for the black temple of Vishnu farther away, and the closer ones that were under the living quarters of the Living Buddha, located exactly in the middle of the lamasery, between the heavens of the air and the stars, and the abysses of the underground world.

To get to the public ritual, the Living Buddha came out on the southern-most terrace and only had to walk down forty steps of the monumental staircase to arrive at the level of the Veda Buddha temple.

On May 28, at 7 a.m., in the their rooms, Saint-Clair and his friends were waiting for the lama to bring them to the temple. Their clothes were spotless because they had been scrubbed clean the night before, along with their shiny boots and leather accoutrements. Except for Saint-Clair, who had always kept his Browning, the others had been given their weapons back, which they carried visibly. So, these five men looked like a small group of military explorers, well rested and fit, thanks to the generous hospitality of their hosts.

Never before had it happened that foreigners, especially westerners like Saint-Clair, Brown and Soca, had been admitted to a ritual of the Living Buddha. But with her omnipotence, Jing Pusa had not hesitated to make the Nyctalope and his friends an innovative precedent.

Was it the woman in Jing Pusa wanting to show herself to her lover in all her lavish, priestly, even quasi-divine splendor? Was it the Living Buddha trying to show the priests and pilgrims and countless faithful followers milling about that this public ritual would be the start of a new, modern world, one with diplomatic relations with the other temporal powers of the planet? No doubt both these reasons had been present in Jing Pusa's mind when she had made her decision, without which Saint-Clair and his friends would have had to stay outside the temple during the entire ritual of the Seventh Star.

She had told the Grand Lama, the head of the 33 brahmins of the sacrifice, who gave orders to all the inhabitants of the lamasery, and to the 333 cohorts of

231

the underground world as well, and he had bowed, smiling, asking permission from the Living Buddha to approve of the decision. The Grand Lama, named Driva Gô, was broad-minded and open, having traveled in Europe and even staying in France for the last three weeks of the World Exposition in 1900. He was tall and strong at 65 years-old, anti-Russian by instinct and by logic, and thought that the Living Buddha had to learn to keep up with the times, like the Pope of the westerners.

It was this very morning that he had succeeded the old Dai Lama who had died suddenly after breakfast, which had surprised no one because the old man had been weak and sickly. Neither Jing Pusa, nor Driva Gô and his Brahmins, nor Saint-Clair and his friends, suspected that a sinister plot had been hatched by men with spies and assassins afoot, recording minute by minute details of the intentions, conversations and behavior of everyone involved in the Seventh Star ritual, which they planned to be Jing Pusa's last, and Om Jahan's first as the new Living Buddha.

Saint-Clair and his friends were armed with guns, hunting knives and combat rifles, but not because they were expecting an attack, or felt the need to defend the Living Buddha. They were simply following Jing Pusa's orders.

"You will be armed because weapons are normal trappings for men adventuring in lesser known countries," she had said, "Of course, they'll be astounded by your presence, but no one will notice that you're armed. Anyway, a Mongol general from Urga and his officers will be there and they will be carrying a lot more weapons than you."

As she spoke, she did not think for a minute that all these instruments of death would ever actually be used. They were just part of the costumes.

It was 7:15 a.m. when one of the doors opened and Saint-Clair and his friends saw the lama they knew well by now. He was the one who had gone to get Gno Mitang and then Soca to reunite them with the Nyctalope. Since then, he had always served as the official go-between for the Living Buddha and her guests.

Learned and fluent in French and English, he was always smiling, very polite and cleverly attentive. His name was Sontang. On several occasions, he had eaten with them and enjoyed the conversations that taught him about them western world; in return, he had taught them about Buddhism and Brahmism, and things which even Gno Mitang had been unaware of.

This morning, Sontang showed up lavishly dressed in a yellow robe embroidered with golden tints and a tall, four-cornered hat of the same colors. On his feet he wore nothing but thick, ebony soles with yellow straps. He bowed and with a French lilt said:

"Greetings. Please follow me. The ceremony will begin in fifteen minutes. If you come early, you can watch the crowd of the faithful arriving. It's a colorful display and you'll find a place where you won't miss any of it, especially the magnificent procession of the Living Buddha."

"Thank you," said Saint-Clair, speaking for them all.

They had to go down a long corridor, one hundred yards or so, to suddenly emerge onto a huge terrace at the end of which stood the Veda Buddha Temple, a giant dome on a relatively high, circular wall, supported by tall columns with entrance doors built between some of them.

At the other end of the terrace, and therefore facing the temple, was a stairway with forty steps going up to a tall, broad, square fortress with bare, windowless walls and a crenellated roof—the building reserved for the Living Buddha and the 33 brahmins of the sacrifice. At the foot of the wall on the last step was an open door, a black hole in the white wall sparkling in the sunlight. It was morning, a beautiful, pure spring morning, with a clear blue sky.

The huge terrace was already teeming with people who had gathered into dense groups around the farthest part of the temple, where a high, wide porch protruded between sculpted columns, marking the main entrance. As Sontang had said, it was quite a colorful sight due to the diversity of clothes of every hue and shade glistening in the bright sun.

"Are there only men here?" Saint-Clair asked.

"No," the lama replied. "There are women, maybe a quarter of them. But they're dressed like men and you're too far to see their faces."

"Let's mix with the crowd," Gno suggested.

"I was just about to suggest the same thing. But we won't go in with them. We'll stay closer to the porch so you can see the procession of the Living Buddha when it comes down the stairs."

Saint-Clair and his friends walked forward and were soon lost among the long column of Tibetan mountain folk covered in natural furs or dyed red, blue, purple, yellow and green, wearing tall fur caps and soft leather boots. Among the men, a few women stood out, thanks to their more delicate faces or especially because of their softer, less direct, glances. All of them, even the women, were armed, most with a long hunting knife sheathed in their belts, but a few carried rifles.

In this column, just like the others, when they came onto the terrace from below, nobody made a sound. It created an almost oppressive atmosphere of silence, broken only by the thousands of leather and wooden soles scraping against the paving stones.

Following the lama, Saint-Clair and the others were dragged with the crowd toward the huge porch where the separate groups huddled together.

When he got next to the groups of people to their right, Sontang only had to raise his arms and speak a few words for the Tibetans around them to step away and reveal a seat made from a huge, square, black marble monolith on which the lama jumped up. Saint-Clair and the others imitated their golden-robed guide. Standing together on the monolith, they could look over the crowd.

They were directly facing the forty steps lined with eighty statues representing the main types of countless Buddhas, Vishnus, Shivas, Brahmas, Shakyamuni, his father Suddhodana and his mother, Maya Devi. The stairway was facing southeast, therefore toward the rising sun.

Then, up above in the darkness of the open doorway, the first brahmins of the sacrifice appeared, dressed in gold-embroidered white robes, wearing golden caps, each holding in his left hand a long, red rod topped by a golden, open lotus. They sparkled in the sunlight, which created a cascade of glistening white and gold as they descended the stairs.

The triple column of brahmins was framed on both sides by the servants who had come up from their sacred duty in the underground world. They marched down with the same slow and solemn step as the brahmins. They were almost naked, covered only from their belly button to mid-thigh by a black loincloth. They were gigantic, broad-shouldered, muscular men, with light gray skin. None of the westerners had seen one of these men since they had been in the lamasery. The servants in the buildings were shorter and thinner with Tibetan faces. But the giants of the sacred guard, besides their colossal size, had oval faces with thin lips, protruding noses and reddish eyes behind long, white eyelashes. Their eyebrows and hair were shorn, making two white stripes on their foreheads and a white dome on top. Each of them held a broadsword before them, their blades glittering in the sunlight. Saint-Clair and his friends saw these details clearly only when the crowd parted to make way for the front line approaching the porch.

"Those sword-bearers are albinos!" Saint-Clair murmured. Then leaning toward Sontang, he said, "Those men are coming from the underground world. How is it that they're not blinded by the light?"

"The light of the sun is not blinding to them," the lama answered, "because the natural darkness in the underground is constantly offset, extinguished even, by the intense but soft luminescence from the telluric gases."

Saint-Clair might not have heard this because the Living Buddha had just appeared at the top of the stairs.

The 33 brahmins of the sacrifice, whose front ranks were now entering the temple, had been followed and accompanied by the 333 chiefs of the underground cohorts. They were wearing round, metal helmets that looked like tarnished silver, dressed in black robes with silver sparkles that were relatively short, ending at the knees, under which they wore white leather boots. Their right hands hung down while their left rested on the pommel of a long sword in a black leather sheath hanging from their black belts. After the 333 chiefs came the Living Buddha.

Her legs were crossed with her heels resting on top of her thighs; her right hand lay flat on her calf and her left arm was bent at a right angle, so that the back of her hand was against her belly button with the thumb and index finger making the symbolic circle of the *yoni* sign. Jing Pusa was sitting in the hieratic

234

position of the Buddha. Her thighs, legs and arms were bare, but each toe had a ring with a precious stone—diamonds, rubies, sapphires, emeralds—and thin, gold chains encircled her ankles. No bracelets or rings were on her fingers. The scarlet robe clung to her chest, but her shoulders were bare. Around her neck was a triple row of pearls. She wore long pearl earrings as well. Her face looked like it had been powdered with gold, along with her shoulders, arms, hands, legs and feet. Her fingernails and toenails were the same bright red as her silk robe. A blue circle, the hermetic symbol, was painted on her forehead between her elongated, waxed eyebrows. To top it all off, her hair was hidden under a concentric circle of golden rings, smaller at the top, which blossomed into a golden lotus encrusted with rubies.

Saint-Clair and his friends noticed these details gradually as the distance closed between them and the Living Buddha. Sixteen enormous, magnificent, black porters in yellow loincloths were holding the 32 rods sticking out on either side of the ebony platform incrusted with mother-of-pearl. On that platform was a smaller, round platform with inlaid gold. On this platform was a huge cushion made of white satin. And on this cushion sat the Living Buddha.

Behind the platform rose straight up a big flaming circle with rays, inside which was a screen of white silk. Against the whiteness of the silk and in the middle of the golden circle stood out the living statue in scarlet and gold.

As the porters walked down the stairs, they did not change their positions: the two in front standing tall, the two behind them bent down a little, and the others behind bent more and more until the last were almost on their knees. Thus, the ebony platform descended always horizontal. When it reached the terrace, the porters straightened up in pairs, gracefully organized so that the platform did not wobble an inch.

Behind them came the ordinary lamas of Chong Koum in plain white robes with yellow pants, escorted by a double row of servants from the first cohort whose small, muscular bodies were only half-covered by a goatskin from their left shoulder to their right hip. All these servants carried short swords—pointed, triangular blades that were razor-sharp.

Like the crowd of people still outside the temple and frozen on either side of a long, wide path from the stairs to the porch, Saint-Clair and his friends were standing at the base of the twin columns with Sontang and watched the Divine Virgin pass by them in absolute silence.

A crowd gathered inside the temple and the one outside made no sound at all—not a whisper, not a breath. The bright sunlight was already warm. The air was pure and fresh in the high altitudes of the cloudless, windless May morning.

What an apotheosis! The silence, the light, these stunned crowds, the procession before and behind the beatific platform.

The Living Buddha, Jing Pusa, the Divine Virgin, did not look at the procession or the crowd or the sunlight. Her big, blue eyes were like two precious stones, two aquamarines, staring ahead, unfathomable, hieratic. Only a faint smile on her red lips, the enigmatic smile of the Living Buddha, symbolic of the Immutable, gave something human to this divine incarnation.

A second before passing under the porch, when the platform came parallel to the twin columns, the head of the Living Buddha turned a little, just a nudge to the right. And for a moment, her blue eyes fixed on the eyes of the Nyctalope. It was a warm and caressing glance, full of joy and delight as well as youthful exuberance—the glance of a woman in love, proud, happy… and having fun!

Saint-Clair looked back without a smile, but his face expressed his fervent, passionate spirit from the depths of his soul.

Half an hour later, everyone was in their place inside the temple as the rites ordained. In the huge room with a high dome and a wide gallery behind a ring of columns, the ebony platform had been set on eight porphyry pillars about three feet high and forming a rectangle at the back of the temple, facing the main door that opened onto the terrace. The doorway had been cleared by the servants, although the whole crowd of pilgrims was not inside—thousands were still milling about outside, near the side doors. The giant servants of the sacred guard were lined up from the main door to the porphyry pillars, creating an empty space as wide as the porch. The crowd on either side were on their knees.

Right away, in front of the pillars, therefore in front of the Living Buddha, a semi-circle formed from the groups of high-ranking dignitaries and delegates who had the right to talk to her during this ritual of the Seventh Star, as was written in their Book of the Law.

There were four of these groups today: that of Om Jahan, the lama from Tengri Nor, a dignitary from the Buddhist Orders; that of Hai Feu, representative of the Shanghai schools; that of Alin Sikha, military chief of the Mongol horsemen from Urga; and the fourth was made up of the lamas from Lhasa.

At first, all the members of these privileged groups stood up while the crowd around them were kneeling. But when an invisible gong was struck three times, Om Jahan, Hai Feu, Alin Sikha and the lamas dropped to their knees and prostrated themselves on the stone floor with their foreheads on their crossed hands. They stayed in this worshipful position for several minutes, then the gong rang out again and everyone in the temple stood up.

It was the lama from Lhasa who spoke first. He did so in a language that was obviously sacred, purely ritualistic, because Gno Mitang knew not a word of it. He wanted to ask Sontang about it, but the interpreter was no longer there. Gno nudged Saint-Clair and whispered:

"I don't understand his speech."

"Me neither," the Nyctalope whispered back. "But that's not what interests me."

"What then?" Gno looked at his friend.

"It's the attitude of the three other groups, the line of men behind them. Take a good look at them."

The Japanese heard the worry in Saint-Clair's voice. He looked at the three groups of men lined up close together. Right away, he noticed that they were all armed, even the Chinese from Shanghai and the lamas from Tengri Nor.

"Yes," he said softly. "They're behaving strangely. There's an obvious tension in their bodies and some kind of excitement in their faces. Their eyes look alert, but agitated, even angry..."

"Even stranger," Saint-Clair added, "because all the other faces in the crowd show only devoted worship. But then..." He stopped.

"Then what?" Gno pressed.

"I've always had some kind of sixth sense about things like these... In those three groups, who are suspicious, and above all in their three chiefs, I sense the quivering that precedes a riot, the lurking pressure of expected violence, organized upheaval, which some signal will unleash. What does it mean?"

Following the logic of his thoughts, Saint-Clair turned his gaze upon Jing Pusa. Sitting dignified, unmoving, her extraordinary blue eyes wide open as if dilated, staring like precious stones, uncut aquamarines, the Living Buddha was like a statue, a gold and scarlet idol.

"Is she looking at them?" the Nyctalope asked. "Does she see these men like I do? Does she feel what I feel—this growing sense of dread? Or is she completely absorbed in her sacred role, nothing but inner thought with no regard for the outside, nothing but a blind and deaf incarnation of divinity? She sure seems to me like she sees and hears nothing..."

He whispered his thoughts to Gno and the Japanese also looked at Jing Pusa. A lama from Lhasa was just stepping forward toward the sacred podium.

Saint-Clair and his friends stood on a wide platform about a foot and half off the ground to the left of the pillars holding up the Buddha throne, about four yards away. Therefore, a little to their right was the throne of Jing Pusa, and right in front of them was the semi-circle of the crowd. They had nobody behind them, but all of a sudden the Nyctalope felt a hand on his shoulder. It was Soca who had leaned over to whisper in his ear:

"Boss!"

"What?" said Saint-Clair, leaning closer.

"Sneak a peek at that Mongol Cossack, the gilded Chinese and the scruffy lama who look like the chiefs of these three groups over there. I heard what you said. I've got a bad feeling too. I'm keeping an eye out automatically and I'm telling you, those guys look kind of funny, but menacing at the same time. Like they're thinking, 'What we're gonna do is nothing like these foreigners or anyone is expecting!' I feel it, boss."

Saint-Clair just nodded to his smart and loyal friend. His mind was already made up. Gno's too. Shoulder to shoulder, their heads almost touching, their eyes focused on the venerable, long-winded lama who was giving a speech. Saint-Clair and Gno Mitang were talking, whispering, barely moving their lips. First, the Nyctalope told is friend about Soca's misgivings.

"He's right," said Gno. "Only the three chiefs are glancing over at us from time to time. The rest of their men are focused on the Living Buddha."

"There's something foul afoot" said Leo, "but what? Obviously, it's against the Living Buddha. There are only five of us here. We're easy prey for an attack that might rear its ugly head… but here? Now? It's unimaginable. And yet, there's a plot brewing. Where's Archibald?"

"Just behind me," Gno said.

"Pretend like you're telling him something about the speech and see if he's got the same intuition as we do."

"Got it."

Gno's completely natural movement made Brown step forward so that he was now standing to the right of the Japanese. He pointed to the orating lama and pretended to tell the Englishman discreetly about the long speech. But in reality, he asked Brown:

"Have you noticed anything suspicious?"

"Yes," the Intelligence officer answered. "Soca just told me what he was feeling."

"Your opinion?"

"The threat of an incident, no doubt of a religious kind, is very real. There are schisms in Eastern Buddhism like in Western Christianity. What bothers me is that there are hundreds of men in the three suspicious groups. And Jing Pusa seems to see nothing."

"The Living Buddha has to keep her hieratic pose as long as she doesn't have to answer the speakers. According to the rites, she will have to answer them, but later."

"True!" Archibald said.

After pursing his lips and furrowing his brow, and then shrugging his shoulders as if to tell the Japanese that he did not understand a word of what was being said, he added:

"We can't just wait and do nothing."

"I know," Gno sighed.

"All five of us are on guard."

"I'm not worried about us," Gno smiled. "Jing Pusa, by simply willing it, could stop any attack directed at us. But what about her…?"

"Right! What does the Nyctalope think?"

Gno turned to Saint-Clair and said:

"Archibald shares the same feeling. He's asking what you think of Jing Pusa's ability to use that mysterious power of hers in the event of trouble?"

"I'm wondering," said Leo, sounding uneasy. "She admitted to me she has the divine power, but explicitly refused to give me any details about the Eighteen deaths that we blamed on Leone Alzac and her partner. Even alone with her, in our most intimate embraces, she never promised to open up the impenetrable third sanctuary and initiate me into its formidable mysteries. She told me, to wait for a message from Dumont-Warren, and she would act according to what's happening in France, but she was never more specific. She said to me once, 'Maybe I'll act without saying a word.' Of course, I didn't press her. So, I wonder, yes, and I can't help feeling nervous about it. I'm wondering if..."

Saint-Clair stopped talking because at that very moment, one after the other, in three seconds, two things happened. The first was that the lama stopped talking and bowed deeply; the second was a particular gesture from the Living Buddha, which caused a sudden quiver of fervent emotion to run through the huge crowd. Her right hand slowly lifted off her thigh, the arm moved, stretched out, stopped and her fingers wriggled three times. Then her mouth opened.

Saint-Clair could not understand the words but her voice shook him to the core. That musical voice, so smooth and pure, soft, unavoidable, penetrating... A divine voice that Saint-Clair's friends did not know, because with them, Jing Pusa had just been a perky young woman. But the Nyctalope had heard her uttering deep, passionate, fervent words. The voice of love! The divine voice!

The Nyctalope's thoughts wandered away. He heard nothing but those sweet tones. Deep in his mind and body, he relived those moments when this voice had lived only for him. Li! Beautiful, wonderful Li! Li sprawled on the pile of white furs... Jing Pusa without her throne, without her scarlet robes, without her gold makeup, without her worship, without her divinity. Li, lover and beloved, who, even in the transports of love, still kept so many of her virginal charms. Saint-Clair closed his eyes, as if in rapture.

Then suddenly Jing Pusa stopped talking. The silence struck Saint-Clair like a shockwave. He opened his eyes. He saw the Living Buddha aloof again, her arm lowered, hand flat on her leg again. He heard Gno whisper in his ear:

"Why does that one look so angry?"

That one was the speaker from the second group, the ragged lama from Tengri Nor, who was already talking, almost shouting.

Right away, Saint-Clair and his friends noticed that the three suspicious groups were fidgeting after staying completely still during the previous speech. The armed men lined up behind their leaders were clearly responding to the excited words and gestures of the new speaker. No doubt about it—they were agreeing with him.

This time, Gno understood a little of the Tibetan dialect being spoken. He nudged the Nyctalope's elbow and murmured:

"Leo, this is crazy! This lama is shouting at Jing Pusa and directly insulting her... hold on..." A moment later, "He's criticizing her inaction when... yes, that's it, when she holds the divine secret of Gedhun Grub!"

The raging speaker stopped talking.

Archibald Brown, who also understood Tibetan pretty well, told Gno:

"Watch out! The three groups and the closest part of the crowd look like they're ready to do something nasty. A lot of those guys have their hands on their weapons."

There was total silence in the vast temple. But there were too many souls for that silence not to carry some strange undercurrents. Unvoiced threats hung in the air. Saint-Clair and his friends felt it. But what kind of threats?

At that moment, the Living Buddha made a gesture identical to her earlier one. Her right arm stretched out, her hand wriggled, and the voice of god incarnate spoke out, this time with cold determination, with sovereign power, and a little arrogantly. Gno translated to Saint-Clair:

"She refuses to respond to the sacrilegious accusation. She's ordering the lama to stay quiet and withdraw."

Right away, the group of Mongol warriors moved *en masse* toward the throne. But Saint-Clair, Gno and Brown saw their leader step away from his group and go around the throne, on the opposite side of the furious lama who continued to scream and swear.

"Ah-ha!" the Nyctalope cried out.

He jumped, but too late!

The Mongol chief was now running and jumping onto the platform. He drew his sword and stabbed Jing Pusa's side. She toppled over and fell out of sight behind the ebony base.

Two explosions followed in a row. It was Saint-Clair who had just shot the assassin in the back and was now on top of him. Other shots rang out. The Nyctalope's friends were firing into the three suspicious groups. The shouting lama from Tengri Nor fell.

"Cover me!" Saint-Clair yelled so loudly that his order rose above the din of the panicking crowd and the brouhaha of the smaller servants, the huge albinos and the brahmin chiefs of the cohorts.

The four friends ran around the porphyry pillars and the ebony platform. They saw the Nyctalope bend down and pick up the limp body of Jing Pusa. They turned their backs to him, facing the crowd, and with their guns reloaded they started firing into the front ranks of their attackers.

They heard Saint-Clair shout, "Keep me covered!"

The lama Sontang was near him. He shouted orders to the brahmins of the sacrifice who ran in from all directions to completely surround the throne and give them some space. In less than a minute, the Nyctalope and his precious cargo were protected by five rings of brahmins and lamas under the command of Driva Gô. The servants and the albinos shared the painful task of clearing the temple while keeping the central path free. They managed thanks to the panic that carried the innocent crowd through the open doors while the conspirators and their men were mowed down by the guns of the westerners. With the Mongol chief dead, the lama from Tengri Nor dead or dying on the ground, and the Chinese mandarin having vanished into the crowd, there was only the violent but reckless hostility of their guilty followers to deal with.

Shortly afterward, a small retinue formed, at first compact, but soon growing wider and longer, around Saint-Clair and his four friends. The lama and the brahmins who were not busy in battle gathered all around them. The group left the temple, went down the central path of the terrace, and started marching up the stairs.

Gno Mitang turned to Driva Gô who was still there with them and with irresistible authority said:

"Brother, you must obey Monsieur Saint-Clair like we do. Jing Pusa told you that he is the Nyctalope. Only he can save the Living Buddha, if it's still possible. In the interests of the higher mysteries of Chong Koum, and especially with a sedition in the works whose extent we know nothing about, Saint-Clair must be obeyed!"

Driva Gô was a man of experience. He had traveled and lived in Europe. He had heard of the Nyctalope, knew his reputation, and he had lately seen, or at least guessed, what this extraordinary man meant to Jing Pusa. So, he responded to Gno Mitang, whom he held in high esteem:

"I and all the lamasery, including the underground world, will obey the Nyctalope."

Gno told his friend:

"Leo, you can talk and act as master here. From Driva Gô to the humblest slave of the underground world, they will obey you."

"We'll need it," Saint-Clair growled back.

He was thinking that the revolt against Jing Pusa had only one goal: to give the traitorous chiefs the power of the murderous will. These chiefs themselves had a master. Was he among the guilty groups? If so, was he dead or injured, or had he gotten out of the bloody battle unharmed? Saint-Clair had no doubt that the Mongol assassin had been just a pawn. He also figured that the lama giving that angry speech was merely a distraction.

If I save her, he looked at her painted blue eyelids and her red lips, *everything will be alright. If she dies, I will be the one to enter the third sanctuary and open the book of the supreme secret. And I will avenge her!*

He could think *If I save her* or *If she dies* because at the moment, Jing Pusa was still alive. He held her in his arms, tightly against his chest. With his right hand, he pressed the wound in her left side to stem the flow of blood. His other hand was flat against her chest, over her heart, with as much hope as fear, feeling her heart beat weakly…

CHAPTER VI
Om Jahan

Om Jahan had heard Saint-Clair shout out and lunge into Alin Sikha, who had been killed before he had time to stab twice. Then she saw the four Brownings being whipped out by the Nyctalope's friends. So she fell to the ground when the guns started firing.

At first, she lay flat on her stomach, playing dead. But as she risked being trampled, she started crawling between swinging legs and writhing bodies. When she figured she was in the middle of the panicking crowd rushing toward the exits of the temple, she grabbed at legs, thighs, hips, and pulled herself back to her feet. She felt only minor bruises as she was carried away with the crowd, yet kept a clear head throughout.

Of course, a failure like this had not been anticipated. Their plan was that as soon as Jing Pusa had been stabbed, all the Chinese would fire at the foreigners since Hai Feu's group was closest to their targets. But Saint-Clair's sudden leap and the westerners' immediate armed reaction had foiled that plan. Such a failure had not been foreseen.

There was more: despite Jing Pusa dead or dying, the brahmins of the sacrifice, their cohorts of lamas and albinos, had not lost their heads. Instead, they had gone on the offensive and their stand had prevented an immediate victory for the conspirators. However, they had anticipated this, and all their surviving soldiers had been instructed to retreat to the smaller temple of Vishnu where they had secretly hidden supplies and weapons in case of such a setback.

This temple was located on a terrace far from the main buildings of the lamasery, and was a veritable fortress behind its three solid, bronze doors. The priests of Vishnu, all 77 of them, as well as their hundred guards, servants and slaves, had been privy to the revolt. But their own beliefs had forbidden them from taking part in the Living Buddha's public ritual.

In case of an immediate and total victory, the members of this temple would have served as Om Jahan's special sacred guard. In case of a delayed victory, the temple was to be used as a meeting place after the retreat—a refuge where they could wait, a headquarters for planning a second offensive that would surely prove decisive... since they would not have to fear Jing Pusa's power.

Indeed, in all their planning, one fact was absolutely certain, undeniable: Jing Pusa would be killed in a few seconds by Alin Sikha's sword. The conspirators would only have to defeat the brahmins and the lamas, along with the albinos and the servants. Om Jahan was sure of winning that fight by hook or by crook, with superstition or religion, but mostly with real, physical weapons.

So, Om Jahan was fleeing through the chaos, across the terraces, toward the temple of Vishnu. And in her flight, she was so distressed that she could hardly control her thoughts. What she was thinking was:

Is Jing Pusa really dead?

If the Living Buddha was alive, if she regained consciousness and control of her will, the thick walls and bronze doors of the temple would be no better than a spider's web against the death awaiting them.

Despite the swell of the crowd and its constant waves of screaming hysteria, despite her own fears, Om Jahan had lost neither her sense of direction nor her cool head. Through the zigzagging people dragging her with them in their flight, she managed to head for the temple of Vishnu. Soon she realized that she was not the only one fleeing this way. She recognized a few lamas from Tengri Nor, some Mongols from Urga, and even some Chinese from Shanghai.

Suddenly, she saw Hai Feu!

She called out to him, but at that very moment a huge commotion arose on one side of the crowd, flowing to the other side and filling the sky with its din. This terror had been growing since the first outbreak of panic in the temple. A group of men or women started screaming, then another and another, until it ran wild over the terraces, up the stairs, through the courtyards and past the esplanade outside of the lamasery. The esplanade was the final destination for the crowds being herded and guided by the armed servants who called up the brahmin chiefs of the cohorts to take over.

Om Jahan squeezed out of a group and scurried over to join Hai Feu. He was at the head of around fifty Chinese. She grabbed his arm and marched alongside him.

"What do you know about Jing Pusa?"

"Less than I know about you, Om Jahan," he said calmly.

"What's that supposed to mean?"

"It means I saw you fall without being struck or shot. As for Jing Pusa, I saw Alin Sikha stab her once but once only. He's dead. I'm sure because when I was crawling away, I touched his body... But Jing Pusa? What do you know yourself?"

"The same as you. Did she die?"

"I hope so for our sake. But be careful, Om Jahan."

"Of what?"

"Even if Jing Pusa died, we still might not win."

"Why?"

"Because the Nyctalope still lives. Turn around and take a look."

Two or three Chinese had heard him. Like Om Jahan, they stopped and turned around. Soon all their companions followed their lead. They had just climbed a staircase and were at the far west end of three stacked terraces, the highest one to the east with the black temple of Vishnu in the middle. A hundred yards or so below them was the huge terrace bordered on the right by the temple of Veda Buddha and on the left by the monumental staircase. On this terrace, on both sides of the double row of giant guards, the crowd was still pushing and pulling. On the staircase, the brahmins, lamas and albinos were spread out, protecting the foreigners. Saint-Clair in the middle of them all was carrying Jing Pusa. The day was so clear that Om Jahan could see the face of the Nyctalope—a mask of quiet strength.

"Yes!" she spit out. "Yes, Saint-Clair will become a big problem, even if Jing Pusa is dead, or if she dies without regaining the conscious use of her will. There'll be a big problem from him and his friends. Also, because Grand Lama Driva Gô and, therefore, the whole underground will be with him when the time comes to choose a new Living Buddha."

"Well, now that you've seen and understand the situation, let's go."

"No, wait!" Om Jahan commanded. "We're safe for the moment. The servants are busy with the crowd and we're far from them. Just wait. I want to see what they do."

Behind Om Jahan and Hai Feu, the Chinese troops stayed put. As time passed, they were joined by Mongol warriors and lamas from Tengri Nor who were following the plan to escape the chaos and head for their refuge, the black temple of Vishnu.

They then watched the head of the procession reach the top of the monumental staircase and enter the vestibule of the rooms and secret temples of Jing Pusa and her household of brahmins and lamas. They saw Saint-Clair and the westerners being led by Driva Gô and Sontang into the holy places that should have been, according to the rites, strictly forbidden to them. And the whole procession followed behind them. The albinos went in last. The huge golden doors swung closed. All that was left outside was the troop of a hundred giant guards. They were not only armed with long swords hanging from their belts, but also with rifles given to them by the servants. Directly beside the golden doors eight of them set up a battery of two machine guns.

Om Jahan put her hand on Hai Feu's shoulder and whispered:

"Driva Gô can't be too optimistic about Jing Pusa's chances if he's taking such precautions."

"Maybe," replied Hai Feu, skeptical.

He was turning around to give orders to get back on the march when he stopped short and looked up. At the same time, Om Jahan and everyone else raised their eyes to the sky.

What they saw was totally unheard of and had never been seen before in Chong Koum. An airplane!

The noise of the crowd in perpetual panic kept them from hearing the sound of the engine, but when the plane got closer, everyone heard it. All the men and women from the stairs to the esplanade became silent, stood still and looked up. Every eye was focused on that strange mechanical bird rumbling through the sky.

Not having received the message from Saint-Clair, which the Living Buddha had entrusted to one of her warrior lamas and three servants to bring to the Refuge, because Alin Sikha's Mongols had killed the messengers, Vitto and Timor were coming to the lamasery following Saint-Clair's earlier message delivered by Timor on May 10.[25]

So, these instructions being the only ones he had received from his boss, Vitto had flown straight to the lamasery. Now he was starting his 15-minute holding position over the roofs.

Om Jahan was extremely intelligent and Hai Feu terribly clever. Neither of them knew about Saint-Clair's first message, but they had read the second one intercepted by their Mongols. In it, Saint-Clair had given Vitto orders to stay at the Refuge until he received a radio message from Paris, which would decide matters one way or another. Then, he could take off and come to the lamasery. It was obvious that this was a follow-up to an earlier message.

When Om Jahan and Hai Feu saw the plane, they both thought the same thing. The Hindu-Tibetan woman was more impulsive than the Chinese man, so she expressed herself more frankly:

"Hai Feu, since the plane is here, that means that the message from Paris arrived. Whatever it's about, we have to get it—and only us. We have to be there when the plane lands. Look around. Outside the walls of the lamasery there's the scattered crowd. On all the terraces of the lower temples, the same crowds. The only place that's empty are the three terraces of the Vishnu temple. The first, the one we're on, is long and wide! It's the best place for that plane to land without crushing or killing a mob of people. Quick, get your men on the stairs and keep everybody off the terrace. I'll stand alone here and wave the plane down."

"Yes," Hai Feu smiled. "Mobs are everywhere but here. I'll send the men to guard the stairs. You signal the plane. Here, use this!"

The Chinese tore off from one of his men a long, red scarf made of fine silk that the man had wrapped around his chest.

Both of them did as they said. The woman—looking like the ascetic lama from Tengri Nor—went to stand in the middle of the terrace. She raised her arms and started waving the red scarf in the air.

Hai Feu's task was harder but quickly and expertly carried out. The more heavily armed Chinese and Mongol soldiers stood at the bottom of the stairs while the others lined up around the edge of the terrace like a welcoming committee.

The plane flew low over the temple roofs, including that of Vishnu, rumbling in the absolute silence that had fallen upon nature and men alike. It glit-

---

[25] On page 208.

245

tered in the bright sun like a graceful mechanical bird soaring through the heavens.

When the plane showed up in the sky over the lamasery, the brahmin in charge of the giant guards on the monumental staircase sent one his men to inform Driva Gô of this unusual event. Word spread from guard to lama, then to the brahmins of the sacrifice, then to Sontang, and finally came to Driva Gô. At the same time, Gissa heard it and passed it on to Archibald Brown and Soca. They were all in the grand vestibule before the holy chambers of the Living Buddha where the Nyctalope had found Jing Pusa sleeping during that unforgettable night. And in this room, on this morning of the Seventh Star, following Saint-Clair's strict orders after he had carried Jing Pusa inside, only Gno Mitang was allowed to enter.

After he had laid her down on her bed, the Nyctalope clapped his hands just like Jing Pusa had taught him. Right away four women appeared, one of them a Hindu around 40 years-old who spoke English fluently. Her name was Laya. She was a doctor who had graduated with honors from the University of London. The three others, all younger, carried out duties as nurses and masseuses. All four of them were the private servants of the Living Buddha.

"Doctor," Saint-Clair told Laya, "Jing Pusa has been stabbed on her left side, a little above the hip. I stopped the bleeding with my hand, but I can feel a lump forming. We have to save her!"

From the look on her face, the doctor was deeply upset, but her reflexes were swift and skillful. She issued quick orders to the three nurses and knelt down to examine the wound. The nurses were back in an instant wheeling a table full of medical supplies and surgical instruments. Laya took a pair of scissors and split open the scarlet robe. Then, under the flashlight held by a nurse, she tapped around the wound.

"Well?" Saint-Clair asked her.

"I think the blade hit a rib and didn't touch the bowels. I'll clean and sterilize the wound first. I'll work better if I'm alone with my nurses."

"We have confidence in you. My friend Gno and I will be in the vestibule with Driva Gô. If anything happens, good or bad, call us in."

"Of course."

"Thank you."

Saint-Clair and Gno went straight to the door. Before the door had even closed behind them, Driva Gô was in front of them, talking:

"A plane is flying over the lamasery."

"A plane!" Saint-Clair exclaimed. "Quick! All of you, please, get out there! If the crowd is still in a panic and our enemies are free, I fear…"

He stopped. He wanted only to stay there and wait for the doctor's diagnosis, but he knew his duty and fought against his desire.

"No, I can't stay here. I'll come with you." To Driva Gô, "Please, if Jing Pusa calls me, send Sontang to get me. I'll be out where the plane is landing."

"What if it's not landing?" Driva Gô asked.

"It will."

Saint-Clair made sure that his Browning was loaded and immediately ran after the others. As soon as they were outside, they saw the plane flying directly over the lamasery. The Zig was circling low over the buildings. Surprised that the plane was still flying around instead of landing on the esplanade, which was not too crowded, the Nyctalope stopped and looked around. He watched and reflected.

"Gno!" he exclaimed at last.

"Yes?"

"Did my second message get to Vitto?"

"I think so."

"But if Vitto had gotten it, he wouldn't be doing what the first message had asked him to do, which is exactly what's happening now. He would have landed already on the esplanade. Look, there's enough space over there."

"You're right," agreed Gno. "We know our enemies were hatching a plot, so we were probably all spied on over the last two weeks. So I guess we shouldn't be surprised that the messengers were attacked. And naturally, Vitto is following the first orders because he never got the second ones."

"That's what I thought," Saint-Clair said.

"Boss!" exclaimed Soca.

"What?"

"I noticed something..."

"Go on."

"There's panic everywhere, except at that one place: over to the right, where the stairs lead up those three terraces to that temple."

"The Temple of Vishnu," Gno remarked as the Nyctalope turned to look.

After a moment's observation while the plane kept rumbling in a circle, the Nyctalope said:

"No doubt about it, those stairs are being blocked by armed guards. They're part of the plot. And higher up, those lamas in black robes, they're the ones from Tengri Nor. They're the enemy."

"Leo," Gno said, "the lama up there waving the red scarf is the one who was talking and instigating the attack on Jing Pusa. They obviously want to keep that big terrace clear for the plane to land."

"Good Lord!" Saint-Clair shouted. "That's Om Jahan! That's the name Driva Gô cried out when..."

"Yes."

"There's no doubt about it now! Om Jahan stole my second message. He thinks Vitto is bringing us a message from Paris. He figures he can use it against us—maybe hold it for ransom."

"Yes," Gno repeated as Archibald Brown nodded in agreement.

"So, here's a plan," Saint-Clair was as calm as could be. "Let's bring all the guards here. They've got rifles and two machine guns. If we attack from here, we're in a better position over the Mongols, the Chinese and the lamas."

He paused suddenly.

"Or?" Gno asked impassively.

"Can you guess what I'm thinking?"

"I think so. You're counting on Vitto being disciplined and following the orders of the first message, throw a box onto the esplanade and land only if..."

"Yes!" Saint-Clair cut him off. "Let's get to the esplanade."

"But let's still bring fifty guards and a machine gun with us" said Gno. "I'll go talk to the brahmin in charge. We don't have to rush since Vitto will be up there for fifteen minutes and he only got here five or six minutes ago if Driva Gô is correct—which I'm sure is the case. So, we've got a good eight minutes before Vitto starts down."

"Let's get going!" Saint-Clair was barely holding back his impatience.

It took only a two minutes talk between Gno and the brahmin in charge of the guards lined up on the monumental staircase, and immediately afterward, Saint-Clair, Gno, Brown, Soca and Gissa were leading a squad of fifty armed men, including four machine guns, across the terrace of the Veda Buddha temple. They cut over to take stairs down to an inner courtyard, and came out on the huge esplanade where countless people were slowly starting to calm down and gather together. Many just stood there looking up at the mechanical bird—a new and wondrous sight for many of them—as it came and went behind the higher buildings of the lamasery.

When Saint-Clair figured he was roughly five hundred yards from the outer wall, he stopped and told Gno:

"The guards have to clear off a landing space. Can you take care of that? I'll keep Soca with me. But be careful. When Om Jahan sees that the plane isn't landing on the Vishnu terrace, he might come down here with his gang and attack."

"I'll set up the machine guns over the porch, which is the only way for them to get in," said Gno. "Ten riflemen will back them while the others cordon off a runway."

"Great! Archibald, you take charge of the guards providing cover."

Now that Saint-Clair felt more confident, he could wait calmly the two or three minutes it took for the plane to finish its rounds and begin its descent.

But someone had seen, watched, and remarked on everything that was happening: the five strangers showing up at the top of the stairway, recognizable even at a distance by their clothes, then the fifty guards with their machine gun filing out onto the esplanade and getting into formation. That someone was Hai Feu.

During this whole time, Om Jahan was still waving the red scarf over her head, a little slower now from fatigue.

Hai Feu was standing at the edge of the terrace on a decorative base. From there, he was almost level with the monumental stairs and the terrace of the Veda Buddha that directly overlooked the esplanade. After watching closely and considering their options, he made up his mind. He went straight to Om Jahan.

"Om, enough!" he said firmly but amiably.

"What?" she lowered her arms, somewhat surprised by the order given so informally.

"Enough," Hai Feu repeated dryly. "Whatever the message is from Paris, that plane is none of our business anymore."

"What?"

"Look!"

With two, slow, gestures in a row the Chinese pointed to the monumental staircase, then to the esplanade. Om Jahan was keen of eye and mind. She first realized that there was only one machine gun and fifty giant guards now left to defend the entrance of the sacred chambers where Jing Pusa was either dead, or dying, or being healed. And she thought that the odds were good that the Living Buddha's mind had dissolved into the infinite, or fell unconscious in a coma, or just passed out. In all of these cases, her deadly will would not be working. The doors would open to anyone who could get rid of the guards.

Then Om Jahan saw the foreigners and the guards setting up on the esplanade, and she reasoned that the albinos and the servants, relatively few of them to boot, who were still outside in the courtyards or on the esplanade were obeying orders to disperse the crowd calmly... She looked fiercely into the Chinese's watchful eyes.

"I've seen. And I understand. Thanks to you, clever Hai Feu."

They walked side by side to the stairs.

"Whose scarf is this?" Om shouted.

One of the Chinese raised his hand.

"Here!" the female lama tossed it over. "Tomorrow, you'll ask me to take it back. You'll make it into a kind of bag that I'll fill up with gold."

Hai Feu made immediate preparations for the lamas of Tengri Nor, the Mongols from Urga and the Chinese from Shanghai to form one big group ready to attack the guards with their rifles and machine gun on the monumental staircase. Against the fifty guards, they had 382 men, whom this time would not be taken by surprise and unnerved like they had been in the temple where their superior number would have enabled them to massacre their enemies if only they had kept their cool.

Meanwhile, the Nyctalope's orders on the esplanade had been carried out. Archibald Brown was in charge of the four servants on the machine gun. The lama chief of the guards and Gissa were overseeing the set-up of the riflemen in

249

a semi-circle. Gno Mitang had joined Saint-Clair and Soca in the middle of the big, clear space that would have to be defended.

They were soon overjoyed to see that they had not been wrong in thinking that Vitto would turn down the inviting runway at the Temple of Vishnu and come to the esplanade to drop the metal box.

"Here it comes! Here it comes!" Soca shouted.

The plane had indeed stopped turning round and was veering down toward the esplanade.

"Plus, he can see us now," Saint-Clair said.

"No doubt about it," Gno agreed.

Filling the space with the rhythmic hum of its engine, the Zig skimmed barely 300 feet over the three men. A shiny object fell out and curved through the air before dropping straight down.

Saint-Clair ran over, bent down and picked up the box right after it hit the ground. It opened easily because the cover was attached with a simple wire twisted three times. He pulled out a thick piece of paper, unrolled it and devoured it with his eyes.

"Bravo!" he exclaimed, and immediately he lay down on the ground.

What followed was all according to plan. Vitto and Timor must have seen the man lying down. Maybe they even recognized their boss? The plane flew up over the lamasery and came back, lining up with the runway. The wheels bounced off the ground a couple of times before the brakes were put on the plane came to a stop a hundred yards away.

Saint-Clair was already up and running with Gno and Soca. The Zig's engine fell quiet. Everywhere was quiet—until the silence was suddenly broken by the rattle of a machine gun and bursts of rifle fire.

"Uh-oh," said Saint-Clair, stopping in his tracks.

He turned around and saw Brown standing by the inactive machine gun and the riflemen on the esplanade just holding their weapons. But guns kept firing. The Nyctalope understood.

"It's on the stairs!" he shouted. "Get back to the Zig!" he said to Soca. "Come with me!" he told Gno. And as they passed by Brown, he added, "Archibald, protect the plane. You can keep the rifles here, but I need the machine gun."

Gno gave orders in Tibetan to the four men manning the machine gun. They picked up the weapon and the cartridge belts while Saint-Clair and Gno pulled out their Brownings. The small group immediately started running toward the monumental staircase. Men were fighting fiercely all up and down the steps. Gun shots were less frequent than the glint of swinging swords and knives. At the very top, the battery of machine guns was firing right and left on the attackers coming over a wide ledge in waves between the rain of bullets. Saint-Clair did not hesitate.

"Gno, we might kill a few giant guards, but we have to fire into that mess. It's a necessary diversion."

"Good God!"

At two hundred yards from the bottom of the stairs, the machine gun was set down. Saint-Clair gave the orders. And they started firing right away. Gno wisely pulled together a hundred servants out of the remnants of the dwindling crowd. He conferred very briefly with their commanding lama and lined them up on either side of the machine gun. They were armed with short rifles, a new English model. Given orders to shoot at will, they carefully picked off their targets on the stairs.

The troops of Om Jahan and Hai Feu had met with unexpected resistance in front of the sacred chambers. Saint-Clair found out later that this was due to a suspicious lama who had seen the Chinese, Mongols and Tengri Nor priests gathered at the Vishnu temple. He had kept an eye on the gathering and soon realized that it was made up of the same men who had been fighting the foreigners and the albinos in the temple. When some of them had lined up and disappeared below, and others had headed for the monumental staircase, this clever lama had taken the necessary measures to prepare a defense.

At the same time, he had sent a messenger to Driva Gô. But by then, Saint-Clair had come up with the machine gun and the servants riflemen led by Gno.

Om Jahan and Hai Feu had attacked. Now they were taking shelter behind a balustrade running from the highest terrace of the Vishnu temple to the narrow forecourt of the sacred chambers. They saw their men trapped between two firing squads and caught on all sides in hand-to-hand combat with the giant guards.

The female lama gritted her teeth. The Chinese furrowed his brow. The former was swearing. The latter spoke calmly.

"We've lost again, Om, because of that damned Nyctalope. What did I tell you?"

"He's a bad omen!" Om spat out. "You've got wisdom. The second round is yet another defeat for us. So be it. But there's still a third option, and you know it!"

"Under the Vishnu temple?" the Chinese raised his eyebrows.

"Yes."

"Isn't it a legend?"

"We shall see!" Om Jahan barked. "In the meantime, let's save what we can here."

With her mouth closed, she breathed through her nose. Her wide nostrils quivered sensually. Then she opened her mouth and started yelling, turned into shrieking, a terrifying cry that ripped through the battle like lightning ripping through a crack of thunder.

Almost right away, an eerie silence fell over the entire lamasery because the Chinese, Mongols and Tengri Nor lamas who were still standing suddenly stopped fighting and beat a hasty retreat back to the Vishnu temple. And thus the machine guns, rifles and blades found nothing in front of them but empty air.

The abrupt end of the battle kept the victors in suspense. And that was when the door of the sacred chamber opened.

"Driva Gô!" Saint-Clair shouted. Then he called out, "Gno Mitang! Gno!"

He ran over, soon joined by his friend. Leaping over the dead and dying, skipping around the pools of blood, they scrambled up the monumental stairs as fast as they could. Soon, Saint-Clair stood before the grand lama and asked:

"What is it?"

"They just told me that the guards were attacked," Driva Gô said calmly.

"Yes, but it's over. It was the same people who attacked us in the temple before. The guards put up a strong defense. I managed to come to their help just in time. It's over. What about Jing Pusa?" he asked anxiously.

Without his dark eyes or his austere face showing any emotion except for his usual serenity, the old man answered with a simple invitation:

"Come."

But the Nyctalope, no matter how he felt, was always thinking a step ahead. He turned to Gno and said:

"My friend, can you deal with Vitto and the plane? I've got the message from Paris and we'll look at it together soon enough. I've got to go see Jing Pusa."

"Of course! Go, Leo."

Following the highest dignitary in the great and complicated hierarchy of the court of the Living Buddha, the Nyctalope went back into the sacred chambers.

PART FIVE: THE MASTER OF DEATH

CHAPTER I
The Bikhunis of Shiva

When Saint-Clair entered alone, Doctor Laya and the nurses quietly with-drew from the room. On the couch of piled up white furs, a large, white, silk sheet had been spread out. Jing Pusa lay on top of it, half-sitting, surrounded and supported by cushions. She was covered from neck to toe with a dark purple, Persian shawl. Only her bare right forearm stuck out and, of course, her thinned face. Her eyes were open and she was smiling.

Trembling with joy and hope, Saint-Clair knelt beside her and stared into her soft, blue eyes. He smiled back at her, took her hand, and brought it to her lips. He heard her gentle but strained voice:

"Leo, I can't talk much but I can tell you that my injury isn't serious. I passed out because the sword hit my lumbar plexus. The man who stabbed me was the Mongol chief, wasn't he?"

"Yes. I killed him," Saint-Clair murmured.

"Obviously he was trying to hit my heart. His name is... was Alin Sikha. It is good that you killed him, but I think he was only carrying out orders. There was a plot by Om Jahan, the lama from Tengri Nor, who was shouting at me, and by Hai Feu, who came with his Chinese delegation from Shanghai. What has happened since?"

Saint-Clair told her. He kept holding her right hand and they did not take their eyes off each other. When he finished, she just nodded. Then, without a trace of anger, she said:

"I understand it all. If you don't find Om Jahan and Hai Feu among the dead, I know where they'll be hiding. In the Temple of Vishnu whose high priest has always been reluctant to obey me. The nest of vipers is there. Don't worry about it. My will is alive and active now. No one will be able to leave that temple without being summoned to appear before my justice."

She sighed, closed her eyes and her face became hard and cold again, but only for a moment. When her eyes opened, she was relaxed again.

"You saved me, you and your friends. If you hadn't been there, the assassin would've struck again and again until my lifeless body was... My life belongs to you now, Leo, all of me..."

She sighed again. He saw her eyelids fluttering and begged her:

253

"Li, stop talking. Rest. We'll take care of everything in the next few hours."

"Yes," she replied, sounding exhausted.

"But listen to one more thing," Saint-Clair said, watching her blue eyes calm down again. "My plane has arrived. I've got the message from Paris. I'll tell you about it tomorrow. Until then, rest and get better."

Jing Pusa smiled amorously.

"I'll do as you say."

Her body sank into the pillows and she closed her eyes. He heard her mutter:

"Kiss me on the lips, my love…"

He stood up and leaned over. For a long time, they breathed as one with their lips joined. Then Saint-Clair went to the door where he had seen Laya and the nurses leave. He opened it but he did not have to say a word. The doctor came in followed by her aides. As she passed by the Nyctalope, she said:

"Please, don't come back until tomorrow."

"That's exactly what I told her," he replied.

"Good. Don't worry about complications. It's a simple wound. No vital organs were hit, only a few nerves of the lumbar plexus. Very painful, but not dangerous. I've seen many like it. I was an intern in an English hospital in Shanghai during the Communist insurrection. You can trust me."

"I do—and I thank you."

"Go now," she said.

He kissed her hand with respect and gratitude, and then left.

At the end of the day of the Seventh Star, Friday, May 28, the whole lamasery had returned to its usual calm, except for the Vishnu temple and a tiny part of the esplanade by the surrounding wall where the plane had been moored behind a wall of rocks built on the spot in an hour by a team servants.

After a meeting with Saint-Clair, Gno and Archibald Brown on one side and Driva Gô, Sontang and a grand lama from Lhasa called Souradah, all necessary measures had been swiftly taken to clean up all visible signs of the tragic panic and the bloody battle of the morning.

What of the thousands of pilgrims, armed or not, men and women, who had survived the drama? Gathered by their lama and brahmin chiefs, they had been led back through the mountain passes north, west and east to their respective lands. Only the southern pass, which went over the esplanade and through the Chaos of black rocks, down the ledge all the way to the shores of Lake Chong Koum, had been forbidden to them. It was declared a sacred path of the Living Buddha, the *still living* Living Buddha, as announced out loud to the crowd assembled on the terrace of the Veda Buddha temple by the 33 brahmins of the sacrifice, each in his own language or dialect, to spread the crucial news: the Living Buddha survived the sacrilegious attack.

Those with lesser injuries had been helped by their companions. The others had been kept in the lamasery's hospital service until they either died or were healed.

As for the dead, they were lay to rest with logs and branches of resinous wood, and turned into flammable pyres that were sprinkled with oil. These pyres were lit late in the afternoon on the highest terrace of the Vishnu temple and all around it, and burned down before the sun had set behind the mountains.

Everywhere in the Veda Buddha temple, on the terraces and stairs, in the courtyards inside and out, the blood was mopped up. The mosaics, tiles and paving stones were washed, scrubbed and polished—completely purified. The servants picked up and burned everything thrown, dropped and abandoned—coats, scraps of fur and cloth, weapons, tools, all kinds of things.

Another issue that Saint-Clair was the first to think of and that was resolved in a few minutes was about the prisoners in the big room. For the Nyctalope and his friends, only the Russians and their Chinese companion were crucial. A quick inquiry by Sontang found out that, during the hour or so of panic and fighting, all the prisoners had stampeded out of the room, crossed the courtyards and ended up on the esplanade. They had been so astonished, curious and captivated by the ebb and flow of the crowd, by the rifle fire and machine guns, by the plane in the air, and then by all that had ensued, that they had not thought of checking if the mysterious invisible wall was still active. No one had thought of it, not even Liang Fong or Lazov or Rikevitch. Lined up and counted by Sontang and a squad of servants, all the prisoners were brought back into their spacious cell. To Rikevitch's questions, Sontang answered with a smirk:

"What happened today is no concern of yours, gentlemen. However, I can tell you that, thanks to the gracious intervention of Monsieur Saint-Clair and Marquis Gno Mitang, your stay here will last no longer than another four or five days."

Vitto, Soca, Gissa and Timor had no need to guard the plane, which was perfectly safe, so they were all together again. With a few servants to attend to their needs, the two Corsicans and the two Mongols stayed ready to do whatever the Nyctalope required of them.

Throughout the huge lamasery with its 100 courtyards, 50 terraces, 33 temples and seven residences, all built over the holy mysteries of the underground world, the night of Friday, May 28, was as peaceful, calm and quiet as the previous had been tragic, chaotic and noisy.

Nevertheless, before going to bed, which they had sore need of, Saint-Clair and his friends took time to find out what was going on in France. In front of his friends, Saint-Clair read the radio message from Paris. Only the conclusion was important:

Impossible to get confession or any useful information from the culprits. They are imprisoned and watched around the clock. Can't do anything more. What news at your end? We are worried. D-W.

Having read this aloud Saint-Clair added:

"The first message said Leone Alzac's partner is called Oryas Zabad Khan? Vitto and Timor, I'll repeat for you what I learned a few days ago and already told the others: the Living Buddha identified him when I told her about the strange case of the Eighteen deaths. This Oryas Zabad Khan is a brahmin from Benares who spent three years in this lamasery and then suddenly disappeared. Jing Pusa remembered an incident that could have allowed him to learn part of the terrible secret of the lethal will."

"That means they're still in danger over there if their precautions aren't tight enough," said Vitto.

"I'm sure they took good precautions," Gno broke in with a smile. "You can trust Yori Koto. He's not the kind of man to take any chances with a captured enemy."

"I'm with you," Saint-Clair added. "I have no worries on that front. Plus, Jing Pusa has her reasons for thinking that Oryas' power is limited in the time and space it can be used effectively. I imagine that Yori Koto figured that out already."

"Undoubtedly," Gno agreed.

"Therefore," Saint-Clair concluded, "first, we have to send a radio message to Dumont-Warren to reassure them about us. As for eliminating Oryas and Leone once and for all, we'll leave that to Jing Pusa to decide what to do."

Since Vitto and Gissa still looked startled and anxious to know what had happened, the Nyctalope took pity on them and, without revealing any intimate secrets, ran through the recent events at the lamasery leading up to the attack.

A few of the incidents were discussed in short order and then they all went to bed.

One person in the drama was not where Jing Pusa and Saint-Clair thought—Om Jahan!

When she saw their bold offensive being trounced by the guards on the monumental staircase and in the sacred dwellings, Om Jahan started to retreat into the Vishnu temple. But another idea popped upon her mind:

I don't know the incantations for the will to kill and paralyze, but I do know that, to use it, one has to follow certain rules, particularly this one: the will has no effect at a distance, except on people already identified and located. Now, Om Jahan, the lama from Tengri Nor in the Vishnu temple, is the enemy Jing Pusa will target and whom she'll strike if I hide here and keep this identity. But I'm not a man, and I'm not the real grand lama of Tengri Nor. My real name is not Om Jahan. Even Hai Feu doesn't know what it is. If I don't go to the temple, if I shed this stolen identity, if I become just another woman in the lamasery, or better yet one of the bikhuni priestesses of the Shiva temple, Jing Pusa's lethal anathema against Om Jahan won't affect me. I've done this before, before Om Jahan took me away. Even clever Hai Feu doesn't know about this...

With this thought and its ramifications in mind, Om Jahan used her thorough knowledge of all the nooks and crannies of the lamasery to slip away from the gang of traitors fleeing toward the Vishnu temple. She snuck off and hid for hours in one of the big, empty vases that were purely ornamental standing on decorated bases around the columns of the Shiva temple, which was the northernmost temple in the lamasery.

No wave of panic or separate skirmishes had reached here. Until sunset the whole area around the Shiva temple remained deserted. But at twilight, the bikhunis, the lamaic priestesses and nuns, came out as usual for their evening stroll. Behind them, the temple rose in tiers of hanging gardens, recently cleared of its winter glass roofs. Most of the bikhunis preferred the gardens to the galleries or circular terraces, but there were always a few who chose to daydream in solitude among the columns.

At least, this is what Hoya Devi was hoping for. For Hoya Devi was the fake Om Jahan's real name, a strong woman who was already starting to forget her previous identity. And destiny was kind to her. *Audentes fortuna juvat* [26] is just as true in Tibetan as it is in Latin. Hoya Devi had dared, and she was favored.

A solitary priestess came to sit next to her vase, legs dangling over the base. Through the open latticework on top of the vase, Hoya Devi watched her strolling over. The last lights of the setting sun were still bright enough for the bold adventurer to see clearly.

She's pretty much the same size and age as me. She's also the same race. I'd prefer to not have to kill her, because thanks to her, I will be safe to hope and plan. As Om Jahan, I learned all the rites of initiation into the Seventh Degree. I only have to say the word and all uninitiated priests and priestesses will obey me. But will she obey me as the woman I am now? A woman has never before been initiated into the Seventh Degree. It doesn't matter! I'll try to convince her and compel her at the same time. If she refuses to do as I say, then I'll kill her and steal her clothes. Later tonight, I'll throw her body into the pit where the Shiva waters flow into the Chong Koum. Then I'll return to the temple and take her place. The rules of the order demand humility, keeping silent and one's eyes lowered. Only whispers and furtive glances are allowed. I know all the ins and outs of this temple, and it will take me where I want to go, or else, this time, I will accept defeat and die. Die...? This pretty bikhuni is certainly not thinking that her death is only a few feet away, only minutes away... If she doesn't surrender. But I hope she does, because I hate killing if it can be avoided.

During this internal monologue, the lonely dreamer leaned back against the vase and kept dangling her legs over the base. Her big, black eyes watched the dying lights of the setting sun. Was she dreaming of one of the 33 brahmins of the sacrifice who alone, on certain days of first lunar quarter, had the right to

---

[26] Fortune favors the bold.

participate in the ritual dance of the priestesses around the statue of Shiva Linga, the procreative god? Her breasts heaved under her white, silk robe with red stripes. She sighed and moaned softly.

Suddenly, she froze in surprise and let out a little cry. A human figure had dropped in front of her as if fallen out of the sky. But this figure did not crash to the ground. It barely bent its knees before standing straight up and putting one hand over the priestess' mouth while the other grabbed her throat. The stunned bikhuni was not too befuddled to hear and understand the holy word that represented the powers of the seventh degree, the word that demanded humility and obedience. At the same time, she saw that it was not a brahmin or a lama speaking this word but a woman.

With her eyes wide open, the priestess calmly but firmly unpeeled the hand that was gagging her. In a steady voice she asked:

"Who are you, a woman, who dares to pronounce a word that only a few men have the right to use, that women must obey when heard?"

Bringing her face up close, recognizing the unforgettable sound of that voice, the attacker almost cried out in joy, but she knew how to control herself. Her aggressive hold suddenly turned affectionate and she answered tenderly:

"Oh, Yusé, my old friend, don't you recognize your darling Hoya Devi?

The next day, Saturday, at 9 a.m., when Saint-Clair, Gno and Archibald Brown had finished their breakfast and were getting ready to go out on the terrace to smoke the English cigarettes which Sontang kept bringing, the lama on duty announced the arrival of Driva Gô.

As soon as Saint-Clair showed him in, the old man was all smiles again. He asked if his new friends had slept well and answered Gno that he had too. Then he turned to Saint-Clair.

"Jing Pusa is waiting for you. She sent me to tell you also that in an hour His Excellency Gno Mitang, the Honorable Sir Archibald Brown and myself will convene before both of you to discuss the affairs at hand and a few more to come."

Saint-Clair flicked away his cigarette.

"See you soon, my friends."

And he left alone since he knew the way.

Gno Mitang figured it good diplomacy to talk with the old lama who was—with the exception of Jing Pusa—the highest spiritual priest and the supreme leader of the strange universe formed by the lamasery and the underground world. The conversation did not just revolve around abstract speculations, but turned to worldly matters. Archibald Brown backed up the clever Japanese as soon as he understood what he was doing.

Gno was telling Driva Gô about the three radio messages from Paris. After relating the facts, he casually dropped this comment:

"In our forthcoming meeting with the Living Buddha and our friend Saint-Clair, we'll talk a little about Oryas Zabad Khan and Leone Alzac, so I'd like you, my dear and venerable brother, to know everything we do. If I've forgotten anything, or if you have any questions, I'd be glad to fill you in."

"Thank you, wise brother," Driva Gô smiled back at him. "You know the Living Buddha was kind enough to inform me of all she had learned from the Nyctalope. What you just told me is a useful addition which I am honored to hear from you."

The three men sat in the sun on cushions at the edge of the terrace with a view extending over the esplanade and the outer wall all the way to the jumble of black rocks and apocalyptic chasms called the Chaos. Their conversation was a free and open exchange of ideas and opinions, sometimes abstract and sometimes very concrete, which these wise and intelligent minds judged worthy. In good spirits, they left no stone unturned concerning the extraordinary events that had brought them together.

But time flies during such conversations. They could have gone on talking for hours when a young lama in a yellow robe appeared on the terrace.

"Let's go," the high priest said.

With Driva Gô walking between Gno and Brown, the young lama led them to the private rooms of the Living Buddha.

CHAPTER II
"Is that all we can do—kill?"

In the middle of white cushions arranged to support every part of her upper body, Jing Pusa was sitting on the white fur couch. A scarlet robe covered her, with sleeves halfway down her hands and a collar that rose up to her chin and over her ears. She wore a round cap of the same color, with a little golden loop on top that came down across her forehead, over her temples and back to the nape of her neck. Not a single strand of hair was seen. And with the high collar from below and the cap on top, her face looked barer with its delicate, slightly gaunt features. Everything about this unique being radiated a natural hieratic bearing that was in no way diminished by the ungraceful position of her stretched out legs, because they were hidden under a dark purple, Persian shawl.

Her big, blue eyes looked very serious as they watched the three men approaching and bowing before her. Her lips, closed but not too tightly, showed no sign of smiling when the men stood up from their third reverential bow. The high priest, in his severe tranquility, the Japanese and the Englishman, clearly stirring beneath their outward calm, stood in a line and waited respectfully.

Between them and the foot of the couch of furs sat three armchairs in a semi-circle facing Jing Pusa. To her right was a fourth chair placed at an angle to be able to see both her and the other chairs. Standing next to this separate chair was Saint-Clair. He, too, looked serious, unsmiling, and greeted his friends with a simple nod.

The door behind them closed without a sound on the long, empty vestibule where not a single brahmin, guard, or other dignitary was present. The little lama had snuck away right after the three men had been let in.

Everything in the sacred chamber was just like when the Nyctalope had come in for the first time, except that the rounded ceiling, partly made of glass, filtered the sunlight into a soft glow. Nevertheless, a flame still floated over the tripod in the subtly perfumed air.

The Living Buddha let the men stand for only a few seconds after their last bow. She made a little gesture toward Saint-Clair with her right hand and with her left, a broader sweep for Gno, Brown and Driva Gô. In a hushed, calm voice that did nothing to soften the hieratic severity of her face she said:

"Take a seat, Messieurs."

She spoke in French, indicating that the council would be held in this language. But obviously, it was not Saint-Clair's lover who was talking, or even the regal Jing Pusa welcoming guests without the pomp and circumstance. No, this was the Living Buddha, the Divine Virgin, the bearer of unimaginable religious authority with incalculable social and political influence. Furthermore—and this the four men felt sharply at the moment with a sudden chill running down their spines—she was only all, a twenty year-old woman lying there, looking frail, with an injury that would keep her bedridden for a few more days, *but she was also a woman holding the power to paralyze and kill any person at a distance by simply willing it.*

It was this woman, more than the others, who invited them to sit down. This did not surprise Driva Gô or the two men at his side. But what did astonish them, although no one showed the least sign of it, was that it was not Jing Pusa but Saint-Clair who broke the silence:

"My dear friends, the Living Buddha has to avoid any unnecessary effort because she might need to use her energy, which will result in a great loss of her vital forces already weakened by her wound. That's why she has given me the responsibility of opening and leading the discussion that revolves around two main points and which holds the life and death of certain people in the balance. The Living Buddha will listen to our discussions and give her opinion at the end. Then Her Potency will make a decision inspired by the gods. But first of all— and this comes from me—I believe it best to keep our debate short because, as she knows, these events must have a rational outcome…"

Here, Saint-Clair hesitated. Driva Gô jumped in with severity:

"Rational, yes! Therefore, categorical, conclusive, and definitive!"

"There's nothing more definitive than death," Gno said softly.

"Indeed!" said Brown, curtly.

But Saint-Clair, like many Frenchmen, was both philosophical and senti-mental with respect to human life. He dropped his forced indifference and re-vealed his emotions.

"Is that all we can do—kill?"

"I don't believe in the human reincarnation of criminal souls," replied Driva Gô. "I believe the gods forever deny these demon-possessed souls to re-turn as a man or woman, and karma sentences them to a miserable life in the bodies of dirty, filthy, not even dangerous animals. Therefore, the death of a criminal is a rational, categorical, and definitive end.

"So, in the present context, we have to a duty to kill if we want a rational conclusion to this business with Oryas Zabad Khan and the dangers he presents, not only for certain individuals like us, but also for humanity as a whole. Frag-mented, limited, partial—the power to kill at a distance, which he possesses, is too strong for this man who broke the vows he made in his initiation into the seventh degree. Cold and ambitious, half-crazed with pride, dreaming and plan-ning to be master of the world in some way, is the kind of man you could ex-cuse, Monsieur Saint-Clair?

"If during his years in residence here, he had showed himself to us as a gentle soul, full of intelligence, faith and kindness, we might conceive that he is only trying to save humanity and turn it into something based on understanding, fraternity and love. But Oryas Zabad Khan never inspired any particular respect here, and he turned out to be a criminal, as proven by the way he stole part of the secret from the third sanctuary, and the way he extorted large sums of money from Mrs. MacCross... but I've said enough. Yes, when it comes to Oryas Zabad Khan, we have a duty to kill."

The Nyctalope did not blink an eye.

"Marquis Gno Mitang, what do you think?" he asked.

"I agree with Driva Gô," replied the Japanese

"What about you, Captain Archibald Brown?"

"We have a proverb in England: Dead dogs don't bite."

Saint-Clair turned his head slightly to face the Living Buddha.

"I heard them," she said. "Let's move on to the other case."

Saint-Clair nodded along with the unforgiving judges in their three arm-chairs. He went on:

"Driva Gô, would you care to tell us what you think of the other case?"

"If we'd also like a rational end, death is called for in that case too," the austere old man said. "First of all, as a punishment for the conspiracy and sacri-legious rebellion whose three leaders were Om Jahan, Hai Feu and Alin Sikha. The latter was justly executed by you, Monsieur Saint-Clair, at the scene of his crime before he could strike a second time. But Om Jahan and Hai Feu are still alive. They are responsible for all the corpses we burned after our victory, which, by the way, we owe to you, Monsieur Saint-Clair. Moreover, they're guilty of attempting a second attack against the guards of the sacred chambers. Their crimes are many, their sacrilege deliberately repeated. And now, what are they doing? Are they horrified by their crimes? Have they surrendered, repent-ant, to the justice of the Living Buddha? Do they ask forgiveness to atone for the bloody crimes in some ascetic lamasery? No! They've taken refuge with their surviving soldiers in the Temple of Vishnu!"

Driva Gô had a hard time holding back his fury. His whole body trembled. He took deep breaths. Forcing himself to focus, he continued.

"You three don't know what the Vishnu temple is here, and what its col-lege of priests and novices are. I will try to explain as briefly as possible because you must know. In the beginning, Vishnu was the second person in the Vedic trinity: Brahma, Vishnu, and Shiva. He fulfilled the role of the Preserver of the World. But little by little, over the centuries, sects formed that gave Vishnu pre-dominance and made him the supreme, eternal, infinite god, the universal soul that pervades and energizes everything that exists. All the Living Buddhas have had to fight against this disruptive schism for centuries. On the outside, the Vishnu cult members all submitted. On the inside, they are continually plotting a spiritual revolt.

"Which brings us to the present. The fact that Om Jahan and Hai Feu are taking refuge in the Vishnu Temple is proof that the priests of this temple knew about the murderous plot and approved it, that their hopes were placed in the ultimate crime of assassinating the Living Buddha, that they would have legiti-mized and sanctified the murder. Obviously, their high priest, whose name is

Krishna Mâ, would have joined Om Jahan and Hai Feu as one of the advisors and tutors of the new Living Buddha with the Mongol chief Alin Sikha as head of the armed cohorts.

"So, I ask you, what would these abominable criminals, these god-killers do with the divine secret from the third sanctuary? Before answering, think about this, for it is crucial! Krishna Mâ brazenly preaches to his brahmins and novices that only the tenth avatar of Vishnu is real, powerful and venerable. Of all the avatars over the ages, this final one, under the name Kalki, is the apocalyptic form in which Vishnu will appear on the day of the destruction of the universe."

With these ominous words pronounced in a deep voice, Driva Gô ended his speech. Soon the silence was broken by Brown's blunt voice:

"In short, anarchy deified. Anarchy leading to its logical end: the annihilation of everything that exists."

Gno spoke up with his usual gentleness:

"I knew this. I also know that the number of worshippers of Vishnu-Kalki is growing in Asia. Stalin knows this too, and is sending Bolshevik agents among the Kalkists. If the temple of Vishnu in Chong Koum is really the seat of apocalyptic Kalkism, as you think, Driva..."

"I know it!" the old man stated.

"In that case, it won't do any good to send off all the members here into twenty different lamaseries for punishment or reform. It'll be like sending missionaries out to make new proselytes in the very places where this anarchy ought to be strictly forbidden."

"Well said! Bravo!" the Englishman said.

There was a silence. Then Saint-Clair added very calmly:

"Basically, in this last case, it seems to me that there are two kinds of people here: those who chose Om Jahan and Hai Feu as their leaders, and those who chose Krishna Mâ."

"Sorry, mate," Brown spoke again, "but your distinction is acceptable only if you refuse to admit that the two are also accomplices and would benefit substantially from their victory."

Playing the devil's advocate out of generosity, the Nyctalope was too reasonable to deny logic. Without hesitating, he replied:

"I admit it."

"I think they're one and the same," Gno said.

"It's obvious," added Driva Gô.

There was another long, heavy silence full of terrible thoughts. Finally, Saint-Clair said:

"Archibald Brown, what's your conclusion?"

The Englishman pronounced his verdict coldly:

"For all the people and the monks who chose to take refuge in the Vishnu temple, for their chiefs and their soldiers, for Krishna Mâ and his priests, for everyone alike—Death!"

The Nyctalope shuddered. But he forced himself to stay calm.

"What about you, Gno?" he asked.

The Japanese looked long and amiably at this French friend, but he still uttered the final word:

"Death."

"And you, venerable Driva Gô?"

"I'm old and on the verge of death. I've never wanted anything more than to serve our divine trinity for peace in this world and the serenity of mankind. I believe that this peace and serenity have no greater enemy than these sacrilegious conspirators, these rebels full of hatred, these bloodthirsty criminals and their accomplices who are being held prisoner right now by the all powerful will of the Living Buddha. Such is my belief and my faith. It is because of this faith that I, too, sentence them all to death!"

Saint-Clair could not hold back. His whole body was shaking. He stood up and after glancing at Jing Pusa, who lay there inscrutable, he spoke clearly, firmly, obviously struggling to contain his emotions. And he spoke his mind without mincing words:

"Gentlemen, I leave Om Jahan and Hai Feu to you because they're apparently guiltier than Alin Sikha in planning and carrying out the attack against the Living Buddha. And they are indisputably responsible for all the victims of the fighting. Therefore, for Om Jahan and Hai Feu, death!

"I will also give you Krishna Mâ, the high priest of Vishnu. He certainly took part in organizing the plot, because if he hadn't known about it earlier or, at least, if he had done his duty and recoiled at the consequences, which he couldn't ignore, then he would have refused them shelter in his temple. Even now, Krishna Mâ must believe or be hoping that the Living Buddha is dead or in a coma on the verge of death, because if he knew she was alive and conscious and getting better, he wouldn't risk continuing his complicity knowing the inevitable result will be his death. Therefore, like you I hold Krishna Mâ responsible in the same way, perhaps worse, because of his long and constant treachery He is just as guilty as Om Jahan and Hai Feu. So, for this third unrepentant, hardened criminal, death!"

Saint-Clair paused for a moment. Then, more calmly because his deeply felt emotions were surfacing, he went on:

"But I ask for mercy, total mercy, a full pardon with maybe some purely moral and religious penitence, for the men and women, the soldiers and pawns, who were just following orders during the battle. Do you know what kind of devious thoughts, what kind of 'brainwashing,' as they call it now, these simple combatants were victims of? Weren't they told, and didn't they believe, that by obeying their chiefs, even unto death, they were fulfilling a sacred task? This wouldn't be the first time that good people were turned into fanatics to serve the selfish interests of a few, all the while believing in a noble ideal.

"I feel the the same about the priests and novices in that temple. You, venerable Driva Gô, know better than anyone what kind of prestigious authority is given to the high priests by brahmins and lamas, and all those who are trained and disciplined, glorified or humiliated, by them. For everyone in the Vishnu temple, except Krishna Mâ, I ask for mercy and forgiveness.

"We have to kill! That is what you three said. I understand, because you judged according to a disinterested justice with noble motives. But I, myself, am not so calm and composed when faced with inflicting death towards men whom I believe are not equally guilty. Your idea of justice is certainly defendable, even when it's blind and absolute, but my own idea is more humane, because it comes from my firm belief that there is no absolute truth in this earthly existence, only relative ones."

After another glance at Jing Pusa, who still looked like an idol, Saint-Clair bowed respectfully and sat down. This time the silence lasted for several minutes. Driva Gô, Gno Mitang and Archibald Brown were all in the same position, head held high but eyes to the ground, hands resting on the arms of their chairs. Saint-Clair watched them calmly. And Jing Pusa was now looking at the Nyctalope, but not with the eyes of an impassive idol.

In the end, Driva Gô raised his right hand. Then he raised his eyes, stood up and bowed. He turned to the man who was risking the Living Buddha's ire by defending people he did not and probably would never know. And the old man said:

"I want to thank Monsieur Saint-Clair whom we owe for executing a criminal before he could complete his crime. And, after reflection, I agree with him." He turned to face the Living Buddha, bowed and added, "I beg your all-powerful will to spare the soldiers, priest and novices."

Then he sat down again. Gno Mitang made the same gestures of veneration to the Dalai Lama and said:

"Under such dire circumstances, my heart remains with my friend, Leo Saint-Clair. Therefore, I humbly ask to join my esteemed brother, Driva Gô, in asking for their forgiveness."

Finally, Archibald Brown, always blunt and a little sarcastic, said:

"My government doesn't always agree with the government of His Excellency here, but men alone are often wiser than their governments. So, I share Monsieur Saint-Clair's views because, sometimes, it's good to forgive after theoretically condemning. And I join his appeal."

Saint-Clair thanked his three friends with a warm smile. And the four men stared at Living Buddha. Her face was again inscrutably impassive. It remained frozen for a long time. But suddenly, the beautiful lips parted and they heard the sovereign voice say:

"Has Monsieur Saint-Clair, then, forgotten a crucial point? More than Om Jahan, more than Hai Feu and Krishna Mâ, much more than these three men who are now harmless prisoners, there is another guilty party. You three also sentenced him to death."

Her holy lips closed. Right away the Nyctalope replied:

"Against Oryas Zabad Khan, guilty of eighteen deaths, two probably out of vengeance and hate, one for money, and one out of cowardice, for this extremely dangerous criminal who knows part of the divine secret, I, too, ask for a sentence of death."

He paused then raised his right hand.

"But after Oryas, there is another who is, if not directly guilty, but at least an active accomplice, and whom neither Driva Gô, nor Gno Mitang, nor Archibald Brown mentioned: the woman Leone Alzac. I won't sentence her without more information. First of all, is she really acting of her own free will? Is she under some kind of spell or influence cast by her formidable companion? He wouldn't be the man we think he is if he shared with her any part of his occult power. Therefore, Leone Alzac should be judged only to the degree, more or less conscious, of her complicity with the sacrilegious, thieving, and murderous brahmin. I ask that Leone Alzac remain prisoner pending full disclosure of her actions."

He turned to his three friends.

Driva Gô simply said, "I agree."

"Me too," Gno approved.

"I'll grant you that," Brown said, sounding very magisterial.

Again the four men turned to the supreme judge. The Living Buddha said:

"The sun tomorrow will shine with justice."

She raised her right hand. This gesture was meaningful. It was understood and obeyed. The four men stood up at the same time, bowed deeply and walked backward, bowed again, and then a third time after taking three steps, repeated according to the rites until they reached the door, which opened as they approached, even though there was nobody in the vestibule. Just as they were stepping through the doorway, the sacred chamber went dark, totally black because even the flame over the tripod was snuffed out.

Only when they were completely out of the room did the four men turn around. And the door shut behind them.

CHAPTER III
The Fifth Avatar of Hoya Devi

Basically, the word "avatar" is the generic name used in Hinduism and Brahmanism for the divine incarnations of Vishnu. By extension, the word has become associated with the transformation or metamorphosis of a human being, animal or plant, in a simple or compound body. In this sense, a Buddhist believer could have seen it used multiple times for the novice bikhuni Hoya, first becoming the priestess Hoya Devi in the Shiva temple, then the reincarnation of the traveling lama Om Jahan, and finally being reincarnated again as Hoya Devi, hard and cold, but now caressing and holding the dreamy, sentimental priestess of Shiva, Yeusé.

Her quick thinking, her cunning, her scorn for the naïve faith of the bikhunis, enabled her to exert her tyrannical authority over a tender soul, quickly devastated and then corrupted by her complicity in the perpetration of this new avatar!

So, next to the parapet at the south end of the round terrace of the Shiva temple, the woman whom we knew as Om Jahan, and who was once again Hoya Devi, had recognized the voice more than the face of Yeusé. And the novitiate had recognized Hoya, whom she believed she had lost forever, right away.

For a long time, maybe an hour, the two women sat there sharing the warmth of a warm, wool coat, talking like two old friends meeting again after a long separation. Hoya Devi seemed to enjoy the sentimentality of the situation because she now had a complete, precise plan, worked out down to the minutest details. And to accomplish it, she needed Yeusé who, unwittingly, revealed two things: Mani Soun, the high priestess of Vishnu, was seriously ill with something the medical matrons said was in her lungs, and her death was inevitable. She, Yeusé, was standing in for her while she decided in which bikhuni, novice or priestess, young girl or grown woman, her soul would reincarnate so that her age-old virtue would multiply the latent virtue of the chosen one.

My destiny! Hoya Devi thought.

And cleverly, little by little, she changed the conversation about the sentimental past and future into a more realistic talk about present possibilities. Then, while Yeusé was talking about something, she jumped in with

"But, my dear, I've been hearing about this every day for the past month!"

"How is that?"

"I was here. For four weeks, I've been living in the lamasery. Oh, how often I thought about you! But I was bound by a vow. I could only see you again after the day of the Seventh Star."

"Oh, what kind of vow?" Yeusé was again touched by the thought that Hoya Devi could have surprised her in her evening reverie a month ago.

267

Telling her just enough of the truth to make her understand, embellishing the facts and ennobling the ideas so that Yeusé would approve, making promises so that Yeusé would accept, and finally, sanctifying everything with lofty religious and political and social, universally human concerns so that Yeusé would be filled with passion, Hoya Devi revealed the reason for her past avatars which was also the reason for her next one. Because this new avatar—the next to last for Hoya Devi's ambition—needed to come to life as soon as possible, in a few hours!

"But the high priestess Mani Soun might still live for days," the naive Yeusé objected.

"She might also die in a few minutes from what you've told me."

"Yes, that's true."

"So, take me to her bedside so that we can do what's needed first, no matter how long we might have to wait."

They did not have to wait long. Fifteen minutes later, Hoya Devi was brought into the room by Yeusé, who was enslaved but ecstatic. Hoya Devi wore two rings on the middle and ring fingers of her left hand that she never took off. One ring had a black pearl, the other a white one, both remarkably big. But the two natural stones had been artificially hollowed out and carried tiny metal capsules. The black pearl bore one containing a poison that took an hour to kill; the white pearl held the antidote that was effective, even if given at the last second before death. Of course, Yeusé knew nothing about this.

A young Bikhuni nurse was watching over Mani Soun. A quick word from Yeusé sent her away. The girl did not see Hoya Devi, who was hiding behind the curtain covering the door. Then, leaning over the sick woman who already looked dead, Yeusé whispered hoarsely:

"Mani Soun, can you hear me? It's me, Yeusé."

The eyes stayed closed but the mouth cracked open and a barely audible voice escaped:

"What do you want?"

"Listen. Shiva has inspired me. Your soul is not to be reincarnated in me. I'm not worthy. Do you understand?"

"Yes."

"Do you remember my close friend Hoya Devi who also loved you so much?"

The eyes opened and suddenly lit up.

"Hoya Devi," the voice forced out. "Oh, yes…"

"Well, she's back. Shiva sent her at the same time he visited me in my sleep. She's back, sanctified by years of pilgrimage in the most ancient temples throughout Asia. She alone is worthy of receiving your soul."

With great effort the high priestess raised her head and chest, leaned on her elbow and feverishly asked:

"Where is she?"

Only then did Hoya Devi come out. She was nude as the rites decreed. Her gorgeous body was like gilded bronze in the flickering light of the flame floating over the tall tripod. Mani Soun watched her walking slowly toward her. She held out a trembling hand. When she was next to the bed, Hoya Devi took the hand and kissed it reverently. She kept holding it when she knelt down. A bright smile flashed briefly on the wan lips of the sick woman. And her voice was vivid and musical again when she said:

"You're more beautiful than the night, blessed Hoya. Thank Shiva for sending you. I obey his divine will with joy."

Then to Yeusé waiting attentively:

"Sound the gongs."

Yeusé sprinted out and disappeared. Shortly after, every nook and cranny of the Shiva temple resounded with the vibrations of the gongs, all the way to the hypersensitive ears of Mani Soun and those of Hoya Devi at her side.

But during those brief minutes alone, the deed was done by the ambitious against the dying. Mani Soun had already given up on living by ordering the gongs to sound. So, a simple prick in the hand was all it took. The rings were fitted with a tiny mechanism under the pearls that shot the poison out of a grooved tip.

The victim did not even feel the prick because what was left of her energy was focused on Hoya Devi and the memories that her beauty brought back through those magnificently hypnotic eyes…

All of a sudden, three doors were opened and soon the room was filled with bikhunis of all ages, some in pure white robes, others with a red stripe running from the left shoulder to the right hip, others too in red robes with a white stripe. All of them prostrated themselves on the ground. When the doors closed again, the heavy drapes falling straight down over the openings, Yeusé helped Mani Soun to sit up.

Hoya Devi, however, was not to be seen. She was lying on the carpet under the black silk drapes that covered the sick bed.

Using the last of her vital force Many-Soun declared:

"By the inspiration of Shiva, I, high priestess whose flesh is about to die, I give my immortal soul to the flesh of Hoya Devi, thrice blessed."

After the ritual prostration all the bikhunis raised their heads, watching avidly. Behind the bed of the high priestess who had fallen back into the sheets, a nude human figure rose up with her arms raised and her hands held together like in prayer over her head. She was a hieratic statue, but alive, with proud breasts and open eyes that sparkled with commanding authority.

Letting loose three shrill cries, all the bikhunis prostrated again, then sat up and froze in the sacred position, arms held high and hands held together over their heads.

Hoya Devi walked slowly around the long, narrow bed and stood before it so that her tall figure hid the dying body in the bed. All eyes converged on her. In a deep, solemn voice she said:

"By our god Shiva I accept Mani Soun's soul to be united with mine!"

Yeusé took the big, black silk veil from the bed and threw it over Hoya Devi's left shoulder, then wrapped her nudity in the precious fabric so that nothing more of the new high priestess was showing but her majestic face, her perfect arms, slender hands and her arched feet.

Thus Hoya Devi's fifth avatar was brought to life.

On the voluptuously curved but still well-defined lips of this woman born of pride and desire, a smile formed. Hoya Devi was hoping that this avatar would not be her last.

CHAPTER IV
A Day goes by

Life inside each of the seven temples of the Chong Koum lamasery was relatively independent. Only the big events were reported, first to Driva Gô, who then gave an edited version to the Living Buddha. Furthermore, the high priests were never in a hurry to send their reports. That was why on Saturday morning, May 29, before and after Driva Gô, Saint-Clair, Gno Mitang and Archibald Brown had passed judgment, the news of the death of Mani Soun the night before and the reincarnation of her soul in a young priestess called Hoya Devi never reached the Living Buddha.

Moreover, even if the news had been delivered to Jing Pusa, she would have given it only cursory attention, strictly for protocol. First of all, because as the Living Buddha, she always lived above the everyday workings of the seven temples, but also because at the moment she had bigger and very different things to deal with—burning issues that were much more serious regarding her own life!

But Hoya Devi, as the new high priestess of Shiva, was certainly expecting that Driva Gô would learn about her coronation, especially since she was in the dark about Jing Pusa's condition, whether she was dying or already dead.

So, the day after the Seventh Star, after the judgment had been passed, Driva Gô had just left the sacred vestibule and was going down the hallway to his own rooms with the three foreigners when he saw, standing before his door, next to the yellow lama on duty, a human form in a white-striped red robe with a pure white veil.

A bikhuni of the third degree, he thought. *What happened with the women?*

No rite was prescribed for the Grand Lama, the supreme director of the seven temples, chief of the underground world, and official representative of the Living Buddha when an emissary came from the seven high priests, even with foreigners present. So, no rite kept him from acting as he did with informal simplicity.

The veiled figure knelt down before him. He touched the shoulder lightly and it stood up. The lama on duty opened the door for them and led the figure in by the hand. Even though there were more important things to think about, Saint-Clair, Gno and Brown were deeply interested in the incident.

Since Driva Gô did not ask them to leave, they followed him in. The newcomer's gender was hidden behind a white veil. They knew that the Shiva temple was akin to a nunnery, but they were not sure about this figure until they were in Driva Gô's study—a room furnished in typical Victorian English style—and they heard her voice. It was a gentle, musical voice, very feminine, whose words the three foreigners did not understand. Nor did they understand Driva Gô's response.

But after ten minutes of talking, after the woman had left, Driva Gô explained to his three friends:

"Nothing important. Mani Soun, the high priestess of the Shiva temple, passed away last night. Her soul is reincarnated according to the dogma. The new high priestess is one Hoya Devi. Forget about it. I'll put it in my report later. The Living Buddha has more important things to worry about since tomorrow is the day of justice, and today…"

He paused before thinking of everything he had to do for the administration, which was no bed of roses, both for the lamasery and the underground world.

"My venerable friend," said Saint-Clair, "I think we should leave you to your duties. But will you do us the great honor of having lunch with us later?"

"Yes," the old man answered with a smile. "You have plenty to do, too. Don't you have to send a radio message to Paris? It'll probably be more to comfort them than to explain to someone over there all the intricacies of what's been happening here…"

His smile turned into a quiet laugh, a little ironic. Saint-Clair laughed heartily. He had his reasons to be happy and so took the opportunity to express it. Gno and Brown brightened up, but only nodded.

"Well, then, see you later in your rooms," Driva Gô said as he showed the three men to the door.

"Are we going to the plane?" Gno asked next.

"Yes," Saint-Clair replied. "Our men are waiting for us. Archibald, you're going to see the inside of our Zig and you won't be disappointed by its comforts."

Vitto, Soca, Timor and Gissa were inside the rocky fence around the plane. The two Mongols were polishing it. The Corsicans were inspecting the engine, tools in hand.

An hour later, Saint-Clair had sent his first message to Dumont-Warren in Paris. It read:

We're victorious and safe. Stop. Keep close watch on prisoners and wait for next step. Explanations impossible over radio but can confirm that universal threat has been averted. Still a critical mystery remains. Saint-Clair.

For Driva Gô, Saint-Clair, Gno and Brown, between cup after cup of mint tea, cigarette after cigarette, questions and answers, the lunch lasted long, until 4 p.m. There was no discussion about anything arcane concerning the underground world, nor the occult power of Jing Pusa. But overall, the Grand Lama was able to satisfy the curiosity of his three companions.

Then, duty called and it was also time for Saint-Clair to see Jing Pusa, so they went their separate ways. Gno and Brown had decided to go and see the prisoners in the big room, especially the Russians Rikevitch and Lazov and their enigmatic associate Liang Fong, not to mention the wise but temperamental secretary Manassé.

The Japanese diplomat and the English Intelligence officer were figuring that they could make them talk, because it would be easy to pique their curiosity, feed their anger and irritation, exploit their desperation and hope, and maybe pull even more information out of Manassé who could give them a lot of useful data.

Thus ended the Saturday, May 29, like every day since the dawn of time.

CHAPTER V
The Day of Justice

Sunday, May 30, 1937, was, perhaps, the most important day for humanity since the birth of Jesus. But humanity knew nothing about it. For the drama that changed the destiny of the world was known only to a handful of men and one woman, who spoke about it rarely and only in secret to very few people.

Among those people was a novelist—Saint-Clair's biographer. And this man told the story without causing a stir because it is generally accepted that everything a novelist writes is pure fantasy and is published only to entertain the masses. This novelist can smile philosophically, but he smiles more ironically on the inside when he thinks about where we would all be now if certain events had not happened on May 30, 1937 in Tibet, a little north of Lake Chong Koum, 35 degrees latitude north and 86 degrees longitude east...

But let's get on with the story.

So, this day, which for Christians all over the world was the Lord's Day, was the day of justice at the lamasery of Chong Koum. But the tremendous importance of this special Sunday came not from the public act of sentencing and executing, but from a secret, unbelievable act, never seen before and never to be seen again.

When they woke up, Saint-Clair, Gno and Brown were invited by the master of ceremonies Sontang to meet at the entrance of the sacred chambers. They were allowed to bring Vitto, Soca, Gissa and Timor. The group stood together on the left side of the wide landing at the top of the monumental staircase. They could not have been more than six feet from the door.

"The right and left," Sontang explained, "will be facing the grand terrace of the Veda Buddha temple. A yellow lama who knows English will be waiting for you there. He can tell you everything you will surely want to know about the ceremony of justice."

During the meeting with Jing Pusa the previous day after their long lunch, Saint-Clair had been hesitant about asking what would happen on the Day of Justice. He quickly saw that it was Li meeting him, alone, and not the Living Buddha. They had a sweet, tender conversation like two passionate lovers, one of whom, the woman, was almost completely bedridden because of her recent injury now healing under the bandage. Li was adorable. But the Living Buddha, Jing Pusa, said nothing. When Gno Mitang had asked Saint-Clair about it, as any old friend would, he could only answer:

"Jing Pusa didn't say a word about her decision and the sentences."

The three worthy foreigners were therefore brimming with curiosity and a little anxious when heading over to the place indicated by Sontang. Just as curious but with no anxiety were Vitto, Soca, Gissa and Timor, who knew nothing about the debate in the justice council.

Three in front, four behind, the group of seven men moved to where a yellow robed lama was waiting for them. He bowed and in perfect English said:

"Good morning, gentlemen."

This official *speaker* stood next to Gno Mitang, but a little in front and turned so that he was almost facing the three friends as they all stood before the monumental staircase at the bottom of which spread the vast terrace all the way to the great temple of the Veda Buddha.

There was beautiful weather throughout the region. Only a slight breeze blew in from the northeast. In the clear, blue sky, the splendid sun rose gloriously. The terraces, stairs, monuments, white and red marble and black or purple-brown basalt all sparkled. But everything was silent and deserted.

Were they only waiting for the arrival of Saint-Clair's group? As the Nyctalope and his friends stood motionless, waiting anxiously and curiously, music suddenly filled the world. It seemed to come out of everywhere. It was the music of thousands of gongs of hundreds of sizes made of dozens of different metals, but whose tones, which were very distinct at first, blended together as they rose in the air, a harmony of gold, bronze, silver and crystal. And the big doors of the sacred dwelling opened.

A lavish pageant of brahmins and lamas came out, followed by two rows of the strange giant albino guards. Every step on the monumental staircase was occupied by colorful robes, white, black, yellow, green, orange, lined up together.

Then Jing Pusa appeared. Like on the morning of the Seventh Star, the Living Buddha sat on a white silk cushion that was on a round, golden stand itself sitting on a black, pearl-inlaid platform carried on the herculean shoulders of sixteen muscular men. She sat in the hieratic posture of the Buddha, but instead of the crimson robe hugging her chest, she was dressed in a kind of ancient black cloak pinned at the left shoulder with a big emerald which covered her just to her bare legs. She wore a tall, black tiara carved out of basalt and sculpted so that, despite its blackness, it looked like Breton lace.

As soon as Saint-Clair and his friends saw her, they realized that, except for her sixteen bearers, they would be the closest human beings to her. The Nyctalope could have reached out and touched her. He just looked at her.

Jing Pusa made a slight movement of her head, turned her face to him and gave him a long look with those beautiful blue eyes and a furtive smile. It warmed his heart. Even in this solemn ceremony, she was for him alone not the quasi-divine Living Buddha, but the very human, very feminine Li.

Then the invisible gongs fell silent. Now all the stairs leading up and down to the terrace of the Veda Buddha were filling up with multi-colored processions.

The yellow robed lama did not wait for questions. He had his instructions. He obeyed them. His gestures were discreet and his voice low, but he was understood by the foreigners watching and listening.

"That procession is the priests of Balma Veda. That one of Shakyamuni. There is Buddha Kapôla and that one is Buddha Yidam." A moment of silence and then, "There are the priestesses of Shiva, who are also bikhunis of the goddess Shakti of the four arms, the spouse of Buddha Kapâla." Lastly, with sudden emotion in his voice, "And here are the priests of Vishnu!"

Saint-Clair and his friends gave their full attention to this final procession that the lama had pointed to directly. All the priests of Vishnu wore the dark gray robes of penitents because, during the night, Driva Gô had informed Krishna Mâ of the sentence of the Living Buddha, the decision of the Divine Will— *alive and well!*

Krishna Mâ had bowed and accepted his fate. What else could he do? But holding a grudge against the terrible, seductive woman who had pushed him into death, instead of lifting him into a life of power, he had told Driva Gô:

"Following your orders, Hai Feu will be at my side, but Om Jahan will not be there."

"Why?"

"Because he disappeared and I have no idea where he is. Or rather…"

"Or rather what?" the venerable envoy had pressed him.

"Where *she* is!" Krishna Mâ had spit out,

"*She?* What do you mean?"

"Om Jahan is not Om Jahan. The lama born with that name is dead. A woman replaced him. She's the one who cooked up and organized the plot."

In Driva Gô's long life, he had seen and heard things much more astonishing. So he had not blinked but asked calmly:

"Where is she? Do you really not know?"

"I swear on my next reincarnation, which I pray the gods will not make a vile disgrace—I don't know what became of the woman who called herself Om Jahan."

"Do you know her real name?"

"Sorry, but that, too, I am ignorant of."

Now, as vast and complex as the world of the lamasery was, a woman could not just get lost in it if she chose to stay there. As for the real underground world, even the reincarnation of the terrible, wily goddess Shakti could not have entered it. So wise Driva Gôhad had thought:

A woman who dared what this one did won't run away as long as she still has hope of succeeding. She probably—no, certainly—believes that the Living Buddha is dead, since no news of the injury was announced, and no one has seen her since, except for Sontang, I, Saint-Clair and his friends. So, the criminal hasn't fled. She's hiding…

"Ah-ha!" he had said aloud, smiling.

"Do you know something?" Krishna Mâ had asked impatiently.

"I think I can guess, but I have to find out for sure. If what I'm thinking is correct, she will be at your side, Krishna—this woman who led you astray."

"Oh, Driva Gô, you to whom I am nothing now, but a shameful brother, I will accept the next reincarnation in the vilest form if, on the Day of Justice, I have beside me that thrice-cursed woman who must be one of the rare incarnations of the demonic Shakti!"

The vindictive high priest of Vishnu had raised his arms, hands open, stretched out, so that his vow to accept vile ignominy could reach the ears of the gods.

Saint-Clair told Gno Mitang:

"The person walking on the right of the high priest of Vishnu, is he Chinese? I can't tell."

"Yes, it's Hai Feu."

"What about the loud-voiced lama? Om Jahan was his name, I think…"

"Yes, Om Jahan."

"I don't see him. He should be on the left of… What's the name of the high priest?"

"Krishna Mâ."

"Right, well, the two main schemers should be on either side of the main accomplice. They're missing one."

Of course, in the solemn setting, majestically religious at the moment, the two friends were whispering like their lama interpreter. And Driva Gô was standing in front of the ebony platform, alone in the ten square feet at the top of the monumental staircase. He could not hear what the two foreigners were saying; otherwise he would have informed them of his recent discovery.

Moreover, Archibald Brown was also showing his surprise, along with Vitto, Soca, Gissa and Timor. The first Corsican even dared to lean over and whisper into the Nyctalope's ear:

"Boss, that Om Jahan guy isn't there."

"I'm sure Driva Gô will explain it to us later."

Their curiosity and their emotions were piqued because even the Nyctalope did not know what sentence would be pronounced by the Living Buddha. But they all felt—like the brahmins, lamas and even the albinos—that something tragic, never before seen or heard, was about to happen.

On every step of the monumental staircase and everywhere on the vast terrace of the Veda Buddha, the processions stood still, grouped in squares or rectangles or semi-circles depending on their custom. The six groups of men and only one of women were gripped by so much worry and growing confusion that the foreigners could feel the anguish of this crowd filling the air around the lamasery, in the light of the sun, on this wondrous spring day, in the fragrance wafted on the breeze from the hanging gardens!

At last, when the groups from the seven main temples were in their places, Driva Gô raised his right arm at the same time as he raised his clear voice:

"The light shining on us is the light of justice of Jing Pusa, the Living Buddha, the manifestation of the Divine Will, all powerful over the lives of humans."

His clear voice certainly reached the farthest away of the hundreds of men and women gathered there, but it was an old man's voice that could not sustain a long, loud speech.

Then Sontang appeared. He went to stand at the right of Driva Gô. He was dressed in a scarlet robe and wearing a tall, triangular cap of the same color. He was holding a bundle of stiff, white paper in his hands. He untied a black string and his voice boomed out as he read slowly.

What he read, what was written, was in classical Tibetan and constituted what one might have called the criminal charges. The sacrilegious plot was described in such detail that one of the conspirators would surely give a complete confession, not necessarily to gain a pardon in this life but at least to spare his soul the disgrace of an inferior reincarnation.

Still reading, Sontang recounted the violent attacks on the Living Buddha, first the one in the Veda Buddha temple, then the one before the sacred dwelling. After a brief silence that fell over the crowd like a marble slab in the bright morning air, Sontang, even more slowly than before, read the sentence out loud:

"In accordance with eternal justice, the priests and novices of Vishnu will be punished for three moons to spending every hour of the day and night in rigorous meditation and undergo the seven mortifications of the body during a fast in which they will receive only water with one tea leaf.

"The Chinese from Shanghai, the Mongols from Urga, and the lamas from Lhasa, guilty of murder and propagating sacrilege, will devote three moons to work in the underground world, after which they will be banished from Chong Koum forever with just enough provisions to get them to the edge of the desert.

"As for the three leaders..." He marked a pause, before reciting their names in a funereal voice: "Krishna Mâ! Om Jahan! Hai Feu!..." There was another pause, more ominous than ever, then, "Divine justice condemns you to a slow death by the inescapable will of the Living Buddha! Step forward into the sacred triangle."

Two men stepped out of the formation of the Vishnu priests. Only two! And their names were murmured from mouth to mouth. Where was Om Jahan?

The two condemned men walked forward. The light of the sun threw their short shadows in front of them on the white slabs.

In the exact center of the huge terrace, a black triangle had been drawn on the narrow slabs of basalt. The high priest of Vishnu and the Chinese Mandarin, their backs to the sun, stood on the East and West angles of that equilateral triangle. The north angle remained empty.

They knelt down and bowed, their foreheads on the ground between their arms with their hands open.

Suddenly Sontang shouted:

"Om Jahan! Om Jahan!"

Everyone stood still, waiting, utterly silent. If the bees from the garden of Shiva had come buzzing over the terrace, their sound would have been deafening.

Minutes passed. No human form came out of the multi-colored crowd.

Driva Gô motioned with his hand and Sontang announced:

"The night before last, the night of the Seventh Star, Mani Soun, high priestess of the bikhunis of the Temple of Shiva, died. By the holiness of her life, she had the right to choose the honored soul in which her own soul would incarnate for another period of earthly existence. She chose one of the bikhunis who was and once again is called Hoya Devi..."

With this name, which all the bikhunis knew, and probably some lamas remembered suspiciously, Sontang made a dramatic pause. Hundreds of pairs of eyes, including Jing Pusa's, Saint-Clair's and his friends', turned to the white and red cohort of Shiva's holy women.

A little in front of the three rows forming a tight semi-circle, one woman stood out in her white robe with wide red stripes: Hoya Devi, the new high priestess. She did not budge.

Sontang went on:

"Last night, the venerable Driva Gô, obeying his duties, which demand that he blesses the sacerdotal college in which a new high priest of priestess is chosen in the name of the Living Buddha, visited the Shiva bikhunis. He greeted and blessed Hoya Devi, according to the rites. He kissed the forehead of Mani Soun before she was given to the fire and her ashes spread to the four winds. Then, not following the rites but his own instinct, the wise Driva Gô counted all the bikhunis, and he counted up to one hundred..."

There was a brief silence, then hundreds of mouths started mumbling. But Sontang continued with a little bit of irony in his calm voice:

"A criminal doesn't always think of everything! Mani Soun was dead and her soul was reincarnated in one of her bikhunis, so there should have been only ninety-nine living bodies..."

There was another silence, followed by more murmuring through the restless crowd. Sontang went on:

"The venerable Driva Gô knew that Mani Soun, even before getting sick, had thought of reincarnating in the body of her subordinate, a priestess of the third degree called Yeusé. She had mentioned it to him several times. So, an hour after counting to one hundred, the venerable Driva Gô went back to visit Mani Soun's body where Yeusé kept vigil. Yeusé's soul is naturally virtuous, but her character is weak and her heart vulnerable. By this vulnerability and weakness, she sinned. By her virtue, she repented. When Driva Gô, acting as both a father figure and a commander, questioned her about this miracle of a hundred living bodies Yeusé didn't have the demonic perversity to hide the truth... wherefore, by the supreme will of the Living Buddha, Yeusé will be made high priestess of the Shiva temple. As for Hoya Devi..."

After announcing this name, stressing the final, piercing syllable, he stopped again.

A few feet away from him, Saint-Clair and his friends struggled to contain their emotions, no different from the rest of the motionless, breathless, passionately attentive crowd. The Nyctalope leaned over to Gno and whispered:

"A woman!"

"It's logical," Gno whispered back. "Since a woman has become the Living Buddha for the first time since Gedhun Grub, another smart and brave but unscrupulous woman could very well hope to replace her. But her plan had holes. First, because she used violence, which is always futile. And then, because she forgot that ninety-nine does not add up to a hundred."

"How exciting!" Brown commented drily.

They turned their attention back to Sontang who started talking again.

"Hoya Devi was the one who called himself Om Jahan! Hoya Devi!" Here, he took a deep breath and shouted, "More criminal and more perverse than Krishna Mâ and Hai Feu, your death will be twice as slow than that of your accomplices, who were also obviously your victims."

Then more urgently, he concluded:

"Hoya Devi, step into the sacred triangle!"

Oh, how that terrible woman must have been regretting the shot of poison into the dying priestess' hand. One drop would have been enough for a weary, withering body, but as a precaution, she had injected all of it, and now there was no more poison in the black pearl that might be jabbed directly into an artery to put her into a coma and a quick death. Now, she would have to suffer the boundless humiliation of being vanquished by another woman barely out of childhood and suffer in agony for hours on end.

In her humiliation and rage, in horror of her future physical suffering, in her mind's hatred of death, Hoya Devi rose up to a fevered climax of what might be called negative courage. Positive courage would have been to obey with simplicity, dignity and stoicism, like her two partners in crime. But Hoya Devi would not obey. Hearing Sontang's order, she howled out in fury and revolt, rose up on tiptoes, stretched her arms to the sky, fists clenched and without taking one step forward she cried out

"Jing Pusa! You whore! You won't..."

But among the bikhunis were some tough women. Last night, the Grand Lama had summoned a handful of them to his office pretending to organize a pilgrimage so as not to awaken any suspicions in Hoya Devi. Yeusé had not been included because she was needed for the cremation and spreading the ashes of Mani Soun.

After reminding the women of their sacred duty of obedience, and that revealing a secret would earn them a slow and painful death, he gave them instructions without telling them the reason for the furious revolt he had been expecting. Therefore, Hoya Devi was kept from saying more because the six bikhunis jumped on her, threw her to the ground, bound and gagged her with their scarves. Then, they carried her to the sacred triangle and dropped her on the north angle. The body lay on its back, panting, face turned to the sun while the bikhunis hurried back to their place.

Something else happened that had never been seen before. On her white cushion, the Living Buddha rose up gracefully, using only her leg muscles. The bandage under her robe was held fast by a tight shirt. And there she was, standing up, all draped in black.

All the eyes of the crowd were focused on her. There was another silence in which the vibrations of the sunny air were almost palpable. And in this silence, a pure, clear voice arose, which all ears heard while all eyes watched the divine arms rise up, bend a little and the palms joined above.:

"May the souls of Krishna Mâ and Hai Feu leave their bodies! The soul of Hoya Devi will leave hers only when the sun has disappeared behind the mountains."

At that very moment, in the huge silence that fell again, they heard the dull thump of two bodies falling to the ground. And they were two corpses lying on the slabs.

All of a sudden, an uproar broke out—a muddled uproar from countless mouths, followed right away by the sudden prostration of the terrified humans in awe. Even Sontang and Driva Gô were stricken to their core by the force of the lethal will. And among the group of foreigners, Gissa and Timor hit their foreheads on the stone slabs. Only Saint-Clair, Gno and Brown, along with Vitto and Soca, remained standing, but they bowed deeply.

The Nyctalope was the first to look up. He was pale. His hands were shaking. He saw the body of Hoya Devi twisted in its bindings, rolling on the ground, then stiffening. What hellish pain was torturing the woman? He could not stand it any longer. He stepped forward until his chin was almost touching the platform borne by the sixteen giants.

Jing Pusa looked down and their eyes met. He touched her hand and whispered so softly that it was probably understood more than heard. He pleaded\

"Li, I beg you, don't let her suffer any longer. Kill her!"

He was answered with a gentle look and a tender smile. He went back to his place trembling.

Again the pure, clear voice as heard:

"Hoya Devi! Hoya Devi, do you hear me?"

The convulsive body on the ground stopped moving.

Jing Pusa was vibrant now.

"In the name of love, I will have mercy on you. Hoya Devi, you are a woman. You understand me. Do you want to live? To live in penitence for your sins of pride, ambition, betrayal and murder? Do you want to live? To live, perhaps, and love?"

Like everyone, Sontang had heard. Like many he was thinking:

The gag! She can't answer!

He leaped down the stairs and ran to the woman. He leaned over and untied the scarves. Then he helped her to her feet while whispering with a kind of religious terror:

"Answer! Answer!"

But pushing the brahmin with all her strength, the terrible woman cried out:

"Damn you, Jing Pusa, you bit..."

Her curse was cut short. Anger flashed from the blue eyes that promptly turned cold. And the body of Hoya Devi collapsed to the ground.

Nothing but a corpse.

CHAPTER VI
Sunday Morning, at the Rose Garden

The radio message sent from the lamasery, or rather from the plane, by the Nyctalope on Saturday morning, May 29—just before the Day of Justice—arrived in numbers and letters on a yellow sheet of paper at the office of Dumont-Warren that afternoon. He decoded it, read and reread it, and thought about it for a long time.

Then he got on the phone with Saint-Honoré-les-Bains and the villa. Jacques Fitou was on the other end of the line.

"Hello, Fitou. What's new?"

"Nothing at all, boss. Since you and Garnoch left on Thursday, things are *copacetic*, as we journalists like to say."

"OK. I've got news."

"Yes, boss?"

"I want Yori Koto to hear this."

"Easy enough. Wait a minute."

A minute went by and he heard:

"Hello? Yori Koto here."

"Good! Listen up both of you. I just received a message from Saint-Clair..." A double gasp was heard over the phone before Dumont-Warren continued: "One of you get a pen and paper. I'm going to give you the whole message. No place of origin was mentioned so it must be coming from Chong Koum. Are you ready?"

"Yes, sir."

"So here it is: *We're victorious and safe. Stop. Keep close watch on prisoners and wait for next step. Explanations impossible over radio but can confirm that universal threat has been averted. Still a critical mystery remains. Saint-Clair.* Did you get all that down?"

"Yes."

"Read it back to yourselves, but stay on the line, I'm not done yet." Another short wait. "OK? Good. So, is there anything in particular that strikes you?"

"Yes. Jacques and I are both wondering what the next step is?" said Yori.

"That's exactly it. I won't be sleeping tonight. In five minutes, I'll alert Garnoch. In an hour, we'll take the car. This time, I'll have a chauffeur because I don't like to drive at night. Tomorrow is Sunday. The next step might be tomorrow. I want to be there for it. Anything else to tell me?"

"No, sir. Except that Jacques and I agree with your decision."

"Thank you. See you soon."

With that Dumont-Warren, hung up.

In the Morvan, and especially in the big, mountainous and wooded valley of which Saint-Honoré is the center, Saturday evening, May 29, was one of the most beautiful, warmest, clearest and sweetest-smelling day that nature had given to springtime on earth. The living creatures felt lighter, younger, filled with sweet and smiling melancholy.

In the dining room of the Rose Garden villa, they were lingering after dinner. The doors were wide open onto the balcony. Florence de Salsis, Fabienne Blancat, Yori Koto, Jacques Fitou and André Black were still all there. The food was served as always by Alfred and his wife, Louise. After the coffee was served, Florence let them know they were free to retire.

They were discussing what the "next step" might be when the door opened and Isha came in. It had been agreed that Florence would be the "lady of the house" with Fabienne as her friendly partner, but Yori Koto was in charge. So, it was to him that Isha went straightaway and with some nervousness in his voice.

"Oryas Zabad Khan is asking to talk to you and Monsieur Fitou," he said.

"All right!" the journalist blurted out.

But the Japanese said nothing. He got up and, with a nod, invited Fitou to follow him. Barely one minute later, the two men entered the room they were calling their "prison." It was a big and comfortable bedroom with a connected bathroom. In truth, they had arranged it so that two rooms made up the prison—windows barred and watched so that escape was impossible, and even if someone from outside shot into the room, they would be immediately spotted by a permanent armed guard. This last step was a necessary precaution in case Oryas used his power on one of the servants of the villa.

Isha closed the door and stayed in the hallway. Yori Koto and Jacques Fitou stood side by side and bowed slightly to Leone Alzac sitting in an armchair. Then they turned to face the brahmin standing in the middle of the room.

"You called for us," Yori Koto spoke coldly but with no hostility. "What do you want?"

Fitou was annoyed by the semi-darkness of the room. In the final minutes of twilight, they had not turned on a lamp. He stepped back to the door and switched on the bright ceiling light. Both men were struck by the new expression on the normally serene and inscrutable face of Oryas Zabad Khan. His lips were taut, his face tense, and his eyes full of anguish.

"Well, what do you want?" Fitou almost shouted. Instinctively, he turned to Leone Alzac who looked pale and stressed.

"What happened?" Yori asked.

The brahmin swallowed hard and in a hoarse voice:

"I don't know. Since the sun set behind the forest, I've had a growing sense of anxiety. I feel like I'm suffocating. And yet, Madame Alzac assures me that it's a beautiful, cool evening. My body feels normal. I've taken my pulse and my temperature. All are normal. And yet, I'm suffering. Please, allow me, allow us, to get a little fresh air..."

As Yori and Fitou did not try to hide their bewilderment, the brahmin continued more calmly:

"I can tell you that, right now, I think all your precautions are of no importance. Yes, I have the power to kill at a distance with my will, and I have used it before, but I swear to you that it's only partial, limited by time as you've already guessed. It's only during certain phases of the moon relative to its position with the sun. Since April 27, the day of the 18th death, conditions haven't been favorable. I'll only have the power again after the new moon, on June 8. Therefore... But what a sense of dread I feel! Please, let me go out and walk around..."

Yori and Fitou were stunned, but convinced that this crazy speech was the truth. Plus, this extraordinary man looked frightened, like an animal being hunted by some unspeakable peril... The Japanese decided on the spot:

"I believe you, monsieur, and we will do all I can for you. You and Leone Alzac won't be followed or watched. Just give me your word, both of you, that you won't try to escape."

"I give you my word!" Oryas raised his right hand over his head.

"Me too," Leone panted.

Three minutes later, the two prisoners were walking quickly over the field, which was lit only by the countless stars of this paradisal evening.

In the dining room, in the bright light of the seven-bulbed chandelier, Yori Koto, Jacques Fitou, Florence, Fabienne and André Black were sitting and smoking, or not, speaking little in the grips of this new mystery that they felt powerless to solve. In fact, they were doubly anxious—anxious to see the two dark forms come back from their walk in the dark, and anxious about the arrival of Dumont-Warren and Garnoch.

Isha had gone out to meet the car on the highway where it forked off into the forest road. Daloz stood guard at the service gate to open it when he heard the hum of its engine. Alfred, Louise and the cook Adelaide had been ordered to watch from the office. The other servants were also under orders to stay in their rooms.

Dumont-Warren and Garnoch arrived before Oryas and Leone had come back. In the dining room where they were given a cold meal—since they had not eaten before leaving Paris—Jacques Fitou brought them up-to-date on events.

"Is this psychic-telepathic foreboding the next step Saint-Clair was talking about?" Garnoch wondered aloud.

Everyone was wondering the same thing, but they said nothing. They could not come up with ideas, or express them. After the meal, they went into the rose garden. There were still canvas lounge chairs and rattan armchairs. All the men and the two women felt the same confusion, the same perplexity, the same apprehension as they sat in silence watching out the field. No one even smoked. The air was cool but neither Florence nor Fabienne, both wearing sleeveless dresses, felt cold. Quite the contrary! It soothed their nerves, cooled their blood and calmed them down. They just waited.

The twelve strokes of midnight from the bells of Saint-Honoré were carried lazily on the breeze. Presently their watchful eyes saw two human forms moving in the field. Dark on the gray ground, they stood apart from each other. The taller one on the left was the mysterious brahmin. They both came on slowly, walking directly toward the rose garden.

All of a sudden, Garnoch stood up and marched out to meet them. And they stopped right away.

"I'm going too," Yori whispered to Dumont-Warren.

"Yes."

Like many naturalist scholars, Garnoch was not pretentious, but he still had a little unconscious arrogance. It showed itself when he stood before the couple with Yori Koto beside him.

"Monsieur, you recognize my voice, correct? If a conversation with a man of science would be useful and desirable to you in your present state, I am at your service."

Without hesitating, in an eerily detached voice, Oryas replied:

"Thank you, Monsieur Garnoch, but Madame and I only need some rest."

Yori felt it his duty to take the lead:

"Please follow me back to your room."

"With pleasure."

Soon, all the occupants of the villa were in bed. But how many would sleep during this strange night?

At 6:30 a.m. in the morning, now Sunday, May 30, they were back in the dining room for breakfast. The weather promised to be as splendid as the day before, even though the air was fraught with an obscure fear. It felt like the bedroom of Oryas Zabad Khan was exuding invisible waves of evil.

"My God, what's going to happen today?" Florence muttered, staring at her untouched cup of chocolate and cream that she usually adored.

No one answered. But eyes were so full of such blatant anxiety that Fabienne could not help saying:

"I'm ashamed of being afraid, because I am so afraid. Not for me. I don't know for whom or why."

The last to arrive, because he had taken the last prison watch, was André Black who spoke gravely:

"They didn't go to bed. They sat on the couch next to each other, holding hands. Sometimes, she put her head on his shoulder and he caressed her cheek or her hair. They kissed once for a long time. Then she sobbed. He consoled her in a really soft, gentle voice. I felt embarrassed listening in, so I stepped away from the peephole."

No one made any comments.

André was a stoical, down-to-earth man with a healthy appetite so he sat down and started eating. Suddenly, slapping his forehead and exclaiming "Ah", like someone who forgot something he wanted to say, he added:

"Their window was wide open. They didn't close it once, even when it got cold."

Everyone looked up automatically and turned to the open French doors, because the window of the prison bedroom was located directly above them.

A few minutes later, in a silence that was broken only by the clinking of silverware, porcelain or crystal, Florence de Salsis blurted out in a nervous and therefore intuitive voice:

"I'm sure that this 'next step' will happen today."

Her eyes glistened, full of tears. Yori Koto was sitting to her left. He took her hand, squeezed it gently and said:

"My dear friend, be calm. I think we all feel the same thing. Since last night, everything's turned strange. We have to wait and see."

"Yes, let's wait," Dumont-Warren agreed. "Right here so that we can hear anything that might happen up there."

But André, who was unquestionably the least affected of all, proposed:

"Boss, I think it'd be good if one of us kept an eye at the peephole up there. Things could happen that wouldn't make any more noise than the blink of an eye."

"Right, but who?"

"I'll do it," said Jacques Fitou, standing up.

"Sure."

So, Fitou left the room under the worried eye of Fabienne who did not dare move a finger or say a word.

The meal dragged on with sips and nibbles. Florence drank her chocolate. Louise had set out two big dishes of freshly picked strawberries. They started eating them distractedly, rolling the fragrant fruits in powdered sugar.

The general sense of dread settled down and their spirits felt stuck in a murky nightmare with a clear sensation that they were going to suddenly wake up and chase away the dark and hazy dream. In this state, they talked, but only to say a couple of meaningless words about a strawberry, the sugar, or whatever else they saw on the table.

More than an hour passed like this. Yori chanced to look up at the clock on the wall and saw that the hands pointed to 10 a.m. Without thinking, he said, "It's ten o'clock."

Florence and Fabienne jumped up, turned pale. The men also pushed back their chairs and stood up. At that very moment, a scream ripped through the latent dread—a woman's ear-splitting scream that turned into the howl of a wounded animal.

"Leone Alzac!" Florence babbled.

She ran to the door followed by Fabienne. However, Yori was faster and closer than them. Dumont-Warren, Garnoch and Block hurried after him. The group reached the upstairs landing together. Halfway down the hallway, the door on the right, the door to the prison, was wide open.

Only Fabienne and Florence went in. A kind of modesty had made Fitou stop the men in the doorway. For, on the carpet in the middle of the room, lying with its arms out to the sides, was the body of Oryas Zabad Khan. Dead, for sure! His eyes were wide open, rolled upwards, his face belonged to a dead man.

Leone Alzac was kneeling down, her head swaying, no longer wailing, just moaning softly, almost whining like a child, choked by sobs. She let herself be supported by Florence and Fabienne who knelt on either side of her, but said nothing. Fitou whispered to the other men in the open doorway

"I was watching through the peephole from the second I got here. It must've been four or five minutes. Zabad Khan got up, started pacing the room while Leone Alzac was just sitting there, watching him nervously. Sometimes he stopped, opened his mouth, took a deep breath... I heard him grumbling aloud, 'Leone, I feel like Jing Pusa knows what I did and where I am. She's going to kill me. Leone, she'll kill me.' He turned to the door, towards me! Oh, the terror on that twisted face! Leone Alzac got up to go to him and that's when he just fell backwards, his arms spread out... like a tree cut off at the trunk and blown over by the wind."

What could they do? The five men stepped back into the hallway. Yori closed the door quietly and whispered with the others. Decisions were made. The first was, naturally, to leave the two women to take care of Leone Alzac. Then, they agreed to move the body to a bed in another room and to call a doctor from Saint-Honoré. All the formalities, including the burial, would be seen to.

"Well, there's no doubt about the diagnosis," Yori said. "Cerebral hemorrhage. It's logical."

"It's the next step," Dumont-Warren said.

"And remember what Saint-Clair wrote— *close watch on prisoners*."

"Yes," Garnoch added, "while waiting for the next step."

"But who's Jing Pusa?" Fitou asked.

As he pronounced the name his whole body shuddered.

Yori spoke with a kind of religious solemnity:

"Remember what Leone Alzac said: '*This is all bigger than us, unfortunately, bigger than you or me, Gno Mitang, his friend the Nyctalope, even Zabad Khan himself... Oh, gods!*'—well, friends, Jing Pusa must be one of the *gods* she had in mind."

"And the Nyctalope knew about it," Fitou said simply.

CHAPTER VII.
The Third Sanctuary

Striking down Oryas Zabad Khan was not the crucial event about the fate of mankind on Sunday, May 30, 1937, any more than the executions of Krishna Mâ, Hai Feu and Hoya Devi had been. These corpses were four more to add to the Eighteen dead and basically closed the portion of this adventure that was limited to mostly criminals, and had been concluded by four acts of sovereign justice.

But the element that was both the origin and the instrument of all these acts? This element still remained. It could start another cycle in the same way. Maybe even a worse one. And to what end? With what results?

Leo Saint-Clair was thinking of this while the corpse of Hoya Devi was growing stiff in the sun on the white slabs inside the black triangle in the very center of the huge terrace of the Veda Buddha temple. He was thinking of this—and getting dizzy.

At that moment, Driva Gô made a gesture. The giant guards raised up their big swords, which sparkled in the sun, high and straight. Right away, the gongs rang out. The breeze carried the sound throughout the lamasery.

Then the sixteen muscular giants started moving. The ebony platform turned around. Driva Gô and Sontang led the Living Buddha's procession back to her sacred dwelling. On all sides, the brahmins and lamas, the bikhunis and the rest, got going.

Watching and contemplating, the foreigners saw the huge terrace empty out. Soon, there was nothing but the three corpses lying in the triangle, one in a dark gray robe, another in golden yellow, and the last in white with red stripes.

Saint-Clair heard their lama-interpreter say calmly:

"Gentlemen, would you be kind enough to go back to your rooms. You can wait there for the Living Buddha to call you."

They did not have to wait long. The Nyctalope and his friends were only back two or three minutes when the rather heavy silence was broken by Driva Gô's entrance. He looked very grim but he managed a smile for Saint-Clair. After looking around, he said:

"Leo Saint-Clair, Gno Mitang and Captain Archibald Brown, please follow me. The Living Buddha would like to see you."

Leaving Vitto, Soca, Timor and Gissa, the three marched out. But Gno whispered to Saint-Clair:

"My friend, do you know what's happening?"

"No," the Nyctalope answered. "Jing Pusa gave me no idea about what's going to happen next."

He was deeply worried. He did not doubt Jing Pusa's love; the depth and breadth of her feelings had already proven themselves in different ways. He loved the young woman like a hardened adventurer can when a virgin offers herself in such unusual circumstances, meaning that he loved with both passion and concern. Because this virgin turned into a woman by him was also the most extraordinary being, the most exceptional of all human beings: the Living Buddha! And she was endowed with a power that put her above and beyond humanity, since this power was one of the fundamental attributes that countless men have always and probably always will ascribe to divinity. Jing Pusa was unique in the world because she was the Living Buddha, because she was the Master of Life! How was such a woman going to resolve such a common, humdrum, human situation as a love affair? Saint-Clair had the feeling that this situation was now going to be resolved. It was inevitable. But how?

In any case, one thing was true, foregone, and undeniable: the decision belonged to Jing Pusa alone. Saint-Clair was sure that the decision had been made and that she had decided their future during the council of justice. But what had she decided?

To the great surprise of Gno, Brown and Saint-Clair himself, it was not the Living Buddha who welcomed the three guests and Driva Gô in the huge salon completely decked out in the purest, noblest style used during the youth of Empress Shen Shi, a time that, in China, was the great modern era for interior design and furniture.

One whole side of the sumptuous but comfortable room was taken up by three bay windows that looked directly out upon a flowery, shaded terrace.

The very young woman who was standing there, almost in the very center of the room, was a beautifully ambiguous European with slightly slanted, blue eyes, a golden brown, oval face and an outfit that was even more surprising with its contrast of the small, red turban hiding all her hair and the black, silk, sleeveless dress, a little low-cut at the neck, which could have been made by the best Parisian *couturier* from the Rue de la Paix. Black silk stockings and dark red shoes matched the turban.

Her laugh, joyful and youthful, greeted the clearly stupefied men. Saint-Clair could not help crying out:

"Ah, it's Li, it's *her*!"

And he was so happy that he turned pale after he felt his heart stop for an instant. But already the young woman was coming to him, holding out her hand bare of rings and bracelets. She was speaking simply, casually, as naturally as could be, as if talking about a normal, everyday matter.

"Leo, didn't you convince your friends that I'm a woman, a simple woman, a woman like all the others?"

Then while Saint-Clair took her hand and kissed it, she turned to the Grand Lama.

"And you, Driva Gô, who watched me play when I was a little girl, didn't you tell these guests who you so rightly respect that I really love to have fun and that my name is Li?"

She looked again at Saint-Clair and spoke softly:

"Great gods, what mysteries!"

And she laughed. Then, with a hint of gravity in her voice, she added:

"Obviously in an hour, I will become once again a powerful, religious entity, tremendously unique... but only for a few minutes, and for the last time."

There was a brief silence. She smiled for Saint-Clair with a squeeze of her hand, and continued:

"But for now, it's time for some Porto, Madeira, or even a cocktail if you want."

She looked at Driva Gô who clapped his hands three times. Like a flock of doves, a group of young servants came in wearing white robes. A low table was put in one corner by the couches and armchairs. In a flash, it was covered with a lace tablecloth, bottles and glasses. One of the prettiest girls stood there holding a cocktail shaker in her hands. Others kneeled or sat around her ready to take orders for the tasty concoctions. Others still stood quietly apart in the room or on the terrace watching for a sign from Sontang who had come in with them. He greeted them, shook hands and asked simply:

"What will you have?"

The Frenchman, the Englishman and the Japanese came from a rather refined world so that their idea of comfort, through their traditional upbringing, was modeled on this. Right away, the guests had everything they wanted.

After sipping the cocktail, Gno Mitang began his praise with "My dear hostess," which seemed completely natural in the relaxed and elegant environment that needed no ceremonious displays of protocol.

They spoke in French and English, mixing the two. When complimenting Brown on his good cheer during his solitary confinement, Jing Pusa used English. Driva Gô had lived in Europe for a long time and Sontang had spent several months in France and England. They had not been brahmin and grand lama then, but educated tourists or wealthy foreigners mingling in the socialite world of embassies.

So, on the whole—despite the different emotions running through their minds—the cocktail hour was exactly what it was meant to be. But all of a sudden, because of that subtle *aura* that can be felt in big crowds as well as smaller gatherings, the room fell silent and still. Driva Gô bowed to Jing Pusa and slowly, gravely said:

"In a few minutes the ritual to enter the third sanctuary will begin."

"Yes."

She stood up. She did not even look at Saint-Clair who was sitting next to her. Following Sontang to the back of the room, she vanished into the darkness of a doorway that opened automatically for them. All the young servants disappeared as well. The Nyctalope stood up with Gno and Brown and looked at Driva Gô, who had stayed behind. But the old man just closed his eyes and put a finger to his lips.

When she came back, Jing Pusa was once again the Living Buddha in the scarlet robe with the gilded cap and strapped sandals. Sontang walked in front of her and Driva Gô followed after signaling to the three men to get behind them.

They left the salon and went down hallways and stairways that Saint-Clair was not familiar with. Soon, the natural light changed to natural gas in conch shells on tripods or hanging from the ceiling. They were descending into the underground world.

The doors in front of Sontang were opened by semi-nude albinos. In the long vestibule there was a double row of blue-robed lamas, all bowing deeply, palms together over their heads. Then there was a huge room of golden columns, followed by one of silver columns, and finally a third one, smaller, at the end of which stood two statues of Buddha, one male and one female, and between them a shrine on ivory elephant legs surrounded by completely motionless flames stretched out in almond shapes over huge, emerald shells.

Before the shrine, Sontang took three steps to the right and Driva Gô stepped forward and to the left. The Living Buddha stopped between them. She turned around immediately to face the three foreigners who stood stock still. And she spoke in a soft, slow, deep voice:

"We are in the third sanctuary. In this shrine is the 77th book of the Rig Veda, which contains the secret of the will to paralyze and kill. In bringing you three here, just like Driva Gô and Sontang, I have violated the supreme law that allows only the Living Buddha alone, or carried by a brahmin in case of sickness, to enter the third sanctuary. I have violated the law because I have decided to do something of utmost consequence, and I want to do it in the presence of men who will not speak of it because I ask them not to, but who will be believed if I ask them to break their silence one day."

Jing Pusa paused and her majestic eyes looked from one man to another. Troubled and nervous, the five men forced themselves to stay calm and they bowed. They swore never to betray the secret of what was about to transpire unless Jing Pusa allowed it.

When they were standing straight again, they saw that the Living Buddha was touching the edges of the shrine, which was in the shape of a closed lotus, made of a tarnished looking metal with rubies and sapphires embedded around it. She was performing the ritual to open it, presumably known to all lamas of the seventh degree.

And the lotus opened. The big front petal dropped down slowly and rested on its base. Jing Pusa reached inside with her left hand and brought out not a book, but a scroll, a rolled parchment or, as they saw right away, several rectangular parchments rolled up together. She turned to face the others and raised the yellow roll above her head.

"We didn't need the sacrilegious theft and murderous acts of Oryas Zabad Khan to imagine what a human being could do with a power that partakes of the divine. Man is imperfect. Even the best, the holiest, the wisest is prone to error. He can be tempted by his passions and give in. Leo Saint-Clair, I admire you and I love you, and I believe that if you held this supreme power, you would use it only for what you believe was good and just. And I am also sure you would make mistakes that would not give more joy to mankind, but only change the form of its eternal punishment.

"But imagine a man like Hai Feu, a woman like Hoya Devi, the student of Om Jahan the fanatic. Imagine one of the tyrants who are enslaving people with their ideologies today. Imagine anyone who got hold of this book and became the Master of Life and Death! Woe unto Man then!"

She stopped again. Now she was shaking. Her voice had rung out like a gong. During the long silence, she tried to contain herself, and at last, she succeeded. In a softer voice, she continued:

"By the inexplicable will of the gods, I have used the most fearful element of their power. I have now decided to forget it. I have already wiped it from my mind. But I have also decided that no other human being should ever know this dangerous secret in the future. I have consulted the superior wisdom of Driva Gô. His mind and heart have agreed. I was expecting no less from this sublime old man who has seen so much more than I, and knows the passions of men. So, here is what I'm going to do..."

With a slow, calm gesture, she pulled one sheet of parchment off the roll and offered it to the flame. It sparked and crackled, smoked a little, and then the whole thing dropped out of Jing Pusa's hand and was swallowed by the emerald cup where it vanished in flames.

The sacrificial act was carried out six times in a row, slowly. When the seventh parchment was destroyed, Jing Pusa smiled radiantly and her incredibly blue eyes looked directly at Saint-Clair.

But the emotions stirring inside the five men were so strong that all of them, even Driva Gô the old grand lama, even Gno Mitang the stoic Japanese, even the stolid Englishman Archibald Brown, were holding back tears. They felt no shame. They were fully aware of witnessing a miracle and, despite the limits of the human spirit, enjoying a boundless, infinite serenity.

EPILOG
The End and the Beginning.

"I think, my dear, that you will be just fine," Saint-Clair said.

"I'm sure I will," Jing Pusa giggled. "Especially if you're next to me."

"Yes. Vitto and Soca will be in the pilot's seats in front of us. The fifth seat in the back is for Gno. Timor will be at the radio and Gissa, with his habitual dignity, wants to take on the important job of steward. He's right not to feel humiliated but to be proud of it. Everyone ought to know that a steward is not so much a waiter in a restaurant, like we think in France, as he is a butler, a quartermaster, a director, a supply officer responsible for the needs and comforts of everyone. He knows that at the English royal court, the Lord High Steward is none other than the Grand Seneschal!"

He laughed. He was joking around. He was happy, madly and consciously happy, because he was seating Jing Pusa in the plane. They had cleared the path and rolled it onto the esplanade facing the huge, empty space with its tail only a few yards from the wall that surrounded the lamasery.

To the right and left of the plane a dozen men were standing against the light, their backs to the slowly rising sun on the eastern plains: Driva Gô, Sontang and four other lama dignitaries, Archibald Brown, the scholar Petrus Rikevitch, the Stalinist officer Grigori Lazov, and the Chinese explorer Liang Fong. Before leaving the lamasery Jing Pusa had said goodbye to her high priests with no regrets, but with a great deal of emotion.

During the night, before a gathering of all the brahmins and lamas, before Yeusé, the new priestess of Shiva, and the other five high priests, she had solemnly delivered into the hands of Driva Gô the golden lotus with the ruby fruit, which was the secret insignia of the Living Buddha. Driva Gô told her for the first time the name of the child whom they would prepare to become the new Living Buddha —a name that Jing Pusa was not unaware of. Because the death of the Living Buddha is always anticipated, so that there will be no interruption. Until the child was old enough, Driva Gô would act as regent, and then Sontang if Driva Gô died.

Moreover, this was not the first time that a Living Buddha had stepped down from the sublimely holy office. But every time before, it had been for philosophical reasons, for a retreat into humility in a small monastery of contemplative lamas buried in some oasis in the middle of endless plains or inaccessible mountains, completely unknown to the profane.

Such would not be the fate of Li Jing Pusa. Her predecessors who had renounced their role had left Chong Koum with nothing but their monk's robe, a simple fur coat, a sack, a gourd and a staff. Jing Pusa was carrying two suitcases covered with yak skin. One contained linen, dresses, a luxurious sable coat, beautiful shawls and precious scarves. The other, smaller but heavier case held an immense fortune: hundreds of rare, precious stones and twenty bars of that tarnished-looking metal they used to make their simple plates and cutlery—a metal that was none other than platinum!

One of the few things Jing Pusa had been willing to share with Saint-Clair concerned the inviolable mysteries of the underground world—this secret "basement" made of compact rock and pockets of sand that had never been measured, but extended over many square miles of surface and was 177 yards deep. For centuries the servants and the albinos had gradually chipped away the rocks to create support columns and draining the pockets of sand. Little by little, the excavated material had been put through an ancient process that would be the envy of modern science in their underground factory whose chimneys, most of them naturally formed, rose into the inaccessible regions of the mountains around Chong Koum. Thus they fashioned gold and other more common metals, but especially platinum, which makes up 88% of what they found there.

With the precious stones and rare metals that Jing Pusa was bringing, she could make the jewelers in Europe swoon in admiration. It was enough for her to live a generous and even luxurious life, if she so chose.

But for independence, the young woman had thought only of the strictly material aspects. She had told Saint-Clair with the serenity of someone who had made up their mind for good, with the happy fatalism of her love that was now flowing through her entire being:

"She who was a kind of goddess and obeyed by millions of human beings, is now your slave and proud to be one, and hopes she will always be so. She is called Li and doesn't want any other name."

After he had seated Jing Pusa in the plane, Saint-Clair climbed out. Gno was waiting for him at the bottom of the ladder. The two of them went to the group that Driva Gô was naturally presiding over.

The Nyctalope shook the hands of Rikevitch, Lazov and Liang Fong not without a touch of friendly irony. To wrap up what he had told them the night before, he said:

"You can assure Comrade Stalin that, just like in the past, a man can be a dictator over other men only by relying on the old ways known to us since the age of clans, since chiefs have led their followers, since mobs are ready to obey those who are ready to command... for good or evil! Goodbye, Messieurs, and no hard feelings, right?"

Gno was smiling next to him, nodding his head slightly. He, too, but in silent ceremony, shook the hands of the Russians and Chinese.

Then the two friends bid a warm farewell to Archibald Brown who was staying in Tibet. He was going to be a tourist with a small escort arranged by Driva Gô. When he was tired of traveling around, he would go back to Bombay and probably London again.

"So, we'll see each other again in Paris someday," Saint-Clair told him.

"By the grace of God," he recited religiously.

Finally, Saint-Clair and Gno exchanged bows and formalities with the high lamas and Sontang. But Driva Gô opened arms. They embraced each other like close friends.

Then, they turned and went back to the plane.

Meanwhile, Vitto, Soca, Timor and Gissa had taken their respective posts.

The door closed and the engine started. Two servants, trained by Timor the night before, pulled out the wheel stops at the right moment. The plane taxied onto the esplanade. Slowly, smoothly, it took off.

A few days later, the Zig landed at the private airstrip of Nevers-Sermoise. Three cars and a van were waiting for the passengers who were greeted on the runway by Dumont-Warren, Garnoch and Yori Koto along with Florence de Salsis. All the luggage was packed into the van with Soca at the wheel and Vitto in the passenger seat.

The blue convertible was for Jing Pusa and Florence de Salsis alone together. Florence drove. Yori Koto took Timor and Gissa in the Torpedo. Finally, the big limousine driven by Isha sitting next to Pierre Daloz carried Saint-Clair, Dumont-Warren, Garnoch and Gno Mitang.

Except for some instructions for the flight, mostly at the end of their voyage, they had said nothing over the radio. Therefore, in the limousine, they were asking each other all kinds of quick questions to get updated on the situation. There would be plenty of time for details later. The first question Saint-Clair asked was:

"What about Leone Alzac?"

"She's dead," Dumont-Warren answered.

After a moment of silence, he explained:

"Right after taking over the villa, Yori had searched the place for anything that might be used as a weapon, even poison. After Zabad Khan's body was put into a coffin, and before we hammered in the first nail, Leone Alzac asked to be left alone with him for seven minutes to pray according to their rites. She had seemed calm, resigned to her fate, but was obviously grieving with brief fits of tearless sobbing. So we agreed to her request. None of us thought she could commit suicide. Besides, we had placed the coffin in a small room on the ground floor, taken out all the furniture and decorations. It was nothing more than a bare cell, following her own instructions according to some special ritual for the brahmin he had been. After her seven minutes were up, Florence and Fabienne went in and found Leone Alzac lying in the coffin on top of Zabad Khan's body, both under the shroud. I'll skip the calls, the running around, the doctor's trying to revive her... She'd killed herself. She had taken great pains to use a method devised by the ancient Yogis and probably taught to her by Zabad Khan. The desperate woman had stuffed up her nose with rolled up tissue. Then she had stuck her tongue back in her throat and, with the shoulder pads from her shirt, she made a slip knot, tied it around her neck and pulled."

Dumont-Warren was upset. He wiped his forehead and continued in a low voice:

"I bought a plot in the cemetery of Saint-Honoré for two coffins, side by side. It's surrounded by a chain hooked up to four stone pillars. There's a black marble headstone for them. Yesterday, they finished engraving their names, Oryas and Leone, and a date, May 30, 1937."

He was finished.

Saint-Clair kept his eyes closed. He was pale and had nothing to say. Gno said softly:

"You did well."

On June 10, after everyone had left and the whole staff had been let go, the Rose Garden villa was handed over to a local real estate agent to be put up for sale. Enough money was given to the agent to take care of the property for a year if a buyer was not found. When sold, the money, minus his commission, would be deposited in the social assistance fund of Saint-Honoré.

On the grounds of the Nyctalope's Blingy estate, near Versailles, there was a big, charming 18th century pavilion in which Li Jing Pusa set up house with a personal servant brought in from Bombay by plane.

Gno Mitang left for Tokyo, summoned by the Emperor who was eager to hear his report. Naturally, Yori Koto accompanied his boss, but Florence de Salsis went with them since she had become Mrs. Yori Koto by a specially arranged marriage at the Japanese embassy in Paris.

Naturally, Fabienne Blancat and Jacques Fitou were also married. Dumont-Warren and Saint-Clair were their witnesses.

The only characters whose fate after June 10, 1937, we cannot know for sure were Mrs. Melody MacCross and Patrick O'Dougal and his butler. On that morning, after a brief phone conversation with an unidentified person who had sent her a copy of the death certificate, duly signed and stamped, of Madame Leone Medwin, born Leone Alzac, Mrs. MacCross had asked for her bill, packed her bags, paid off her maid handsomely, and, with her chauffeur, left in a car accompanied by an older Irish gentleman and his butler who had been waiting for her. The small house on rue Hallé was not rented, but its monkish owner had also left. Would he return some day?

The papers reported that Mrs. MacCross, the richest woman in the world, had bought a yacht in Cannes and was taking a long cruise along with an Irish friend. But then the American press found another "richest woman in the world," much younger, who was about to marry for the fourth time after divorcing three times in two years, with a child from her first marriage, and they forget all about Mrs. MacCross in editorial rooms.

As for Leo Saint-Clair, he gave some thoughts to writing his memoirs. The fact that Li Jing Pusa was living next door in her pavilion made him believe, reasonably enough, that the Nyctalope wouldn't be ready to embark on any new adventure in the immediate future.

Even if we accept the transmigration of souls, the idea of reincarnation, the dogma of metempsychosis, death is always the end. But love, too, is always the beginning. Thanks to Li Jing Pusa, who was really starting to live for the first and maybe only time in her life, Leo Saint-Clair, too, was embarking on a new chapter in his life.

www.ingramcontent.com/pod-product-compliance
Lightning Source LLC
Chambersburg PA
CBHW060432030726

47495CB00003B/841